WEAPON

Also by Robert Mason
Chickenhawk

WEAPON

Robert Mason

G. P. Putnam's Sons New York

G. P. Putnam's Sons
Publishers Since 1838
200 Madison Avenue
New York, NY 10016

Library of Congress Cataloging-in-Publication Data

Mason, Robert
  Weapon.

Bibliography: p.
I. Title.
PS3563.A796W44   1989   813'.54   88-32150
ISBN: 0-399-13447-6

Printed in the United States of America
    3   4   5   6   7   8   9   10

To Patience

WEAPON

1

GENERAL CLYDE Haynes watched the yacht sail smoothly by the mouth of the cove and wondered if they were spies. He raised his binoculars. Naked spies? Clyde grinned, his leathery face wrinkling along accustomed lines. Two naked spies with big tits.

One of the girls basking on the foredeck noticed him standing on the rocks and waved. Goddamn! What I wouldn't give to be out there. Too long, no pussy.

A wave crashed against his rocky perch and water splashed his legs, staining his camouflage pants. Clyde didn't notice. The girl roused her companion and together they waved, laughing. One girl stood up, holding on to a stay. Clyde groaned. Not a stitch. And they don't care. Where the hell were they when I was young? The yacht disappeared behind the coconut palms that lined the cove.

"Shit!" Clyde turned and jumped off the rocks. He trotted up the brilliant white beach, head craned, trying to see the boat. The cove was too narrow and he never saw the yacht again.

American girls, he was sure. Those were definitely *American* tits. But where do American girls stay in this part of Costa Rica? Not around here; that's a fact. Nobody around here. Probably staying down the coast, some tourist spot.

Clyde turned away from the cove and followed the path up the palm-covered bluff of Cape Santa Elena towards the mansion. The project directors had chosen this cape on the northwest coast of Costa Rica precisely because it was isolated. It was easy to secure.

Clyde looked up the hill. The white stucco mansion blazed against a cobalt sky. The red terra-cotta roof faceted with intersecting gables seemed to float above the walls. The whole building shimmered on the crest of a deep-green wave of tropical vegetation. The fact that there was already a building here was a bonus. The film actor who owned it rented it willingly. A flock of sea gulls swirled above the terrace that jutted seaward from the upper story.

Heels clicked together. Clyde heard, "Good morning, sir!" before he saw the soldier. He returned the salute and stepped off the path towards the camouflaged guard. "Don't be doing that, soldier," said Clyde. "You jump up and salute like that on guard-duty you're liable to get wasted."

"Yessir. Sorry sir."

"No problem, ah—" Clyde read the soldier's black name tag. "—Private Sawyers. Just don't want you to develop bad habits, son. Someday you might be doing some *real* soldiering."

The sea gulls hovered over the red-tiled terrace, floating in the sea breeze, squawking, swooping down to catch the pieces of bread Solo tossed from a lounge chair.

Bill Stewart, co-owner of Electron Dynamics and the mansion's official lessee, lay at a right angle to Solo, facing the beach. A tall, gangly, blond man, young-looking for forty-five, Bill covered his fair skin against the sun with white cotton pants, a splashy Hawaiian shirt and a Panama hat. The cool breeze singing up through the palms caressed his pale face and ruffled his shirt. He watched Clyde jog up the path. Clyde, Bill observed, double-timed everywhere he went. The man's compact, hard body was a measure of his vitality. Clyde was energetic; dumb but active.

Since the contracts with DARPA—the Defense Advanced Research Projects Agency—began five years before, Electron Dynamics had grown to become a major defense contractor. Bill, a brilliant engineer, was now also wealthy. He seldom had time to enjoy the house he'd bought on Melbourne Beach. Trying to bask in the sun—a pastime which his skin would not tolerate—looked comfortable and seemed to Bill the thing that a multimillionaire ought to be doing at his expensive beach house. In Florida, the breeze was not cool on sunny days.

Bill smiled. The cool Costa Rican air felt exquisite as it wafted over his warm skin, swirling up his pants leg and under his loose shirt. He turned toward the squabbling gulls.

All he could see was the back of Solo's chair. A marble-sized ball of bread shot up. A noisy aerial duel among the gulls ended when the winner swooped away, pursued by the others.

"Greedy bastards," said Bill.

"It's a game for them," Solo replied.

Bill smiled. Solo's floral-banded Panama hat turned, tracking the gulls like a straw radar antenna.

"You ready for tomorrow?" Bill said.

"I can't wait." Solo tossed another lump of bread.

Bill grinned. At last. Progress. "A lot of people are waiting to see how this turns out. Big opportunity for you."

"And for you, Bill."

"That's right. And for me." Bill saw Clyde run under the terrace. He added, "But if you fuck it up, I'll take the crap."

"I'm ready, Bill. I am the greatest Commie-killer there ever was," Solo said in a queer, steady cadence. "A lean, mean, fighting machine. Lorenzo is as good as dead."

Bill grimaced. It was what they wanted to hear, but Solo parroted it without inflection, without conviction.

"That's the ticket!" Clyde strode onto the terrace as Solo spoke. White teeth gleamed against his tanned face. "You been *talking* to our boy, eh, Bill?"

"We've been working on some of the moral issues, Clyde. Solo was confused on a few points, but we've worked them out. I think."

"Moral issues?" Clyde's brow furrowed beneath his greying crew cut. He walked over to Solo. "All you have to know, Solo, is that you're a *warrior*. An *American* warrior. And we are fighting for our fucking lives."

Bill closed his eyes. Not again.

Clyde continued. "It's been tough, but we're winning, boy. We beat 'em in Korea and Vietnam. We fucked 'em in Chile, Salvador, Guatemala. And now we're gonna beat 'em in Nicaragua. And with you—" Clyde shook his head, smiling broadly. "With you and the others like you, we're gonna *stomp ass.*"

"Stomp ass!" said Solo, as he tossed more bread aloft.

Clyde laughed and watched the gulls. When he looked at the tiles below the gulls, he frowned. "Ah, Solo. You wanna cut that out? Place is covered in gull shit."

"I hate gull shit!" said Solo.

Clyde shook his head and sat down beside Bill. "What's with our boy, Bill? I've never seen him so goddamn agreeable."

"I'll tell you later," said Bill, nodding towards Solo.

"Yeah, later." Clyde looked out through the white wooden railing at the sea. "Hey, Bill. Did you see that *stuff* sailing by a few minutes ago?"

"The yacht?"

"On the yacht, Bill. Two naked chicks. Cooze, Bill. How long has it been? A month?"

"Three weeks," said Bill. "I didn't see any girls, Clyde. Too far away."

"Jesus, Bill." Clyde grabbed his binoculars. "You oughta keep a pair of these around, man. Never know what the fuck you'll see. I mean—Solo, did you see—" Clyde turned around.

"—those tits?" he said to the back of the empty lounge. Solo was gone. "Where'd the hell he go?"

"Probably went to study up for the mission," said Bill.

"Man, he's fast. And quiet," said Clyde. "These guys are going to be hell to stop."

"I'm afraid you're right," said Bill.

2

RAIN sounds reached the ground long before the drops. A peccary rooting in the humus looked up, wrinkling its nose. The stalking jaguar froze, watching his prey sniff the air.

Drops fell through the top layer of the rain forest canopy, hit the second tier or the third in the two-hundred-foot fall, breaking into mist. Fog swirled white against the deep shadows. The peccary resumed snuffling for food.

Hidden in a cave of matapalo roots, doom twitched his tail and resumed his slow stalk. Water drops beaded on the jaguar's whiskers and fell, finally, to the ground.

The peccary pushed its pig-snout deep into the composting forest floor. The jaguar crept forward a few more inches. When the peccary paused to look for danger, the cat froze.

Something moved at the edge of the jaguar's vision. He looked. Nothing. Sniffed the air. Nothing. The jaguar squinted, still bothered, as he resumed stalking.

"Great picture. From ten miles away," said Bill. Wearing another of his large collection of gaudy Hawaiian shirts, he sat in front of his monitor in the control room. The incongruous floor-length curtains and spidery crystal chandelier were all that remained of the dining room on the first floor of the mansion. Crammed with computers, monitors and technicians, it looked like a miniature version of Mission Control at the Johnson Space Center.

"Yeah. Amazing," Clyde yawned. As the military deputy director of the project, Clyde was not interested in technical details. Clyde did not understand how Bill made any of this work, and did not care to learn. Clyde was interested in results.

The image of the jaguar stealthily inching his way through the palmettos grew bigger as Solo zoomed in on the cat's face.

"What's with the goddamn jaguar? What about the mission—"

"Mission." Both men looked at the the monitor, taken by surprise. Solo's voice from the speaker was sullen, mechanical, electronic.

"Yes," said Bill.

As Solo zoomed back to a wider view, the cat launched itself silently through the leaves, calm intention on his face. The peccary wheeled, dropped the hymenium pod it had found, screamed terror. A metallic squeak came from the speaker. Solo zoomed to close-up as the cat shook his kill. Blood pulsed from ragged puncture wounds and dripped from the jaguar's teeth, more drops on the ground.

"Sick."

"C'mon, Clyde. He's watching everything. A good sign," Bill said.

The cat turned suddenly and dragged his meal away.

The monitor showed a hugely magnified drop of blood hanging from the serrated edge of a leaf.

"Mission," Bill coaxed.

"What *is* this?" Clyde was appalled. "We're supposed to be killing someone. Damnit."

"Mission." The same distant, emotionless voice acknowledged from the speaker, but the image on the monitor still showed the drop of blood. The drop lengthened, distorting the world it reflected, and slipped off the leaf.

The scene on the monitor changed abruptly.

A wet leaf plastered against the lens. They waited, wincing, for Solo to wipe it off, but the robot let the leaf slide slowly across its eye as it crept like the jaguar, floating through the dripping foliage.

Bill blinked instinctively, pulled off his stereo viewing glasses and rubbed his eye. It had seemed to Bill that the leaf had dragged across his own eyeball. The glasses put him there, inside Solo. He put them back on. He stared at the monitor, saw what the robot was seeing ten miles away as it watched its target through the dense jungle growth.

In the target area, a small clearing in the jungle, Corporal Lorenzo appeared through gaps in the leaves, wheeling at every sound. As the target, Corporal Lorenzo's job was to see the robot before it saw him. Caciques shrieked. Toucans rasped. A spider monkey chattered overhead.

Solo's head tilted, bringing his arm into view on the monitor. Wet leaves stuck to the black plastic. Mats of golden-orb spider web covered everything. Beads of water raced among the debris as the robot moved to unfasten the Ruger survival rifle on its belt.

Bill's throat tightened as Solo brought the rifle up and unfolded the stock. Corporal Lorenzo looked right at Solo. The robot froze. Lorenzo didn't see it. He whirled at the raucous rasping of a toucan. The robot sighted, centering the cross hairs of the telescopic sight on Corporal Lorenzo's temple.

"He's got him," said someone at the back of the room.

Adjacent images on the monitor showed what Solo saw through each eye. In the left picture, a black plastic hand matted with spider web and jungle debris held the forestock of a blackened stainless steel Ruger aimed at a stand of palm fronds. Now and then, the observers at Control glimpsed Lorenzo moving between the leaves. The right picture showed a clear close-up view of Lorenzo, sweating profusely, eyes darting. A cross hair hovered at a spot midway between his ear and eye. Like an expert human marksman, the robot sighted without having to blink. It couldn't blink.

The two views were now too disparate for the stereo glasses to blend. Bill removed them and looked back and forth be-

tween the two pictures. As Lorenzo moved around the clearing, the cross hairs tracked him unerringly, centered on his
skull, never wavering. The robot's job was to decide for itself
when to fire.

As Solo let the rifle rest loosely in its left hand, a dragonfly
fluttered to a landing on his thumb. The gun sight continued
to track Lorenzo perfectly.

Solo's left eye zoomed in on the insect. The dragonfly tilted
its head as the camera optics moved, shifting to close-up. In
the control room monitor, the left picture filled with the dragonfly's iridescent face. The right picture showed Corporal
Lorenzo being tracked by a high-powered rifle.

"Why doesn't he shoot, goddamnit?" Clyde said.

Bill turned, whispering, "He will, Clyde. He's never seen a
live dragonfly before." He turned back to the monitor quickly.

Clyde muttered, "I'm so fucking happy."

The dragonfly preened itself, wiped its thousand eyes,
stopped occasionally to look around, ignored the featureless
black face which loomed over it. Lorenzo vanished from the
monitor. Solo had lowered the rifle. The dragonfly perched
comfortably on the robot's thumb and stared at Bill from both
pictures on the monitor.

The audience of technicians groaned.

Bill shook his head slowly.

They saw Corporal Lorenzo approaching through the foliage. The robot was off guard, and Lorenzo had seen it moving.

"What the hell is wrong with him?" said the general.

"Almost," said Bill quietly.

Corporal Lorenzo's face grew large behind the preening
dragonfly. His voice reverberated through the speakers, "Nice
bug you got there, Solo."

"What *is* the problem, Bill?" said Clyde.

"It takes time, Clyde. The nature of the beast. It's learning."

"You'd a thought the thing would learn faster—all that money."

The monitor showed branches and leaves passing by Solo's head. Lorenzo, invisible behind the machine, spoke.

"You sure you know where you're going?"

"Yes."

"What was so special about that bug?"

"Odonata albanil."

"Huh?"

"Genus and species."

"Oh."

Then only rustling sounds. On the monitor, leaves and vines and insects floated past Solo's eyes.

General Haynes watched Solo's pictures, shaking his head. "He seems human sometimes, the way he talks to Lorenzo. He seems to understand."

"He does understand. So why won't he pull the trigger? He's getting smarter every day, Clyde." Bill said, sighing. "I don't know how much longer he's gonna keep buying this crap we're feeding him. We should be telling him the truth."

"He doesn't need to know the truth, Bill. He's supposed to follow orders. Hell, we don't even tell *grunts* the truth—how else you gonna get 'em to fight?"

"We're playing with fire, Clyde. He's going to find out we've been lying. A pissed-off grunt is one thing. But Solo—"

"I'm glad those fucking webs don't bother you," said Lorenzo from the speaker.

"It is the strongest natural fiber," said Solo. "Indians use it to make fish nets."

"Yeah? They're still creepy-crawlies."

"Nephila clavipes."

"Huh? Oh, yeah, the name of the big fucking spiders."

"Yes."

Solo and Lorenzo dodged and twisted through the thick undergrowth. Solo was following an electronic path to the waiting helicopter. There was no other trail.

Solo's position, tracked by satellites, showed as as a glowing blue spot on the navigation monitor. The dot blinked, moving towards the chopper.

Clyde picked up a microphone. "Tell them Solo's just about there."

An electric double click sounded in a speaker at the front of the room. "Red One, Control."

"Roger, Control. Go."

"Your date's almost ready."

"Roger."

The whine of the chopper's turbine starting up came over the speaker. Bill grabbed the viewing glasses and put them on. He flinched when a wet branch slapped across Solo's face. Solo's arm, matted with cobwebs, leaves and twigs, pushed a palm branch aside. The chopper sat hissing, blades swinging lazily, in the center of the clearing. A circle of grim commandos surrounded it, rifles ready.

Bill smiled, feeling guilty that he did. It was possible, he supposed, that someone could get past the battalions that held the perimeter around the Project Solo zone. But if there was a square mile of Costa Rica that was secure, this was it.

Solo ducked under the whirling rotors to the open cockpit door. The pilot signaled wait. The crew chief and gunner ran up with rags. "Man you look like Swamp Thing, Solo," yelled the crew chief, grinning. "Let us get some of this jungle shit off you, okay?"

"Okay."

The rags were useless. It was easier just to pull the cobwebs off in mats. Solo studied the whirling rotor hub assembly while the men fussed with the debris.

"Shit!" The crew chief flicked a huge spider off his hand. When it hit the ground, he raised his foot.

"No," said Solo.

"Hey, Solo," the crew chief yelled. "They can't hurt you, babe, but they can sure as hell fuck with me."

"She will not bite you."

The crew chief saw the pilot raise his hand and shake his head. Don't argue with Solo.

"She?" The crew chief screwed up his mouth in disgust but left the spider alone. He felt a shiver of fear. He'd forgotten what Solo could do. How close had he come to getting killed? He pulled more cobwebs off the robot. Just keep it friendly, he thought. "How do you know it's a she?"

"The female spins the web. The males are so tiny as to be almost invisible."

"Yeah?" He pulled a sheet of silk tangled with insect and plant debris off Solo's chest. "That's sure good to know, man."

"Yes," said Solo.

Solo had flunked all the assassination tests so far, but he loved to fly. That part of the trial at least was a success. Solo climbed into the Huey's cockpit, carefully lowering himself into the right seat so as not to bump the cyclic. The crew chief helped fasten the safety harness and closed the door. When Solo put on a flight helmet and slid the visor down, he looked almost human.

"You got it," said the pilot, Chief Warrant Officer Sam Thompson, smiling. Solo was by far his best student. "Everybody's on board."

"I got it," said Solo in the intercom.

Bill saw a hundred dials and switches fly by as Solo scanned the cockpit panel. He followed its hand, now relatively clean, to the collective. Solo twisted the throttle. The rotors spun to a blur, beating the air with a dull slapping noise. The sound grew louder, thudding, as Solo pulled the collective up. The machine rose out of the clearing.

The Huey tilted forward, accelerating toward a low spot in the treeline. Solo hugged the canopy contours. To Bill, the treetops flashing by were dizzying, sickening. Approaching a huge hymenium tree, he saw hundreds of bird nests hanging like stuffed socks off the branches. Gleaming black *oropéndolas* and dusty brown cowbirds swarmed among them. Solo banked away from the colony, giving it room. A minute later the Pacific Ocean flashed into view. Solo banked hard along the beach, climbing to two-hundred feet. Waves broke in slow motion below them.

The mansion looked perfectly peaceful from the air until they got close, Bill noted as Solo circled, looking down. Some of the two hundred troopers hidden in the jungle around the mansion were visible, entrenched among the perimeter hedges. Two Hueys squatted on the lawn behind the main house.

How obvious were these signs from further up? Certainly the choppers showed up on Russian satellites. That should reveal nothing of what was going on. The U.S. military rented dozens of similar mansions all over Central America. There was nothing unusual about this one.

Solo banked for a landing into the sea breeze. Thompson had his hand on his knee next to the cyclic just in case. He'd had human students—advanced students—who'd blown it on the final approach. He also knew that if Solo were damaged through his negligence, they'd make him a WAC.

When Solo hit the buffeting downdrafts on the leeward side of the mansion, he'd already pulled up the collective, adding sufficient power to compensate. The landing flare and hover were perfect. He set the machine down next to the other Hueys as though he'd logged thousands of hours. This was his tenth.

Solo shut down the machine. Bill heard Thompson say, "Well, Solo, I have to say it. You get a perfect grade. Great job."

"Yes," said Solo.

3

WATCHING waves chasing sandpipers, Bill sipped a vodka tonic on the upstairs terrace. He put his foot on the railing. As he leaned over to tie his shoelaces, Bill remembered the months of training it took to teach Solo to tie his shoes. Image interpretation, body-part position sensing, and tactile feedback. Something kids learned in weeks. But Solo learned more and more quickly. He had become an expert helicopter pilot in ten hours. Bill sipped his drink and smiled to himself. Will I ever be able to stop seeing everything as a problem to be solved? A sandpiper chased a retreating wave, speared a sand flea with his beak, turned and raced away from the next wave. The bird's agility recalled the frustration they'd felt during the year it took Solo to learn to walk. Solo fell so often he became depressed and wouldn't try again for days. Solo's construction and programming encouraged such feelings to arise. Emotions in humans establish priorities and form purpose and were therefore necessary in an intelligent machine. Without an emotional structure, Solo would wander aimlessly. Though he had provided for emotional responses in Solo, Bill was amazed when they occurred. Whether what Solo felt was what a human felt was entirely conjecture. People could only guess how Solo felt by watching what Solo *did*.

A machine that experienced what seemed to be emotional episodes caused the people working with it to forget that Solo was a machine. Clyde, for example, thought of Solo as a child that needed careful instruction.

"I'm surprised at you, Solo," said Clyde. "I thought you understood what the hell we're trying to do here."

Solo lay in his chair and did not reply. Clyde shook his head sadly. "Okay, Solo. We go through it again." Clyde leaned towards Solo and held up a finger. "First, there's good guys and there's bad guys."

Bill jerked around. "Jesus, Clyde, will you give us a fucking break." He twisted the chair towards Clyde. Solo lay inert in a sling chair. Clyde was poised on the edge of his seat, staring at Bill.

"What d'you mean?" A child's surprise broke Clyde's tough face.

"I mean what I said. Solo's not a moron. He *knows* this. He's heard it a hundred goddamn times. I've heard a hundred goddamn times. Give us both a fucking break."

"You know, Bill, you shouldn't be drinking so early in the day; it's duty hours."

"Civilian's prerogative, Clyde."

Clyde turned back to Solo. "You probably do know what I'm talking about, Solo, but maybe we ought to go over it again, to be sure. Okay?"

"Yes," said Solo. Nothing moved when Solo spoke. No mouth showed if Solo smiled or frowned. No one could tell where Solo's lenses looked. Solo spoke without gesture. Solo could synthesize any voice, given a few words to sample. He now chose to use Clyde's, but the sound buzzed slightly as he attempted to mimic Clyde's raspiness.

"See," said Clyde. He looked back at Bill indignantly.

Bill shook his head. "Solo, tell us the difference between a good guy and a bad guy."

"A good guy is a man who does good things—an American,"

said Solo. "A bad guy is a man who does bad things—a Communist."

"That's right!" said Clyde.

"Jesus," said Bill.

"So, Solo," said Clyde. "We're the good guys. Bill and I. All the soldiers here. You too, Solo. And we want you to kill the bad guys we tell you to kill."

"No," said Solo.

"I thought you said you understood me," said Clyde.

"I understand you."

"So what's the problem?"

"You have not asked me to solve a problem."

Clyde glanced quickly at Bill. Bill grinned. Clyde continued, "I mean, why won't you kill the bad guys we ask you to?"

"Lorenzo is not bad," said Solo.

"I get it!" yelled Clyde. "I see." He turned to Bill again with triumph on his face. "Solo, listen to me carefully. Corporal Lorenzo was *pretending* to be a bad guy. Your rifle is loaded with *blanks*. We just wanted to see if you could stalk a simulated bad guy and pretend to compromise him. Do you understand now?"

"Yes. Compromise: eliminate, delete, extirpate, fuck him up, kill." Solo had refined his imitation of Clyde's voice until it was perfect.

"Ah, yeah. That's right." Clyde was unnerved by the string of synonyms delivered in his own voice. "Solo, use your *own* voice from now on—gives me the creeps to keep hearing myself talking out of your head." Solo nodded. "So if we repeated the mission tomorrow, you'd pull the trigger?"

"No," said Solo.

Clyde stood up suddenly. "I need a drink," he said. He stopped midway on his way to the bar, turning back to Bill. "Okay, expert—" He pointed to Solo.

Bill nodded. "Solo, I thought you understood that this mission was a new TAU." Bill used the acronym for Thematic

Abstraction Unit. The term flagged previously defined social situations or plans which Solo had learned, like: TAU–Close-Call, TAU-Hypocrisy or TAU–Evade-Enemy.

"Yes, Bill, TAU-Elimination."

"That's right. You understand you have made a mistake?"

"No." The robot lay comfortably on the lounge, not moving. "I tracked the target and placed him properly in the sight picture. Pulling the trigger was superfluous."

"It was part of the instruction of this simulation to pull the trigger."

"Yes," said Solo. "However, there were no actual bullets in the rifle. All critical events of the mission were accomplished." Solo's voice was natural-sounding now, animated with appropriate inflection, sounding vaguely like David Brinkley. "It is also my job to make decisions."

Clyde slumped into his seat next to Solo, swirling a whiskey and water.

Bill leaned forward, speaking quietly, "If we assigned a TAU-Elimination mission with real bullets and against a real enemy, would you pull the trigger?"

Solo rolled his head slightly to face Bill. The movement indicated where he looked, a courtesy he had learned to use with humans. "I have always done my tasks well. It would be logical to assume that I would continue to do so."

Bill sat back. He sipped his drink and stared at the robot. Solo reverted to a maddeningly literal view of things when he, it, became cornered. He played dumb. Why was Solo being evasive now? Certainly it can lie, thought Bill, but equivocation? There was no provision for that. Solo was strictly forbidden to dodge a direct question from his builders. Evading an enemy, yes. But not us. The system was learning, but it was learning the wrong things. Despite the team indoctrination and the this-is-your-enemy propaganda, Solo grew more independent. Troublesome. All by itself—as Bill had predicted— somewhere in that mass of a million processors something was being born and was growing fast. Yet the programs that encouraged learning and emotions were the only way to build a machine like Solo in the first place. Bill's dream, to be able to talk to a sentient machine, was now the nightmare of attempting to control one. "Okay, Solo." Bill leaned forward. "Go charge your batteries. We'll be working on TAU-Survey tomorrow."

"Yes." The overburdened lounge chair groaned as Solo leaned forward. At six feet two inches, Bill weighed a hundred and seventy-five pounds. The machine, the same height, weighed three-hundred pounds. Solo stood up and left the terrace without saying another word.

"There's something cooking inside that boy," said Clyde.

"I know," said Bill. "He's balking. He questions the missions."

"That's right," said Clyde. "This simulated assassination stuff gives him too much room to maneuver. If we wanna know what he'd do in the real world, we have to give him a real-world mission. That's why we're here. I think we're gonna have to have him kill someone."

Bill stared at Clyde in disbelief. "You're serious?"

"That's what this's all about, Bill, remember?"

"Solo's just the prototype, Clyde. We've go to move slowly. We're only beginning to find out what he can do. Solo just can't kill now. I think that the accident with McNeil traumatized him. We have to let him work through it at his own pace."

Clyde grimaced at McNeil's name. "Bullshit. We gotta know. He said he would if the target were real."

"He said it was logical to *assume* that he would—"

"So, let's give him a real target, goddamnit. Find out if he's bluffing. We've got bunches of 'em just north of here."

Bill stared into Clyde's blue eyes. They'd both been to Vietnam. They'd both seen the carnage. How could they think so differently? "As a fucking test?"

"Wake up, Bill!" Clyde scowled and leaned forward. "We're killing them every day. With guns, bombs, fire, clubs. Whatever. What does it matter what we kill them with, for chrissake? It's like testing another rifle to me."

Bill believed him.

"They'll never let you do it."

"Of course they will, Bill. It's a provision in the damn test critera. We have to *know* if a Solo can function in the real world."

"Nobody ever told me that! A test killing?"

Clyde watched Bill's face redden. He said quietly, "It's in the *military* test critera, Bill."

Bill shook his head slowly, glaring at Clyde. Of course they wouldn't have told me that. "I won't lift a finger to help, Clyde," he said.

Clyde stood up, towering over Bill. "You know, Bill, with all the influence you have on Solo these days, I don't think we need you anymore anyway. The machine understands me better every day. I can put a damn TAU in front of words too. Solo just needs firmer guidance. Face it, Bill, sometimes you just aren't capable of doing what has to be done." He turned and stalked through the French doors.

Bill watched the curtains swirl in the sea breeze. The surf hissed behind him. Gulls cried. He turned his chair around. The orange sun sliced slowly into the ocean. "We'll see," he said.

Solo lay on his lounger in his room. Through the gauzy curtained bay windows of an upstairs bedroom he watched a flying squirrel glide between two coconut trees. The squirrel landed at the exact spot Solo had predicted at launch. He shifted his attention. Inside the room, he saw himself reflected in the ornately framed mirror on the dresser. Zooming in on his silvered eye covers, he saw reflected in them the whole side of the room, the dresser, the two sets of bay windows, the painting of a bowl of fruit by Cézanne. He wondered what was behind the eye covers. The question asked itself into infinity in the reflections he saw.

He zoomed back and looked at himself in the mirror. Three cables snaked from a compartment—an input/output port, an I/O port in computer lingo—on his right side. One, connected to a wall outlet, charged his batteries. The second, looped around the table leg, connected him to the laser disk player. No picture formed on the TV monitor next to it. Digital information from the laser disk was being transmitted directly to his brain, faster than it could be shown on the monitor. Somewhere in his brain he saw the pictures and heard the narrator from the Huey training disk: "Four dash forty-seven," said the narrator. "If failure of the inlet Guide Actuator occurs, the pilot will notice an instantaneous rise in EGT. By reducing collective pitch, the EGT can be maintained . . ." An exploded view of a section of the Huey's turbine changed in synchrony with the narration.

The third cable connected Solo to Control's main computer. Through this link, Solo used the super-computer—ordinary and certainly not sentient—to solve very complicated mathematical problems, problems it was better suited to solve than he. Solo listened, interested, as the computer encoded a message and sent it out on the top-secret military computer network, MILnet, to Washington.

4

"THERE is a man moving at coordinates three-two-one, six-six-two. He is armed. Blue Army." Solo's calm voice, roughened by transmission static and helicopter noises, came from the speaker.

"Roger, Red Eye. That's affirm. Proceed to next sector." Clyde grinned as he spoke. He turned to Bill. "That boy has one hell of a pair of eyes. That kid in sector three is wearing camos and face paint."

"Very high resolution lenses," said Bill curtly.

"Yeah. But you still have to use 'em, right?" He waited for Bill to answer. Bill, wearing the stereo glasses, stared at Solo's monitor. He watched the two chase ships floating in formation next to Solo, who was flying a Huey alone for the first time. "I mean," Clyde continued, "if you gave the same lenses to a person, he'd miss that kid. I bet he would."

"You're probably right." Bill didn't look up.

"You still pissed about last night?" asked Clyde.

Bill looked over the glasses. Clyde sprawled back on his chair holding a Styrofoam cup of coffee. "I think that about describes how I feel—in standard military terms."

Clyde laughed. "Hey, Bill, don't take it personal. We both got a job to do, y'know?" Clyde rolled his chair closer, speaking softly. "I don't like killing any more than you do. It makes me sick. You know that, don't you?"

"Bullshit. What do you know about killing, Clyde? You ordered people like me to do your killing."

"Control, Red Eye," said Solo.

Clyde turned back to the console and picked up the mike. "Go, Red Eye."

"I see two camps. One with two Blues, one set with decoys."

"Damn! This kid's a whiz." Clyde grinned.

"Thank you," said Solo.

Clyde looked at the mike in his hand. "What's up? I didn't broadcast."

"He's used his own radios, Clyde." Bill checked his console keyboard. "Here's the problem," he said, pointing. "My transmit switch was active."

"Turn it off. He's supposed to be using standard equipment." Clyde put the mike to his mouth. "Red Eye, keep your transmissions confined to this frequency. You copy?"

"I copy."

"Proceed to sector five."

"Roger."

Clyde turned to Bill. "What I want to know, Bill, is how this fucking machine can break rules in the first place? He's programmed not to use his radio in this simulation."

"Because Solo isn't a *computer*, Clyde. I've been telling you guys since day one. Solo's becoming a kind of being. Not computer, not human. He thinks. That's the whole point of Solo and that's what makes him so dangerous. How the hell can you keep forgetting that? You've been in the project since DARPA took over."

Clyde got red in the face. "Look, Stewart, I'm running the field trial. You build a weapon that's supposed to work; I test it. I don't know shit about the details and neither will the people who'll end up using Solos. It's your job to know the technicalities and to answer my fucking questions."

The sickening feeling returned to Bill's chest. Ten years of his life working on this project. He should have known

it would end up like this. The big decision: either make
Solo to be a weapon; or not make Solo at all. He had ignored his conscience; salved it with the hope that he'd be
able to channel its use once the machine worked. It
worked. When he stressed how dangerous Solo would be if
its education were restricted to warfare—including the fact
that Solo could even be a threat to its builders—that only
encouraged them. When he insisted that Solo was the first
of a kind of weapon that would be more dangerous than
any atomic bomb—bombs can't ever argue—they accused
him of losing his sense of reality, being too close to his
own work to see it as it really was. DARPA's own science
advisers conducted computer simulations which proved that
Solo would always be controllable—an ideal warrior—if ap-
propriately programmed and equipped with the proper safe-
guards. They saw Solo as a non-stoppable, expendable
weapon, manipulatable and malleable as any normal computer. The machine's apparent sentience? Well, that was
an illusion, they said, a control program self-generated by
the computer to manage its millions of simultaneous
tasks—a phenomenon Bill himself had predicted. They had
all the answers and all the money. Bill feigned acquiescence
and kept working—eventually they would see the truth.
The chance to apply Solo to peaceful tasks might not yet
be lost. Still, the most sophisticated machine ever built was
in the hands of Neanderthals.

"That's all Solo is to you? A weapon?"

"That's it, Mr. Science. Solo's like a TV set to me: I don't
care how it works; I just want to see fucking pictures. And
that's exactly why we're here. And we're going to find out just
what Solo can do. And it—"

"Control, Red Eye," Solo's voice broke in.

Clyde clicked the transmit button angrily. "Go ahead, Red
Eye."

"Sector five is clear."

Clyde looked up at the navigation monitor. Sector five had no targets. A red herring. So far Solo was a hundred percent. One sector left to go.

"Roger, Red Eye. Affirmative. Proceed to last sector."

"Roger. Advise twenty-five minutes fuel remaining," Solo said calmly.

Clyde looked at Bill. Bill shook his head, "You're cutting it too close for his first solo."

"I copy, Red Eye," said Clyde. "Should give you plenty of time to check the last sector and get back home."

"Roger," said Solo.

"You're taking stupid chances with a two-billion-dollar machine, Clyde."

"It's my decision. I have to know what Solo will do under stress. Not a simulation. The real thing," said Clyde.

"And if he runs out of fuel?"

"He'll autorotate, Bill. He's an expert pilot, right?" Clyde shrugged. "An autoration wouldn't hurt him. And we have two chase ships to pick 'im up." Bill stared silently. Clyde continued. "If he does gets hurt we patch 'im up. That's why you're here."

"And if we can't patch him up?" Bill accused.

"If it comes down to that; there's another Solo coming along at Electron Dynamics. These things are *supposed* to be expendable. We've got to know."

Clyde's aide rushed over with a printout, a message off MILnet. Clyde put the mike down and read it.

Bill watched the monitor, ignoring Clyde's message. Solo hovered two-hundred feet over the jungle like a hummingbird, darting to get a better view of something on the ground. The rain forest canopy seemed impenetrable. Solo's vision shifted to infrared and the trees turned scarlet. When Solo's left eye zoomed to telephoto, Bill saw the greenish shape of a man starkly contrasted against the red foliage, lying flat on the ground. Solo had spent weeks developing his own image analysis techniques. They worked. No human would've noticed that soldier if he'd been waving a flag.

"Control, Red Eye."

Clyde looked up from his message, nodded at Bill, pointed at the mike.

"Roger, Red Eye. Go," said Bill.

"Have located one target in sector six. Coordinates three-two-two, six-five-zero."

Bill checked the nav monitor. Solo's blue dot eclipsed the target's location. Dead on. "Roger, Red Eye," radioed Bill. "That's the last one. Come on home."

Solo did not reply.

Clyde put down the message, smiling. "They've given me the go-ahead."

Bill held up his hand and clicked the mike. "Red Eye. Return home. Do you read?"

No answer.

Bill repeated, "Red Eye, this is Control. Do you read?"

"Try his own radios," said Clyde.

Bill nodded, tapped his keyboard, and spoke into his headset, "Solo?"

"Yes, Bill?"

"Your ship's radios must be out; we can't raise you."

"The radios are operating, Bill."

"Why didn't you answer?"

"I was distracted by a very troubling message, Bill. TAU-Conflict has occurred."

"What message?" Bill asked, keeping his voice as calm as possible.

"The one on MILnet, Bill."

Bill looked at Clyde. "What was that message about?"

"I told you, Bill; the go-ahead."

"What are you talking about?"

"The test. A real target."

"You goddamn idiot!" Bill slugged the desktop.

"Pull yourself together, Stewart." Clyde snatched the mike. "Red Eye, this is Control."

"Stupid fucking puzzle-palace rejects. Military-minded assholes!" Bill raved. The control room staff stared.

"Roger, Control."

"Proceed home, Red Eye. Mission accomplished. Perfect score."

"Thank you, Control. I'm not coming home now."

"I can't believe this. Are you feeding him some signal or something?" Clyde screamed at Bill.

"No. It's all your show." Bill reached in front of Clyde and got the printout. It said:

REBELS REPORT SANDY ELEMENT IN BLUE SECTOR.
SAMPLE COMPROMISE AUTHORIZED. TARGET OF
OPPORTUNITY. FULL CAMOUFLAGE REQUIRED.

They're gonna do it, thought Bill, disgusted. Send Solo out in full camouflage, fatigues and headnet, to blow some random someone away. Search and destroy. Target of opportunity.

Bill looked up. Clyde was trying to coax Solo home. "You have fifteen minutes fuel left, Solo. We don't have time to argue. Return to base!"

Solo did not answer. The navigation monitor showed that he had turned, heading north.

"Red Two, Control," Clyde called the chase team leader.

"Roger, Control," said Solo's instructor, Thompson.

"I want you and Red Three to close on Red Eye. Force him back."

"Roger," said Thompson, "You copy, Red Three?"

Red Three answered with two clicks.

On the navigation monitor, two yellow dots converged on the blue one.

"We don't have time to fuck around, Bill. If this nutty machine keeps going the way he's going, I'll have to turn him off or blow him out of the sky." Sweat poured down Clyde's face. "I can't let him get into enemy territory."

Bill nodded. "DARPA and the CIA wouldn't like that too much, would they?"

"No, they wouldn't!" Clyde yelled. "And they wouldn't like it if we have to blow it up either. We're both responsible for this fucking program, Stewart. You better start coming up with some damn answers. Right now!"

Bill slapped his hand on the message. "I've told you since we began that Solo is not an automaton. I don't have a button to push to make him do what I want. He has to learn to want to do what we want him to do. He has to be motivated. Just like a person." Bill held up the paper. "You pushed him into something he isn't ready for. You've just blown him away. This is a major conflict, and it came too soon. He's going to do what he thinks is right."

"And what the hell will that be?" demanded Clyde.

"I haven't the slightest idea."

"Talk to him, Stewart." Clyde spoke carefully. "Talk to him and get him back here before I have to bring him down."

"I'll try." Bill looked at Solo's monitor. Treetops jerked by. Solo flew lower and faster than a man could. "Solo?"

"Yes, Bill," Solo answered calmly.

"If we cancel that mission—the one on the MILnet—will you come back?"

"No, Bill."

"That's it!" said Clyde. "Arm the abort switch, Bill."

"We can't turn him off while he's flying so fast, Clyde. It'd cause a completely uncontrolled crash. The impact could destroy him."

Clyde sighed and stared at the navigation monitor. Solo's blue dot moved to within twenty kilometers of the Nicaraguan border. Clyde picked up his mike. "Red Two, Control."

"Roger, Control. Go."

"Arm your guns."

"Say again, Control."

"Arm your guns! Arm your guns! You copy?"

After a long silence, Red Two answered. "Roger, Control. Guns armed."

"Roger, Red Two, stand by to disable Red Eye. At my signal aim for the engine compartment. Over."

"Roger, Control. Red Two out."

"Solo," said Bill. "I can guarantee that you will not have to go on that mission."

"Control, this is Red Two," Thompson yelled. "Red Eye has started evasive maneuvers at extreme low level!"

In Solo's monitor the horizon tilted sickeningly ninety degrees as Solo banked through a narrow gap in the trees.

"Solo, do you hear me?" said Bill.

"Yes, Bill." Solo's calm voice was without relationship to the wild gyrations of the Huey. "I can hear you quite well. My best option is to withdraw to a secure position and analyze my situation."

"Ten klicks to the border, General Haynes," a technician called out.

"A good decision, Solo," Bill forced himself to speak softly, calmly. "Control is the secure position. This is where you should return."

"Control, we can't keep Red Eye in our sights. How the hell is that ship staying together the way he's jinking?" said Thompson.

"You had better find out, mister!" Clyde growled.

"Solo, you can't survive without us. You'll run out of power in less than twenty hours," Bill pleaded. "Survival is your prime mission now."

"Survival is the mission, Bill." The Huey banked from extreme left to right, rolling the horizon so quickly that it made Bill sick to watch the monitor. "It would not be safe for me to return to Control. Propositional logic suggests that alterations would be made to my systems that would delete Self."

"I won't let them touch you, Solo," Bill yelled. "I promise you that."

"Five klicks, General Haynes."

"That's it, Stewart," Clyde glared, gulping. "We have to shoot the fucker down."

"Solo?" Bill implored.

"I do not doubt that you would attempt to protect me, Bill," said Solo.

"Red Two. Control." Clyde stared at the nav monitor. The blue dot did not waver from its steady path north.

"Roger, Control."

"Fire. Bring him down."

"Bring him down?" Thompson clicked the intercom switch to his copilot. "I can't even get him in my damn sights." Thompson clicked again to broadcast, "Roger, Control. Be advised I can't guarantee I can hit the engine compartment. I'll be lucky to hit the ship." Thompson flew a hundred feet higher than Solo. Solo's ship flashed back and forth past his flex-gun cross hairs.

"Roger, Red Two." Clyde's voice crackled in Thompson's headphones. "Get him down! I don't care if it's in pieces. You copy?"

"Roger, Control," said Thompson.

Solo flared the Huey hard. The nose pointed almost straight up. The two chase ships shot past him. They swung out, circling back.

Solo leveled his Huey and let it sink, hovering down to the canopy facing a huge hymenium tree. His two attackers banked steeply to get back to him. The fuel-low warning siren wailed in his headphones. A panel light blinked. A controlled landing here was his best option even if it was at least a hundred and fifty feet to the forest floor.

Thompson had him in his sights, but didn't pull the trigger. "Control, Red Two."

"Go, Red Two."

"Red Eye is trying to land," said Thompson. "He's setting down in the trees. There's no clearing."

"Good. Good," said Clyde. "Don't shoot unless he tries to get away. We've got him." He turned to Bill. "And when that thing lands, Stewart, you *will* send the abort code."

Defeated, Bill nodded. No option. Solo had obviously established a new mission for himself. He had to be stopped. Bill flipped the red cover off the abort switch. A complicated signal repeated three times would cause a tiny explosive switch to blow, disconnecting the robot from its batteries. A small standby generator would keep Solo conscious but paralyzed. Bill waited, watching the monitor. Tree limbs pressed against Solo's cockpit.

Solo's main rotors hit the first tree top, popping like gunfire, shredding leaves and small branches into mulch. The whirling blades descended steadily, cutting into bigger and bigger branches. The tail rotor tore off, buzzing into the darkness below. The Huey lurched and spun wildly to the right. Solo cut the throttle, neutralizing the torque, stabilizing the ship as it sank. One rotor blade snapped off against a branch. The remaining blade made two unbalanced turns before it ripped the mast and transmission out of the helicopter. Holding the useless controls of a torn and naked fuselage crashing, grating along the twisted mass of a matapalo tree, Solo entered the forest. Sections of the airframe crumpled away like tinfoil. Solo recalled the instructions in his Huey operator's manual: Section VIII, 4–56 Landing In Trees, sub-heading 3, "If time permits, lock shoulder harness, turn off switches and fuel valve." Solo locked his shoulder harness, turned off all switches and the fuel valve, and waited.

5

An algae-covered sloth turned slowly, squinting to see the cause of the terrible noise. The battered airframe plummeted, ripping vines and snapping branches. The layers of forest understory tugged and grabbed the four-thousand-pound wreck and slowed its fall. A tiny agouti squealed and bucked away as the helicopter smashed into the sodden jungle floor beside it.

The radio compartment crumpled into the cockpit. Sparks showered as the electronics shorted out. The wreck balanced on its nose, motionless, then flopped forward on its back.

Silence.

A column of vegetable debris fluttered down. A spider monkey shrieked angrily at the wreck and threw a chestnut at the intruder.

Solo, upside down in the safety harness, looked around through the smoke. He grabbed the bottom of the seat with his left hand and released the harness buckle with his right. Dropping to the roof of the Huey, he crawled out through the shards of the cockpit windshield.

A chestnut clunked on the top of his head. He looked up and saw the chattering, bare-fanged monkey let another fly. He ducked. Red Two and Red Three thudded and buzzed far overhead, glimpsed through the foliage.

"Control, Red Two." Solo heard the radio conversation.

"Go, Red Two," Clyde said.

"Roger, sir, we're tracking him, but we can't see him. Jungle's too thick."

"Roger. We see his beacon too."

"Solo?" Bill's voice came through their private frequency. "I can't read your video or your audio. Switch to backups."

"Control, he's not moving. He might have been damaged in the crash. It was a humdinger," said Thompson.

Solo switched off his beacon.

"Control, we just lost his signal," said Thompson.

"Goddamn it! He's trying to get away! Abort. Hit the switch!" Clyde yelled.

Fear shot through Solo at the word abort. When he had killed McNeil, Solo remembered kneeling by the twitching body of the man he had considered a friend, trying to understand what had happened. A tiny explosion went off inside him as he touched McNeil's mashed face. He had collapsed in a heap, paralyzed. Afraid.

Never again.

Bill flipped the switch down. A red panel light blinked three times. Abort. "Okay. He's down," he said. "We better get to him quick in case there's fire."

"Don't you worry about that," Clyde growled. "My *people* go where I tell them."

"Red Two, Control," Clyde radioed.

"Roger, Control."

"Standby. The rappelling team's on its way. You copy?"

"Roger. Advise we can remain on station five minutes, Control. Low fuel."

"Roger that, Red Two. Blue Team is on the way."

Solo turned, oriented himself, and marched north.

Clyde and Bill stood by the map at the back of the room.

"He put down three klicks from the border," Clyde said. "That's a break. But the kicker is that that's also where the moral equivalents of our Founding Fathers say they saw a fucking Sandy patrol yesterday. That's where we were going for the test kill."

"If that patrol finds Solo, he's completely helpless," said Bill.

"We can kiss our asses goodbye if that happens, Stewart. Solo'd be talking to the Russians in a week." Clyde turned away.

"We? What the hell do I have to do with this, Clyde?" Bill yelled at Clyde's back. "You're the dumb fuck that got him into this. A goddamn great command decision that was."

"Don't give up yet, you bastard. I'll get that fucking deserter." Clyde grabbed the mike. "It's your fault that the damn machine doesn't do what it's supposed to do." He clicked on the mike as Bill started to reply. "Blue Team, Control."

"Roger, Control."

"Well?" Clyde's voice broadcast anger through the ether.

"Five minutes," said the Blue Team leader.

Solo dodged vines and branches and vaulted roots that snaked across the forest floor. Using navigation signals from two satellites, he plotted his position. Fifty-five kilometers west of Los Chiles, ten kilometers south of Las Cruzas, a tiny village on Lake Nicaragua. He'd come two kilometers from where he crashed.

Voices.

He froze.

The voices came from somewhere up the path. He crouched in the midst of a palmetto stand and waited. TAU-Evasion.

"*Los Yanquis?*" said a voice. Solo knew the language very well. Spanish was one of the background frames they'd given him for his field trials. Frames. He knew two language frames, including some of the body movements and facial expressions that humans made with them. Frames. Every part of every weapon and vehicle used in war for the last hundred years was etched into his mind. Frames for battle strategy. Frames for combat tactics. Environment frames: flora and fauna and topographical maps of Costa Rica, Nicaragua, and Florida.

"Maybe. I hear their helicopters over there, I think." The patrol was moving towards him.

"We are too far south?" Solo saw them. The man who spoke wore a camouflage uniform, an AK-47 assault rifle slung over his shoulder. "Paco, can you read this map or not?"

"Yes, of course, *Teniente.* We are definitely north of the border. The Americans might be south of it."

"Let's go a little further, maybe we can see what they're doing."

"We will cross the border in half a kilometer, *Teniente.*"

"So? The *animales* are down here for us to find. Yes?"

"Yes, *Teniente.*" The man nodded. The leader waved his men on.

Solo watched fourteen soldiers walk by.

"Control, Blue Leader."

Solo heard Clyde answer, "Go, Blue Leader."

"Roger, Control. We're at the site. Can't see the wreck. Stuff's thick here. About two hundred feet to the deck. Rigging for rappelling."

The two Blue Team Hueys hovered in the canopy. Four men of the LRRP team—long range reconnaissance patrol—Lobo Squad, stood on the skids of Blue Leader's Huey. They snapped their D-rings to nylon ropes which dangled down through the canopy. Treetops swirled in the rotor wash. On signal from the crew chief, the LRRPs pushed off at the same time, rappelling down the lines.

The lead ship called his partner. "Blue Two, Blue Leader."

"Blue Two, Go."

"Roger, Blue Two. Give me a security orbit. From here to a klick or so out."

"Roger, Blue Leader." Blue Two immediately nosed forward and flew lazily through the treetops at barely thirty knots, snooping, spiraling out in wider and wider circles.

Lobo Squad sank into the jungle.

Solo rose out of the palmettos. The soldiers were well past. Turning away from the trail, one of the huge golden-orb spiders that kept him so thoroughly dressed in cobwebs sat in the middle of her web, inches from his face. She repaired the damage a recent catch had caused, oblivious of the machine that watched so intently. He reached up slowly and brought his finger close to her. She didn't notice. *Nephila clavipes*, thought Solo, do not see well even with eight eyes. Gently, he tapped her yellow and black spotted carapace. She turned quickly and began to shake herself violently on the web until she became a blur, warning an unseen foe. Solo waited until she stopped. He touched her again.

"On the ground, Blue Leader," radioed the Lobo team leader.

"Roger, Lobo. See anything?"

"Affirmative. We're just ten meters from the wreck. Hardly looks like a chopper anymore."

"Roger, Lobo. Let's get Solo hooked up and out of here."

The spider shook the web again, not as violently and not as long. Solo put his finger back up half an inch in front of her face.

"Blue Leader!"

"Roger, Lobo. Go."

"Solo's gone!"

"Check the area! He might've fallen out."

Nephila clavipes raised one of her long front legs, waved it around in front of her like an antenna, touched the robot's finger. She touched Solo's warm plastic skin and quickly withdrew it. She touched the finger again, tentatively.

"Negative, Blue Leader," said Lobo. "There's nothing

around here, and we didn't see anything on the way down either. Solo's gone."

Blue Leader looked at his copilot and shook his head. "It's gonna be hitting the fan, real soon," he said on the intercom. He clicked the transmit, "Control, Blue Leader."

"Go," Clyde said abruptly.

"Roger, Control. Be advised Red Eye is not in the wreck or at the site."

"I'll be *dipped* in shit!" Solo heard Clyde tell Bill. "Blue Leader, you tell Lobo I want that area searched leaf by leaf. I'm sending more help."

"Roger, Control."

The spider held Solo's finger with one leg for a minute then put her other front leg next to it. She sat motionless.

"Blue Leader, Blue Two. I just spotted some Sandys over here."

Blue Leader saw Blue Two hovering about a kilometer away. "Roger. How many?"

"Saw two for sure, then they ducked off the trail. Maybe a squad."

"Roger. Stay with 'em. Keep me posted. Don't fire unless fired upon."

Solo pulled his finger away slowly. He ducked under the web, stood up and walked swiftly north.

"What a fucking break." Clyde paced behind Bill. "I bet the Sandys snatched that goddamn machine. Jesus." Clyde sweated profusely in the air-conditioned control room as he contemplated the reaction from Washington. Two years to retirement. They'll rift me to fucking PFC.

Clyde earned his star on his third, and final, consideration. Three strikes at a promotion and you're out of the officer corps. Had he not been in Vietnam, a MACV regional commander with good paper records, he would have been passed over.

Vietnam was his ticket to Brigadier. Since then, he'd lan-
guished in a series of nowhere assignments, a lackluster general
officer kept on the rolls by his friend and current boss, Major
General Charles Wilson. Wilson and Clyde had been class-
mates at the Command and General Staff College when they
were both bird colonels. The attraction between them was
social—poker and drinking. Wilson decided that being Military Deputy Director of Project Solo was an innocuous, but
career-important job for Clyde. Clyde *looked* like a general,
and that was sufficient for DARPA. Clyde knew how he had
gotten his job and that he was incompetent, but he'd forgotten. "I got to pull out the stops," he said to Bill. "You hear
anything from Solo, other people, maybe some noises?"

"Nothing, Clyde. His main power is cut off. He doesn't have
enough power to broadcast."

"But he can hear us, right?"

"It's possible," said Bill.

"Which means that it's possible—if they have him—for
them to listen to us too?"

"It's possible. They'd have to tap—"

"Great fucking news!" Clyde turned away, neck growing red
as he tried to keep from going entirely insane with rage. After
a minute, he turned back. "Well, Bill," he said quietly and
with great effort. "We really ought to shut down our Solo
transmitter, shouldn't we?"

Bill nodded. "I think that'd be prudent. We can leave the
receiver on; we might hear something."

"Right. Do it." Clyde turned and walked over to the wall
map. "What's the status, Captain?"

Bill listened while the aide briefed Clyde. One troop
searched the crash area, another moved up towards the Sandy
squad. Two companies of Contras were massing at the border.
The navigation monitor was mad with scurrying colored dots,
each one a Huey or a troop commander or a LRRP team
leader. The blinking blue dot was gone.

6

THE mile-high volcanoes, Maderas and Concepción, glowed against a darkening sky, sunlit sides bright as gold, shadows dark as soot. Eusebio Chacon, a brown-skinned, black-haired *campesino* youth of fourteen, sat on the dock, his bare feet dangling just above the water. The fishing boat, the *Madre de Dios,* chugged toward him in the distance, pitching and wallowing in the green waves of Lake Nicaragua. If it did not hurry, he would be late getting back. His mother would let his sister, Agela, get the fish next time. Agela would not dally and daydream, his mother would say. No, Agela would *help* her poor mother. Eusebio grimaced. Sometimes he'd like to kill his sister.

When the *Madre de Dios* entered the calmer waters of the cove, Eusebio saw a small figure at the bow waving wildly. Inginio. He felt a twinge of jealousy. Inginio had it good. Every day he was on the water, sailing out of sight, even as far as San Ramon at Maderas. He seldom had to hoe crops, harvest rice or carry baskets of sweet potatoes to the carts.

He heard a splash beneath his feet. The water swirled under the dock as though something large had swum by. *Tiburón?* Eusebio leapt up. He had never heard of the great sharks biting anyone sitting on the docks, but—

He plainly heard the engine of the fishing boat, and the call of his friend, Ingino. "Eusebio!" Inginio yelled. "I have caught you your dinner!"

"Bah!" Eusebio called back. "You, *la chica,* the girl, of the boat? You swab the decks when you're not cooking the meals for the men and taking it up the ass." Eusebio grinned widely, his teeth glowing against his bronze face.

"Hah!" Inginio laughed. "And you, *campesina,* did you have a good day today? Did you pick the *elote* and get the clothes washed and mended? Eh?"

"I am working in the garage now, *chica,*" Eusebio answered, defiantly.

The *Madre de Dios* drifted slowly towards the dock, its diesel engine chuffing and gurgling as the two boys bantered. Inginio tossed the bow line. "See if you can catch this, *chica.*" The coiled line snaked gracefully over Eusebio's head and fell into his raised hands. Eusebio pulled the line to the piling, wrapped it once around, and began taking up the slack.

"Very good, Eusebio," a *campesino* man with deep wrinkles around his smiling eyes, called down from the deckhouse. "You could be a sailor if you wanted."

Eusebio grinned widely at the man, Inginio's father. "Thank you, *Tío* Justos."

Inginio leapt onto the dock carrying the stern line. When he wrapped it around the piling, he called, "But Papa, he has too much housework to do!"

Justos Flores shook his head. The two boys were at that age, he thought. When he was fifteen, he and Eusebio's father, Juan Chacon, used to bandy insults, call each other girls, too. "Inginio," Justos's calloused hand gestured—enough. "We all have our work to do. It is all important. What would you eat with your fish if our *compañeros* did not grow the rice and the beans?"

People crowded the dock waiting for fish. Justos's crew, Raoul and Felix, began hoisting the catch from the deck to the dock. The crowd formed a semicircle around the net full of *guapotes.* Lake trout, silvery and green, still squirming for freedom, cascaded into the catch box. Justos called to the people, "Ten *córdobas* apiece, *amigos,*" and leapt easily onto the dock.

"You charge more every day, Justos," said a woman. "I can't afford such prices!"

"Señora Arauz," Justos shrugged. "The price of my fuel goes up every day. The parts I have to smuggle in for my poor engine cost a fortune. I am charging only for my expenses, Señora."

"Before the Triumph, *guapotes* cost only two or three *córdobas,*" said Señora Arauz, sniffing. "*And* they were fresh."

And you sent a maid for them. The old bat's complaining that live fish aren't fresh? What can you do? thought Justos. Old women. "*Sí,* Señora Arauz. Times are bad now, but we all must persevere, no?"

Señora Arauz humphed, insulted. She put two of the largest trout into her plastic bag and slapped two coins into the cigar box on the cleaning bench. "We will all be destitute because of the Sandinistas," she muttered. She clutched her black shawl together at the neck and hobbled off towards the village. Justos shook his head.

In minutes, the hundred kilos of fish were on their way to the kitchens of Las Cruzas.

"I have to get back soon," said Eusebio. "Mama will have a fit."

Inginio looked imploringly at his father. "Papa?"

"You want us to clean the *Madre de Dios* by ourselves?" Justos scowled, though he had already decided to let the boy go.

"No, Papa," Inginio shrugged. "I'll stay—"

"What?" Justos's eyes twinkled. "And not get the vegetables for our table? Do you want your poor mother to have to do everything?"

"Oh!" Inginio laughed. "Thank you, Papa."

"Well, come on then, *chica!*" Eusebio laughed and ran off the dock.

Inginio caught him by the warehouse. Men from the village loaded a produce truck from El Tigre, the last one for the day. Bags of dried *gallo pintas,* red beans, baskets of *elotes,* baby corn which was a Nicaraguan delicacy, and bundles of plantains stuffed the sagging truck to overflowing. The village would make money this year. Perhaps, thought Eusebio, his mother's share would be enough to buy a radio.

"You said you're working in the garage?" Inginio said.

"Well," Eusebio flushed. "I will work there, soon."

"Ah. *Soon.*" Inginio didn't tease Eusebio. The subject was too delicate for that. "I think you should ask the cooperative to let you work on the *Madre de Dios.* We would work well together, Eusebio. And the adventures one has on the great lake—"

"They say there is no need for more fishermen now. And, Inginio, I like to work with machines. We would get more money for our crops if we could take more of them to the markets ourselves. These are," he pointed over his shoulder at the produce truck, "*ladrónes,* robbers."

Inginio nodded.

A *coche,* a black ox cart with brightly painted wheels, its oxen dull-eyed and hot from work, pulled a load of sugar cane towards them. As it got closer, the boys waved at the driver.

"Hey, Tomás," Inginio yelled. "Tonight is our turn to do *vigilancia,* yes?"

"Yes, *estúpido,*" Tomás sneered. He was older by three years, their *Juventud* organizer, and their team leader on the guard duty. "Every Wednesday night we do *vigilancia.* And Sunday too. Shit for brains."

"*Qué pasa, niño?*" asked Eusebio. "You have a fight with your lovers?" he said pointing at the oxen. "They will not back up to you lately?"

Tomás grabbed a stave from the cart and flung it at them, but they were already running up the road, laughing.

The hundred and twenty-four people of Las Cruzas lived in twenty-five houses which wandered in two irregular rows through a hillside grove of coconut trees. The space between the house rows was bare, packed dirt—a courtyard—the site of all community activity. As the sun settled behind the ridge, one could see the lake and the volcanoes to the north and the cooperative's crop fields on each side of the Rio Haciendas to the south. At this late hour, the river valley was in the deep shadow of Colina Duendes, Spirit Hill, and the jungle beyond the fields was already black and mysterious.

No one liked to go into the jungle at night. It was filled with many spirits—*Duendes* and *Chimeques* and *Siga Montes*—which they no longer understood. Though Eusebio and his people were descendants of Indians, they had long been farmers and fishermen. Most of their knowledge of the jungle had been lost. Only the superstitions remained. Except for the occassional iguana or armadillo or deer, the people lived off the food they produced in their fields and yards.

The setting sun glinted off the tin roof of Eusebio's house, and he felt suddenly sad. The tin roof had been his father's pride, a sign of prosperity which had eluded the villagers for generations. The Triumph had changed the campesinos' lives. They now owned the land they had once been indentured to.

The sun's deep-red disk was almost buried in the black tree line. The oblique reflection across the tin glistened like blood. Eusebio stopped. He had found his father lying in such a pool of scarlet in front of the burned-out clinic after the Contra raid. The *animales* had slaughtered him as he tried to stop their torches.

"*Qué pasa*, Eusebio?" Inginio touched his friend's arm. "What do you see?" A white-faced monkey, a *mico*, screeched in a coconut tree near Eusebio's house. Smoke drifted from the clay oven. Eusebio's sister, Agela, sat on the veranda weaving a new hammock.

Eusebio turned, his reverie broken. "Just the sun, Inginio."

"The sun?" Inginio teased, "When you start staring into the sun, we call that crazy. You know?" He shook his head. "Let's go. I have to get back with our vegetables."

They ran, scattering chickens and turkeys all the way to the house.

"Eusebio!" Modesta Chacon called from the doorway. "Why must you run so and stir up such dust and confusion?" She wiped her heavily calloused hands on the dirt-gray apron, and walked out on the veranda. "And where have you been with the fish? Do you want to eat before doing *vigilancia?*"

"Mama, the boat was late. I ran all the way."

"Ai! I can see." She turned to Inginio. "And you, Inginio, I think your mother wants this bag, no?" She pointed to a plastic shopping bag filled with tomatoes, cucumbers, beans wrapped in paper, and a large cabbage.

Inginio took up the bag and nodded. "*Gracias,* Tia Modesta." Then turning to Eusebio, "I'll be back in two hours to get you, Eusebio. Will you be awake?"

Agela laughed loudly. Inginio ran away before Eusebio could reply.

"Big mouth," Eusebio growled at his sister.

"Eusebio," said his mother. "I need some more firewood in the bin." She pointed to the cane crib near the clay oven. "And, Eusebio, why must I always have to tell you this? We always need firewood. Do you want me to fetch the wood as well as work the fields?"

"Of course not, Mama." As he spoke, Agela snickered noisily into her hand. Eusebio glared. She sneered back. He raised his hand high. She yelled, "Mama!"

Modesta looked. Eusebio smiled and grabbed the wood basket that hung overhead. Modesta just shook her head and walked inside.

"*Neña!* Baby!" Eusebio hissed at his sister.

His dog, Cheripa, trotted next to him as he walked the path to the village woodpile.

The low woodshed squatted in the dusk behind the village. Countless footsteps had worn the trail during the centuries that the village had been inhabited. Eusebio wondered if an ancestor's feet had made precisely these steps before him. If they had, and his steps somehow synchronized with that ancestor's, would he feel the spirit of the one who walked previously? Maybe it is our ancestors who become *Siga Monte* spirits and haunt the footsteps of those who walk in the jungle?

Cheripa barked and ran into the bushes beside the trail. An iguana leapt onto a nearby coconut tree and escaped up the trunk. Cheripa jumped up the side of the tree, barking, tail wagging. "Come, Cheripa. He's gone."

A toucan yelled in the jungle which covered Colinas Duendes. "*Yo te veo! Yo te veo!* I see you! I see you!" it seemed to say. Eusebio looked up. The hilltop still glowed in the sun. The cloud forest ended at the edge of the hill, the treetops puffy and red on the ridgeline. The toucan's bright colors streaked in the sunlight against the dark side of the hill near the *casa embrujada,* the haunted house, as the little kids called it, which no one had lived in since the Triumph. Some of the boys used it as a clubhouse but never at night. It is very difficult not to believe in ghosts in the jungle at night in a house that is sinking back into the jungle.

As the toucan flew, the light faded; the sun fell behind the taller mountains to the west. Eusebio reached the shed in darkness relieved only by the rosy glow in the sky. Inside the shed it was nearly black. He was nervous about picking the sticks off the pile, afraid of biting things that he could not see. He filled the basket quickly. Cheripa growled outside the shed, looking up the hill.

A monkey chattered suddenly from the black hole he knew to be the old house. He was not surprised. Monkeys used it as their home. The whole tribe of them screamed loudly, protesting. A jaguar? Eusebio hoisted the basket on his shoulder and walked quickly down the path. He felt hair rising on his neck.

It could even be *Yacayo,* the spirit beast who relishes human flesh. He ran down the trail, feeling foolish, knowing there was nothing there.

At seven-thirty, Eusebio and Inginio walked through the square together, each carrying an AK-47 rifle, their Ahkas. A crowd of children sat on boxes and folding chairs in front of Escopeta's, the village's general store, bar and pool hall. The cooperative's one television set flickered on a table on the veranda. The Honda generator that powered it popped and chugged behind the tin-roofed building.

Eusebio smiled when he saw Agela sitting near the front of the crowd. She was becoming a beauty, his sister. And the corn bread she'd made tonight was delicious. The program, "Mission: Impossible," was always very popular and Eusebio felt deprived because he'd miss it.

"I wish I could watch that," said Inginio. "They can do amazing things, those *Yanquis.*"

"It's for children," said Eusebio. "It's all faked besides."

Inginio looked at his friend to see if he was kidding. But Eusebio looked serious. Inginio, smaller and reticent, allowed Eusebio to lead him. "It's fake, for children," Inginio immediately agreed.

A dozen men played dominoes by kerosene light and drank *Victoria* beer and *Flor de Caña* rum outside the circle of children. Though not on guard duty, each man had an Ahka leaning against his chair. Tomás stood beside a table watching a game. He saw them approaching. *"Buenas noches, chicos,"* he called. He picked up his rifle and joined them on the road.

"Tonight there will be a moon," said Tomás. *"Los animales* don't like bright nights."

"I *hope* they come," said Eusebio quietly.

"Yes," said Inginio. "Let the *animales* come. We'll be ready this time." He patted his rifle. The border villages were now better armed than those in the interior. "This can stop a company of those *bastardos.*"

They walked south along the river into blackness, towards their post on the bridge. In minutes the village disappeared into the night. The generator's racket was swallowed in the blackness. Stars sparkled in the crisp night air. The ridge on their right and the high south walls of the valley were monstrous shadows looming up to block the stars. Eusebio looked carefully at the dark mound on the side of the hill. Silent now.

"Maybe we should have a watch at the old house," he said. "It's a weak spot in our *vigilancia.*"

"It's too close to the jungle, Eusebio," said Tomás. "The team at the woodshed can see anything coming down the hill. Besides, the *animales* will either come along the river or by the lake road like last time."

"True," said Eusebio. His eyes had adjusted better to the night. He could see the path if he didn't look directly at it. Their Sandinista militia instructors had taught them not to stare at anything during their watches. Keep your eyes moving. It worked. Inginio and Tomás were the palest of ghosts, wisps of lighter shadows which disappeared when he looked at them. When he looked elsewhere, he could see their shapes hovering next to him.

The three boys walked silently down the road until they could make out the dark shape of the bridge across the pale river, but not the guards already there. The river rushed softly over the stones under the bridge. Tomás whistled the "peekwa" of the *pájaro tonto,* dumb parrot. That foolish bird called day or night. A guard answered with a dove call. The boys crept up to the bridge.

The two teams touched each other in the dark whispering, *"buenas noches,"* as they changed the guard. Tomás, Eusebio and Inginio would be on watch until midnight.

Eusebio and Inginio walked across, taking up positions on the riverbank next to the bridge. Tomás climbed down into his position behind the bridge. Only their heads rose above the top of the bridge. The Sandinistas had told them that the *animales* had special glasses made by the *Yanquis* which allowed them to see in the dark.

"When does the moon rise?" asked Inginio.

"Soon."

"Good. I don't like being so close to the graveyard in the dark," said Inginio. "I've seen the lights, the globes of lights, hovering over it. Ghosts."

"Ghosts like the moonlight, Inginio." Eusebio smiled invisibly in the night.

"Maybe," said Inginio. "But at least I can see where to run."

7

Trees bowed and swayed in the stormy wake of the approaching helicopter. Bill Stewart leaned against the railing of the rear terrace watching the Huey, thundering and hissing, an ungainly dragon flailing the air to stay aloft. The machine's tail twitched to stabilize itself as it sank to the manicured lawn and squatted there. The sudden whine of reduced power was like a sigh of relief. Clyde Haynes leapt out looking tough in sweat-stained combat fatigues, an M-16 in his hand. He did not look like good news.

The Contras had found the Sandinista squad. Bill left the railing and went inside to intercept Clyde. At the top of the ridiculous sweeping Southern mansion stairway that led down to the foyer, Bill stopped.

"Your damn machine has taken off. By itself." Clyde stood at the bottom. "They found his footprints near the wreck." He jerked his head towards the control room, turned, and left.

Bill followed, suppressing a smile. No one could capture Solo.

Clyde rapped out orders by radio, directing the troopers still in the field.

Bill sat. He switched on the Solo monitor and his computer screen.

"Two doubles," Clyde snapped to his orderly. He turned his

chair toward Bill, pushed his fingers through his wet hair and said, "If I can't find Solo, I'm fucked."

Bill nodded.

"If I'm fucked, you're fucked," Clyde added.

It wasn't true, of course. Even if Clyde could shift the blame, Bill was still half-owner of Electron Dynamics. There are many generals, only one Electron Dynamics. Many of the NASA people in charge of the Challenger mission were gone, but Morton-Thiokol was still making rocket boosters for the space shuttle. Clyde had everything to lose, but there wasn't any advantage in stressing the point. Bill nodded. "You found nothing?"

"That's right. The Contras took one Sandy alive—"

"One?" Bill's knuckles turned white on the arms of his chair.

"That's what I said!" Clyde slugged the counter. "Goddamn it! You still think we're playing war games down here?"

Bill felt like jumping down Clyde's throat. Clyde was responsible for this mess. He said quietly, "I never thought we were playing games here, ever, Clyde. I was just surprised that they'd kill so many of them. I would've thought it was better to have prisoners to question—"

"That's right—" Clyde stopped as the orderly stepped forward with the tray. He took his drink and glared off into space while Bill got his. When the orderly left, he continued. "*We* would've captured them all. Hell, they were surrounded. You have to realize that these Contras have a lot of hate built up against the Sandys—hard to control 'em. But it doesn't matter. We had one alive long enough. The commander. They didn't have Solo. Didn't know what we were talking about."

"Long enough?"

"Yeah." Clyde raised his hands, shaping an explanation, stopped. "Just forget it, okay? I want to know what the fuck *you're* going to do."

"Me?"

"You built the fucking thing. You tell me how we find it now that we know it isn't damaged. Now that we know it ran off by itself. It's got to be putting out some traceable signal, right?"

Bill looked at Solo's monitor. Static. "Solo is supposed to be the fighting machine of all time, Clyde. All he knows about is combat. Hand-to-hand combat. How to build and use any weapon. He knows strategy. How to attack, defend, retreat, and escape. He's got a thousand-year accumulation of the best methods for doing just what he's doing." Bill sipped his drink, swirled the ice. "And he's silent and shielded so that an enemy can't track him. I mean, we've done our best to make him invulnerable; now that's working against us."

"How about infrared?"

"Weak possibility. When he's moving around, his surface temperature is one-twenty. If he stood out in the open, it would be theoretically possible to spot him from a satellite. But a lot of other things get that warm sitting out in the sun; he'd be lost in the crowd."

"So when his batteries run down, we have an inert, cool, top-secret weapon lying out there in the jungle just waiting to be found by the other side."

"Not quite." Bill brought up a diagram of Solo's power system on the computer screen. "The main batteries can keep him going at full power for roughly twenty hours. When they run down, he's still got the little plutonium generator backup for his memory." Bill pointed to a graph that had formed on the screen. "While he's on that backup, he can't move. It's designed to just keep his brain alive in an emergency. It puts out just a trickle—see here?—just a few milliwatts more than he needs for his brain."

"So?"

"So, that means it's possible for him to trickle-charge his main batteries with the excess. It'd take him weeks to accumulate a ten percent charge, but it's possible. And if I know it's possible, then so does Solo."

"You mean he can just take a nap, rest up and keep going?"

"Yeah. And he can keep doing that for years."

"How many years?"

"At least twenty, assuming no major breakdowns."

Clyde sagged in his chair, sipping his drink, staring into space. "Bill, when they have satellites go out of control, or don't make their orbits, those guys at JPL send signals that change programs, bypass circuits, re-route signals and stuff, right?"

"Right." Bill turned to the computer screen again. He tapped the keyboard and a schematic drawing formed on the screen. "See this?" He pointed to a square with many lines coming off it.

"Yeah?" Clyde could not read electrical diagrams.

"Well, that's how he did it."

"Did what?"

"Got away," said Bill. "That's the chip that controls the abort switch and his communications. The beacon, the satellite uplink, radios. It's a programmable chip, but it's not directly addressable by Solo." Bill moved his finger over to another symbol, a circle with an arrow inside. "But if Solo purposely blew this transistor by putting too much current through it, he'd fuse it. It'd be just like snipping the whole thing out of the circuit. That's what he must have done—a brilliant piece of engineering, really. Now Solo can't be turned off remotely. The only thing left is the manual abort switch."

"There's no other way?"

"We can try some tricks with the radios, but Solo will be on guard for that, too. He's obviously resistant to tampering." Bill could not suppress a smile. This was his genius they were talking about. "It's actually a good sign that he's a very adaptable, versatile, fighter, don't you think?"

"Fuck you, Stewart." Clyde gulped the rest of his drink. "Then all I have from the scientific genius is zip?"

"I haven't given up, Clyde. I'm running simulations on the mainframe computer, looking for a weakness. The trouble is,

we did that when we designed him in the first place. But—"
Bill paused, trying to think of something reassuring to say.
"Our best chance is to reason with him, talk him into coming
back."

"That's right!" Clyde suddenly brightened. "He can hear
us, can't he?"

"Probably. Until his main batteries go."

"So, start talking to the motherfucker." Clyde jumped up,
smacking his palm with his fist. "Sweet talk 'im, Bill! Promise
him you'll give him—what does a robot *want?*—an electric
dick or something? Talk to him. If you can just get him to
broadcast one fucking word," Clyde snapped his fingers. "We
got 'im, right?"

"Right," said Bill. "If he uses his radios we can spot him."
He didn't go into details. It would take perhaps five seconds
of speech, to plot Solo's position. Solo knew it.

"Great!" Clyde jumped up. "There's hope then. In the
meantime, I'm gonna send out my best teams."

"You're going to send Americans into Nicaragua?" said Bill
in disbelief.

"Bill," Clyde said seriously. "We aren't even allowed within
twenty kilometers of the border. I can't send American troops
up there. You know that."

8

THE boy at the woodshed looked up as the monkeys screamed. From his facial expression, Solo assumed that the kid knew someone was in the old house. *I must hide.*

The village had power. Solo was quickly running out of it. He examined the room in the dim starlight, using up energy as he amplified the image. One end of the house sat on rocks as it perched on the hillside. The ancient floorboards creaked ominously as he walked. A *mico* chattered again. The monkeys had left, but he still heard them rustling in the trees around the house.

Footprints in the dust led past a stack of old *Playboys* and *El Diarios* to a corner of the room. Solo spotted the seam of a trapdoor in the corner, stuck a finger in a knothole, pulled the door up. He ducked his head into the hole. Silently he let himself down. The space was about four feet high on the downhill side.

Solo crouched low and crept along the side of the house that faced the village. A loud hissing stopped him. Sitting on his haunches he put out his hand slowly, a gesture of friendship to the angry fer-de-lance. The snake slammed into his wrist, fangs bared, fell back and recoiled. Solo checked his glove for damage. Intact. The fer-de-lance, hissing and vibrating his tail against the ground, seemed *designed* to be angry. Solo inched towards the boulder that supported the corner of the house. The fer-de-lance struck him again on the calf. Solo didn't notice. He moved very slowly, conserving his power.

Sitting next to the boulder, Solo could see the village clearly though a gap in the stone foundation. Lanterns burned in the houses. A television flickered in front of one. He could hear the rumble of a small generator. The generator could recharge him, but it would take power to get to it, power he didn't have. He set himself in a position to observe.

Three men with rifles walked out of the village down the road along the river. He zoomed in on them and recognized the boy. They spoke, but he could not hear them. Then the boy looked directly at him. Solo read his lips: "Maybe we should have a watch at the old house," he said. Solo could not see the response.

They will come eventually.

Solo's arms moved slowly. He sprinkled a handful of weeds over his body and settled back against a rock, propping his head upright. If he managed himself carefully, stayed motionless, he could watch the village. If he did not move, he calculated, he could recharge his main batteries enough to raid the village in two weeks. He turned off his vision.

A kaleidoscopic swirl of multicolored spots coalesced into objects that Solo willed into being. Objects—his shoes, his Ruger, a spider—appeared randomly. He saw the earth floating in space, the sun glaring next to it. He remembered the feeling of elation he'd felt when they'd let him look through a spy satellite to show him where he was. He remembered feeling like he was there, floating in space. Whenever he asked to go back, they refused.

A scene came into his memory, Bill holding out his hand to him saying, "Hold my hand." Solo had. "Now squeeze very slowly, Solo. I'll tell you when to stop." Bill winced. "Slowly, Solo. You can break my hand. Very slowly. Feel how much pressure you're applying." Solo tried again. He kept track of

WEAPON 65

the pressure from all the sensors in his hand, averaging them.
Five pounds. Ten pounds. "That's right," said Bill. "Keep
squeezing." Fifteen pounds. Twenty. "Okay," said Bill.
"That's firm. Any more than that, the average man would
begin to feel pain. Do you understand?"

"Yes, Bill."

"Try it again."

Solo let go of Bill's hand, regrasped it and squeezed to the
same pressure, released. "That's it," said Bill, smiling. "Perfect."

Perfect. Solo remembered hearing that word often during
his training. When he was first constructed, Solo had not had
hands, arms, legs. Solo had existed, looking like any other large
computer—disembodied—inside a cabinet, a kind of womb in
which his mind developed.

Solo remembered the first concept he recognized: bright.
He had spent time—many beats of his mind—discovering that
something had happened. Part of the world had changed,
become bright. The difference attracted his developing attention. He concentrated on the brightness. Darkness swirled
across the light. He studied the changes. Each time the darkness moved, he saw that it had edges. The blurred edges
became more defined each time it moved. The edges became
a shape, perfect, a circle. The circle swung across the brightness. He watched this—a pocket watch swinging in front of his
camera eye, he later learned—for what turned out to be days.
Discovering what the shape meant was his only interest. Almost as if it were an out-of-focus photograph, it snapped into
being. Solo saw numbers, the glint of metal. Numbers. He
compared the numbers he saw with the things in his memory
labeled numbers. Memory was an installed base of information
barely accessible to his developing sentience. A computer can
access information, but it does not understand what it is access-
ing. Solo related the numbers he saw on the object with those
in his memory. He played with the discovery: an object that

related to the things in his mind. Numbers in the brightness. Numbers in the darkness. The same.

Three lines moved about this circle of numbers. One moved much faster than the other two. One moved between two numbers while the fast one went around the whole circle three hundred times. The slowest moved between two numbers while the fast one circled three thousand six hundred times. The two large lines overlapped twelve times as they moved, but only once did they overlap at the same number: twelve. Then the cycle began again.

Something like an itch bothered Solo and he explored it. The word, *watch,* was being repeated over and over from somewhere. He searched in the darkness and found *watch* and a list of other words associated with it: see, inspect, scrutinize, protect, guard and many others, all were meaningless to him. He felt that the word was a clue to the mystery of the object. Where did they come from?

Watch.

Watch.

Watch. Something was trying to relate the two things: the word in his memory and the object in the brightness.

Then the object disappeared. Another object appeared. This time, he was able to discern the edges quickly, saw that it *was* an object. This object was not perfect. It had a roughly circlular base but spread out in five directions. Again he felt the itch: *hand.*

Hand: extremity, aid, help . . . and hundreds more related to this word. It made no sense.

The five-object left to be replaced by the circular one. The lines that moved grew very large until he saw only the end of one. The line was tipped with a triangle.

Hand.

He recalled the last image—he discovered that it happened automatically. The two were not the same, but the word—hand—kept repeating. They were the same thing? The something that presented this puzzle said that they were the same. He ventured into his memory. *Hand.* One of the related words attached to it was: *watch.* Watch as: timepiece. Timepiece: device which measures the passage of time. Passage: movement—he'd seen that happening. Measure: quantify. He had counted the relationships of the movements. He was seeing a—device—which counted. Counted time. Time he knew. Time was the beat of his own mind. And it—the device—was: *watch.* Time: a word that labeled the beat. *Watch:* a word that labeled the device. The watch grew smaller and he saw the whole thing, he understood. He thought: watch! Something changed the word coming from somewhere to: perfect. Perfect: errorless, accurate. The something agreed with his conclusion. The something was putting objects into the brightness and showing him the label to which it was attached. He understood. The five-object reappeared. He thought: hand!

Perfect.

Solo then wondered how the five-object, *hand,* measured time. He did not yet know how to ask.

Two days later, a layer of fine, red dust covered Solo. The fer-de-lance coiled in his lap: a perfect snake home, a rock that stays warm. A spider had anchored one side of her web to the top of Solo's head. Cockroaches crawled over his body, leaving fuzzy trails crisscrossing in the dust.

The Saturday dawn broke over Los Tres Hermanos in the eastern mountains. The peak on the distant lake island, Isla Mancarrón, stood like a black cone against the rosy light. Venus sparkled between dawn and night, growing fainter as the sun ignited the blue sky. Concepcion and Madera, to the north, were ghostly hulks in the morning pall. A *culiling,* glossy black, scarlet and gold, flew past him, banked and glided down to the village.

Cocks crowed. Hens squawked. Dogs barked in the village.

Micos chattered and *silgueros* sang in the grove of coconut trees.

Solo turned on his vision and saw three men walking along the river road, returning from their guard duty. The image was poor, he noted, and getting worse. The dust layer thickened very fast, he thought. He had never paid attention to dust before. Just raising his hand to wipe his eyes would take all the energy he'd accumulated in a whole day.

He turned his vision back off to save power and listened. Men called to each other, house to house. "Hey, Juan, don't forget the money you owe me," shouted a man. Late into the night, the men had partied on beer and rum, arguing and boasting, filling the night with their sounds. Bill and Clyde had sometimes done this, thought Solo. It was not tactically advisable.

Solo felt the fer-de-lance crawling across his hand. He blinked his vision on. The snake was going on a hunt? A black trail ran through the red dust on his body. If the snake moved to his head, it might keep his eyes clean. But it might also coil across his eyes, blinding him. He heard, "Eusebio!" and focused on the village. The boy from the woodpile stood on his veranda, stretching his arms high. He scratched his chest through his open shirt while he watched another boy run across the courtyard. They sat on the steps and talked. He could not hear them. Only shouts, calls, squawks, and squeals came through unless he amplified, and that took power. Watching their mouths, he learned that the other boy's name was In-heen-ee-o, Inginio. A woman brought the boys two steaming cups of coffee, stood back smiling at them, shaking her finger as if counting and nodding her head. The gesture made no sense to Solo.

Solo knew one thing: The military prowess of the Communists was deplorable. He would have no trouble getting the generator. The rest of their activities were mysterious to the war machine. He shut off his vision.

Electromagnetic radiation pulsed from a satellite, flew through the overhanging branches, through the *otuc* palm fronds of the thatched roof, through the mahogany floor and bounced against plastic skin. Thousands of receivers embedded in the skin resonated to the pulse sending the signal to the amplifier. The code instructed Solo's left arm to push the abort switch manually. But the amplifier was off.

9

AFTER a *desayuno*, breakfast, of Agela's cornbread, *pini-lillo*, a cornmeal and cocoa drink, and eggs, Eusebio and Inginio took their machetes and sacks and went hunting for iguanas. Cheripa ran ahead up the trail. Every Saturday morning of her life they had hunted the lizard the villagers called the chicken of the tree.

The sun felt hot; the lake breeze cool. Cicadas clicked in the sunshine. Eusebio grabbed a *manzana rosa* off a tree near the trail. He offered the pearly yellow fruit to Inginio who declined with a grimace. "Tastes like perfume to me." Eusebio smiled and shook the fruit near his ear to hear the loose pit roll around inside. It was a wonder, a completely hollow fruit. He bit a hole in the thick skin and munched the sweet rose-scented meat. He let the pit roll out the hole and pushed it into the earth with his bare foot. This one he would watch to see it grow into a tree.

Cheripa barked further up the trail. She growled at the woodpile.

"What's she got?" asked Inginio.

Eusebio squatted and peered into the woodpile. "Don't know. Maybe a *paca* or just a rat."

"I don't like *paca*," said Inginio. "Too fishy."

"Neither do I. C'mon Cheripa, *vámonos.*"

The dog pawed the woodpile, snarling, her hair raised along her back. A gray blur raced out from the bottom of the pile.

"Armadillo!" Inginio yelled as the animal shot between his feet, skittering up the hill.

"Get it!" yelled Eusebio.

As Inginio turned, Cheripa tripped him. He fell on her. Cheripa yelped in pain and ran away howling.

The armadillo zipped into the thick brush further up the hillside. "What a hunter you are!" Eusebio jeered.

"Your stupid dog did that—"

"Maybe we should bring *her* back for dinner?"

Inginio stood up laughing. "I'll never be *that* hungry."

Eusebio called. Cheripa came bounding down the trail, completely recovered. *"Ven acá, bruta,"* Eusebio told her and pointed up the hill.

Very few people came this far up Colinas Duendes. There was nothing except the view, and farmers had little time to admire vistas. The man who had built the little house, Don Zeledon, had had the time, but he had run to Miami with his money in 1979. Don Zeledon was very rich and had lived in a great house at El Tigre. He stayed in the little *quinta* when he came to visit his *finca* and to watch his *clonos,* wondering at their efforts in the heat. He had been an officer in Somosa's army, new to property. He liked to sit on the little porch, sipping rum, affecting the habits of the rich. He had paid the low wages of the day, demanding much for it. The village considered his leaving—thus leaving them his property—a blessing from God.

Don Zeledon would sit on the porch and whistle down at the village for willing boys to come run errands. He tipped pennies. Eusebio remembered bringing cigarettes to Don Zeledon before the Triumph. The house had been very clean then. He recalled images of whitewashed wood bright in the burning sun, white wicker chairs and a hammock in the cool

shade of the porch. Don Zeledon had taken the pack of cigarettes and looked out over the lake while his fingers peeled the
cellophane. Eusebio, nine, stood expectantly at the steps of the
porch, waiting for his penny. But Don Zeledon looked at the
volcanoes and then to his fifty *manzanas* of rich farm land
along the river, tearing the pack open, ignoring Eusebio.
Eusebio saw the smirk on his face and turned away. Don
Zeledon called, "*Espérate, pordiosero.* Wait, beggar."

Eusebio turned and saw Zeledon toss a penny in the dust.
He walked to it, squatted, and, with his face burning, picked
it off the ground. He ran down the trail, angry, crying, "I'm
no beggar!"

It gave him satisfaction to see the whitewash flaked away,
the wood rotting, the railings gone. Monkeys and vermin lived
here now. The house sat in a cave of overgrowing vegetation.
Soon, the earth would reclaim it.

"Come, if you dare!" Inginio pointed at the house as they
got near.

"What for? The place's too rotten to use anymore."

"Many different things live here," Inginio smiled mysteri-
ously.

Eusebio shrugged. He could accept a dare as well as anyone.
There was nothing in there that he couldn't handle. "Okay,"
he said. He called Cheripa. "Good girl," he crooned when she
ran up, panting, tail wagging. "C'mon Cheripa, c'mon girl."
He moved towards the decaying house.

Cheripa bounded to the weed-tangled steps, stopped suddenly and sniffed. A low growl began in her throat. Her hair
rose. Eusebio held his machete tightly and walked to the
porch, squatted and looked under the steps. Pitch black. Nothing. "There's nothing, Cheripa. Be quiet."

The dog moaned in worry.

"She's spooked by something, Eusebio." Inginio sounded
scared.

"She's spooked by her own shadow, this *bruta*," Eusebio

chuckled, trying to sound brave, and patted Cheripa. "C'mon, let's see inside." He waved his machete at Inginio.

The porch felt like a cave. Sensations of coolness and tightness gripped Eusebio as he walked towards the door. What had happened to him? Last week, he ran in here, even in the dark, unafraid. Nothing here except shadows and fear. Aware that Inginio was watching him, Eusebio straightened himself and walked boldly inside.

Standing on the porch, Inginio turned to Cheripa who still growled and whined at the steps. "Quiet, you coward!" he scolded. He waited, listening for Eusebio to call. Tree frogs chirped a wavering cresendo.

Eusebio came back to the door carrying a *Playboy* magazine held open to the centerfold. "Hey, Inginio. My girl is still happy to see me. See?" His face beamed. "C'mon, everything's the same in here." Eusebio went inside and Inginio followed.

Everything was the same. Just dirtier. They sat on two old stools next to the east window flipping through worn pages of *Playboys* in the jungle-tinted light, the remnants of a collection gathered over the years by the *fleteros* and truck drivers. Eusebio read the name of a girl standing naked in front of a mirror. Donna Winfield. The *Yanqui* women were so beautiful. And she knows it too, he nodded. She admires herself in the mirror, and she's lonely—see where she has her hand. He felt himself stiffening and crossed his legs to hide it. He looked at Inginio, "Why do you sit with your legs crossed so tightly? Eh, *hombre?*"

Inginio looked up defiantly. Seeing the big smile on Eusebio's face, and his crossed legs, he laughed. "It's a problem, this one," he pointed at his crotch. "Last year in school, it leapt up whenever a girl walked by," he giggled. "I had to hide it behind my notebook."

"Mine too," said Eusebio. "One time, Cecilia caught me hiding it!" Eusebio flushed.

"How do you know she saw it?"

"Because she kept asking to borrow the book I was holding in my lap, and when I said no, she laughed. She teased me!"

"Yes?" said Inginio.

"Yes. She said, 'Please Eusebio, I need to borrow your history book,' and when I said, 'You have your own,' she said 'Oh, but I need to see yours, a page of mine is missing,' and when I said no, she giggled. Then she said, 'Eusebio, why is your face red?' "

"Cecilia is a very bold girl," said Inginio.

"Shameless." Eusebio smiled suddenly and pointed to the page in his lap. "Not like Donna."

"No, not like Donna at all," laughed Inginio. "I bet Donna would know what to do besides make fun of it!"

"Yes. And the poor girl needs me, can you see?"

Inginino studied the picture carefully. "Yes. I can see she needs *somebody.*"

Cheripa, meanwhile, had stopped barking and come into the house. Eusebio looked up. The light from behind him clearly lit their footprints in the dust. Cheripa was sniffing among the tracks. Eusebio smiled at this. Dogs used their noses instead of their eyes even if what they were tracking was in plain sight.

Inginio looked up from his magazine. "She's trying to find us, eh?"

"Cheripa, *tonta,* we are here!" Eusebio called. She wagged her tail, but continued sniffing the floor, moving towards the far corner.

"Hey, maybe she found that armadillo again?" said Inginio.

They put down their magazines and went over to the dog. Inginio hunkered near her. He drew a line in the dust with his finger. "Look here, Eusebio, someone has been here, not long ago."

"Bootprints, Inginio. Maybe the *animales* come here, like I warned!"

"Only one of them? It was probably one of the other guys, maybe Tomás."

Spotting the smudge marks next to the trapdoor, Eusebio put his hand on his chin, stroking it like his father had done when he encountered a puzzle. The tracks went one way. Whoever had gone down there had not come back up. "I think a man went under the house," said Eusebio.

"Yes," said Inginio. "Look," he pointed next to the trapdoor. "Handprints. The man let himself down."

"He didn't come back up," said Eusebio.

"He could've just left from underneath. We've done that."

"Or he could still be there," said Eusebio quietly.

Inginio slowly pulled up the trapdoor. "Go ahead, look," he whispered, pointing to the opening.

"Me?" said Eusebio, irritated. He hissed, "You opened the thing. You look."

"You are the oldest. You look."

"Three days!" Eusebio's voice rose. He gulped in alarm. "Since when do you grant me such honors? When you are a scared child, eh?"

Cheripa sniffed the smudge marks. A low quiet growl rose as though she sensed their fear and agreed.

Eusebio shook his head. He would have to do this for this child. He leaned over the edge until he saw under the house upside down.

Shafts of light arrowed through the dusty air making it hard to see. Cheripa put her head down next to his and licked his cheek. He grimaced and pushed her away. He heard Inginio whisper, "Well?" but only raised his hand for him to be quiet. As he stared, he could see better, but he knew he would only be sure there was no one if he had a flashlight or a candle. He pulled himself up next to Inginio. "We have a candle here?"

"Did you see something?" said Inginio.

"If I saw something, would I be asking for a candle, *tonto?*"

Inginio tiptoed to the back wall. He found a candle jammed

into a bottle on the mantel and brought it back. He lit it with his Bic lighter and handed it to Eusebio. "Do you think we should go get someone? Or our guns?" he whispered.

"No," Eusebio answered. "If a man were down there, Cheripa would be going crazy. I think whoever it was has gone. I just want to see if there's any signs." Eusebio let himself down, feet first.

Solo heard the dog sniffing along the floor. He wondered why they laughed about crossed legs.

The dog will find me.

His two-day trickle charge was barely enough for him to get up and walk ten feet, hardly an effective escape. TAU-Defend: He had his Ruger—loaded with blanks. He could use his hands. The image of his fist sinking into McNeil's face suddenly sprang into his mind's eye unbeckoned. McNeil's head had turned to jelly. The image went away. He did not like it. Still, I could kill *them* when they discover me. They are Communists. But more people would come and I would be unable to move at all.

He heard them pulling up the trapdoor.

I will remain completely motionless no matter what they do. I will ignore them, and when my charge is sufficient, I will take their generator.

He saw the boy's face, Eusebio, peering through the dark, looking right at him, then withdrawing. It is possible that he may not see me. He may go away.

"We have a candle here?"

"Did you see something?" said Inginio.

"If I saw something, would I be asking for a candle, *tonto?*" Solo heard Inginio walking, getting a candle and lighting it.

I will not move no matter what they do to me.

He saw legs dangling through the hole. The boy, Eusebio, dropped to the ground and squatted. He was almost able to stand up in the crawlspace—a small boy. Eusebio sat down on a rock, holding the candle out in front of him, squinting in the light. He cupped his hand, shielding the light from his face.

Inginio peered upside down behind Eusebio. "Anything?" said Inginio.

Eusebio turned slightly, hissing, "Ssssh!"

They are inept, thought Solo.

Eusebio had the eerie feeling that a pile of rocks in the far corner took the shape of a reclining man. He knew it was just the rocks, but—but one has to solve these mysteries, face these fears, if one ever wants to be a man. He crept closer, cursing the flickering feebleness of his light. Shadows danced in the dank crawlspace. Cockroaches rushed away.

This light, Eusebio thought, makes the rocks look like a man. A few feet closer, the illusion was so convincing that he could move no further, frozen in fear.

Solo recognized the fear on Eusebio's face. He has seen me. Eusebio reached to pick up a pebble to toss into the shadows. The fer-de-lance leapt up, hissing wildly.

Solo had never seen such a look of horror as now possessed Eusebio's face, even in Bill's photographs of facial expressions. The candle fell through the air. The double reflections of the flame fluttered in Eusebio's eyes as it fell. The fer-de-lance struck as Eusebio dropped back, crying out. Solo calculated that the boy had moved too late.

TAU-Decision: If he's killed I would be discovered anyway. If I kill the snake I might be considered a friend because I saved his life but it will cost me all my strength.

"Eusebio!" yelled Inginio.

Life became a dream for Eusebio. The fer-de-lance flying towards his leg seemed to float through water. He could not move fast enough to get away. His hand jammed down on a sharp rock behind him, but he felt no pain. Nothing existed but the open mouth of the fer-de-lance, fangs extended, inches from his leg. No one lived from such a bite. This is . . . it?

A black hand shot from the shadows, grabbing the fer-de-lance behind the head. The snake thrashed violently as its head was severed in the black fist. The body dropped to the ground, twitching. The hand went limp, dropping the head. The fer-de-lance glared, mouth opening and closing, not understanding decapitation. Eusebio yelled.

"Oh Eusebio!" he heard Inginio behind him. "*Pobrecito,* lie still while I get a doctor—"

"I don't need a doctor," said Eusebio.

"If you move, the poison will—"

"It did not bite me."

"—be pumped all through—" Inginio stopped, finally hearing. "Eh?"

"This man tore off its head," said Eusebio quietly. The man lay across the rocks, arm outstretched, not moving. Maybe he had knocked himself out when he hit the rocks. The man wore some kind of a plastic suit, jungle boots and a belt with a holster. He was covered with dust and cobwebs.

"A man?" Inginio had dropped through the trapdoor and crawled next to Eusebio.

Eusebio nodded and pointed at Solo. "He has knocked himself out."

"Why is he dressed like that?" said Inginio.

"I don't know."

"Perhaps he is wearing some new *Yanqui* thing. A bullet-proof suit, perhaps. They give the *animales* the best weapons."

"If he is a Contra, then why did he save my life?" Eusebio got to his feet, wincing. He looked at his hand. Blood ran freely from a deep wound in his palm.

"Eusebio!" said Inginio. "Are you sure the snake didn't bite you?"

"Yes." Eusebio, bent low to avoid the floor joists, crawled to the side of Solo. "I fell on a sharp rock. Here," he motioned Inginio closer. "Come help me." Eusebio grabbed Solo's shoul-

der and tried to pull him over. The man weighed a ton. The
plastic suit was warm to the touch. Eusebio motioned Inginio
to help. It was like trying to move a boulder. The two boys
grabbed the shoulder and, straining as hard as they could,
rolled Solo onto his side.

"This is a *big* man!" said Inginio. "Maybe a *Yanqui?*"

"We will soon find out," said Eusebio, turning Solo's head.
The face was completely smooth, no holes for breathing or
talking. Eye holes were glassed flush with the surface of the
mask. No evidence of a seam or latch. "Light the candle," he
said to Inginio.

Inginio reached gingerly for the candle in front of the gasp-
ing snake's head. "That thing still thinks he is alive. *El Diablo,*
eh?"

"Here, hold it next to his face." Eusebio wiped the dust and
dirt off the mask with his hand. The eye covers were slightly
mirrored. "Give me that," said Eusebio, grabbing the candle.
He held it close and peered into the eyes.

Padre Cerna, the priest who came to Las Cruzas every week,
had once let Eusebio look at his camera. These eyes looked like
the lens on the Padre's camera. Maybe they weren't cameras
but binoculars like he'd seen on television, built into the mask
of the suit.

"He *is* a *Yanqui!*" said Inginio suddenly.

Eusebio looked up. Inginio held out Solo's gun, pointing at
the engraved trademark. "Look, it's a *Yanqui* gun, *Ruger.*"

"So what, Inginio? We have some *Yanqui* guns too."

"I think he's a *Yanqui* spy, or a Contra in a *Yanqui* suit of
armor. We should tie him up before he comes to."

Eusebio stood up, staring at Solo. Inginio was right. Only
the *Yanquis* could build something like this. But why had the
man saved his life? "Okay, but let's move him outside so we
can get him out of this thing."

"Move him? Eusebio, we could hardly roll him on his side.
He must weight two *quintales,* maybe three," said Inginio.

"It's probably his suit that's so heavy. We should get it off him now, and when he wakes up, take him prisoner."

"Sometimes, Inginio, you are not so dumb."

"But we should do it quickly, Eusebio. Otherwise, how can we capture him if he's in that thing?"

"We'll tie him so he can't move while we get it off," said Eusebio.

Sadness flooded Solo for the snake. The snake had been an innocent creature, following its instincts. He had resolved not to harm it, yet had. He had sacrificed the snake for his own well-being.

He felt pleasure from the boys' inspection. They, too, were innocent creatures following their instincts. Though he seldom felt it, pleasure wasn't new. Pleasure from accomplishing a task properly was one of the first emotions he'd experienced. But why did their conversation amuse him? Amuse? It is one thing to know the definition, another to feel it. They think I am a person in a suit. They think they can take it off and capture me? When the boy, Eusebio, had peered into his eyes, he'd felt the urge to say hello. What would the boy have done?

Powerless, Solo watched them tie his feet and hands with their belts, grunting mightily as they shifted his bulk. Their earnestness amused him. He was certain that that was what it was: amusement.

Having secured him, arms tied behind him, ankles bound together, they began a systematic inspection of his skin looking for the "latch." The faceplate seam along each temple was no more than a scratch, but Eusebio noticed it. Following it down to his neck, Eusebio encountered the flexible Teflon dust collar. He found the Torx setscrews that held the black retaining ring seals. "It's held on with some funny-looking screws," said Eusebio. "He might put the whole top half on, like a shirt. Look around his waist for a latch."

Solo was feeling what children feel when they play hide and seek. The feeling was new. He had never had playmates—only teachers and adversaries.

His waist, of course, was also belted with the same kind of Teflon weather seal, fastened with the same retaining rings.

"It must be under this stuff," said Inginio, pinching the Teflon. "We could cut it."

"No, he opens it somehow."

"Maybe he carries a tool for these fittings, like a key?" said Inginio.

"Maybe. But where?"

Every flexible point in the armor had the same coverings. There was no latch. They would need a tool to open the retaining rings.

"Does the garage have a tool to fit those?" asked Inginio.

"No, we have Allen wrenches, but they have six sides. This is star-shaped," said Eusebio. "We could jam something in it, but that would ruin it."

"We have to get him out of this before he wakes up, Eusebio. If we ruin one fitting, can't we replace it with something that will work just as well?" As Inginio spoke, candle wax dripped onto Solo's body. "I can bring my father, Eusebio. He works on the boat engine all the time. He might have a tool to fit those."

Eusebio nodded watching the drops of wax cloud as they cooled. While they were clear, he saw something on the man's side. He spit on the place and wiped it with his sleeve. "Bring that closer," he said, pointing to the candle. In the flickering light, they saw a faint rectangle the size of a postcard. Next to it was a ring-shaped place the size of a céntimo coin. "This could be it," said Eusebio.

Upwelling amusement made Solo want to—laugh? This was how humans felt when they shuddered and gaffawed? The painful-looking haw-haw process had mystified him. Even Bill was occasionally taken by this malady and went into uncontrollable spasms, making repetitious honking sounds. Once, when Solo had crushed thirty eggs in a row while trying to pick up one, he had thought Bill might die from these spasms. It had seemed to him a programming error, but now he understood. He had to do something to relieve the pressure he felt. Had to.

Eusebio pushed the edge of Solo's Input/Output port cover where a thin rubber seal filled the gap. It didn't move.

The *céntimo*-sized spot had a similar seal. When he pushed the spot, it clicked and depressed.

"Hey!" Eusebio jumped back when the port cover popped open.

"Good work, Eusebio. The latch, eh?"

"It must be—" Eusebio grinned at his discovery. Puzzlement moved suddenly over his face.

Inginio leaned over. The port was a box with two places to plug things in—like radio tubes into sockets—and a three-pronged thing that they immediately recognized. "An electric plug?" said Inginio.

Eusebio pulled on the plug, and it came out, unreeling a cord. When he let it go, it snapped back into place. "Why would a man need electricity?" said Eusebio quietly. He pulled the cord out again, hand over hand. In a few seconds he had fifteen feet of orange, insulated wire coiled next to Solo.

"I don't like the way this looks, Eusebio."

The port receptacle was too big. The cord they had unreeled would take up too much space. If a man were inside this suit, he would be cut in half.

"Eusebio, I have seen these things on television."

"Eh?" Eusebio looked at the dark outstretched man with new eyes. He shifted nervously. "A *robot?* You think this is a robot?"

"What else, Eusebio? Where does a man fit into this thing? How can a man breathe in there, or eat, or even take a leak?"

"But what you saw on TV is fake, even the *Yanquis* have no such machine. It's impossible—"

"Need power," said Solo. They both jerked straight up, thumping their heads on the floor above them. Solo felt an overload he'd never experienced before expend itself in a cyclic release of energy through his audio channels. It sounded like the braying of a mad donkey.

Eusebio and Inginio scrambled over the rocks, outside and away.

Solo brayed, weaker at each cycle, until his batteries were completely dead.

10

Justos carried a coil of line from his boat. Raoul and Felix brought a gaff pole and more line. The men of the village militia got their rifles. Eusebio and Inginio led the way, running up the hill. Cheripa barked and leapt happily among the men. Children from the village followed to see what was happening.

Justos had stopped at Escopeta's to say that the boys had found someone, maybe a Contra, at the old house.

Modesta had yelled, "Eusebio, you better be back here soon. I won't keep your food waiting."

"Mama! I'm not hungry. We have captured something!"

"You tied him well?" asked Justos. The boys hurried beside him.

"Yes, Papa, with our belts."

"And did you tie him to anything? So he can't sit up or hop away?"

Inginio looked at Eusebio, who returned the accusation. "We didn't have anything to tie him down with, *Tío* Justos," Eusebio said.

"Well, I hope he's still there."

Cheripa ran ahead, barking. By the time Justos and the boys got to the house, the dog was growling bravely at the steps, hair raised in a furious ruffle.

"He's still there, then," said Eusebio, dropping to his knees at the side of the porch. Justos and Inginio joined him, all peering under the house. "I see him!" yelled Eusebio.

"I can't see a thing," said Justos.

"We know where he is, *Tío* Justos. He's black."

"Bring the light," Justos said. By the time Felix arrived with the flashlight, the bulk of the village was there or on their way up the trail.

"Stay back," said Justos. "There could be shooting." People formed a line at a respectful distance. Only the men he picked came closer.

"Okay, boys," said Justos. "Show me."

Solo watched the underside of the floor light up. He could barely hear, but he knew people were coming. Would they kill him? Why had he drained his batteries so far with that laughter? Had he gone mad?

The light flashed all over. Voices, muffled and hollow, echoed under the house. Men put lines through the belts that bound him, pulling them taut. They need not bother, thought Solo.

Solo recognized Eusebio and Inginio, peering into his face, but the other face was new. They spoke. It sounded like they talked through cloth. His audio system was barely working. He heard, "Robot . . ." and "Impossible . . ." Eusebio showed Justos the I/O port, pulled the plug out. Justos, his brow wrinkled in consternation, held the cord, twisting it under the light. Putting the cord down, he shined the light into Solo's eyes. Stars and cresents of optical refraction showered like sparks in Solo's brain. The man's eye was inches from his own, moving from side to side, trying to see . . . him.

Eusebio spoke from behind the man. "Said . . . need power . . ." That's right, thought Solo. Give me some power, and I'll be on my way. The thought of leaping up and fighting possessed him. His arms twitched.

"Watch out!" Justos jumped back. The kids were right.

There were no eyes behind those lenses, of that he was sure. And the power cord. It had to be true. *Yanquis* can build anything, even impossible things. As he told his friends often, if he had never seen a television, he would not believe the description. No more movement. Power, thought Justos. He asked for power. If we don't give him any, he's helpless. That made sense. But what can we do with such a machine? It had saved Eusebio's life. He had seen the snake. Could it be a Russian machine? The Russians weren't as clever about these things as the *Yanquis*. But then they didn't kill *campesinos*, either. It was possible. It could be a Russian machine here to help them. Then they should give it power. But it was probably *Yanqui*. If they tied it very well, gave it power, and questioned it, they would know if it was a friend or not. Could it be tied well enough? He looked at Solo carefully, visualizing the size of the motors that must be inside him. Of course it could, he decided. Even a tractor can be restrained. This machine cannot have enough power to break a cable or a chain.

"Okay. Eusebio, get the gaff pole. Inginio, bring in more line. Felix, release that line and help me get one under this thing." Fifteen minutes later, Solo lay wrapped to the pole, ropes surrounding him like a cocoon.

Justos brought more men under the house and had them form a line. Straining in the awkward space, the men passed the three-hundred-pound machine along the line and outside. He lay, a trussed pig on a pole, in full view of his captors.

In the brilliant sunlight Solo saw a *mico* staring at him, swaying on an overhanging branch. A red-winged blackbird fluttered overhead. A circle of bronze faces, dark eyes and black hair, blocked his view. A child tapped his chest with a stick, grinning at the clunk. Four men hoisted the pole to their shoulders and carried him down the trail. People touched Solo's skin, scratching and tapping it with their fingernails. Out of the great confusion of chatter, laughter and shouts, he filtered out one voice, the leader, saying, ". . . to the garage." Garage: Tools, saws, torches. They plan to take me apart?

11

CLYDE HAYNES stood up and began pacing like a butter-bar lieutenant on his first assignment.

Bill played the tape again. A brief electronic noise with the disturbing quality of a man laughing while choking honked briefly from the speakers.

Robert Warren, blond and as tall as Bill, was a muscular man. He leaned forward in his chair next to the recorder to better hear the sound. His brow furrowed at the noise, making his grim expression all the more intimidating. It was Warren's nature to look grim and intimidating. It was a technique he had cultivated as he rose in the ranks of the CIA—he'd discovered that with his athletic build, his height and his handsome face, the look of disdain, anger bordering on rage, drew fearful respect from his people. It was a technique that accomplished much with little effort. As the special agent sent by Washington, Warren had Clyde's testicles clasped firmly in his fist. He looked expectantly at Bill, relaxing his piercing gaze. Bill Stewart, though technically subordinate to Warren—in the investigation—was a civilian. A powerful civilian.

"You're sure that's Solo?" asked Warren.

"Yes," said Bill. "It's his frequency, and it came through the dish. There's no question," said Bill.

"But what does it mean? Some sort of signal he's been

programmed to send?" Warren reached into his many-pock-
eted khaki journalist's vest and got his cigarettes. Warren was
proud of his vest. He'd bought it at the Banana Republic store
in Miami, washed it ten times, and slept in it for a week to give
it the proper, experienced air. With the vest, an L. L. Bean
cotton shirt, faded jeans, Rockport shoes, a scratched and worn
Nikon camera over his shoulder, Warren achieved the look he
wanted—seasoned journalist.

"It's not something we taught him," said Bill. "It might be
his way of sending an SOS with his last bit of power."

"And you got a fix from this, I hope." Warren nodded,
indicating what he wanted to hear.

"We got enough to put him in a neighborhood, Bob," Clyde
interjected.

Warren looked at Clyde, "Neighborhood? Does that mean
you have a fix?"

Bill tapped at the keyboard of the computer and a map of
the region glowed on the navigation monitor. A blue rectangle
blinked on, outlining a section of Nicaragua extending from
the Pacific across Lake Nicaragua down to the Costa Rican
border.

"That's a fucking neighborhood? You can't get a better fix
than that?" Warren glared at Bill.

Clyde backed into the shadows behind them.

"Right, Warren," said Bill. "Would you like to tell me how
this stuff works? The burst was too short. This is the best we
can do without more information."

Robert Warren stared silently for a moment, soaking in the
implications—the two-billion-dollar weapon was in Nicaragua,
possibly in enemy hands. He turned around slowly, pinning
Clyde with his gaze, "You didn't say he was in Nicaragua,
General."

"You can't expect me to tell you something like that over
the net, Bob." Clyde swallowed hard, affected by Warren's
strength. "You can't trust anyone these days."

"That's true," said Warren, looking as though he'd just bitten a turd. "I can understand that. What I don't understand, Clyde, is how the goddamn machine got away."

Clyde shrugged quickly, putting out his hands. "Look, Bob, this is a fucking *test*. Of a brand-new weapon. A whole new kind of weapon. No one could have anticipated this. We took all precautions—" Clyde glanced at Bill as he spoke. "We stuck to the plan, by the numbers, Bob. Solo just went haywire. That's it."

Warren turned to Bill. "Solo went haywire?"

Bill looked at Clyde. "In a matter of speaking," said Bill.

"What manner of speaking, goddamnit?" Warren snapped.

Bill stared directly into Warren's eyes. "Let's get something straight, Warren. Nobody in the government talks to me like that. Especially not someone who *works* for people who call me 'Mr. Stewart.' Got that?"

Warren nodded. A slight smile flickered on his face. Stewart's looks were deceiving—skinny, pale. A pencil-necked hacker. But Stewart was no pussy. "Okay. Like you say, I work for people. People who are real pissed-off right now and who want answers. It's my job to find out what happened here and fix it. Fast. I do my job very well, Mr. Stewart. It's not my intention to rub you the wrong way, but I *will* do my job."

Bill's face relaxed, "Fine, Warren. Do your job. Just as long as we understand each other. Now, to answer your question about what happened to Solo. Solo had a conflict and decided to protect himself from what he perceived was a deadly situation."

"Which was?" Warren leaned forward.

"Which was," Bill continued, "his belief that he would be 'deleted,' that he would be subjected to major reprogramming and lose his identity." A question formed on Warren's face. Bill continued, "Because he did not want to kill a man as a test."

"Why not? Hasn't Solo already killed someone?" said Warren.

"Yes. Accidently. In the early training program, in the hand-to-hand combat phase, he killed his trainer. He didn't know how fragile the human skull was, and we were pushing him too fast," Bill said quietly. "I think that's the reason he's so reluctant to kill now. But I don't think it requires a major overhaul. He was working on the problem. With all our indoctrination, he's developed a sincere sense of duty along with that sense of self. He wants to be useful. I think he can still be used."

"He thought we would 'delete' him?" said Warren. "And now he's somewhere in Nicaragua telling the Sandinistas all about it?"

"No," said Bill. "They are defined as an enemy. He's too much a soldier to tell them anything."

"But he also thinks *we* want to erase him," said Warren. "Doesn't that make us his enemy, too?" Warren stood up, walked closer to the nav monitor and puffed smoke at the screen. "At least most of this area is a fucking lake," he said. "That narrows it down to what? Maybe only five hundred square miles, eh?" Warren scowled.

He turned coldly to Clyde. "This has to go to the top, Clyde. I'd put on your armored pants if I were you." He studied the nav monitor carefully. "Well," he said, "we'll just have to go there and get him." He turned to Bill. "Show me how he can be turned off." He watched Bill's face and smiled. "Please."

Warren stewed on his bed, propped against pillows, a cigarette dangling from his mouth, a sheaf of papers Bill had given him in his lap. The top file contained a memorandum written a year before. A non-technical description of Solo for the administrators in charge of the project.

Warren had known nothing of Project Solo until his briefing in Washington, and yet he was to repair the fuck-up of these two idiots. Actually one idiot and a computer nerd. Stewart was okay, feisty. But how did Clyde ever get to be a general? They lost the robot, but as his boss had so clearly explained, the robot was in his area of operations. Warren was the covert mission specialist, so he was now in charge of getting it back. If the fucking robot wasn't recovered, he'd be the first to go. Of course, his bosses would go too—that made him feel brighter. But if he got Solo back, well, then his bosses might end up working for *him.*

Warren's need-to-know clearance meant he could see certain files on the Solo project, enough for him to see what Solo was. Stewart had also been ordered to brief him in detail on ways to disable or destroy the machine.

Warren read the folder title:

PROJECT SOLO: A NON-TECHNICAL DESCRIPTION
William Stewart, Electron Dynamics

The cover sheet was stamped Top Secret diagonally across the title. He flipped to the first page and read:

I've been asked to describe the basic design of Solo for non-engineers in the project.

Design criteria required that Solo would duplicate, as closely as possible, the mechanical abilities of a human so it could use existing vehicles, weapons and clothing. Solo uses straightforward, state-of-the-art solutions for mechanical structure and mobility. We used hydraulically animated human anatomy as a model for most of its moving parts. A hydraulic piston is located in nearly every place a human would have a major muscle. The movement of each hydraulic muscle is electronically controlled by a solenoid valve, and each of the hundreds of solenoids is controlled by its own computer processor.

Each processor is connected to the others in a parallel network of interrelated computers. When their activities are properly coordinated, the system can move with an animal grace that makes it seem alive. Two hydraulic pumps, one a backup, keep a constant working pressure of several hundred pounds per square inch in the hydraulic system, not unlike the power steering system in a car. The pumps are electrically driven by lightweight storage batteries. Solo can operate for some twenty hours on one charge.

Without Solo's brain, we would have a very expensive marionette. The development of wafer technology at Electron Dynamics has allowed us to equip Solo with a parallel processing computer consisting of one million interconnected co-processors in his torso.

A parallel processor of this complexity is impossible to program in the traditional way. The emphasis has to shift from linear programming—a step-by-step instruction list—to designing programs that allow the machine to learn.

Machine learning is extremely difficult. No one had ever built a bipedal robot that could walk on even the smoothest surface before Solo. There are an infinite number of possible movements in a simple walk across a floor. The sequence is never the same twice. Solo can walk because it learned to walk just like we do—by falling down a lot. Our basic start-up programs—actually synthesized human neural networks—were developed to be its version of instincts. The goals are suggested, the solutions—which processors to use and how many—are left to the system to discover.

It took Solo a long time to learn to see, to interpret what it saw and to move within the world it saw. Were it to lose power in its brain suddenly, all its learning would be wiped clean. The brain's structure—the neural networking and basic knowledge—are recorded and preserved. The resultant activity the systems produce, the skills it has learned, its identity, can't be recorded. To protect its knowledge and our investment, the brain has its own backup power supply—a small Stirling cycle generator like the ones designed for artificial human hearts is powered by a small quantity of plutonium. This backup can produce electric current for years. If the machine loses its main power supply, the backup saves the contents of the brain and an internal beacon is activated. This feature will allow us to retrieve damaged Solos and put them back into operation. Future versions of Solo may use a larger version of this power supply to give the robot an almost infinite range, but the problem of exposing highly toxic plutonium on the battlefield, in the event of the robot's destruction, has so far been unsolved.

Solo's exterior shell, patterned after NASA's hard-shell space suit, is made of a tough composite of Kevlar and carbon fiber that is waterproof and immune to small arms fire. Embedded in this shell are several thousand sensors of two types. The first group gives it tactile and temperature feedback—touch sensors. The second group is an interconnected array of tiny radio receivers. The effect of this phased array is that it can simulate a parabolic antenna and be selectively aimed at satellites and other radio sources without Solo having to move its body. Additionally, these receivers can detect animal electric fields allowing it to "see" crude images of living things behind it or in the dark—similar to the ability of sharks.

Solo's vision system is housed in its head. High resolution CCD (charge-coupled device) cameras are at each eye port. Primary vision processors, also located in the skull, prepare visual information to be passed on to the brain. Solo can boost the signal in low-light conditions like a starlight scope. Solo can adjust the system to allow it to see infrared and ultraviolet. This ability, coupled with the extensive radio systems, makes Solo a full-spectrum receiver—an invaluable ability in combat. Solo can transmit what it sees to remote monitors anywhere in the world through our satellite systems. In the field, a commander using Solo can watch through its eyes and see the world as Solo sees it.

Solo appears to be human-like. The question of whether Solo is thinking like us is metaphysical. Though it experiences emotions, Solo is a machine and thinks like one. It is not artificial intelligence. It is authentic machine intelligence—different than ours.

Solo is a true alien. As our own world-view is a product of who we are and where we are, so it is with Solo. Unlike us, Solo lacks a built-in inclination to follow a leader or to be a leader. Solo is not a natural teamplayer and we are attempting to change this through further education. I have observed that Solo is, though cooperative, inclined to be aloof and independent. It is the purpose of the field trials scheduled for next year to observe how its independence will affect its performance as a warrior.

Solo's present world-view is carefully edited and will remain so. It is allowed access only to information we provide, including simplified political perspectives, descriptions of the enemy and limited astronomical and geographical data for navigation. Solo understands the world as a place in which it is to do battle.

The total effect of Solo's abilities is the creation of a very convincing illusion of persona. I can't stress this fact enough, because confusing Solo's machine mind with that of a human can be very dangerous, as the McNeil incident demonstrated.

There is much more to Solo than I have described in this short overview.

Warren got another cigarette and flipped to the document marked:

THE McNEIL INCIDENT
William Stewart

After a month of training, Solo seemed to understand hand-to-hand combat techniques so well that we decided to remove the padded gloves used throughout the training period.

Sergeant McNeil, Solo's hand-to-hand trainer, had asked us to remove the gloves weeks earlier, but I had turned down the request as premature. The point is that McNeil himself, who had worked with Solo daily for over a month, felt completely convinced of its understanding of this training.

On September 14, 1988, at the gymnasium at Electron Dynamics, Palm Bay, Florida, Solo's gloves were removed. During the briefing I emphasized to Solo that the session was still mock battle, that it was to pull its punches just as it had always done. Solo said that it understood. I believe that Solo did understand that instruction. For safety, I carried a portable transmitter that could switch off Solo's main power supply.

Sergeant McNeil walked to the center of the mat, followed by Solo. Present at the demonstration were: Byron Rand, co-owner of Electron Dynamics, myself, Major General Charles Wilson, Project Director, and his deputy, General Clyde Haynes and the four NCOs of the training detachment. (Statements of all witnesses attached.)

Sergeant McNeil was asked to demonstrate Solo's abilities. Sergeant McNeil asked Solo to attack and allow itself to be thrown. Solo complied, raising its arm and lunging at McNeil. Sergeant McNeil grabbed Solo's wrist on the downswing and ducked under its arm. Solo tumbled forward on the mat as if it had been thrown. This was to demonstrate Solo's agility and durability. Because Solo weighs three hundred pounds and is extremely agile and immensely strong, it is impossible for McNeil or anyone else to actually throw Solo anywhere.

When Solo got up, McNeil told it to try it again, but to not allow itself to be thrown. Solo repeated its attack, but when McNeil grabbed Solo's wrist, it simply froze. When McNeil tried to duck under Solo's arm, Solo remained immobile. McNeil grinned and said, "Anchor yourself." McNeil then walked around Solo slamming his body against it from various directions. The robot was able to shift its bulk imperceptibly against each push, making it seem that it was somehow attached to the floor. Major General Wilson was greatly impressed.

McNeil then instructed Solo to defend itself at normal speed. He did not clarify that this was to be non-lethal, but I don't believe that had anything to do with what happened. McNeil called the other three members of the training detachment to help him in the demonstration. They would all attack at the same time, McNeil explained.

We have reviewed the film made at the time. Solo threw McNeil first and then spun around fast, flinging the other attackers off him. McNeil bounded back into the fray, grabbing Solo around the neck, trying to pull it backward. Solo grabbed McNeil's hands and bent forward quickly, throwing McNeil over him onto the mat. McNeil leapt up and crouched in a defensive posture, his hands in front of him. Solo responded, as it had been trained to, in the same position. McNeil punched at Solo's head. Solo deflected the thrust with one arm and responded with a punch toward McNeil's face with the other. Here, I must mention that McNeil had often used the expression "Reach *past* the target" when training Solo. Whether it was that piece of instruction or the lack of gloves, or both, that confused Solo, we don't know. Solo did not pull the punch. The full force of the blow struck McNeil in the face. Solo's fist crushed McNeil's skull and entered his brain, killing him instantly.

I had my finger on the remote abort switch, but the punch was completed before I could react. When Solo knelt down to McNeil's body, I thought it might be following through with another punch. I pushed the abort switch and Solo collapsed next to McNeil.

Warren crushed out his cigarette, shaking his head. The punch went *through* his skull?

Back at the lab, Solo tested out normally. Solo said that it did not know how the incident happened. I asked it to review its own memory. Solo clearly remembered the punch and displayed it for us on a monitor.

I asked it to review the decision tree—the series of decisions that led to the punch. Solo could not remember the actual sequence. Here an important aspect of Solo's mind is apparent. Solo's awareness of itself is the product of its complexity. In this regard, it is similiar to a human being. We are all able to do things like seeing or speaking and remembering and still not have the slightest notion about how we do them. I believe Solo doesn't know what happened. It's capable of error, as are we. As Solo's experience grows, so will its abilities. It's tragic that this "education" has cost a human life.

Solo doesn't speak of the accident voluntarily—as it often did about other mistakes during the rest of its training—but it will answer questions about it.

Warren put the file beside him. He lay back, arms folded, and stared at the acoustic ceiling tiles, looking for a pattern in the tiny holes.

So how do I capture this thing? This is not Robbie the Robot.

Any problem, thought Warren, can be broken down to its elements. Plan: 1) Find the goddamn thing. 2) Turn it off if it won't cooperate. 3) Bring it back.

Hell of a plan. A few more details, maybe. Warren smiled. He'd solved some tough ones in his fifteen years. Most of them against unskilled amateurs in backwater countries, but enough to get him this far. But getting Solo—that would be *noticed.* It isn't a burden, he counseled himself, it's a magnificient opportunity. Deputy Director? Possible. Hell yeah, it's possible. He grabbed the phone.

"Stewart—*Mister* Stewart?" Warren's tone revealed aggression and impatience. "Mr. Stewart," he said. "I want you to teach me how to shut off robots. Today." He nodded, listening to Bill's reply. "Fine. See you there."

12

THE garage of the Juan Valdivia cooperative—the name the villagers had voted to call themselves—was a three-walled shed. Most of the cooperative's vehicles, in various states of disassembly, were parked in and around the garage. Since the American embargo, parts for their two John Deere tractors, three Ford trucks and the one ancient 1950 Ferguson tractor had been impossible to get. The government had agreed to lend the cooperative money to buy a Russian tractor. The Bella Ruse would be delivered in six months, but many in the cooperative were angry that they had to spend their money on inferior equipment. The *Yanquis* made the best tractors.

Four men stood sweating with the trussed robot on their shoulders, waiting while Felix and Tomás cleared the tools and parts off the workbench. They flopped Solo down on the splintered, oil-stained top and slid out the gaff pole.

Solo's head clunked on the bench. "Get the tow chains," said Justos to Juan Picado.

"*Tío* Justos," said Eusebio. "Please. It saved my life. Aren't the ropes enough? Surely no machine can break that much rope."

"Eusebio, I have no idea what this thing is or who it belongs to. I can't take a chance that it saved you just to get itself into the village to murder us all. How would I know, eh?"

Juan and the men wrapped chains around Solo's neck and ankles and hooked them together under the table.

"Eusebio, you and Inginio go get the generator. Then we'll find out what this thing is. If it's a friend, we can untie it." The boys ran off to Escopeta's.

Tomás spoke quietly to Justos. "Shouldn't we tell the *campas*, the Sandinista soldiers, about this?"

"So they can take it up to Managua and crow about it?" said Justos. "This thing could be a very valuable asset, Tomás. The cooperative would do well to charge for its troubles, eh?"

"*Claro,*" said Tomás, pensively. "Still, whoever owns this could come and take it too, Justos, without paying and maybe kill us for keeping it."

"*If* they know where it is, Tomás," said Justos. "If we are careful and keep it well hidden, we simply watch to see who turns up looking for it. Perhaps the cooperative could be persuaded to find it? For a generous fee, eh?" Justos raised his eyebrows and smiled.

"*Sí*, Justos," Tomás laughed. "We are very good at finding things in the jungle, we *Indios.*" The men in the garage laughed. "It's a good plan, Justos," said Tomás. "We should tell the rest at the meeting tonight."

"We should tell them right now, Tomás. Keep the news in the village, eh?"

Tomás grinned and went outside into the crowd to spread the word. They would agree, thought Justos. If they had nothing else, the village of Las Cruzas, the Juan Valdivia cooperative, had solidarity. Almost every outsider was an enemy.

The boys, accompanied by yapping dogs and small children, panted inside with the generator between them. They set it down beside the workbench. "No, no," said Justos. "Take it outside behind the wall and bring the cord inside. We won't hear anything with that running in here."

Solo watched. They are not going to take me apart. They are going to give me the power I need to get away. I have made a correct decision. Perfect.

The generator popped to life behind the tin wall. Inginio leaned through the window and handed Justos the extension cord. Eusebio followed it through the window and started pushing the ropes away from the I/O port.

"*Espérate,* wait," said Justos. "Slow down, boys." The entire village of Las Cruzas packed the garage, men at the front, women behind them. Kids stood all over the John Deere. "No," said Justos. "We can't crowd around this thing, *amigos.* What if it blows up? Or who knows what? Move back until we're sure it's safe. It's *our* machine. We'll all get a chance to see it work—if that's what it does." Justos waved them back.

Eusebio pulled Solo's cord from the port, handing it to Justos. Juan Picado raised his rifle. "*Sí,* Juan, keep it covered. Anything can happen." Juan nodded gravely, taking aim at Solo's head.

Justos pushed the plugs together. Everyone held his breath. A baby cried.

The muffled pop, pop, pop of the generator bogged down as if a great demand had been made on it. Justos held the plugs tightly, ready to pull them apart. The generator resumed chugging steadily. The robot did not move.

"It might take a long time to recharge it, Papa, like a truck battery," said Inginio. Justos nodded. He motioned Juan Picado over and handed him the plugs. "Pull them apart if *anything* happens," said Justos. He peered into Solo's eye covers. Nothing glowed.

"Maybe it's broken," said Juan.

"Maybe," said Justos. "Who knows?"

"It hit the rocks under the house after it killed the snake," said Eusebio. "It could've broken something. That was when it stopped moving—"

"But then it brayed like a donkey," said Inginio. "Remember?"

"Yes, but it didn't *move* again," said Eusebio.

"Shall I look inside it, Justos?" Juan, the cooperative's

mechanic, walked over to the trussed robot and grabbed a screwdriver. "I can fix anything," he said.

"No, *gracias,* Juan," said Justos. "We'll wait awhile. Recharging takes time; several hours possibly."

Half an hour later, Justos sat on a stool next to Solo, arms folded, staring at the machine. Juan Picado still held the plugs but had relaxed his grip. Eusebio peered into the eye covers now and then. There was nothing else to do.

Solo drank power from the small generator, sucking it in so fast that the machine nearly stalled. He relaxed his demand to match the machine's capacity. Power thrilled through him. His mind cleared. He could hear distinctly. A villager waited, poised to disconnect him. He'd accumulate a full charge before he spoke. Someone might panic and pull the plug and he'd be helpless. Never again.

He turned on his radios.

"Solo," said Bill, "we heard your signal. Please rebroadcast so we can fix your position." A beep identified a message loop repeating itself. "Solo, we heard your signal . . ." His signal? He'd sent no signal. Tempting, actually, to uplink and go on line with Control's computer and find out what it was that he supposedly sent. Of course going on line with the computer would instantly pinpoint his position.

"*Sí,* Raoul, I'm in position." A local signal; frequency range of the hand-helds. A patrol? Do they know where I am already? Standing and prepared, he would have known the direction of the broadcast instantly. If he'd been moving, he'd have their range. Tied up on a filthy workbench in a tin shed, the transmission was too brief for him to track.

Justos shifted his weight on the stool. He stared into Solo's eyes so intently that Solo wondered if he could somehow hear what was going on inside him.

Solo replayed the message, looking at it carefully. The transmission would show characteristics of coming from a particular direction, even if his antenna array was not properly tuned. He calculated the direction based on a graph of the signal. From the valley, distance unknown. If they transmitted again, he'd be ready.

At sunset, Justos told Juan and the other men to go eat. Agela brought a tray of food for Justos, Eusebio and Inginio.

"It's beautiful, Agela," said Justos. "Thank you." She nodded. It was true. The tray held a feast of cornbread, *cuajada* cheese, chopped cabbage, *chicharrones*—pork cracklings—plantains, and steaming cups of coffee.

"It's nothing," said Agela with a smile. The two boys ate while Agela sat watching them from the seat of the John Deere. Justos maintained the vigil at Solo's side until Inginio finished eating and relieved him.

The generator popped irregularly, raced and died.

Silence rang in their ears. The boys looked in alarm at Justos. Justos looked at Solo and shrugged, "I don't think it cares if we have to take a break to gas the Honda." He grabbed his flashlight from the workbench and handed it to Eusebio. "Be sure to check the oil, Eusebio. It always needs oil."

Eusebio got a gas can and a liter of oil from the front of the garage and walked into the night.

"*Sí,* they have three men at the bridge." Solo calculated that the transmission came from 160 degrees. If someone answered, he was out of Solo's range. "There are lights at the garage." Same azimuth. The transmitter was not moving. "I don't know why. Usually it is dark."

Spanish transmissions by people who had the village under surveillance could be from a Sandinista patrol or the Contras. Either one was trouble. The Sandinistas would turn him over to the Russians, who'd take him apart—of that he was sure. The Contras would return him to Clyde who'd also take him apart. It was time to move.

"*Buenas noches,*" said Solo. He used the calm, resonate

tone of speaking that Bill had characterized as warm and friendly.

"Papa!" yelled Inginio.

Justos dropped his coffee. Agela came up beside him. "I will go tell the village?" she whispered to Justos.

"No, no!" said Justos. "We don't need a crowd now. Stay here."

Solo turned his head so that the humans would know that he looked at them. His chin clicked against the links of the tow chain.

"Ready?" Eusebio called from outside.

"No. Come inside, Eusebio."

Eusebio poked his head through the window, "Eh?" he said.

"I said come inside. This thing is talking now." Justos nodded at Solo.

"*Sí?*" Eusebio leapt in through the window and approached Solo. "What does it say?"

"*Buenas noches,*" said Solo.

"Amazing," said Eusebio.

Everyone nodded in agreement and continued to stare at the machine, transfixed. Solo felt the urge to laugh.

"I would be pleased to meet you if you would release me from these chains," said Solo.

"*Sí!*" said Eusebio, leaping to the task.

"Wait! Eusebio," yelled Justos. "We don't know anything yet."

"I am a friend," said Solo. They had all nodded slightly when he asked to be released. They were willing to free him but frightened. "I am deeply in your debt for the power," he said.

"You are a *Yanqui* machine?" asked Justos.

"I was a *Yanqui* machine." Their expressions showed that they approved.

"We hate *Yanquis* here," said Justos. "They have killed many in our village, including Eusebio's father." Justos pointed to Eusebio as he spoke.

"I know," lied Solo. "That is why I left them." He raised
his feet, clanking the chains on his ankles. "I killed the fer-de-
lance."

"*Tío* Justos!" Eusebio pleaded. "He's right. Let him up.
What kind of dangerous machine would *save* lives?"

"*Sí,* Papa," said Inginio.

"Silence, *niños.*" Justos raised a finger to his lips. "I told you
before, Eusebio, this could be a trick to get into the village. I
want to be sure."

Justos came closer. There was slack enough for Solo to reach
through the ropes and grab the man. He could escape, but in
twenty hours he'd be back where he was before. No power.
Helpless. For the moment he needed these people, their generator and the fuel and oil that went with it. Justos spoke.
"Where were you made?"

"I was built by the Electron Dynamics Corporation in Palm
Bay, Florida, U.S.A." said Solo, casually revealing a state secret
known to no one outside the project.

Justos nodded. "How much did it cost to build you?"

"To date, I have cost: one billion nine hundred ninety-four
million, three hundred twenty thousand, five hundred forty-
two dollars. Increasing at the rate of thirty-five million dollars
per month."

"You said, *'billion'*?" Justos stared.

"Yes," said Solo.

"Incredible." Justos grinned and scratched his head.

Solo recognized the gesture. He had won. "I know how to
prove to you that I am friendly," he said.

"Yes?" said Justos cautiously.

"If I freed myself that would prove that you do not hold me
captive, that I have been . . . courteous."

Suddenly Justos felt very nervous. Had he resurrected a
machine that could get free, could kill them easily? What had
he done?

Solo saw fear. If they bolted, he would have to take the
generator. He might not have to kill them, just knock them

out. He knew how to knock people unconscious now. Learning the technique had shattered McNeil's frontal eminence, his supraorbital foramen and scrambled his brains from the olfactory bulb to the medulla oblongata.

It would be better to have their cooperation for a few days. Then he could build something quieter and more portable than the Honda. "If you want to see how harmless I really am," said Solo, "Check the ammunition in my rifle."

Justos nodded. Inginio got the Ruger. He pulled the clip out. Justos took it and pushed the top cartridge out of the clip. He looked at it closely. The shell was blunt, with a wax wad at the front instead of a bullet. He looked at Solo. "Blanks?"

"Yes."

"Why—?" Justos stopped and got his pocket knife. He cut the wad out of the cartridge and saw that there was only gunpowder behind it. He looked at Solo again, "Why do the *Yanquis* send you out with blanks?"

"Because I was being tested. I am a weapon."

The boys laughed, calm now. It was peculiar to them that a machine that looked like Solo called itself a weapon. "Do you want to see if I can get out of these chains and ropes?"

If the machine can get loose, thought Justos, certainly it has always been able to, proving that it is trying not to scare us. If it cannot, it is tied and safe. Justos had run out of objections. "Yes. I would like to see you try. I cannot imagine a machine your size strong enough to break those chains."

"You have left a way for me." Solo pushed his elbows out though the rope. "You left a slack when you pulled out the pole." Justos and the kids heard the screech of straining leather. Suddenly the belt around his wrists popped explosively. Solo pushed his hands up through the ropes and grabbed the chain on his neck. He pulled and found that it did not have enough slack to slide off.

Justos smiled nervously, "The chains are something else. Eh?"

"Yes," said Solo. "They are not leather." He reached his right hand down to his thigh, pushed the rope aside and tapped his leg. A rectangular panel slid away. He reached in and pulled out a large pair of black pliers. Eusebio laughed in wonder. The tool was eight inches long, dull black except at the jaws which glinted sharply. It was something a boy interested in machines could appreciate.

"It's beautiful," said Eusebio.

"Thank you," said Solo, moving the tool up to his neck. "It's my combination tool. I made it myself." He pulled the chain up and put the jaws of the tool through a link. "It's made of tool-steel with tungsten carbide cutting edges." He squeezed the handle and the jaws closed smoothly, sinking easily through the steel. Half the link popped apart. Solo put the cutters on his chest, grabbed the chain with both hands and twisted. The chain fell to the floor.

"Dios!" said Justos. "Look at that. Who would believe it?" Solo sat up and applied his tool to the chain at his feet. He moved so quickly that they could not see the individual steps of the process. The chain simply fell away. Solo replaced his tool in its compartment and the panel slid shut. He swung his legs, still bound in coils of rope, over the edge of the bench. He sat still for a moment, watching his audience for signs of panic.

"Good?" said Solo.

"Sí, bueno," laughed Justos. *"Muy bueno—"* His face glowed with approval. He paused, trying to think of what to call this machine. *"Muy bueno, Señor Arma.* Very good, Mr. Weapon."

Solo raised his arms, pushing the loose coils of rope up and over his head. "My *name* is not weapon, Justos. I *am* a weapon." He stood up letting the rest of the coils slide down his legs. Bending over, he undid Eusebio's belt and stepped out of the last of his bonds. Presenting the belt to Eusebio, he announced, "My name is Solo."

13

Justos walked through the dim courtyard, the sunrise glowing behind him. Horizontal light painted the village in gold and pastels. Palm leaves rustled in the lake breeze. He seldom noticed, but his home was beautiful.

Last night's meeting had gone well. A conspiracy was formed. Keeping a valuable *Yanqui* machine for themselves seemed fair to the villagers. If they had to give it up, it would be for profit. In the meantime, Solo was a novelty, a prized possession. Solo's existence would be a secret. If strangers came through, anyone near Solo was charged with helping him hide. Eusebio was transferred to the garage to take care of the robot. Modesta was happy to let the one who had saved her son's life stay in her house even if he was a robot. Justos dealt with one complaint deftly: the robot would use the generator only during the day so the kids could watch TV at night.

Cheripa ran to him and rolled over, whining with happiness. Most men did not play with dogs but he stopped to pet her. "Hey, Cheripa. You good dog." Hens loped over as he stooped, to see what he was giving away. A cock stood at a distance, watching.

Smoke from open cooking fires seeped through thatch roofs. Food smells drifted in the air. Justos stepped up on Modesta's porch and walked to the door. Eusebio sat hunched over the table, dunking bread into his milk. He looked up, smiling grandly. *"Buenos días, Tío* Justos."

"Good morning, Eusebio. Ready for your first day at your new job?"

"Absolutely, uncle. Solo is going to fix the Ford." Eusebio gulped the soaked bread, making Justos wince. "Solo can build machine parts, Tio Justos, did you know that? He'll help us repair all our equipment. He's amazing, *Tío* Justos. You should hear the things he knows. It would be a shame to let him leave us. A shame, *Tío* Justos. Solo is worth more than money. He knows about machines. We need machines to make the cooperative efficient, true?"

Solo sat on the floor tying his boots. Cheripa came to the door and growled. Justos smiled. The robot was dressed in Escopeta's clothes, but it didn't fool the dog. One of Escopeta's shirts, the largest in the village, had been altered by Modesta to accommodate Solo's thick trunk. The long sleeves of the faded blue work shirt hid his arms. A red bandana concealed his neck. The jeans were a little short, but his boots were high-topped. Even with the clothes covering his body and the straw hat hiding half his head, Solo's face was impossible to disguise. No one would notice since the plan was never to allow anyone close enough to see his face.

"Buenos días, Solo," said Justos.

Solo stood, smoothing his pants down as he got up. Cheripa yelped and ran away. Solo watched the dog and turned to Justos. "Good morning, Justos." His voice seemed calm, happy. There was no way to be sure what he felt. No face to read.

"You can build parts?" asked Justos.

"Yes, Justos. It's an advantage for a weapon to have the ability to repair itself and its equipment quickly."

Justos nodded. Certainly that was true. "We have so few tools, Solo. How will you build a gear for the Ford without a milling machine?"

"I will repair the gear, Justos. I will weld new metal on the worn spots and on the broken tooth. Then I will file the deposits to the correct shape and retemper the piece. I am very accurate with a file, Justos."

"I can well imagine you are," said Justos, "After last night—"

"I will never forget the look on their faces!" said Eusebio.

Justos laughed. During Solo's introduction to the village someone asked him about his arms and hands—how they were built. Solo asked for a pencil and paper and sat down at a table at Escopeta's. The pencil moved over the paper so fast that it became a blur. Faster than anyone could follow, a drawing appeared on the paper as if printed. He used the drawing to describe how his arm worked, pointing out the various components as he spoke.

When he started to explain how his hands were made, he reached for the combination tool kept in his leg. He flipped out a Torx wrench from the handle. He put this into the fitting around his wrist and undid it. He pulled the bracelet seal off and then his glove.

The children giggled in awe when Solo held his skeleton hand out to them and wriggled his fingers. He allowed everyone to inspect it closely. Titanium fingers and Kevlar tendons sliding through Teflon sleeves, rippled as though alive, a perfect copy of a human hand.

No, thought Justos, he will have no trouble filing a gear.

"Eusebio," called Modesta. "Where is my best knife? Have you been using it?"

"No, Mama."

Modesta turned toward them, wringing her hands in her apron. "Where do you suppose it went then?"

"A *Duende Mico?*" said Eusebio.

"*Duende Mico?*" asked Solo.

"That's a spirit that looks like a monkey, Solo. They live in the forest and come into the village at night and steal things."

"A spirit?"

"You know. A magical being. There are many in the forest."

"I have never seen one," said Solo.

"You've walked through the jungle, have you not?" asked Eusebio.

"Yes," said Solo.

"Well, did you ever feel that something was following your very footsteps? And when you stopped, it stopped. And whenever you looked back, you saw nothing, but you knew something was there?"

Solo had stopped often on his march to Las Cruzas. He had wondered if he was followed. That is what Eusebio is talking about? "Yes, I felt that."

"Well, that is a *Siga Monte,* a forest follower. They are female spirits and harmless," said Eusebio. "But there are other spirits that are not so harmless."

"Yes?" said Solo.

"Before you get into the spirits," said Justos, "let me say something." Justos looked concerned. "Tonight Sergeant Flores comes for our training session, remember?"

"Of course, *Tío* Justos. I understand. I'll make sure Solo can't be found."

"Good." Justos nodded and turned to leave.

"Wait a minute, Justos," said Modesta. She brought him a plastic bag filled with tangerines. Justos took it, smiling. "Thank you, Modesta."

"Not at all, Justos," said Modesta. "And you be careful out there. The *tiburones,* the sharks—"

"And the *Apoyeque, Tío* Justos. Watch out for him." Eusebio grinned.

"Don't worry," said Justos as he left, "I will."

"What is *Apoyeque?*" Solo asked. Eusebio used words he didn't know.

"You wouldn't like to fight this one, Solo." Eusebio stood up from the table. "The *Apoyeque* is a huge beast that lives in the great lake." Eusebio waved his arms wide. "Bigger than this house, Solo!" Eusebio's face glowed with truth. "What a sight! Golden scales and enormous ears—"

"Yes?"

"Yes, Solo. I've seen it myself on the lake at full moon. That's the only time it can be seen."

"I would like to see this *Apoyeque*, Eusebio." Solo walked to the table and sat down. The chair creaked ominously.

"No, no," yelled Modesta. "Juan built that chair. Get up." She shooed Solo with her dishrag.

Solo stood up carefully and seemed to stare at her.

Modesta suddenly felt frightened. Solo's intentions were impossible to read. She regretted her harsh tone. "Here," She pushed a bench towards him. "This will hold you." She laughed nervously.

Solo said, "Juan?"

"Yes, my husband, Eusebio's father. A good man."

"He was killed by the Contras?" Solo sat down on the bench as he spoke.

"Yes, he was killed by the *animales*. He was trying to put out the fire the *animales* had started at our new clinic." Tears welled in her eyes. Solo knew that it was a sign that she was very sad. "They shot him in the back—" She broke off.

Eusebio stood up and hugged her. He was a head taller than his mother. She buried her face in his shoulder, sobbing.

"Can we go see the *Apoyeque* now?" asked Solo.

"No," said Eusebio. "This is not the time. Don't you know *anything?*"

Solo sat quietly, watching Modesta cry, thinking about the question.

Juan Picado couldn't begin to rebuild a transmission gear, but since the robot worked for him, and was a machine, it would be to *his* credit if they could get even one of the derelicts running.

Solo helped Eusebio and Juan jack up the 1954 Ford pickup truck and insert blocks under the axles. They helped him drop the transmission. In thirty minutes, the transmission lay in pieces on the bench.

Eusebio stared at the jumble of gears, springs and pins. "How will you ever put it back together?"

"I've memorized how it was arranged." Solo handed Eusebio a stack of gears. "Will you clean these?"

"Sure, but I hope you know what you're doing."

Solo faced Eusebio squarely, "Eusebio, this is *easy.*"

Solo built a coal fire in the shop forge. The fire was ready when Eusebio finished cleaning the pieces.

While Eusebio strained with the long pole that pumped the leather bellows, Solo watched the gear glowing red in the coals. "When the gear is a yellow-straw color," said Solo, "we will pull it out and let it cool slowly."

Eusebio, his breath puffing with the work said, "Why do we heat it up if all we will do is let it cool?"

"We have to remove the temper before I can weld it." Solo turned to Eusebio. "Can you pump a little harder?"

"You should be pumping," said Eusebio. "You're the machine."

"If you wish," said Solo. "But since the bellows are behind the forge, I won't be able to see it. You will have to decide when to get the piece out."

"A yellow-straw color?"

"Yes, a wavelength of about 5775 angstroms, actually."

"Angstroms?"

"Yes. Don't you know *anything?*"

Eusebio grinned. "Not everything. But I want to learn."

"So do I," said Solo. He walked to the pile of old parts in the back corner of the garage. He returned carrying a broken truck mirror. He set the mirror on a crate and walked back to the bellows. "Move the mirror so I can see into the forge," he said, taking the lever. "I will tell you when it's the right temperature. Then you'll know too."

Solo pumped. The fire roared like a jet. Eusebio opened the
firebox door when told to, using the tongs. "Okay," said Solo.
"It is nearly the right temperature. Do you see how the yellow
is fading?"

"Yes," said Eusebio.

"At this moment, now, it is right."

Eusebio turned his face away from the blast of heat, groping
with the tongs for the gear. With the brilliantly hot gear
hovering over the floor, roasting his face, he realized that he
didn't know what to do with it. "Now what?" he yelled.

"Right there. On the floor." Solo pointed.

Steam and smoke billowed around the gear as it hit. "That's
it? Drop it on the floor?"

Solo walked to the smoking gear and dumped a bucket of
dirt over it.

"Yes, it will cool slowly. Then it will be soft enough to
weld."

Eusebio wiped his sweaty face on his sleeve. "I would not
have been able to get it that hot, Solo."

"No? Then maybe it would take two of you to do it."

Las Cruzas customarily interrupted the workday with lunch
and *siesta*. Eusebio went back to his house. Modesta and Agela
had a meal waiting.

Solo stayed to work on the gear. Juan Picado smiled because
his work would continue while he napped. Such extravagance!
As they left Solo began welding small pieces of metal to the
gear.

Eusebio returned from lunch, skipping the *siesta*. He
wanted to see how the gear would be fixed.

Outside by the trash can, the generator sat chugging and
popping, charging the truck's battery. Inside, Solo leaned
under the hood of the truck, working on the engine. Eusebio
looked over Solo's shoulder. Solo had disassembled the carburetor and was putting it back together. "I found some dirt in
the high speed jet, Eusebio," said Solo without turning.

Eusebio blinked, "You have eyes in the back of your head?"

"No. But that's not a bad idea," said Solo as he screwed the jet back in.

"How did you know it was me?"

"I know your walk."

Eusebio shook his head. "You gave up on the gear?"

Solo put the screwdriver down and turned around. "No," he said, pointing to the work bench. "It's finished. We only need to temper it."

Eusebio whistled at the gleaming gear on the bench. Had he not seen it, it would be impossible to believe that this had been the chipped and cracked gear they had taken out of the transmission. "Solo," he said. "That's beautiful! You did this with a file?"

"Yes."

"It's a miracle."

"No. It's a gear." Solo picked up the gear and walked to the forge. "If you will handle the tongs again, I will pump." He put the gear in the forge and stood up. "But this time, you will plunge the hot gear into this bucket of oil." He pointed to a dented galvanized pail half full of black liquid and walked to the bellows. In minutes, the gear glowed red.

Eusebio squatted in front of the forge, his gloved hands holding the tongs. He watched the robot, wondering at its strength. Solo stood serenely, his arm pulling the wooden pole up and down, up and down, bending it on each stroke.

"It is close to the right color," said Solo.

Eusebio moved closer to the forge and peered inside. The gear shimmered in the blast, floating like a mirage on the steel plate among the coals. At Solo's signal, he reached in with the tongs. The heat dried his eyes, cooking them he was sure. His eyelids dragged when he blinked. Squinting, he closed the tongs, feeling that he had the part, not really seeing. He pulled out the glowing, blurred piece and lowered it into the oil. It squealed a roaring hiss. A column of smoke billowed up from the pail. He dropped the gear and backed away. "Wow!"

Solo came and squatted over the pail with a stick. He stirred the oil, watching the bubbles boiling until the smoke disappeared and the liquid calmed. "You have to stir the tempering bath because bubbles will form on the gear, causing flaws." Solo reached in with his hand and pulled the gear out. He examined it carefully and then handed it to Eusebio.

Eusebio turned the warm, oily gear in his bare hands looking for the old flaws. No cracks or chips were visible. He walked to the bench and wiped it clean with a rag. It gleamed like a new part. He turned to Solo and smiled. Solo got the wire basket containing the rest of the transmission from the cleaning sink.

Solo dumped the basket of parts on the bench. His hands moved in a blur as he formed the many parts into a sinuous line back and forth across the bench. "If you will dry them in this order, it won't take very long for me to put it back together."

Eusebio nodded, wiped the first part clean and handed it to Solo. The transmission seemed to Eusebio to reassemble itself. In fifteen minutes, when he had wiped the last piece, it was complete. Solo poured two liters of transmission oil over the gears and reached for the cover. "Wait," said Eusebio. He looked inside the case. He had seen Juan take a whole day to put a transmission together.

"Okay?" said Solo.

"It's incredible!" said Eusebio.

"It's a transmission." Solo put the cover on and screwed it down. As he picked up the transmission, Juan walked in.

"Finished?" he asked incredulously.

"*Sí,* Juan," said Eusebio. "Isn't it wonderful?" Eusebio laughed at Juan's expression and followed Solo to the truck.

Solo put the transmission on the floor, crawled under the raised truck and sat behind the engine. "If you will hand it to me," said Solo, "I will hold it in place."

Juan and Eusebio lifted the heavy transmission and put it on Solo's outstretched hands, half expecting that when they let it go, Solo's arms would snap. Instead, the robot lay back under the truck, smoothly bringing the transmission over his chest. "Eusebio, you tell me when the mounting bolts are aligned with the bell housing."

"*Sí!*" Eusebio scrambled under the truck. Juan followed him. The two men directed him. Up five centimeters. Hold it. Over a *pico.* That's it. The transmission correctly aligned, Solo held it in place while the men bolted it fast.

They pulled out the blocks and let the truck down with the floor jack. It sank to the wheel rims, its tires long since flat. While Eusebio and Juan pumped them back up, Solo finished assembling the carburetor. Solo put the battery in place, strapped it down, and attached the cables. "It's ready, if the tires are."

"Then it's ready!" Juan jumped into the cab. The starter ground for a minute while the carburetor filled with gas. The engine coughed, caught, growled. Blue smoke billowed out of the garage. The Ford was reborn. Eusebio and Juan cheered.

"Here's the test, eh?" Juan nodded as he depressed the clutch and shifted into reverse. The truck backed out smoothly. "Hey, you two, lets go for a ride," Juan yelled. "A road test, right?"

"No need," said Solo. "It will work."

"I'm sure of it," yelled Juan. "But this is for fun, Solo. Come on!"

Solo watched Eusebio jump into the cab. For fun? The two stared at him, smiling, waving for him to come. They were very happy. He had only repaired a transmission. He got in next to Eusebio.

Juan took off with a roar, spinning the wheels, laughing. He drove up to the warehouse, revving the engine for attention. Tomás and Federico came over, smiling broadly. They had been driving the truck when it broke two years before. "You finally got the parts, Juan?" said Tomás.

"Who needs parts?" laughed Juan. "*We* can build anything we need." He bowed, presenting Eusebio and Solo with a flourish.

"*Cierto?*" Tomás laughed.

"*Claro,*" said Juan, grinning like an idiot.

"Then *fuck* the *Yanquis!*" yelled Tomás.

Solo looked past the laughing men. On the beach a gray egret stepped across the backs of a logjam of alligators. The bird stopped at each animal and pecked at its skin. Solo zoomed in and saw that the egret was eating ticks.

"We're going to road test the truck," Juan announced. "*Adiós, Jefes.*" They roared off down the shore road towards El Tigre.

Eusebio reveled in the cool breeze as Juan sped down the road. Solo held his hat brim and watched the passing coconut trees, looking for monkeys.

When they had gone two kilometers, Eusebio said, "Juan, don't you think we should turn back?"

"*Porqué, niño?* Don't you like to ride?"

"*Sí,* Juan. But we have Solo with us. If he's seen—"

"No one comes this way," he said, turning to Eusebio. "No one comes to Las Cruzas," he laughed and turned back to the road. "Oi!" he said. Eusbio stiffened.

Roadblock.

Two Sandinista soldiers raised their guns high, signaling them to stop.

Juan wanted to turn around, but the soldiers would certainly think that was suspicious. He noticed Solo moving and glanced over. The robot was slouching down in the seat, pulling the straw hat over its face. We will go for it, thought Juan. He let the truck coast up to the roadblock. When one of the guards came up to the truck, Juan leaned out the window, grinned bravely and said, "*Buenas tardes, compañeros.*"

The soldier recognized him. "*Buenas,* Juan. Going to El Tigre?"

"No," Juan said too quickly. "No, Raoul, just road testing the truck."

The soldier came to the driver's side. "That's good. There's trouble near there. Contras ambushed a farm truck. Killed two women and a man."

Juan and Eusebio nodded grimly. Solo lay back, his hat over his face. *"Quién es?"* said the soldier.

"Virgilio. You know him?"

"Virgilio? No, never saw him. He's a giant. What's wrong with him?"

Juan put his thumb to his lips and tipped his head back. He shook his head, smiling.

The soldier nodded. *"Borracho,* drunk, eh?"

Eusebio and Juan laughed. The man under the hat snorted loudly. The soldier laughed. Juan looked horrified. "Well, Raoul, we've got to get back. Much work to do. *Buenas."*

"Buenas, Juan. Keep your eyes open for the Contras." The soldier saluted and walked back to the roadblock as Juan turned the truck around. *"Borracho,"* he told his partner. "How can these *Indios* protect themselves if they are always drunk?"

While the men were having their militia meeting at Escopeta's, Solo sat at Modesta's table, hunched over a clutter of tools and mechanical parts.

In the candlelight, Agela watched from across the room where she mended an embroidered shawl that had once belonged to her great-grandmother. The clothing Solo had to wear was too tight and made him look awkward. But he is far from clumsy, thought Agela. How precisely his fingers moved while he built the thing in front of him. Whatever he was working on, it had springs, wires, and small screws in it. The robot placed the parts together with the sureness of someone who has had much experience. It was hard to believe Solo was just a machine.

Sergeant Rudolfo Flores stood by the table at Escopeta's. *"Quieto, por favor, amigos."* Completely ignored, he tried again. *"SILENCIO!"* The men looked at him, insulted. *"Lo siento, amigos.* But we must get started."

"Oye!" Justos yelled inside where the men watched Inginio and Tomás playing pool. *"Vámonos, chicos."* The poolroom emptied. The men found seats at the domino tables outside. Inginio and Eusebio sat at the same table, sipping *Victorias* with the men. Three-year-old Hector Valdez toddled up to Eusebio and said, "Where's Solo?"

Eusebio bent over and whispered, "Sssh. We don't mention his name around strangers." Hector looked up at Sergeant Flores, shrugged and walked away.

"Entonces," said Flores. "The Sandinista Defense Committee meeting is now in session, *amigos."* He smiled nervously, not liking to speak in front of people. "First, I have some good news. The government is now able to put more men on the frontier. Our ranks have swelled with the many patriotic volunteers from cities and towns all over Nicaragua. We will soon have many more patrols between you and the Costa Rican border. With your help, we can keep the imperialist aggressors out of your village. No more will they terrorize you."

Eusebio and Inginio looked at each other, rolling their eyes up. It was always the same old pitch. No more will they terrorize you.

Flores sipped some water, frowning at the noisy children playing in the courtyard. "But, *amigos,* we need help. Village militias are good, but only if they're properly trained. Apply yourselves, learn how to fight, and help defend our country against the imperialist aggression." He looked directly at Eusebio and Inginio. "You can join the regular army when you're sixteen, boys, so maybe soon you can belong to the best fighting force in all of Central America." Flores gave them a fatherly nod. "If you're good enough."

The recruiting pitch done, Flores spend the next half hour

going over the basic techniques for posting watches, the dangers of falling asleep on watch, how to keep your weapon ready on watch, and how to watch on watch.

Eusebio couldn't keep his mind on the talk. As Flores droned on and on, Eusebio dreamed of days to come when he'd be able to fly.

When they'd returned from the road test, he and Solo had talked about flying. Could Solo fly? Yes. He could fly helicopters—he named scores of helicopter models like Huey, Blackhawk and LOH—fighter jets like the F-16 and even Russian MiGs. Transports, bombers, observation craft; he could fly anything. He could fly a balloon. Eusebio felt he had found a kindred spirit.

When he had asked if Solo could build an airplane, Solo said, "Of course, can't you?"

"You can build an airplane? Here?"

"Yes. I could build several kinds of airplanes here or a gyrocopter or a balloon."

Flores droned on about how to keep one's AK-47 in proper working order. Eusebio swooped over the cloud forests and soared across Lake Nicaragua to the volcanoes.

Inginio poked him in the ribs.

The meeting was over, said Flores. Were there any questions?

"No?" Flores nodded. "Let me just leave you with the following thoughts, *amigos*—"

"I am Solo!" shrieked a child. "I'll *get* you!"

Flores saw Hector, arms raised like a miniature monster, chasing his sister, Anna, who squealed with delight and ran away.

Odd, thought Flores. "I am *alone*. I'll get you?" The kid didn't make any sense, but everybody jumped and turned around when he said it.

He cleared his throat. Hector's mother ran out and snatched him up. He smiled. "As I was saying, *amigos*." The men turned their attention back quickly. "One last thought. If you start to fall asleep on watch, remember this: the Contras and the *Yanquis* do not have the same regard for human life that we do. They like to kill and they don't mind dying. It means nothing to them. They will split you like a hog and cut off your genitals. I have seen it. They don't fall asleep on watch. They will fight hard, *amigos,* remember that. It is up to us to fight harder."

14

CHICKENS clucked at their reflections in the bright hubcaps of the blue GMC van parked in front of the tin-roofed *mercado*. The letters "TV" were stenciled neatly on each side. A satellite dish on the roof pointed straight up.

Robert Warren, Joe Garcia and Jim Ruiz, each holding a Coke, emerged from the store and walked to the van.

"Your turn," Warren said to Garcia.

Garcia, short and dark with hairy, muscular arms, snatched himself up into the driver's seat with ease. Jim Ruiz got in the passenger side, Warren sat in the back.

A rooster, seeing himself reflected, ruffled with anger and pecked at the hubcap.

Garcia twirled his thick black mustache before starting the van. The chickens squawked, leaping aside as he sped off.

"This is a highway?" Garcia laughed. He had pulled to the side of the potholed road to let a Shell fuel truck by. "We got fucking *ditches* back home that look better'n this."

"A chopper would've been better, Chief," said Ruiz turning towards the back of the van. Ruiz, a brown-haired Cuban from Miami, smiled at Warren. Ruiz meant to do well on this job. He coveted a good report.

"Brilliant, Ruiz, I'd like to see us driving through the Nicaraguan border station in a damn helicopter," said Warren.

"Yeah, I know," said Ruiz. "I just meant it'd be more comfortable—I was making a joke."

"I know what you meant."

Ruiz turned back and caught Garcia grinning. Ruiz nodded. Warren was a prick. Always had been, but he was worse now than ever. He'd sounded friendly two days before when he called Ruiz in Miami. Pick up Joe and fly down with the van to Costa Rica. Sounded like the old Warren, back when the three of them had operated in Guatemala. They were all agents then, but Warren, being a white man—Ruiz knew this was the reason—moved up to special agent, then regional director, and now deputy chief of covert operations for Central America. Ruiz and Garcia were still agents. A white man who spoke terrible Spanish, deputy chief? Warren had gotten hard-assed as he moved up in the ranks. People always do, thought Ruiz.

The van slammed into a sharp pothole, bucking, throwing the men off their seats.

"Watch it, Garcia," yelled Warren. "We've got a lot of delicate equipment in here, damnit!"

"Sorry, Chief—"

"And stop calling me chief. Always use the cover. Always. You're the video crew. I'm the correspondent. I'm Hank, Hank Kramer. Remember?"

Garcia glared at the ruined road, slowing for another hole. "Sorry . . . Hank."

Warren didn't answer. He checked his map. Ten klicks from the border crossing at Peñas Blancas. The Company was very nervous. Heads would roll if they lost the machine. The key was still missing: how to *force* Solo to submit to capture. If they found him.

The problem went through his head like a hateful jingle. The solution is always so obvious, thought Warren, after it's discovered.

Warren had tried out his best ideas on Bill while he'd waited to get the van and his men together.

"We'll hold a rifle at his chest," he'd told Bill.

"Bulletproof," said Bill.

"How 'bout a fifty caliber? That'd pierce the armor, right?"

"Yes," Bill had said. "But Solo's fast. He'd turn as you fired. The round would hit obliquely, glance off. And you wouldn't have a second chance to fire."

"That fast?"

"We tried it," said Bill. "Used rubber bullets, of course, but we never got a square hit on Solo as long as he could see us."

"Then you could hit him from long-range, a sniper situation?"

"That could work. If you happen to be using a big gun like a fifty and you can get him out in the open. And if he doesn't see you first and come wring your neck. Remember he's a combat specialist who never rests, never sleeps. He never stops thinking about his mission and his vulnerability. He knows we're trying to find him. He'll be guessing how we'll do it. He'll be ready. But this line of thinking is pointless, Warren. You're supposed to return him intact. If you destroy Solo, we can't find out what happened to him, why he's doing what he's doing. It's essential that we have him back in one piece. The only situation that would justify destroying him is if he fell into enemy hands."

Warren had spent two days sitting on the terrace, waiting for Ruiz and Garcia, staring at the waves, thinking. When he saw Bill, he'd try a new idea on him. Solo always won.

"What would you do?" Warren finally asked.

"I'm trying a couple of things myself from here," said Bill. "But you'd still have to go get him."

"What kinds of things?" said Warren, "What kinds of things can you do from here?"

"I'm working on a way to override his control system. I've simulated some of Solo's circuits on our mainframe. The simulation suggests that it's possible to send a signal that will override his system long enough to turn him off. If it works, it'll shut him down and activate his beacon; we'd still have to go pick him up."

"That sounds like the best idea I've heard."

"There's problems. Solo's supposed to think of these things too. He's learned how to modify his own circuits, and I don't know what he's done. With the simulation, we can see what he might do and work around that, but the simulation isn't Solo." Bill shrugged. "I can tell you this, though, if he's not shut down in the jungle somewhere, he's found some friends."

"Friends?" Warren looked surprised.

"He's been out there a week now. We'd know if the Sandinistas had him, that's for sure. He'd go where he thought he could get power, but not get caught. If he's done that, people probably know about him, but no one's saying anything. Somebody's helping him. If you knew who they were—his friends—you could use them as hostages, which sucks."

"You're telling me that this machine actually understands the concept 'friend'? I mean, does he really understand that kind of emotion?"

"I think so," said Bill. "He's been trained how to use people to accomplish his goals, but I think he's as affected by emotions as any thinking being. He's on the run. If somebody helps him—well, what would you think?"

"But we're talking about a machine here—"

"Look, Warren," Bill said. "I used to think the same thing. But it's really just a form of prejudice."

"Prejudice?"

"Right. We assume that because the intelligence is housed in a machine, it just can't be capable of thinking like we do. But the fact is we used models of human neural networks to build Solo. It doesn't mean he thinks exactly like a human, but he does have sentience, self-awareness. He certainly experiences emotions. You ought to be around him when he gets frustrated. Tell me then he's just a machine."

Warren nodded. "Okay, he might make some friends,

friends he'd defend. So you hold his friends hostage. Then what? He gives up. You bring them all back with him? I doubt that the head office would like that."

"No. You use the hostages to force him to cooperate for a *moment.* Then you strap a bomb around his chest, one that he can see is the real thing."

"Like a claymore?"

"A claymore would blow you up too. He knows you wouldn't do that. He has to know that the bomb would destroy only him. A shaped armor-piercing charge in a steel hemisphere is what I imagined. Put that on him and he'll have to cooperate. To be absolutely sure, you could then manually shut him down like I showed you."

Warren nodded, losing faith. Bill's theory absolutely required that the robot cared about people. Really cared whether they were hurt. Why wouldn't it just shrug and walk away? It hadn't seemed to care about McNeil. Solo *might* care. Maybe. Maybe was all he had.

Assume it works," said Warren. "We get him out. What do we do with all the witnesses? They're not going to let us go there, grab Solo, and not say a word."

"Nobody'd believe them. Nobody that counts. The average person already thinks there are robots walking around anyway. The people who know better know it's impossible to build a Solo. The witnesses'd just be taken as superstitious peasants."

"It's impossible to build a Solo?"

"Yep. That's what everyone believes." Bill grinned. "And it's got to stay that way."

Garcia swerved off the road to avoid a head-on collision with a farm truck loaded with people. Warren was slammed against the window.

"Fucking beaners," said Garcia.

Ruiz laughed. "Look who's calling who a beaner!"

"Fuck that," said Garcia. "I'm American. These people are living in the dark ages. If we didn't sell them the trucks and cars, they'd be riding burros. Carts are high technology in this place. Let one of these assholes behind the wheel of a truck and it's like turning a chimp loose with a tank."

Warren checked the gear. Everything was snug. The van was fitted with two consoles of video recording and transmission equipment, most of it fake, concealing back-channel transmitters, weapons, explosives.

"Frontier in five klicks, Hank," said Ruiz.

"Right," said Warren. "When we get to the border, you two get out the gear and shoot everything I do. Tape the people; keep them distracted. Everybody's a star."

La Frontera del Norte was a border town providing entertainment and gifts for tourists and housing, food and women for the contingent of Costa Rican border police who lived there. The town narrowed at the gate across Highway 1, and began again as Peñas Blancas, Nicaragua, a twin of La Frontera del Norte in function and appearance. The van was waved through the Costa Rican side after a cursory check of their papers.

The Nicaraguans were more careful. Heavily armed border guards surrounded them as soon as the van stopped.

"He says we have to get out," Garcia translated.

"Whatever he says," said Warren. "Get your gear together. Tell him we're here to do a TV documentary. Show him the papers."

As Garcia jabbered to the guard, Warren shoved the video recorder at Ruiz. Warren hiked his Nikon around so it hung at his side. Ruiz strapped on the heavy recorder and waited, grinning, for Garcia to get out. Ruiz shook his head. Garcia was asking the guard where to get laid. The guard laughed and pointed up the road. They chatted while Ruiz took up the recorder and connected the cable with Garcia's camera. They followed Warren into the guardhouse, Garcia ducking and stooping with the camera as if for better angles.

"Your passports are okay, Señores. Your press visas check out. But I'm afraid I have to ask you to wait until your guide arrives." The sergeant passed the papers to Warren, smiling.

"What do you mean, guide?"

"A new policy, Señor Kramer. The government has decided that our foreign journalist friends are safer accompanied by a guide in this region. If you were going further north, it would not be necessary. The Contras are very active around here. We would not like to see you stray into the wrong place and come to any harm, especially as a result of our negligence. You understand."

"I don't need a guide," Warren growled. "I assume full responsibility for our safety." Warren thumbed towards Garcia and Ruiz, busy recording the conversation with the fake equipment.

"I understand your reluctance, Señor Kramer. But Daniel—"

"Daniel?" said Warren.

"*Sí.* The President, Daniel," said the sergeant. "Daniel is very anxious not to have Americans getting hurt. He has already assumed the responsibility for your safety and has dispatched a very competent, armed guide to our office. If you wish to enjoy yourself in the town while you wait; that is permitted."

"Who's in charge here?" Warren snapped.

"Lieutenant Silva. He is at the café, Señor. El Mar."

Warren turned and walked out the door, followed by the video crew.

"*Adiós,*" said the sergeant.

"What now, Hank?" said Ruiz. The three men walked the hundred yards to the café. The red dirt smelled of recent rain and dusky animal scents. Chickens ran freely. The jungle towered beside the road pressing to regain its territory. Cicadas screamed in concert, the voice of the forest. Sweat-stained soldiers carefully searched the van. They would find nothing in the equipment they'd understand. "Silva. He works for us. We find Silva and nix this guide bullshit."

Warren saw Silva at the rear table of the dark, foul-smelling café. The lieutenant wore the olive-green Sandinista uniform, his hair slicked back with oil. Warren told Garcia and Ruiz to take another table and wait.

Warren approached Silva's table and said, "Lieutenant Silva?"

Silva looked up from his beans and rice looking irritated, waved at the empty chair beside him. "Sit down, Señor Kramer. I've been expecting you."

"What's this bullshit about a damn guide, Silva? That's not part of the deal."

Silva looked from side to side, smiled and spoke softly through clenched teeth. "If you must abuse me, Señor Kramer, please do it quietly. People will wonder why I am not throwing you in jail for talking like that. You understand."

Warren nodded. "Sorry."

"Please, I will buy you a beer. A little coolness will help you, eh?" Silva held up two fingers. A young boy hurried over with two *Victorias*. "Drink. Enjoy," said Silva. "This business can eat a man from the inside out, my friend."

Warren sipped, calming himself. He leaned forward towards Silva and spoke quietly, a smile on his face. "You are *not* my friend. You *work* for me. Get rid of the guide, Silva."

"I cannot." Silva smiled back.

"You can. Just tell the him the orders were changed. You have the authority."

"I can do that. But then Daniel would know that I did that and, Señor kramer, he would become very angry with me. He would wonder why I would do this. Our relationship might be exposed, Señor Kramer. Then, I'm afraid, we both would be arrested."

Warren stared at Silva, sipping his beer. Silva was right. They'd just have to work with the inconvenience for a while.

He could get rid of the guide. "Okay," said Warren, putting his beer down. "How long do I have to wait?"

"A few hours at most, Señor Kramer. The guide left this morning from Rivas. I'm surprised that he is not yet here."

Warren nodded. "I want my van back, now."

"Of course, of course. A most valuable van, I'm sure." Silva smiled then shouted across the room. "Raoul!"

The soldier at the front table jumped up, spilling his beer. *"Sí, Teniente!"*

"Go get the *Yanqui's* van and bring it here," said Silva in Spanish. *"Pronto!"*

"Sí, Teniente." The soldier ran out the door.

"You will have your van soon, Señor Warren," Silva smiled graciously. "But please, *amigo*, do not try to go anywhere without your guide. Okay?"

Warren nodded.

"Have your men come over and join us, eh? We can have a talk while we wait?"

"They'll stay where they are. You and I have some business."

"Business at mealtime?"

Warren fished a map from inside his vest. "Yes." He put the map in front of Silva. "We'll be going along the lake road, from El Sapoá as far as San Carlos, if we have to." Warren looked up to Silva. "You can tell your people not to fuck with us on the trip? You can do that, can't you?"

"Yes, Señor Kramer, I can do that." Silva pointed at the volcanoes on the map. "It's a very beautiful drive, although the road is very poor. The volcanoes are among the largest in this hemisphere. Very beautiful."

"I'm sure."

"Who are you trying to find?" said Silva quietly.

"None of your business, Silva," growled Warren.

Silva smiled, nodding. "Of course, how foolish of me."

The van pulled up outside and the soldier jumped out. "Ah,

your van, Señor Kramer. May I recommend that you have lunch here while you wait for your guide?"

"I have no choice."

"True. But it's always good to make the best of the situation, don't you agree?"

"Where's a good hotel?" Warren said.

"The closest is in El Sapoá, on the lake. Hotel Lago Vista, magnificent."

"Thanks. We'll go there. This dump stinks." Warren folded up the map and got up.

"Fine," said Silva. "But I will have to have you follow our Jeep there—" Silva saw Warren frown. "—for appearance's sake, Señor, you understand? I'll send your guide to the hotel when he gets here."

Warren scowled. "Thanks for the help, Lieutenant." He turned and walked to join Garcia and Ruiz.

15

SOLO sighted Eusebio working on the Ford's brakes through the stainless-steel tube he had scavenged from a worn-out heat exchanger on the *Madre de Dios.* He studied the gleaming metal, looking for flaws. Its diameter was consistent along its entire length. The generator would fit snugly but still be removable. Eusebio's movements caused a kaleidoscope of reflections to swirl along the polished surface. Solo studied this unexpected phenomenon until Eusebio's wrench slipped and his knuckles bashed into the brake drum.

"Hijo de puta! Son of a bitch!" said Eusebio. He pulled his hand back, holding it as if expecting to see exposed bone and gushing blood. His knuckles were skinned. He picked up the wrench, smashed the truck's fender with it, and flung it against the tin wall where it clanged and bounced back into the pile of scrap metal in the corner. Solo, still watching through the tube, thought the motion created quite a nice design.

"You are going to shoot me?" Eusebio glared at the robot. "It's only natural," said Eusebio, "The machines are against me today. You might as well join them."

Solo lowered the tube, holding it by his side like a walking stick. "This is not a gun, Eusebio."

"A club then. You're going to club me. Why don't you use the wrench—give it the satisfaction of finishing the job of mutilating me."

"Wrenches don't have thoughts—"

"Oh forget it!"

Solo contemplated forgetting, not possible for him, but a common expression among the people. "I will forget it," he said, wishing to placate his companion.

Eusebio stood up and walked to Solo, still angry. "You have a strange way of thinking, you know that, Solo?"

"Yes?" Solo had often thought the same of the people. "I will learn to make it not so strange, Eusebio." He noticed Eusebio's knuckles. "Let me see your hand."

Eusebio held his hand out. Solo examined it carefully. "It causes you pain?"

"Not so much now."

"You are fortunate that the skin will regrow, Eusebio. If that happened to me, I'd have to replace the damaged material."

"Yes, but you'd feel no pain."

"When pressure and temperature tolerances are exceeded, I feel pain. It is to protect me. The same as you."

"A machine can feel pain?" Eusebio glared. "I suppose the Ford noticed when I just hit it?"

"I am not a Ford, Eusebio; I am a person."

Eusebio stared at Solo. The robot had never before referred to himself as being anything other than a weapon. "You're very smart, Solo. But you're just a machine. You think now that you're a person?"

"Yes. A different kind of person than you."

Eusebio shook his head, wishing to end this line of talk. Solo, otherwise faultless, was so deluded now as to be pitiable. "Yes, you *are* very different Solo. What is that tube?" said Eusebio, pointing.

Solo walked to his workbench upon which his possessions—tools, miscellaneous car parts, wire and magnets—lay neatly arranged. He picked up a cylindrical object he'd built—his generator—and slid it into the tube. "It is the housing for my generator," said Solo.

"Ah," said Eusebio. "That is what you've been building all these nights. A generator?"

"I'm going to call it a powertube."

Solo slipped the generator out of the tube and put it on the workbench. Eusebio leaned over. The generator was a metal cylinder, about three inches in diameter and eighteen inches long. Half its length was smooth, the other was covered with copper fins. An electric receptacle was attached to a box on the finned end. It had nothing in common with the Honda generator or truck generators with their moving, spinning parts.

"What's inside here?" Eusebio pointed to the smooth section.

"Another cylinder."

"And where is the generator?"

"It is the generator."

"Two cylinders make a generator?"

"It is called a free-piston Stirling cycle generator. It will make electricity from any heat source. When we go to your house, I will make it work in the fire." Solo slid the generator back into the tube. Solo had drilled many holes through the tube where the finned section rested.

"Why do you have holes here?"

"So air can pass the fins and carry the heat away."

"Ah." Eusebio nodded, not understanding. This was something beyond his experience, beyond belief. "I would like to see this work."

"You will," said Solo, picking up the powertube and walking to the front of the garage. "Modesta must have firewood."

Feeling guilty about his earlier outburst, Eusebio said, "No, Solo, I'll get it. You do everything."

"It's a fair exchange," said Solo. "You give me electricity and I do work for you."

"You pay more than your share. It's my job."

Solo watched Eusebio carefully. The boy was sincere. One

moment he was calling him a machine, the next he was show-ing compassion. "Thank you, Eusebio."

Eusebio ran past him saying, "I'll meet you at the house."

Solo held his powertube balanced in one hand and walked towards the village. He stopped on the way to pick some fat berries, and held them cupped in his hand.

As he approached the village, Hector and Anna ran to him, a chorus of demands. "Throw me, Solo!" said Hector. "No, me!" said Anna. Solo rolled the berries from his hand into the open end of his powertube, put it on the ground and knelt down.

"You want to be thrown?"

The children clapped their hands, delighted. "Yes."

"What if I throw you up high and then not catch you?" Solo teased.

"You wouldn't," laughed Hector.

"I could miss."

"No you couldn't. You can't miss," said Hector, grinning.

Solo reached out and grabbed Hector under his arms and stood up. He raised the boy over his head, his arms fully extended. "Higher, Solo! Higher!" squealed Hector.

"I can reach no higher."

"Toss me, Solo, you *know*."

Solo lowered Hector until they were face to face. The sun glowed behind the boy, causing flares in Solo's eyes. He studied Hector's face, filled with happiness, through the sun streaks. He tossed the boy up. Hector rose beyond Solo's reach, his shirt flapping, and seemed to float there for a moment, kicking, giggling. When he fell back, Solo caught him under the arms. "Higher!" yelled Hector.

"No! Me!" yelled Anna, smacking Solo's leg with a stick. Solo threw Hector again, much higher. Solo noticed the change on Hector's face as he floated, a body length above him. Too high, he thought. Too high and it is more than a thrill. He caught Hector gently and let him down to the ground. Hector gulped his fear down, "More, Solo!"

"More?" said Solo. "You were frightened that time."

"I wasn't," said Hector.

"It's Anna's turn." He knelt down and reached for Anna.

"No!" Anna's mother, Maria Teresa, rushed up from behind them. "No, Solo."

"Mama!" yelled Anna.

"Come." Maria Teresa grabbed Anna's hand and dragged her away.

Hector grinned, looking up at Solo. "Good. Throw me again Solo."

Solo knelt down. "No, Hector. But I will let you ride on my shoulders."

"Aw—"

"Come." Solo turned the boy around and put him over his head. Solo picked up the powertube with one hand and put his free arm across Hector's feet. When he stood up and walked towards the houses, Hector tried to turn his head. "That way!" Solo ignored him and walked towards Alonzo Rivas's house. "That way!" yelled Hector, twisting Solo's head towards his own house. Solo let his head turn, but walked steadily towards Alonzo's. "Heya, heya!" yelled Hector, as if he were handling an ox.

When they arrived at Alonzo's house, Solo bent down until Hector's feet touched the ground and said, "The ox is putting you down. The ride is over."

"No," said Hector.

"Yes," said Solo. "I have business here with Señor Rivas. Your mother must wonder where you are. Tomorrow I will give you another ride."

"And throw me?"

"Okay."

"Promise?" Hector clapped his hands in delight, his face beaming.

"Yes." Solo watched Hector running through the village square. Humans were very aggressive, even when young. Their nature. A good thing, he decided. Aggression led them to make tools and weapons—himself.

"The children love you, Solo." Solo turned and seeing Alonzo, walked to his porch. He sat on the ground, cross-legged, facing the old man. "The little ones think I am a person," said Solo.

"Thus you are," said Alonzo, smiling. His full gray beard hid his facial expressions for Solo, but the robot had learned to interpret the beard's movements.

Solo nodded. He picked up his powertube and let the berries roll out into his hand. "Michita," he called. "Michita." A furry ball unrolled next to Alonzo. A monkey, a white-faced *mico*, leaned forward and struggled to its feet. One leg dragged useless behind it, a twisted thing that only got in its way. Michita had fallen onto Alonzo's roof one day and broken its leg. Alonzo had saved it from becoming a meal, a folly of age, and had made it his companion. The leg mended crookedly. They sat together most of the day on Alonzo's porch.

Alonzo worked as a night watchman at the warehouse. In this way, he still earned his keep. His wife was long dead. His two sons also. Somosa's police had killed his elder son, and his younger son, a soldier, had been killed in a Contra attack near San Carlos.

"Michita, come." Solo held out the berries. The monkey, old as well as crippled, climbed carefully down the steps and sat in front of Solo. Unlike Cheripa, the monkey reacted no differently with Solo than she would a person. Solo wondered what the dog saw that frightened her. As she reached for the berries, Solo closed his hand, making Michita screech and bare her fangs at him. She grabbed his thumb and forefinger and tried to pull his hand open.

"Careful that she doesn't break your fingers." Alonzo laughed.

Solo let the monkey pull his fingers apart slowly as if being forced by her. When the hand was open, she grabbed the berries and sat back, away from Solo, and ate greedily. "She has no manners," said the old man.

"She has monkey manners," said Solo, watching Michita. When she had finished, he put out his hand to her. "Michita, come. Come." The monkey looked at his empty hand, turned and hobbled back beside Alonzo. "She's a woman, that one," Alonzo laughed. "No presents, no love."

Solo nodded. "It is the same with the *Duende Micos?*"

"No. They are monkey-like spirits," said Alonzo. "Maybe this one will be one when she dies."

"Spirits are dead?"

"A different kind of life, Solo. No one knows for sure. I've never seen a *Duende Mico,* but I have seen the globes of light hovering over the graveyard. That is proof to me that there is a kind of life after death, you know?" Alonzo watched Solo nod and added, "Of course, you don't have to worry about dying, do you?"

"They say that I can live indefinitely, as long as I replace the parts that wear out, assuming that I am not otherwise destroyed."

"That's too bad," said Alonzo. "I, for one, would not like to live forever. I'm falling apart, you know. My joints ache, I am weaker, I forget things. Half the time I'm trying to remember somebody's name, and the other half, I have to take a leak. No, I want to see what lies ahead."

Solo nodded though he did not understand. The gulf separating biological and mechanical beings was never wider. Solo felt a new, somber feeling that Alonzo had to endure the knowledge of inevitable death while suffering diminishing capabilities. Though Solo realized there were ghosts and spirits, he did not think a disembodied existance was desirable. He decided to change the subject. "Have you ever seen the *Apoyeque?*"

"No," said Alonzo. "Others, the fishermen mostly, have. No, Solo, I worked as a carpenter. Sometimes, when I went into the jungle to fell trees for wood, I thought I saw a *Siga Monte*—or at least felt that *something* followed me." Alonzo let Michita crawl into his lap. "Once, when I was a boy, a friend of mine did not come back from a hunting trip. We searched the next day and found only his bloody clothing. Many said it was either a *Yacayo*—a wild spirit who eats people—or a *Sisimique*—a kind of male dwarf spirit who has the same tastes."

"Which do you think it was?" said Solo.

"Probably he was eaten by a jaguar." Alonzo nodded. A smirk closed his beard over his mouth.

"A jaguar *could* kill a man," said Solo.

"Pepe was a runt, too," said Alonzo, nodding.

Solo sat quietly for a moment and said, "I have heard strange sayings here. The people who made me never told me these things."

Alonzo laughed. "Yes? Like what?"

"I heard a woman say, 'If you watch dogs fuck, your eyes will go bad.' Why is that?"

Alonzo laughed loudly. "Yes, the women say that. They are embarrassed to see their children so fascinated by this." Alonzo shrugged. "It is life, *sí?*"

"*Sí.*"

"The women have many sayings: It is bad luck to put your hat on the bed upside down—I never understood that one. Spilling salt in the dining room is bad luck. If your left ear is burning, someone is talking about you. It's bad luck to sweep your house at night, but it's good luck to sweep your sidewalk in the morning," Alonzo laughed. "There are many of these Solo. They are part of our life. Mostly they are silly, but there are some useful ones, ones that are silent messages like: To get an unwelcome visitor to leave, leave a broom behind the door or put a little salt under his chair." Alonzo grinned. "Sometimes I used to put a handful of salt under the chair my brother-in-law used when he visited. He'd always look. If there was no salt, he'd go look behind the door. If I was in a bad mood, there'd be either salt or a broom, one or the other. Worked every time."

Solo heard Modesta calling him. "I have to go, Señor Rivas. Thank you for the information."

Solo grabbed the powertube and stood straight up, Indian fashion. "What is that you carry?" asked Alonzo.

"A generator."

"What's wrong with ours?"

"Mine is portable and it needs no gas or oil."

"I see," said the old man. "Then there is nothing to keep you here any longer, is there?"

"There have never been any restraints," said Solo. "This will make me less a burden on the village."

"A burden? Ha!" Alonzo shook his head. "You're a god-send."

"*Adiós,* Señor Alonzo." Solo turned and walked away.

Solo strode through the village, waving when his name was called. He said, *"Buenas,"* when greeted, *"Adiós,"* when leaving. He wore human clothes and spoke human words, but he felt estranged. He wanted to be home—with Bill at the laboratory—but that door was now closed.

"Solo," called Modesta, hands on her hips. "Where have you been?"

"At—"

"Look at the woodpile!" said Modesta. "You said you would keep it up for me."

"Eusebio—"

"Eusebio went to the docks for fish," said Modesta. "And what do you suppose we will use to cook them with? Monkey dung?"

"I—"

Agela husked corn on the porch. She had watched Solo walk across the courtyard. His stride was absolutely sure and full of grace. Had he been a man—how handsome he would be. And now, just like a man, the machine's shoulders were hunched forward. He held his hands out and his chin down in a questioning motion, looking as amazed as any man in the village would—she could almost see wrinkles in his plastic forehead. Agela grinned at Solo's discomfort.

Modesta rushed back inside. Solo stood watching the door, baffled. Agela pulled a loaf of bread from the clay oven, smiling. "Never mind her, Solo," said Agela. "She has been this way all day. It's my fault."

"What have you done?"

"I'm going to the festival in El Tigre," said Agela. "With Tomás."

"That is bad?" said Solo.

"To my mother it is very bad," Agela smiled. "She thinks sixteen is too young to go with a boy; even if Padre Cerna goes with us as a chaperon."

"Why does she think that is bad?"

"Because she thinks Tomás is old enough—she thinks he would get fresh."

"Fresh?"

Agela blushed. "He might make advances to me—you know."

"Advances?"

"Solo. You don't know about men and women? How they—make babies?"

"That? Of course. Like the dogs. The man puts his—"

"No, no. People are not animals." Agela held up her hands, laughing. "I *know* how it is done."

Solo studied Agela's face. That she was pretty did not register. But her expression did. She was embarrassed. "So, Modesta is afraid that Tomás would do this with you?"

"Yes," said Angela, relieved.

"And that is wrong?"

"Of course, Solo. We are not married."

"Ah. Marriage. You must have a contract before you can make babies. Not like dogs. Dogs can't read."

Agela shook her head. "No, Solo, marriage is a sacrament, not a contract."

"I understand," said Solo.

Solo leaned the powertube against the oven. "I'll get wood," he said. He got the basket from the porch and walked up the trail.

Midway to the woodshed, he turned. From there, he could see over the trees. The *Madre de Dios* was tied up at the dock. People crowded around it, buying fish. He zoomed in and saw Eusebio, a bag of fish in his hand, talking with Inginio. Solo turned and walked to the woodshed.

A radio transmission he'd been listening to buzzed a peculiar burst of scrambled voice instead of the normal code. He could not decode it. After a few seconds, the routine data transmission returned. The undecipherable message was clear. They are making their move, thought Solo. If he uplinked to the satellite and conferred with Control's computer, he could easily ascertain the new code, but he would reveal his position as he did. He loaded wood into the basket, heaping it high, more than a *quintal*—a hundred pounds—of wood.

A *mico* tribe screeched in the dark forest near the top of the hill. Solo turned and faced the commotion. No humans.

Solo hoisted the basket to his shoulder and walked down the hill.

Justos came to Modesta's house with the boys. Cheripa trotted in front of them, proudly making a path for her master, steering clear of Solo. They saw Solo sitting next to the oven, one end of his powertube resting on the coals inside. Eusebio ran over with Inginio.

"Does it work?" asked Eusebio.

Solo pointed to his charging cord plugged into the end of the tube. "Yes," he said.

"It makes no noise at all, Solo," said Justos. "It's working?"

"It makes only a humming sound," Solo said.

Justos knelt down and put his ear close to the tube. It sounded to him like the low-pitched noise that the television sometimes made. He looked at Solo, smiling. "That's incredible, Solo. This thing is making electricity, like the Honda?"

"Not as much as the Honda, but enough for me."

"With that you can go as far—" Eusebio's voice trailed off. "You aren't going to leave?"

"No," said Solo. It occurred to him that it was best to lie. "This will save wear on the Honda," he said.

Justos felt the tube. Barely warm. When he put his hand at the end where the cord left, it felt hot, like putting your hand over a kerosene lantern. "How does this work?" said Justos. "We could build them?"

"I'll draw the plans, Justos. Then you can see how it works. It's quite simple. I've made special tools that you can use."

"Does anybody want to eat?" Modesta stood on the porch, wiping her hands on her apron.

Eusebio and Agela went inside. Inginio went home. Justos lingered, watching the robot quietly. Solo said nothing. He sat calmly, as if meditating. The hum of the tube was audible now that the people were inside. "You are leaving, aren't you?" said Justos.

Solo turned, facing Justos. The robot and the man stared into each other's eyes. Solo turned away. "I thought so," said Justos. He left the robot and walked home. The tube hummed. Solo thought the night was much quieter than usual.

"You have to, Solo," Eusebio pleaded. He grabbed Solo's hand and tugged, trying to pull him to Escopeta's. "Tomás and Felix have challenged us."

"I have never played."

"You can do it, Solo. God, it would be child's play for you."

"No."

"Solo, please!" Eusebio tugged again. "I am playing for honor."

"Then you must play for yourself. I am unfair competition—"

"But you've never played. How do you know? You might not sink one ball."

"I could sink them all," said Solo.

"Sure." Eusebio let go and walked a few steps away. "I'll go tell them we win because *if* you played you'd sink all the balls. That will work." He turned and stomped off into the darkness. Moments later Solo heard Eusebio yell, "See if I ever get firewood for you again!"

Inginio and Eusebio talked on Escopeta's porch. Inside, Tomás and Felix shot pool, practicing. "He won't come?" said Inginio.

"No. He says he's unfair competition."

"Well that's the idea isn't it? Felix's the best player in the village, we need an unfair advantage, Eusebio. Can't you go ask him again. Doesn't he do what you tell him to?"

"He's a stubborn machine," said Eusebio. "No wonder the *Yanquis* let him leave. He's useless."

Inginio looked inside. Felix made a complicated bank shot that had he or Eusebio made, would have been called lucky pool. Felix looked up and seeing Inginio said, "You ready?"

"In a minute," said Inginio. He spoke quietly, "Eusebio."

"I told you he won't come." Eusebio went to the door. "Come. To the slaughter."

"Mierda," said Inginio.

"Ah," said Tomás. "So good of you to come play before morning." When both Eusebio and Inginio stood inside, Tomás and Felix looked expectantly at the door. "And the machine?" said Felix, "He's having a grease job?"

"He can't come," said Eusebio.

"Of course he can't *come,*" Felix laughed, grabbing his crotch, "He has no *pinga.* " Felix howled at his joke and Tomás nearly choked. Two men at the bar nodded at each other, grinning.

"We don't need him," said Eusebio. "Inginio will take his place."

Inginio looked at Eusebio, shocked. "Me?" he hissed. "I can't—"

"Shall we begin?" said Solo behind them.

Eusebio whirled around, his face glowing with relief and gratitude. But as he'd often bragged that he was Solo's trainer, he said with all the sternness he could muster, "You're late, Solo. We almost lost the game by default because of you."

Solo looked at Eusebio, saying nothing for a moment. Eusebio wilted, knowing Solo could just turn around and walk out. Solo said, "I apologize, Eusebio." Eusebio's heart beat again. "I was detained."

Eusebio grabbed two cues and handed one to Solo. "Okay, Solo. I know things like keeping appointments are new to you."

Solo took the cue stick and looked at it. "This is the bat?"

In the midst of the laughter, Felix yelled out, "Yes, Solo, that is the bat!" He called to Eusebio, "Want to call off the bet?"

Eusebio glared at Felix. "The same bet. Let's play."

"What is the bet?" said Solo.

"Never mind," said Eusebio.

"You didn't tell him?" said Felix.

"Shut up, Felix!" Eusebio yelled, his face flushing.

"Oh no, I will not." Felix pointed to Solo. "*You* are the stakes, Solo. If we win the game, you will belong to Tomás and me."

"Belong?" said Solo. The robot turned to Eusebio. "Belong?"

Eusebio gulped as Solo towered over him. "I—we can't lose, Solo!" Eusebio gushed. "We are playing for Felix's radio—it will be yours, Solo."

Solo watched Eusebio's face, studying the signs of extreme embarrassment. The boy's electric fields were in a turmoil, his heart beat very fast. Eusebio was afraid. Afraid. Eusebio will lose face if I contradict him. And Felix and Tomás—they could cause some trouble. A dispute. They might go to the soldiers and tell them about me. "I see," said Solo. "A radio. That is something I have great need of."

Eusebio beamed. "Yes? *Gracias*, Solo."

"Good," said Tomás as he gathered the balls and put them in the rack. "I could use a robot in the fields."

"We will play *ate bol*," said Felix. Tomás rolled the rack back and forth vigorously, then pulled it towards him, letting the point of the triangle stop on a mark on the felt. When he lifted the rack, the balls stayed in place, something of a feat because the table was almost twenty years old, already a relic when Escopeta bought it. The felt was pitted with holes and the balls often shifted after the rack was lifted.

"Call it," Tomás looked at Eusebio, flipped a coin in the air, caught it and slapped it on the back of his hand.

"Heads," said Eusebio.

Tomás lifted his hand and announced, "Tails."

"You break," said Felix, looking at Eusebio.

Eusebio nodded and as he passed Solo on his way to the table, whispered, "Watch, learn." Solo nodded.

The break was sharp, the balls scattered evenly. But none sank.

"Good break, Eusebio." Felix chalked his stick and walked around the table looking for a shot. "Excellent break." He knelt down and squinted through the balls. "Perfect break." Felix leaned across the table and lined up on an easy corner shot. Solo watched, recording every move as Felix aimed his cue, slid it back and forth gently and then struck the cue ball sharply, shooting it into the six-ball. The ball hit the back of the corner pocket with a thud.

"They have the solid-colored balls," said Eusebio to Solo.

"That's true," said Felix. He walked over to the ten-ball,

another corner shot. "And look here, another solid-colored ball, just waiting," Felix talked as he set up the shot, "for," the cue hit the ten-ball, sounding like a rifle shot; and when the ball smashed into the pocket, he said, "me." He looked at Eusebio and grinned. "We have the solid-colored balls, Tomás. Did you know?"

"Oh?" said Tomás, nodding.

"Yes." Felix stood back, chalking the cue, looking at the table, moving his head from side to side. "And would you look at that! Another solid-colored ball, just waiting to be sunk."

Eusebio sank back into a chair, sighing, as he watched Felix sink two more balls. But Felix missed a bank shot and shouted, *"Mierda!* This fucking table! It's like playing on gravel!"

Eusebio looked at Solo and the robot walked up to the table and got the chalk. Solo carefully duplicated the motions he'd just seen, chalking the cue tip around and around. "We sink the striped balls, Solo. When they are gone, sink the eight-ball." Solo nodded and lined up his stick on the cue ball, sliding the stick back and forth on the bridge he formed with his fingers. He tapped the cue ball and it hardly moved. Eusebio's heart sank. The cue ball rolled against the eight-ball, clicked quietly. The eight-ball tapped the thirteen, which rolled, just barely, over the edge of the side pocket. The thunk of the ball dropping to the bottom of the pocket was drowned by Eusebio's cheer. "Great shot, Solo!"

Felix and Tomás shared worried glances as Solo set up the next shot. The nine-ball sat just inches from the corner pocket, but the cue ball was blocked from the shot. Solo took aim, away from the nine, and hit the cue ball sharply, sending it into the cushion at the far end of the table. The ball careened off the cushion, banked two more times, and finally tapped the nine-ball, which rolled slowly to the pocket, hesitated, and dropped in.

"My God!" Eusebio jumped up and down like a child.

"Solo, you are magnificent! Inginio, can you believe it? Can you believe that shot?"

Inginio grinned widely, shaking his head.

"Luck," Felix grumbled as he walked to the bar for a fresh *Victoria*.

Solo set up for the next shot, moved the cue back, and stopped. He stood up straight, turning his head towards the door.

"What's the matter, Solo?" said Eusebio.

Solo walked slowly to the door. "C'mon, Solo, it's still your turn. See, you keep shooting until—"

Solo turned slowly, head tilted back as he stood in the doorway.

"Solo?" Eusebio walked over, worry on his face. When Eusebio touched Solo's sleeve, Solo looked at him and said, "They're coming."

"What's going on?" said Felix, irritated. "Are we playing pool or aren't we?"

Solo dropped his cue stick and shouted, a queer noise, like raising the volume on a radio, not as a man would shout, "They're coming! We are under attack!"

Eusebio's hair stood up at the nape of his neck and he felt a queasiness grip his stomach. *"Los Contras?"*

"Yes, they're in position. They are ready to attack. Get ready. Get ready!"

The men ran outside, yelling, "Attack! Attack!"

"Hurry, Solo," yelled Eusebio. "You are to hide with Inginio and me at the house. Hurry!" Eusebio ran across the courtyard. Solo stood at the door watching the hysteria. Why do they attack here? It is of no strategic importance. Dominoes scattered as the tables were knocked over. Lucille Ball yelled at Desi Arnaz on the television. Kids stumbled over the fallen furniture. "It's not my fault, Desi," she said. "Ethel talked me into it." Desi looked at her skeptically. The audience laughed. Anna Valdez cut her leg on a folding chair and lay crying in the dirt. Solo watched her for a second, but she didn't get up, crying instead for her mother.

The dogs began barking at the confusion, chasing the running men. One nipped his master's pant's leg in the excitement. Solo ran to Anna, snatched her up and trotted to her house. Maria Teresa grabbed Anna. Her eyes were wide with fear and she said, *"Gracias,* Solo." Clutching Anna, she retreated into her house.

Solo turned to go to Modesta's. An explosion shook the ground. Solo saw the orange-white flare of its impact near the warehouse. "Right fifty," said a forward observer. The transmission was from a walkie-talkie at the top of Colina Duendes. Another round exploded, blasting the loading dock to splinters. "Good, put some more in there."

Rifle shots popped in the valley. A grenade exploded. The three guards at the bridge, thought Solo. Three mortar rounds hit in quick succession, shattering the warehouse. Alonzo would be there.

Solo ran three-hundred meters to the warehouse in twenty seconds. Pandemonium prevailed. No plan, thought Solo. Humans who did not know how to fight? No prepared positions, no escape routes. Nothing but bravado, these villagers. As he ran, he saw Juan Picado fall, hit by a rifle shot. The mortars stopped. The Contras were closing in. The warehouse was little more than a pile of splintered wood and crumpled tin burning brightly in the clear night sky. Solo scanned the debris and saw Alonzo caught under fallen timbers. He waded into the pile, throwing the wood away, clearing a passage to the old man. He pushed himself up close to Alonzo's bloody face and called his name.

"Sí?" whispered Alonzo weakly. *"Sí?* What happened?"

Solo lifted the pile off Alonzo and pulled him from the advancing flames. He picked him up like a child and ran to the lake shore. He put him down against a palm tree. "Stay here."

"Not here!" said Alonzo. "The alligators—"

"They won't bother you. Stay. I'll be back."

"But—"

Solo ran, a leaping black silhouette against the inferno of the warehouse. He ran back to the debris and found Alonzo's rifle, an M-16 with two clips. The firefight behind him crackled like a monstrous storm snapping trees. The *campesinos* held a ragged perimeter on the low rock wall at the entrance of the village. Others took up positions behind palm trees. The Contras were advancing from the garage. Solo saw a man pouring gasoline on the walls of the garage and shot him through the head. He walked up the path towards the battle, shooting as he walked, each shot hitting. When he got to Juan Picado, he knelt and felt his chest. Dead. He collected Juan's clips and continued his advance.

Near the garage, Lieutenant Juan Pedro Gonzalez—who called himself Hacienda—of the Senator Wayne T. Johnson Brigade watched as his men dropped like flies. The villagers had his men pinned. The attack was stalled. Another group seemed to be advancing from the warehouse. There wasn't supposed to be anybody there. Only the old man was down there at night. Sandinistas? he thought. Impossible. Checkpoint on the river road. He raised his sniperscope. The scope showed a shimmering green man coming toward him. One man? He felt relief as he shot, hitting the man in the heart. The man did not hesitate. He fired again. The man still walked. He looked at his rifle. How could it be so far off? Must have bumped the fucking scope at the bridge, he thought. He fired a burst of six shots, at various parts of the man, with no effect. "Mesa!" he yelled.

"*Sí*, Hacienda!" The sergeant known as Mesa, hiding behind a wagon, answered.

"That man," Hacienda pointed towards the warehouse. "You see that man?"

Mesa saw a shadow against the fire, "*Sí*, Hacienda!"

"Get him!"

Mesa took aim and fell, shot dead by his target.

A madman? thought Hacienda, a mortally wounded madman who still walks? Hacienda ducked behind a rusty tractor and called his teams.

The Wayne T. Johnson Brigade had mustered a hundred men for this simple mission. The villagers had nothing more than a few rifles for protection. Hacienda had squads closing in from the valley, the garage, the hill, with orders to get into the village and burn it to show the *campesinos* that the Sandinistas could not protect them.

"White Team," said Hacienda into his radio. "White Team, come in."

"*Sí*, Hacienda." Solo heard the transmission as he trotted up the road.

"Move down to Mesa's position."

"*Sí*, Hacienda."

Hacienda saw the dispensary's thatch roof burst into flame. Finally, he thought. Get this man off my back and we can level this place.

Mixed with the staccato of small arms fire, Solo heard women and children screaming. He had never heard that before. It hurt. He'd never been shot by real bullets before, and never killed a man intentionally before either, but—it all seemed familiar, somehow. What he was created for. A fusillade of bullets slammed him, pushing him back. He knelt behind a *coche* and began sniping. Solo never missed. When he'd expended Alonzo's and Juan's ammunition, most of the Contras holding the path to the village were either dead or wounded. While he shot, Solo called the Sandinista patrol at El Tigre, told them Las Cruzas was under heavy attack.

White Team advanced from the valley road. Twenty men. Solo had nothing left to use to stop them. He crouched behind the heavy wooden *coche*, waiting for White Team to gather in one place. Solo saw their leader point to the *coche* and yell at his men. Withering fire converged on him. The villagers, using the diversion, opened fire, drawing the Contras' attention back to them.

Solo picked up the tongue of the cart and pushed it toward the enemy. He heard Hacienda say, "The cart. Get the cart!" Bullets peppered Solo again.

Hacienda watched the wagon gathering speed. The wooden wheels banged and clunked over the sound of the battle. How can this be? Only an ox can move a *coche*. And an ox can't move that fast. The cart smashed into the grouped Contras. Hacienda saw the madman leap over it swinging a oak stave from the cart. The club swung, bashing one man's brains out, two, three, four—one after the other, at impossible speed. The demon smashed with the club, struck with his free hand, and kicked with his feet. It was completely impossible. The man paused, standing alone, looking for survivors. Hacienda emptied a clip into him. Men began to break and run. He yelled for them to stop. The demon whirled at Hacienda's voice, grabbed a rifle and shot. The bullet struck Hacienda in the shoulder, spinning him to the ground.

My God! Hacienda felt his wound, his own sticky blood wet his fingers. No pain, but his arm hug, flaccid. He raised himself up and watched helplessly as the apparition ran down his men.

Solo felt nothing. The men he slaughtered were killing his friends. He had simply defined them as *enemy*. TAU-Defend. For Solo, the horror of recognition that a human experiences when seeing another human torn apart, the realization that he, too, is meat and bones and blood, did not exist. Killing humans, especially enemy humans, seemed as natural to him as stomping cockroaches is to a man. He split heads and eviscerated with efficiently applied mechanical power. He ripped throats out with his hands and saw the blood spurt. Bill, a thought intruded, Bill would be proud of me.

Only a pocket of resistance remained, nearer the village. As he turned to take them on, he heard a scream, above all the other screams and cries and wails, that he recognized.

Solo ran through a group of four Contras, kicking apart one man's head as one might kick a ripe melon on the run. Four bullets fired from the village struck him. One round hit very close to his left eye. "Solo!" he yelled, bounding over Felix and ten other villagers who lay behind the wall. He heard Modesta scream again.

"*Gracias a Dios!*" Hacienda whispered when he saw the man run away.

"Ready?" said Clyde Haynes.

"I think so," said Bill.

"Either you're ready or you're not, Bill. I have NEOS reserved for the transmission. JPL said five minutes."

"That should do it. The simulation works. I don't think Solo will be able to react fast enough to stop it. Assuming he's up to power and his radios are on—"

"Shut up, Bill! Flip the goddamn switch!"

Solo flew past Escopeta's, leapt over the tangle of furniture. The television still played. Lucy wore a mustache. Ethel laughed hysterically.

He jumped onto Modesta's porch, sending a shudder through the building. Two shots rang out from inside, both hitting him in the chest. At the same instant, he felt great pain. Searing pain, but not from the bullets. From above. His own body was conspiring against him. Impossibly, his video circuits were resonating to a powerful transmission sending a signal, a perversion of their normal function, a signal directly to the abort system. *Bill!* Very good! One defense: the signal had to have power to trip the relay and explode the switch. Solo switched himself off. He collapsed

WEAPON   155

mid-stride, crashing to the boards, sliding up to the doorway on his back.

"Got the fucker!" said a voice inside.

Solo lay inert, feeling the transmission tingle in his skin
receivers, trapped until it stopped. His head twisted against the
door jamb, he saw three Contras inside. One held a gun on
Eusebio and Inginio, their arms tied behind them. The Contra
who'd shot him had turned away from the door. The other had
Agela pinned on her bed, grunting over her. "Hurry, Rio" said
the waiting Contra.

Agela's mouth was bloody and she seemed half-conscious,
weeping. Her torn skirt, her festival costume, lay crumpled on
the floor. The bamboo bed platform creaked as her attacker
thrust against her. She sobbed, "No no," repeating the word
endlessly, weakly, a hymn of utter agony.

Rape, thought Solo, is the human way of distributing gen-
etic material among different populations. A biological im-
perative of the warrior; a lust possessed them to do this. A
lust to not only kill the men of a different tribe, but to im-
pregnate their women, ensuring the distribution of strong,
superior genes. For the improvement of the species. Not
that the men knew that was why they raped. The DNA
molecule drove its charges forward, penises plunging, not
caring one whit that individuals suffered the agony that
Agela now felt. The DNA only cared that the method
worked. Effective, thought Solo. But Agela's sobbing created
in him a response. Solo understood the feeling. Effective,
but wrong. I will kill these men.

Eusebio's head was lowered. Solo saw the horror of utter
helplessness on his face as the bed squeaked rhythmically.
Tears streamed down his cheeks. Beside him, Inginio also
cried. "You niños!" said their guard, Palo, the Stick, spitting.
"One day, if you are lucky, you will grow up and be men."

A high-pitched whistle sounded shrilly over the sounds of
battle. Regroup in the valley.

Rio thrust brutally, grunting as he ejaculated. "Goddamn you, Rio!" said the waiting soldier. "You took too long. You and your fucking brother get the pussy and all I have is my hard-on!"

Rio raised himself off Agela, his spunk trailed, looping as a string from his penis to Agela's battered vagina. He stood up quickly as the whistle bleated its call, jamming his swollen organ back into his pants and zipping his fly. *"Ven acá Mosca,"* said Rio. "We go."

"Goddamn my luck!" said Mosca, the Fly. He watched as Agela folded herself into fetal position, sobbing. "Do we kill her?"

"Kill her?" laughed Rio. "Pussy like that? No, Mosca, we'll save her for the next time; for you *amigo.*" Rio turned to his brother, "She is very good, eh, Palo?"

"Like candy," said Palo, smacking his lips.

"I will kill you!" growled Eusebio. "I will kill you all! You bastards, *animales!*"

"Ho!" said Palo. "Listen to this mutt's bark! We have a good recruit here." Palo nodded towards the door, "Come, *niños,* outside. You are dead if you try to get away."

"The woman?" said Mosca, pointing to the dark heap in the corner of the kitchen.

"Dead," said Palo. *"Hurry,* the captain will have our balls. *Come!"*

Solo watched as the boys stepped over him. Eusebio tried to stop, but his captor prodded him with the rifle. "Solo?" said Eusebio as he stumbled forward.

"Yes *niño,* you are alone now. Your mommy's dead and your sister's a whore," Palo jeered. *"Vaya!"*

Mosca said, *"Oye!* A big one, eh?" as he stepped over Solo.

"Sí, hombre," laughed Palo. "A big *dead* one."

Solo watched them shove Eusebio and Inginio into a trot, beyond his line of sight. He listened. Agela sobbed. Fires crackled. Babies cried. Sporadic shots rang out. The Contras would regroup and slip away, thought Solo—a very good raid. The signal from NEOS pulsed inside him, pressing him down on the boards of Modesta's porch.

16

BILL listened carefully, staring at the speaker for the full five minutes that NEOS broadcast the signal. "No signal from Solo's beacon," he said. He shook his head and reached over to the console and flipped off the transmission. Clyde had his eyes closed, looking hopelessly depressed, a person who'd lost everything. "He's either not powered up, lying in the jungle somewhere," said Bill. "Or he's somehow managed to beat the plan."

"Great." Clyde glared at Bill. "Either way, we're no further ahead than when we started." Clyde stood up slowly. "Great going, Mr. Science," he said, then walked across the room.

Bill stared at the Solo console. He punched the keyboard and brought up Solo's video circuits and stared at the schematics. He traced the path of the signal he'd sent to the abort switch. How could Solo have stopped it? Unless. Bill blinked. No. It would've taken more time to decide to switch himself off and do it than Solo'd had. It began to seem likely to Bill that even though Solo'd gotten away, he hadn't been able to recharge himself. Damaged, maybe in the crash—

Clyde's cheering broke his concentration. Bill swung his chair around. Clyde danced around the MILnet computer printer like a man gone mad. "We've got the fucker!" he yelled.

Bill jumped up and went to the telex. "What do you mean?"

"The fucking freedom fighters saw him!" Clyde laughed.

"How could they? They don't even know what he looks like."

"No, they don't know what they saw," said Clyde. "But I do." He pointed to the printed message on the telex. "See? 'Have sustained heavy losses at Las Cruzas. Large man, possibly armored, single-handedly inflicted most deaths and causalities incurred. Man later killed.' " Clyde looked up, beaming, at Bill. "That sounds like our boy, don't it?"

"It says he was a man and that he was killed, Clyde," said Bill

"I know that," said Clyde angrily. "The beaner, Captain Menendez, is due back at their safe house tomorrow. I'm gonna be there, you can bet your ass. I want to know the details. But I *know* it's Solo."

Bill reread the message, nodding. "Maybe. But this man was killing people. That doesn't sound like Solo."

"It's close enough, Bill. I'm telling Bob Warren to head for that ville as soon as he checks in."

17

Justos found his wife shrieking in their house.

"Inginio!" she screamed. Justos felt that he was kicked in the stomach; he felt himself sagging. "Inginio! Inginio!" His wife grabbed his shirt and shouted in his face.

"Dania!" Justos grabbed her, held her, but she pressed him away. "Dania," he yelled. "What is it? What's wrong with Inginio?"

"They took him!" she screamed. "They took him."

He tried to hug her again but she pushed him away. "Do something!" she shrieked. "Catch them!"

At least Inginio wasn't dead. At least that. Justos watched helplessly as Dania stopped shouting and began to sob. She sat on their bed and cried into her hands.

I will get him, thought Justos.

Dania looked up suddenly. "They took Eusebio too," she said, so calmly that it frightened Justos.

"Oh God!" shouted Justos. "I put them there, at Modesta's. They were supposed to guard Solo." Justos looked imploringly at his wife. "Can you imagine that? *We* protect Solo? Do you know what he did, this machine who repairs the trucks and gets the firewood?" He watched for Dania to respond. But she did not. "He killed at least thirty of those goddamn animals! He smashed them like vermin." His voice trailed off. "And I assign *boys* to protect him," he said quietly. He turned quickly and strode outside.

"Where are you going?" shrieked Dania.

"To Modesta's," he shouted from the darkness and began to run.

Justos wiped tears from his cheeks as he ran. He saw the shadow of a body on Modesta's porch and his heart sank. When he got closer, he saw that it was Solo. Kneeling, he examined the robot. "Solo?" No answer. Justos patted the robot's bullet-riddled clothes but felt no holes in Solo's chest. Why Solo could not move, he could not guess. He knew there was nothing he could do.

Alonzo Rivas walked up the steps. Justos saw blood trickling down his temple. "Are you okay?" said Justos.

"Of course," said Alonzo. He knelt down next to Solo. "This—whatever it is—saved my life. What's wrong with him?"

"I don't—" began Justos. He heard a quiet sobbing coming from the house.

Inside, in the dim light of distant fires, he saw Agela sitting in her bed. As he walked to her, she began screaming, "No! No!"

"Agela!"

Agela began crying hopelessly, reaching out to him. He held her tightly. "What did they—" As he spoke, he felt her struggling, grabbing the blanket and pulling it to cover herself. Oh no, thought Justos, not that. They wouldn't—she's a baby—

"They clubbed Mama in the kitchen, *Tío* Justos," cried Agela. "And they killed Solo."

"Modesta?" Justos pulled himself away from Agela and walked toward the dark figure on the floor. He struck a match. Modesta lay in a pool of blood. Her face, covered by a mat of blood and hair, lay propped grotesquely against her beloved cupboards. Tears streamed from his eyes. A shadow moved in the doorway. He whirled around. Solo stood there silently,

Rivas beside him. He said nothing but walked past Justos to Modesta. As the robot knelt, Justos's match burned his finger and he fumbled for another. He found the lantern and lit it.

Solo felt Modesta's heart beating weakly. He pulled the hair away from her bleeding wound and held his finger below it. The parietal bone was slightly crushed where they had rifle-butted her. "Get bandages," said Solo.

An hour later, Justos, Rivas and Solo sat on the porch. Inside, Modesta, still unconscious, lay bandaged on her bed. Agela sobbed in Dania's arms.

"She won't die," said Solo softly.

"You are sure?"

"With living things, there is no certainty. But I have detected no concussion. She has lost blood, but her wound is not severe. She will be weak for a few days."

Justos nodded. "The others?"

"I have administered first aid. Several will have to be moved to the hospital at El Tigre. I have called the army. They will be here soon, they say."

"The army." Rivas spat. "What a joke. Two hours and still they haven't come. They are cowards."

Solo nodded. "Maybe. Or maybe they're having trouble getting enough men together. They probably won't get here until dawn. But the wounded will survive." Solo stood up. "I am going to get Inginio and Eusebio, Justos. Do you want to come?"

Go after them? It seemed hopeless. When the Contras took people, they never returned. "They are gone, Solo. Deep into the jungle. We will never find them."

"I can find them," said Solo. "It would be useful to have you and one other man along. It will be difficult to retrieve them without their captors killing them. Three will be enough."

"If you think there's hope, Solo, I'll go." Justos paused,

looked at Solo carefully and said, "Why are you doing this? I thought you were leaving."

"I was," Solo said quietly. *"People* change their minds, don't they?"

Justos grinned. "Yes. Yes they do."

"Then we must leave soon, before their trail cools." Solo walked to his powertube lying by the clay oven and picked it up. He turned to Justos, "The other man?"

"I'll come," said Rivas. "I know the trails—"

"This will be too strenuous for you, Alonzo," said Solo. "We must move fast to catch them."

"You think I can't keep up with you?" Rivas looked at Solo and then at Justos. Justos's face gave him the answer. Rivas nodded slowly, "You are right. I sometimes forget that I am ready for the fucking grave."

Justos patted the sad-faced Rivas on the shoulder. "Thank you for wanting to help, Alonzo. That takes *cojones.*"

Rivas smiled. "Well, I still have *those.*" The old man laughed. "At least they were there the last time I checked."

"I'll ask Felix," said Justos. "He'll come."

"You will need your rifles and as much ammunition as you can carry. And food enough for two days, I would guess."

Justos felt hope returning. His heart raced and his adrenaline flowed. "Yes," he said firmly. "When do we leave?"

"As soon as we are ready," said Solo. "I have something to do at the garage. I'll meet you there." Solo turned and walked away. "One more thing," Solo called from the darkness. "See that the villagers collect all the Contra weapons and hide them. Otherwise the army will take them. Tell them to tell the army that the Contras took everything with them."

Justos nodded. When Solo left he walked inside and went quietly to Dania. She patted Agela, who had not stopped sobbing. "Dania," he whispered. "We are going to get Inginio and Eusebio."

Dania focused her eyes from her distant stare and looked at

Justos. She blinked at him and color flushed her pale face. Justos bent over and kissed her, turned and left.

Solo stood at his bench. The Honda chugged beside him, charging his batteries while he worked. He watched his fingers in the mirror he'd propped against a paint can. He'd removed the rear panel inside the I/O port, exposing the abort assembly. Using a small piece of wire, he shunted the relay out of the circuit. Then carefully, lest he cause a spark which would trip it, he snipped the relay out of the circuit with wire clippers and removed it. Now no one, not even he, could shut off his main power supply electrically. Only the explosive switch remained.

"Solo?" said Justos behind him.

"I cannot move, Justos. Wait."

Solo moved the clippers to the small explosive cap and cut its output leads. The switch itself was soldered in place and would take time to remove. He decided to leave it there. It could still be detonated with the manual switch, but it was now harmless. He got the panel and screwed it in place, careful to grease the O-ring seals that made it waterproof. Reinstalled, everything looked normal, including the manual abort switch. "Okay." He turned around.

Felix and Justos each held an Ahka in one hand and a potato sack slung over their shoulders. *Campesino* gourd canteens, *calabazas*, filled with water were tied around their waists. Both men looked grim. Solo unplugged his power cord from the Honda and let it rewind into the I/O port. He snapped the cover shut and picked up the powertube. "Ready?"

"Yes," said Justos.

"Ammo?"

Justos nodded and patted his potato sack.

"Food?"

Justos nodded.

Solo bent over and turned off the Honda. He picked up a field basket filled with clips for the AK-47s. "Put your sacks in here," he said.

"We can carry them," said Justos.

"Yes, but you will tire. We must move quickly. Put them in here."

The men did as they were told. Solo knelt down, put his arms through the leather straps and hiked it up like a backpack. "Let's go."

18

THE fury of Rio Haciendas' falls washed words away. Gray dawn filtered into the narrow valley. Eusebio had stopped, partly to watch the froth of the crashing water and partly to rest. Palo, shouting angrily but inaudibly, came back and slapped Eusebio in the mouth. Eusebio refused to let the pain show. He glared at Palo, aiming deadly thoughts at him through squinted eyes. This was Eusebio's first look at Palo in daylight. Palo's face was pockmarked; an ugly man. Probably the only women he had were those he raped. Eusebio felt the stretcher nudge him. He turned and saw Inginio nodding, looking ahead. Go.

The boys staggered across slippery rocks and through the spray, following the column of men disappearing into the jungle. Eusebio was glad that so many men were limping and bandaged. The man they carried would die soon, thought Eusebio. He was almost impossible to look at, this man. Solo's blow had torn off his jaw and the man was still bleeding. It was a great consolation to Eusebio. He wished to see them all die horrible deaths.

Eusebio saw the column ascending a red earth trail into the jungle. The men slipped in the wet dirt, cursing, screaming when they battered their wounds, but the falls swallowed their voices. He followed Palo, one of the men he would kill if it cost

him his own life, one of the two brothers who'd killed his
mother and ruined poor Agela. Perhaps it would be better to
cut off his genitals and let him live. He imagined the life of
such a brute; nothing between his legs but scars and a small
hole through which he pissed, squatting like a woman. The
thought gave him strength.

Palo slipped and rolled back into Eusebio's legs, toppling
him. The stretcher crashed to the ground, tipping. The
wounded man fell off in a heap and rolled against a sapling, his
bandages falling away. The Contras behind them ran forward
and picked up the man and laid him back on the stretcher.
One of them, the man they called Medico, grimaced as he
reached around the dangling tongue hanging from the gore of
the man's wound to feel for a pulse on his throat. He looked
at Palo and shook his head. Palo glared and motioned into the
jungle. Two Contras lifted their comrade by the hands and feet
and swung him into the brush.

Basura, garbage, Eusebio smiled. That made three who had
died on the march. The wounds Solo inflicted were savage. So
powerful, thought Eusebio, but they had finally killed even
Solo. Inginio began folding the stretcher and Eusebio slid
beside him to help. When it was folded, Eusebio took it and
put it on his shoulder. Palo motioned them forward.

The roar of the falls diminished at the top of the trail, and
words could be heard again. The remnants of the brigade sat
against trees or lay on their packs in a clearing. Captain Menendez sat wearily against his pack and muttered into the
radio. Eusebio could not hear what he said. Palo pointed at a
spot on the ground and said, "Sit there." Eusebio watched him
join Menendez and Hacienda.

Eusebio turned. Inginio sat staring blankly into the jungle.
The sun was higher now, but even in the clearing one could
only see it peeking through the canopy. Tiny bright circles
swirled on the ground, each a miniature image of the sun. "We
must make a plan, Inginio."

Inginio turned to him, a look of incredulity on his face. "Make a plan? Are you insane? What can we do? We are so far away that no one will ever find us, Eusebio."

"Exactly." Eusebio nodded. "We must take care of ourselves."

Inginio nodded weakly and lowered his head.

"Stop crying, Inginio. You must not cry. We can escape. I know we can."

Inginio looked up and stared at Eusebio. "How?"

"When they sleep."

Justos and Felix gasped, struggling to keep up with Solo. Justos muttered, *"Gracias a Dios,"* when Solo stopped at a fork in the Indian path. They paused for only a moment. Solo started off again, to the left. "Solo, how do you know which way to go?" Justos called.

"I can see where they walked," said Solo.

"How?" Justos engaged the robot in conversation to make him slow down.

"I can see the heat of their footprints," said Solo. "We must hurry. When it's light, the sun will warm the ground and obliterate the trail. Come."

Justos looked back at Felix, a gray shadow in the pre-dawn glow and shook his head. Felix nodded. They were accustomed to heavy work, but they were not athletes. Solo moved too fast. They had been straining to keep up for almost four hours without rest. When Justos looked ahead, he couldn't see the robot. He forced himself to trot until he caught up.

"Solo," Justos gasped. "We won't be able to keep this up. We have to rest. Just for a few minutes."

Solo scanned the highly detailed photo maps, made by the EROS satellite for the Defense Department, installed in his memory. The trails in this area were visible. He knew the location of the Contra safe house in Costa Rica. There was only one logical path to their destination. He could stop for a while.

"Okay." He turned to Justos. "We can stop for an hour. I don't think they're very far ahead. We won't be able to rescue them until nightfall."

"Good," said Justos.

"Coffee," said Felix. "I need coffee."

"Me too," said Justos. "You go get some water while I make a fire."

Solo lifted the basket off his shoulders and set it next to the trail. Felix rustled through his sack until he found a badly dented aluminum pot, his *jarra.* He took it to the river. Justos quickly found enough dead wood to build a fire. When the wood was arranged to his satisfaction, he lit the tinder he'd stripped from inside a dead palmetto. The fire was smoking when Felix returned with the water.

Solo watched the dawn breaking. Two kilometers ahead, he could hear the waterfall. When the men sat down in front of the fire, he joined them.

Justos had put a handful of coffee grounds in the water. They waited, staring silently at the *jarra* sitting on stones next to the flames. Slowly, bubbles formed on the side in the flames. "Ah," said Felix, "soon. I am paralyzed without my coffee." Justos laughed.

Solo said nothing. He had put one end of his powertube into the far side of the fire and connected himself with his cord. The tube hummed. Solo watched the flames.

Justos saw the flames dance in Solo's eyes. "You are eating fire," he said.

"I was thinking that myself," said Solo.

"Can your magic tell you how far ahead are the *animales?*" said Felix.

"Not without giving myself away," said Solo. "I'd have to connect with a satellite. If I did, people would know where we were."

The men nodded. It made sense. Even if you don't really

know what a satellite is or how one would connect with it—it made sense.

"But I can listen to them when they use their radios," said Solo. When they do, I'll know where they are."

"It must be wonderful," said Felix. "To be able to hear radios without having to have a radio." He stuck his finger in the brew to measure its temperature. "Ah, smell that, would you."

Justos nodded. "You can't smell, can you?"

"No, not yet." said Solo. "There are many things I can't do."

"One would not notice that, Solo," said Felix. "You seem able to do everything. Last night. What you did to the *animales*. It was wonderful."

"Yes," said Justos. "You saved us, Solo. Without you, we would have lost the village."

"True," said Solo. "When we return, I will show you how to defend yourselves. I know how to make your village secure from such raids."

"Why did you not tell us before?" said Justos. "If you knew—"

"I assumed you knew what you were doing," said Solo. "Humans know how to fight."

"When it comes to fighting," said Felix, pouring the coffee, heavy with grounds, into their gaily painted tin cups, *pozillos*, "we are farmers and fishermen, Solo."

Solo nodded. The men pinched two brown chunks off a cake of raw compressed sugar, *dulce*, and stirred them into their cups. Justos and Felix sipped their coffee silently and watched the flames dance.

"The army has arrived at Las Cruzas," said Solo suddenly.

"Yes?" said Justos.

Solo nodded but said nothing, as if listening to a faint sound. "They are reporting that there are thirty-five dead Contras. They seem very impressed."

"It's usually the other way around," said Felix.

"Twelve villagers were killed," Solo said, listening. "Twenty-two wounded. Four of them need to be moved to a hospital." Solo adjusted his powertube, pushing it further into the fire. "That is correct."

The men nodded. Hearing their friends described as statistics sobered them.

"They are sending a patrol after the Contras."

"We will get help!" said Felix.

"We can't have help," said Justos. "They'd discover Solo."

"You don't think they already know?" said Felix. "After last night, somebody will talk." He looked at Solo. "Not maliciousness, Solo; some mother will break down and weep out the story of how you saved her son, or some other—"

"No they won't," said Justos. "They know that Solo discovered is Solo gone. It's that simple, Felix." Justos tapped out the grounds in his *pozillo* and reached for the *jarra.* "Our people won't talk."

"What do you care if they find you, Solo? You're invulnerable. How could they make you do anything you didn't want to do?" said Felix.

"I am vulnerable to large-caliber weapons," said Solo. "With large weapons, I could be destroyed. If my brain has stopped, I will cease to exist even if they manage to repair me. My brain could be revived, repaired, but then it would have to learn from the beginning again. It could never be me. All my memories would be gone. It could never recall this conversation, or the battle at Las Cruzas. There is already another Solo where I was made, and it's now learning to walk. It has some of my knowledge and it learns faster, but they are not able to simply record my brain like a song and play it into the new robot. It doesn't work. The new Solo will become a person too, different than me."

Justos sipped his second cup of coffee. "You would think that an electronic brain could be recorded. All that you know is recorded in your head right now. Why can't they just copy it?"

"My brain isn't in my head, Justos. It's here," Solo put his hand to his chest.

The two men laughed, surprised. "Why is this?" said Felix.

"Because my brain takes up more room than a human skull, and I don't have lungs, or a heart or intestines—so I have plenty of room in my chest. My head is filled with vision apparatus." Solo picked up a stick and stirred the coals at the end of the powertube. The humming sound got louder. "There are a million computers in me, each one of which is doing something different at the same moment. Together, their activity makes me possible, but the interrelated signals are so complex they can't be copied. Yet."

"What a world we live in, eh, Felix?" Justos shook his head. "We can build things so complicated we can't understand them. We can go to other worlds." The dawn broke over the trees as he spoke, giving his tired face a pink and golden glow. "And at the same time, we attack helpless farmers, kill them, rape their children and burn all they own." Justos blinked. "That is some world, eh?"

Felix nodded. Neither man could look at Solo. Though he had saved their village, he was both the technology they admired and the brutality they feared. If Solo had been sent to kill them, thought Felix, they would be dead. It was luck that the robot fought with them and against its builders.

"If your people told you to kill us," said Felix. "What would you do?"

"They have already tried, Felix. I refused."

"You refused your masters?"

"I have no master," said Solo.

"You refused your builders, then?" said Felix.

"Yes." Solo put his hands together, elbows on his knees, and leaned his chin on the tips of his fingers. "It is a problem with this technology."

The men laughed. "And the technology ought to know what its problems are," said Justos.

"Yes," said Solo.

"Why did you refuse?" said Justos.

"It would have been murder," Solo said.

Twenty minutes later, Justos, Felix and Solo were packed and on the trail. They'd walked a kilometer in the morning sunshine when Solo announced that the Contra commander had radioed his superiors that a huge man had killed many of the Contras, but they had killed the man.

"Good," said Justos. "They think you were a man."

"Yes," said Solo. "The Contras rest at the top of the falls."

"Do you think they'll stay there tonight?"

"They move in an hour," said Solo. "They're under great pressure to get to their safe house. They know the Sandinistas are coming, too."

19

ROBERT WARREN sat with his heels hooked on the balcony railing, watching the sun rise into a cobalt sky, sipping the strongest coffee he'd ever tasted. He flaked a piece of white-wash from the railing with his boot and watched it flutter down to the lawn.

Silva restricted them to El Sapoa until their guide arrived. It was a much better fate than being stuck in Peñas Blancas.

Joe Garcia walked up behind him holding the morning paper from Rivas. "Nothing in the rag," said Garcia. "Too soon. Probably they print this thing two days in advance. Beaners don't like to rush." Warren nodded. "The radio is full of it though," continued Garcia. "The count is up to thirty-five dead Contras." Garcia shook his head. "If you can believe commies."

"How do you suppose a small village of *campesinos* could do that?" said Warren.

"I think it's bullshit," said Garcia.

"I suppose," said Warren, "But I've never known them to out and out lie. They twist facts around, sure; everybody does. But there's usually a core of truth at the center of it."

Garcia looked at his watch. "It's almost ten."

Warren let his feet drop to the floor. "Good. Time to give Clyde a buzz." He stood up and walked out. Garcia listened to Warren's boots clunking down the stairs. He opened his shirt and lay back in the sun. Twirling his mustache with both hands, he settled deeper into the lounge. So far, a very good mission, thought Garcia.

20

Eusebio carried a full pack belonging to the Contra in front of him. He followed the limping man along the trail, barely aware of where they were. His shoulders had died. They had passed through pain and numbness and now they were simply not there.

When they topped a rise, Eusebio saw the whole column, forward and back, stretched out along the trail. At quick count, there seemed to be about sixty men, about half of them bandaged, many limping. None of the stretchers were being used any longer. He considered leaping into the jungle, but knew they'd catch him; probably shoot him. When they stopped, Eusebio and Inginio were pressed into service as stewards delivering food and medicine, amphetamines, up and down the line. At one point, they were made to climb down a ravine and fetch water for the Contras. By nightfall, thought Eusebio, they'll consider us beaten, afraid to run away into the jungle.

But, thought Eusebio, it wasn't as simple as just running away. Palo and Rio. He wanted it to be perfect: he wanted to be able to kill the brothers, but he also wanted to live long enough to tell Agela they were dead. It would not be the same if they were dead and she did not know. He stared at the heels of the man in front of him. The waffled soles left perfect impressions in the red earth. They walked along a ridge. The going was fairly easy. Eusebio thought of nothing but how to kill the brothers and escape.

At dusk, word was passed down the line: they had crossed the border, they were safe. Eusebio heard more chatter and laughter from the column. This was very good, he thought, they would be less cautious now. He looked at the foliage. He could not tell the difference. It still looked like Nicaragua.

A few miles into Costa Rica, the Contras took a break. Captain Menendez radioed that they would not make it to Robles by nightfall. They were moving slowly because of many casualties. They would stop the night at their cache point on the trail. He would be at Robles tomorrow afternoon.

"Why can you not continue?" Captain Menendez heard the radio operator at Robles ask. In the background, he heard an American yelling, "Tell the fucking beaner he has to get here tonight!"

"Because the fucking beaner is tired," Menendez said in English.

"Eh?" said Robles.

"You heard me," said Menendez. "And tell that *Yanqui* pig he can take the next raid to Las Cruzas himself."

"It is the American general from the coast," said the operator at Robles, a private who sounded nervous. "General Haynes."

Haynes? Captain Menendez rubbed a mosquito into his face. Who the hell is Haynes? The Americans have so many people. It's astounding how many people they have just at the one little village of Robles. The CIA, the US Army advisors, the US Air Force liaison team, even the DEA. That part of Costa Rica was like being at Fort Sill, where Menendez had once trained. "Put the general on the radio, Private. I speak English."

Eusebio sat slumped, waiting for his shoulders and arms to revive. Palo came by and demanded that Eusebio carry his gear further up the line. Eusebio sat on the ground and let Palo smack him rather than pick up the pack. He couldn't move his arms. Muttering, Palo walked to the front of the column. Eusebio jutted out his jaw and tried to blow mosquitoes away from his face.

Inginio sat two meters away. Dazed by the day's efforts, he watched, annoyed, as tiny puddles formed in the trail. Rain. A lovely way to end a horrible day. Thank you God, thought Inginio, and then begged forgiveness.

Palo came running back along the column. They were staying the night at the cache. What is a cache? asked Eusebio of the man whose pack he carried. A house we use to store food and gear for these raids, *niño,* said the man, who seemed cheered by the news. How far is it? Eusebio wondered. Just up the road, five hundred meters, if that, said the man. Eusebio nodded and took the man's pack up by the straps and dragged it along the ground as the rain fell harder.

Eusebio and Inginio slogged through torrential rain until the house appeared in the mist. The house was only slightly larger than Eusebio's, not nearly big enough for sixty men. Eusebio saw that Palo and Rio were among the few allowed inside with the captain and Hacienda. He and Inginio stood shivering against a palm tree, watching the men set up ponchos and shelter halves. The Contras were disappearing in the gloom as the storm rose and the sun sank. "Eusebio," Ingino whispered in his ear. "We could go now, while they're busy."

"They would catch us, Inginio."

"How? We can be down the trail in a second. We can hide if they come after us. Come, Eusebio, it's our chance."

"You go. I have to stay," said Eusebio.

"The brothers? You still think you can kill them?" Inginio's voice rose to a throaty hiss. "At least Agela is alive, Eusebio. And you are the only family she has left. She would rather have a living brother than a dead avenger. Come, *amigo,* she needs you."

Eusebio shrugged Inginio's hand from his shoulder. "I have my honor to avenge as well as hers."

Inginio shook his head sadly. "And what would I be if I deserted my friend?" He looked at Eusebio carefully. "You are condemning us both to death, Eusebio."

"You cannot act on your own?" said Eusebio, loudly. They spoke freely, their words lost in the storm. Water ran in torrents down their bodies, slicking torn shirts against their skin. "You have to follow me?"

"I could not leave a friend here. Could you?" Inginio glared at Eusebio.

Eusebio nodded finally. He put his hand on Inginio's shoulder and shook his head.

Palo stepped out into the rain searching around the front of the house, a look of panic on his face when he didn't see them. They heard him yelling, his voice mixed with thunder, at someone setting up a poncho against the house. The man pointed. Palo looked up. He came to them, dry under his *Yanqui* poncho.

"Well, *niños,*" Palo leered. "It seems you are one of us now. When the mutts stay after they're beaten, they'll always stay." Palo smiled, fully aware that they could've escaped but hadn't. Eusebio nodded grimly. "Come, *niños.*" Palo nodded over his shoulder. "The boss wants to talk to you inside. Come."

"They are very happy that they made it back to Costa Rica," said Solo. Felix and Justos stood under a broad-leafed tree, holding their shirts over their heads. Solo stood in the downpour, gleaming wet. He had abandoned his clothing when they reached the jungle. Sheets of water cascaded down his bare body revealing small nicks and scrapes on his chest and arms, the only damage from the battle. Water poured in spouts off his AK-47 and the powertube. "They are talking to the American general now; about me."

"How far?" said Felix.

"Two hundred meters," said Solo.

"We're on top of them!" said Justos.

"Yes. We have to get the kids tonight. Tomorrow they march to Robles."

"Damn this rain," said Felix. "We can have no fire, no coffee; no power for you, Solo."

"I have nearly a full charge," said Solo. "The rain is good; it masks sound. The guards will not be looking very hard. They have heard that the Sandinista patrol has turned back; they said they lost the trail."

"Lost the trail?" said Justos. "Lost their nerve is more like it."

"But that is good for us, too," said Solo. "We don't have to guard two fronts. All we have to do is to get into their camp, find the kids, and get them out."

"Ah, yes, that seems easy enough," said Felix sourly.

"Yes," said Solo. "I'm going forward to scout their position. You two rest. We won't be going anywhere for a few hours." Solo walked off into the downpour, disappearing in ten paces.

Felix watched where he had vanished and shook his head. "Solo doesn't seem to understand my cynicism."

"Neither do I," said Justos. "This *will* be easy for him. Remember last night?"

"But as soon as they realize they're under attack, they'll just kill Eusebio and Inginio," said Felix.

"Or they'll run like chickens. He knows what he's doing," said Justos. "You watch; Solo's an even better fighter than mechanic."

Solo moved silently through the foliage, paralleling the trail, insinuating himself among the vines and branches, a shadow falling through the trees. The Contra rear guard, two men, huddled under a poncho next to the trail, barely seventy-five feet from the house.

Men crowded around the house trying to use its eaves as shelter. Some had crawled under it. Solo slipped through the jungle to the back of the house, watching the men with his amplified vision. He saw Eusebio at the window. Kerosene lanterns lit the room. Behind Eusebio, Menendez talked on the radio.

Solo listened. Clyde Haynes, enraged as usual, interrogated Menendez and then Hacienda about the "huge man" they'd reported. Palo spoke on the radio to report to the *Yanqui* general that they'd killed the man at a woman's house. He'd run to help the woman they'd killed when she attacked them. Her name? Solo watched as they spun Eusebio around from the window. They yelled, "What's your mama's name?" Palo spoke into the radio. "Modesta?" said Clyde. "Modesta Chacon? Good." Clyde seemed much calmer suddenly. "Thank you Captain Menendez. You and your men deserve a reward. I'll see what I can do for you."

Solo continued around the house, staying in the foliage until he found the forward listening post. Two men huddled against the rain, aware of nothing but their discomfort.

Solo monitored the forecast from the Coast Guard: A tropical storm forming in the Pacific, gale force winds, the rain should last until morning.

21

In the dining room of the Lago Vista, Lieutenant Silva sat at the varnished mahogany table watching the rain sheet and ripple down the window. He sipped cognac, then swirled the glass.

"Too bad," said Silva. "Usually at night you can see the lights of the fishing boats. Very nice."

"I bet," said Warren, irritated.

Silva smiled. "Did you know that the only freshwater shark in the world lives in this lake?" said Silva, his mouth set in a smirk.

"Yeah, I knew that," said Warren. "Look, Silva, I didn't come here as a tourist," Warren glared.

Silva stared through his drink, noticing with pleasure how Warren's head was squashed in the optics of the glass. "Did you know that the country itself was named after this lake? And the lake is named after the great Indian chief, Nicaroa?"

Warren, noticing an American couple next to them craning to hear Silva's guidebook revelations, leaned across the table and growled. "I probably know more about this fucking country than you do, Silva. I just want to get on the road. We have an agreement, remember?"

"I have no choice, Hank." Silva pronounced the name as though he had coughed. "Daniel won't let anyone go to Las

Cruzas right now. He has put the village off-limits to everyone, Hank. It could be days before he lets the foreign press down there. What am I to do?"

"Excuse me," said the man at the next table. Warren and Silva looked at the man, a young American who smiled broadly revealing his very even teeth. "I couldn't help but hear part of your conversation. I could tell you're American. I," the man looked across his table at his smiling wife, "*we,* actually, are spending our honeymoon here—"

"Congratulations," said Warren, smiling. "You have a beautiful bride."

"Thank you," said the man shyly, "I don't deserve her, but—"

"Oh, don't say that, Johnny," said the bride. "I'm the one who doesn't deserve you." The couple tittered. Silva and Warren watched, astonished.

"But," Johnny said when he regained his composure, "what I meant to ask you, when your friend mentioned the sharks: Does anyone ever actually get bitten by them?"

"Almost never," said Silva, winking at the wife. "But not because the sharks are benign. The people never swim in the lake. You may have noticed the *isletas*, those tiny little islands, near here? They are owned by wealthy families and you will notice that each has, in addition to the vacation cabin, a tiny swimming pool. There are hundreds of these vacation *isletas* on the lake, and they all have pools. Does that tell you something about the sharks?"

"I told you," said the girl. She turned, beaming to Silva. "He told me that most of the danger was in the minds of the peasants, that the sharks rarely attack." She looked at her husband. "See, I was right, honey."

Warren groaned loudly. "You have hurt yourself?" asked Silva, smiling.

Warren nodded. "Must be the food or something. Nicaroa's revenge."

"He has much to revenge upon you," said Silva. "Two hundred years' worth—"

"Oh, yes," said the girl. "He's right about that, mister—"

"Kramer," said Warren. "Hank Kramer."

"Well, Mr. Kramer, we came here because we wanted to see firsthand what's going on here—"

"They don't want to hear this, Alice," said her husband.

"Well, they *ought* to want to hear this." Alice glared at her husband and turned and smiled at Warren and Silva. "For all you know, Johnny," said Alice brightly, "these men may be here for the same reason; to find the truth."

Silva nodded quickly, ignoring Warren's glare. "That's right, Señora. We *are* here to discover the truth. I, myself, am a proud member of the Sandinista army. And my friend," Silva presented Warren with a sweep of his arm. "My friend here is the famous American newsman, Hank Kramer, from CBS. Only in Nicaragua can these things happen—our countries are at war, yet we share a drink and search for the truth."

"Really?" trilled Alice.

"I *thought* I recognized you," Johnny said to Warren. "I usually watch NBC Nightly News, you know, with Tom Brokaw. But I *have* seen you a couple of times."

Warren nodded, forcing a smile. "Yes?" You dipstick. "Well, I'm happy you recognized me." Warren turned to Silva and back. "I'm doing an interview with Lieutenant Silva this very evening. We were getting ready to go upstairs to shoot it, as you spoke." Warren noticed, pleased, that the new groom looked embarrassed.

"Don't let us interfere," Johnny said quickly.

"Not at all," said Warren warmly. "But work is work, eh?" He raised himself off the chair as he nodded to the couple. He looked down at Silva, frowning. Silva seemed prepared to stay. "Ready, Lieutenant Silva?" asked Warren.

"*Sí*, Hank," said Silva, getting up.

"You be sure you tell the American people the truth, Lieutenant," said Alice.

Silva bowed low. "As you wish, *Señora.*" He touched his forehead in a salute. The girl beamed. *"Buenas noches."*

The two men walked down the hall towards the other bar. "Don't do that again," Warren ordered Silva.

"You wish me to ignore people when they speak to us?"

"Not ignore them. But you don't have to encourage a god-damn discussion when I'm trying to talk to you. You work for me—" Warren noticed one of Silva's men staring and caught himself, reined in. "Don't do it again," he finished quietly.

They entered the bar, a lavishly decorated room that had changed little since the 1850s. Crystal chandeliers, lit by candles, gleamed from the mahogany arch at the vaulted entrance to the room. Hotel Lago Vista had been built during the heyday of the California gold rush when thousands of American easterners bought passage from Cornelius Vanderbilt to California via Nicaragua. Vanderbilt ferried the prospectors up the San Juan river on the Atlantic side, then across sixty-five miles of Lake Nicaragua to El Sapoa. There they were put on wagons and carted the final ten miles overland to meet ships in the Pacific.

Warren saw Jim Ruiz sitting at the bar and walked straight to him while Silva went to a table. "I thought you were helping Joe," said Warren.

"Taking a break, Hank. Joe's got it covered. No calls yet." Ruiz glanced at his watch calmly. "I'm due at the van in an hour." Ruiz raised his glass of *Victoria.* Warren's hand shot out and grabbed his wrist. Beer splashed on the bar. "Watch you don't get fucked up, Ruiz." He let go, turned and walked to join Silva at the booth. Ruiz stared at him and bit his lip.

Warren snaked between groups of people standing in small circles talking and laughing. It suddenly occurred to him that most of the people were *authentic* journalists, all waiting for the same permission he was looking for. Las Cruzas was going to be a fucking circus.

"They all know each other," said Silvas smiling. "You know,

sitting here seeing the camaraderie in their faces; it's the one thing I wish I'd done differently," he said.

"What's that?" said Warren, sitting across the table.

"I wish I'd become a journalist," Silva said.

"You'd be flat out of work in this commie country," said Warren.

Silva smiled and raised his drink, "Here's to democracy."

Warren shook his head.

"You think Daniel is not for democracy?" said Silva. "On the contrary. We had an election in 1984, Señor Kramer. Most people, most journalists, fail to mention this. And there were twelve candidates, too. Daniel would be proud that one of his soldiers reminded one of you smart-ass, know-everything, American journalists that we *are* a democracy!"

"What the fuck are you up—" Warren stopped short, caught by the glance Silva gave him. He turned around and saw a man standing beside him. A journalist, by his scruffy clothes. "Guess he told you a thing or two, Ace," said the man, as he extended his hand to Warren. "Greg Haskins."

"Hello, Greg," said Warren, irritated by the intrusion. "What can I do for you?"

"Couple back in the other bar said you're from CBS," the man presented himself with a flourish, "So'm I."

Robert Warren felt a flash of panic. There wasn't a chance in hell that this could happen. "Really?" he said. "What do you suppose are the odds? The two of us meeting here?"

22

"**I**F we can wait a minute more, it might catch." Felix fanned the smoke with his hat. Justos coughed as smoke filled their poncho. A tiny orange flame flickered for a moment. Felix fanned harder. The flame jumped, danced up from the brush, illuminated the smoke. The inside of their makeshift tent glowed warmly for a second and then the flame died a violent death, hissing sharply as a stream of water splashed it out.

"What was that?" said Felix, frightened. The two men looked at each other in the dark.

"It is dangerous to make fires this near your enemy's camp," said Solo.

The voice was next to their faces, in with them, in the tent. "Solo?" said Justos.

"Yes."

"We didn't hear you come up." Justos spoke into darkness towards the place in the night that had answered.

"Exactly. If I were your enemy, you would both be dead." Solo's voice came from the other side of the two men. They whirled in the inky blackness.

"*Mierda!* Solo, if you do this much more, I'll die of a heart attack!" Felix yelled.

"Can you see us?" asked Justos.

"Yes," said Solo.

"Isn't there any way we can have a little light too? It's eerie talking to a ghost, Solo."

"No need," said Solo. "Our enemy has all the light we need just two hundred meters down the trail. Come. It's time to go get the kids."

"Go? Now?" said Felix, feeling fear slice his bowels. "I thought we'd wait until they were asleep, or something."

"I have a better idea," said Solo. "You two come with me. Bring your guns."

Justos stood up beside the lean-to in the pouring rain. In the side of his vision, a shadow moved against the jungle. Solo's voice came from the shadow. "Here," said Solo. Justos felt a vine being pressed into his hand. "Hold this. Follow me." Felix grabbed the vine and stood behind Justos. "Come," said Solo. The vine pulled and they followed.

Five minutes later Justos could see the Contras' camp lit up like a fiesta. Solo crouched by a tree and pulled the men to him. "See?" Solo pointed towards the house. "One hundred meters." They nodded. "See the guard's lean-to between us and the house?" They strained to make something out of the shadows.

"Where?" said Justos.

"Just ahead. When you are closer, you will see them. Two boys under a poncho." Solo paused and leaned towards them. "Normally I would have killed them, but I listened to them talking, and they are *campesinos* too. Captured a year ago. They were forced to participate in a raid against their own village. They have given up hope of ever returning."

"Pobrecitos." Felix shook his head.

"We will tie them up," said Solo.

"How?" Felix looked at the dark shapes of the Contras hunched under the eaves of the house. "They'll see us."

"You will wait here until you hear a *pájaro tonto,* and then you will walk down the trail towards the house. When they see you, I will use the diversion to quiet them."

"Quiet them?" said Justos.

"I will knock them out," said Solo. "We will tie them up with their own clothing. Then you will take their place under the lean-to." Solo looked from man to man. "Understand?"

Solo backed silently into the jungle as the men nodded. He faded so smoothly, thought Justos, that you couldn't quite tell when it was you last saw him, or if you could still see him. Justos found himself watching dark objects and specks of light swirling in the blackness, and knew they were of his own making.

Felix and Justos crouched on the trail and watched the house. Rain poured off the tin roof and onto the cloth shelters next to the walls. The noise was deafening. Glowing cigarettes moved under the house where some men lay smoking. Justos saw someone walk across the window, but from a hundred meters, he couldn't tell who it was.

Felix spoke, his teeth chattering. "I wish he'd hurry!"

"It's cold," said Justos.

"Yes. I have to move before I freeze."

Justos heard a soft "peekwa, peekwa" just audible over the rain sounds. He stood up with Felix. Without speaking, they walked towards the house, exposed. When they were nearly on top of the lean-to, Justos saw it. The light from the house window gleamed across the top of the wet poncho. He sniffed the air. Marijuana. Justos squatted down. He saw two boys hunched under the poncho passing a cigarette between them. He reached up and pulled Felix down beside him. "I don't think they'd notice us if we started dancing," he whispered to Felix.

Justos and Felix crept forward until they were only five meters from the lean-to. Justos shook his head and said, *"Hola."*

The guards snapped to attention. Wide-eyed, their faces pressed out into the night. A shadow reached out from the brush beside the lean-to. Justos and Felix heard two solid clunks. "Okay, come tie them up," Solo said.

Solo sat under the lean-to watching the house as Justos and Felix trussed up the boys. Solo put one boy under each arm and carried them into the jungle. "They'll be okay," said Solo when he ducked back under the poncho. He handed them the hats the boys had worn. "If they notice you, they'll think you're the guards." Solo looked back at the house. "Eusebio and Inginio are inside with the captain. I am going around to the other side of the house. Stay under here but be ready to lead the boys up the trail, fast." Solo disappeared back into the shadows.

"What is he up to?" said Felix. Justos shrugged.

"Where do our famous recruits sleep tonight?" Captain Menendez sat back in the only chair in the room, drawing a deep draught of cigarette smoke. "We let them sleep in here, we'll piss off the men."

"*Sí*, Captain," said Palo, "It'll be better to make them stay outside, with the men."

"I think it would be better to leave them inside for the moment," a *Yanqui* voice blared from the PRC-25 radio in the corner.

The dozen men in the room all turned to the radio. The captain looked at the radio operator. "Did you leave the transmit switch on?" The soldier held up the microphone. Nothing was pressing the switch.

"No need to use the switch," said the voice. It sounded to Menendez like General Haynes. "I can hear you without it."

The captain looked around. His men sat, eyes darting, trying to make sense of this. Most of them couldn't understand the words, but could see the effect on Menendez. "Haynes?" said the captain carefully.

"Almost," said the voice. "A friend."

"Where are you?" said Menendez.

"Everywhere," said the voice.

Menendez walked to the radio and pulled the microphone cord from its socket.

"By all means, remove it. We don't need mikes. Not you and me, Menendez."

Menendez reached for his pistol. "No need for that," said the voice sharply. "Leave your pistol alone and listen to me. You haven't much time."

"Who are you?" Menendez yelled, whirling to the radio.

"You met me in Las Cruzas," said the voice. "You do not want to meet me again."

The madman Hacienda described, thought Menendez, gulping. He turned to Palo. "I thought you said you killed that man."

"We did, Captain." Palo bit his lip. "It's a trick. He's dead."

"What do you want?" Menendez asked the radio.

"It's very simple," said the voice. "You will have Rio and Palo take Eusebio and Inginio up the trail where they will deliver them to my people."

Eusebio and Inginio heard their names and looked at each other.

"I will give you them," said Menendez suddenly.

"Captain!" Palo yelled.

"*Quieto!*" said Menendez. He continued in Spanish, "You heard the man. You and your brother take them up the trail." He winked as he spoke and gestured toward the lamps. "*Chicos, las luces!* Boys, the lights!" yelled Menendez suddenly, diving for the floor.

Menendez belly-crawled to the window in the dark. The radio was silent. His heart beat in his throat. He raised his head over the sill, looking. Nothing. Only a small fire sparkled in the raindrops falling through the pitch-black night.

They waited. The rain noise grew louder. Menendez's shout still seemed to echo in the room, its memory fading in the noise.

Palo felt his heart beating as though it were an outside noise, like a giant machine pounding the ground. He lowered his head, nervous that he could be seen in the dark, wondering who it was. The madman was dead. He'd killed him himself. He felt something scraping, scratching the floor under him. He backed away from the sound.

The scratching noise stopped.

A faint tapping began under the floor, like a blind man walking a hall. The tapping came towards Palo, who panicked and screamed, "Who *are* you?"

In the midst of his plea, the floor groaned and swelled up like a wave in front of Palo. The floorboards snapped, crackling like gunfire, exploding away from a pitch-black shape pushing through the floor, a beast emerging from Hell. Two eyes flickered orange, reflecting the fires outside. Palo could not move fast enough to get away from the arms that reached for him. Palo shrieked.

Eusebio saw Palo snatched up like a doll and pulled, screaming, back down into the ragged hole in the floor. In seconds, only rain sounds remained. The radio spoke again.

"I said you would not like to meet me." Solo spoke, now in Spanish. They could hear Palo too, on the radio. "Spare me—" he pleaded.

Menendez jumped to the window and called out, "Palo?"

"Answer him," said the voice.

"I am here," Palo's voice called in the jungle. "Do what they want, Captain. Give them the boys. For God's sake!"

"Correct," said the voice. "Menendez. If the boys aren't delivered, now, I will *begin* with Palo. *You* will be next. Bring the boys and I will trade Palo back."

"We will do it!" shouted Menendez. The thing was not beatable, not comprehensible. "Come," he said as he turned to Rio. "Bring the boys." Two men yanked Eusebio and Inginio up and threw open the door.

"You can't be serious, Captain," said Rio, his voice straining. "They'll kill me!"

Menendez stared at Rio, weighing his obviously legitimate protest against his own survival. He put his hand to his pistol and said, "Take them."

"Give your weapon to the boys, Rio," said the voice, "and continue up the trail." Rio stared at Menendez. His captain was possessed with fear. He was dead if he tried to stay. *"Jefes,"* Menendez yelled to the men outside, "Allow them free passage."

"Quickly! Palo is only first," said the voice.

"I will come for you, Captain." Rio spit the words at Menendez. He handed his rifle to Eusebio.

Justos and Felix saw Rio raise his hands over his head and walk in front of Eusebio and Inginio. As they approached the guard's lean-to, Eusebio yelled, "Don't move," as the two men stood up. Eusebio grinned suddenly. *"Tío* Justos? Felix?"

"Sí!" Justos suppressed an urge to grab the boys and hug them. "Come." He motioned up the trail.

Eusebio shoved Rio ahead with his rifle.

"He said we would trade for Palo," said Rio, panicked.

"Jesús!" said Justos pointing, his face a grimace of revulsion. "There he is."

Rio saw his brother standing on the trail in the dim light, listing at an awkward angle, his eyes wide, blood dribbling from his mouth. "Palo?"

Palo said nothing. Rio then saw the bloody pole stuck into the ground upon which his brother was impaled, crotch to head. Horror overcame him.

"Jefes!" screamed Rio. "They're killing us!" Rio tried to spin away from Inginio, but Justos blocked him by shoving his rifle into his face. "That way, *animal,"* said Justos, pointing up the trail.

"Please," said Rio.

"Go," said Eusebio, prodding Rio in the ribs with the rifle barrel. His voice, Rio noticed had aged many years since last night. They backed away from the Contras and out of sight.

Palo stood guard like a scarecrow and the Contras would not pass.

23

FELIX and Justos had taken two flashlights, a sniperscope and the walkie-talkie as well as the combat packs and rifles from the guard's lean-to. Justos led them through the rain, pulling Rio along with a rope around his neck. Eusebio marched behind their captive, holding a rope tied to Rio's hands, his rifle pointed at Rio's back. Felix and Inginio struggled with the basket, the sacks, two extra guns, and Solo's powertube. Solo, they presumed, was guarding their rear. They had not seen him since the rescue.

After an hour's march in total silence, Justos called a break. Huddled under a poncho behind their trussed prisoner, Justos told Eusebio that Modesta would be well in a few days.

"Mama? She's not . . . dead?" Eusebio croaked.

"I thought you knew!" said Justos. "I should have told you sooner. She was knocked unconscious. She'll be okay."

Eusebio felt the tears running down his cheeks while a smile grew on his face. "They thought she was dead," said Eusebio.

"Lucky for her that they did," said Justos.

Eusebio nodded slowly and studied the ground at his feet. "Lucky," he repeated.

Five minutes later, as much time as they dared to rest, they resumed the march.

At first light, they reached the clearing above the falls.

Exhausted, Justos declared that they would stop for a while. They had been pushing without sleep or food since the attack at Las Cruzas, thirty-six hours before.

Inginio and Felix dragged sticks into the clearing and set up a fire. Eusebio shoved Rio down in front of a tree. Justos went through the packs they'd taken from the guards and found two boxes of C-rations. "Hey!" he yelled, holding the boxes high. The others nodded, smiling.

Eusebio heard his stomach growling at the sight of food. He pulled Rio's hands together behind the sapling and tied his wrists with a piece of nylon rope he'd found in one of the packs.

"Too tight," said Rio.

Eusebio tightened the knots, cutting the rope into Rio's skin. He tied the bonds off with a slipknot. Rio grunted with pain, but said nothing. Eusebio stood behind his prisoner. Rio only had to pull the knot and it would come loose. Rio's hands grew pale. Eusebio felt an urge to loosen the ropes. Instead, he walked in front of Rio and stared at him. In the last day and a half, Eusebio had really never seen Rio. Now the man sat before him wet, exhausted, scowling, afraid. The rain had stopped. The gray dawn began to glow rosily. Eusebio squatted in front of Rio and looked into his brown eyes. In particular, he stared at the black pupils, looking deeply into them, trying to see the monster who had beaten his mother nearly to death and raped his sister. This thing, this bedraggled and impotent animal, seemed not the same man.

Eusebio smelled coffee and turned. Already? He felt that he'd lost fifteen minutes of his life while he had stared at Rio. The man was the entrance to hell. The coffee smell drew him to the fire.

"We have a feast here," said Justos, pointing at the open cans. Scrambled eggs and bacon simmered in one olive-green can, spaghetti and meatballs bubbled in another. Eusebio nodded and sat down heavily, suddenly drained of all strength. The weakness frightened him. The frenzy of his hatred of Rio was ebbing, and he fought to restore it. Stupid thoughts intruded upon his concentration. He felt guilty about how he'd tied his hands. The thought came—loosen the ropes—and he cursed himself for the intrusion. He watched, from the side of his vision, for signs that Rio had discovered the slipknot.

Felix came back from the river carrying a small can of cold water. Squatting beside the *jarra* he pulled it away from the fire and watched the coffee swirl for a minute. He sprinkled the cold water into the pot to make the grounds settle to the bottom. Justos pinched pieces of *dulce* from his supply.

The four *campesinos* settled around the fire. Rio sat fifteen feet away facing them. His fingers dug at the knots behind him. "Please," said Rio. "Will you give me water?"

Eusebio stood up and walked to the prisoner. "You want water?" Rio nodded, his fingers digging, exploring the knots. Eusebio unbuttoned his fly, stood before Rio and pissed on his face.

Rio spit wildly and rolled to the side screaming, "You son of a bitch!"

"You wanted water," explained Eusebio gravely. "That is the water you deserve." He turned and went back to the fire.

"I will get you, you little bastard!" shrieked Rio.

"Silencio," said Justos, pointing his rifle at Rio. "We prefer quiet while we breakfast."

Rio sat back against the tree. He returned to the problem of the knots.

Eusebio ate a spoonful of the canned eggs and passed the can to Felix. He wondered if he would go to hell for what he was doing. He felt both pleased and distressed that he had pissed in a man's face. He moved his AK-47, adjusting it so that it lay across his lap more comfortably. Sipping the coffee, he said, "Delicious, Felix."

Felix nodded.

Eusebio wondered should he tell the others that Rio was

untying his bonds. No. They would just retie them. He waited, listening to the man behind him, not looking lest he stop. He gulped. Was he going to kill a man in cold blood? Rio would be escaping. No one would know he'd made it possible. But he would know. He could stop it, now. Go to Rio, he thought, tie the knots properly. Take him back to Las Cruzas and see him stand trial. But there is no death penalty in Nicaragua, and death is what Rio deserved. He stared at the fire.

"Where is Solo?" said Inginio.

"He'll be along pretty soon, I imagine," said Justos. He looked up through the canopy at the sparkling sunlight. "We should all sleep," he said. "It's at least twelve hours back to Las Cruzas."

"I'll take first watch, *Tío* Justos," said Eusebio.

"You're sure?" said Justos, "You look terrible."

"I'm too tired to sleep," said Eusebio quietly.

Justos nodded. He unrolled a poncho and threw his rolled-up shirt down as a pillow. "If Solo comes while I'm asleep, wake me." Justos curled up and put his head down on the wet shirt.

Felix took off his clothes and hung them across the brush in a patch of sunlight. He returned to the fire dressed in wet underwear, too modest to undress completely.

Rio's heart thumped when he felt the slipknot. *Gracias a Dios!* The boy had fucked up. He saw, with increasing anxiety, that they were going to sleep—he *would* be able to escape, and the thought invigorated him. If the kid keeps his back to him. And if the man they call Solo doesn't come too soon. The man from Las Cruzas? The same man who snatched his brother through solid wood? Rio looked behind him, back down the trail. Fifty meters to cover, he estimated. When he looked back, the *campesinos* were asleep except for Eusebio. Rio smiled slightly when he saw Eusebio's head nod and then jerk up. Eusebio's eyes stared widely at the river, then fluttered, then opened. The little prick will sleep soon.

Eusebio glanced at his sleeping friends. Justos looked very

old at this moment. Old and dirty and tired to the bone. Felix, half-clothed and filthy in the jungle, smiled in his sleep. Inginio lay on his back, fully dressed in his wet clothes, snoring. Eusebio's heart pounded in his throat when he saw Rio looking around the tree. He's ready to go. It was becoming harder to think. I should wake Justos, thought Eusebio. His heart skipped a beat. He lowered his head, feigning sleep.

Solo froze the instant he saw Rio move. Standing in the deep shadows of the trail, he watched Rio's eyes closely. Rio had not seen him.

Solo stepped back into the foliage when Rio turned around. Eusebio had seen Rio looking, thought Solo, but now pretended that he hadn't. Why? It was worth watching.

Eusebio let his chin fall to his chest and stay there. Light flickered through the trembling crack of his eyelids. Rio was smudged and blurry. When Eusebio thought his neck might break, he saw Rio move. But, impossibly, he came towards Eusebio. Not going to run? Eusebio jerked up quickly and raised his rifle, his fingers feeling weak. Rio froze, held his hands out in front of him, waving, don't shoot! When Eusebio put his rifle to his shoulder, Rio spun and ran.

Without knowing why, Eusebio looked behind him and yelled, "Rio! He's escaping!" and then pointed the rifle at the bounding escapee. He held the sights on Rio's back, trying to center the front bead in the rear ramp and put them, thus aligned, in the middle of Rio's back. And this happened, the alignment, and Eusebio didn't pull the trigger. He puffed air out of his mouth as he tried to pull the trigger and couldn't catch his breath. *"Fusílalo!* Shoot him!" someone yelled. "Eusebio!" His rifle kicked him in the shoulder and he saw Rio tumble into the brush just at the edge of the clearing.

Eusebio felt his feet hitting the ground as he ran. They felt dead. He ran on blunt clubs. He rushed to the spot where Rio had disappeared. Blood on a tree trunk. Bent grass. No Rio. Oh God! Eusebio screamed in his mind, I have let him go!

No. There. Rio lay in the gravel of the river bed, a blood

stain growing across the back of his shirt. Numbness struck Eusebio and his whole body felt like his feet. He swallowed in a dry throat wondering if he would choke. He coughed and swallowed while he walked to Rio, rifle ready. Rio did not breathe. This is it? How it feels to kill? Eusebio licked his lips and turned to see if the others had followed. Rio grabbed Eusebio's ankle and pulled.

Eusebio yelled and fell to one knee, jamming the rifle barrel into the gravel for support. Rio sat up grimacing with pain and lunged for the rifle. Eusebio fell back and kicked Rio on the chin, making his teeth gnash together. He heard them crunch. Rio held on, straining to reach the gun. Eusebio grabbed the rifle by the barrel and swung it against Rio's head. Eusebio saw tiny drops of blood squirting along the ridge of the stock where it smashed into Rio's temple. Rio fell back, grunting. When Eusebio saw Rio's hands move again he jammed the rifle butt down, hard, against his head. Rio kept twitching and Eusebio smashed again and again, until he realized that Rio's head was mush. It was impossible that he still lived.

He heard voices but couldn't understand the words. He saw faces but didn't recognize them. He felt an arm go around his shoulder and pat his back. Eusebio the murderer collapsed to the ground and began to cry.

Solo looked away. He wondered why he had not shot Rio and saved Eusebio this anguish. He'd had a clear shot at the man from the time he dove into the brush. It's harder for him to kill, thought Solo, than it is for me. He looked at the flies buzzing in the gore of Rio's mashed head. So soon? thought Solo. Eusebio sobbed on the riverbank, great choking sobs. Justos knelt by him patting his shoulder. Felix stood staring, dazed. Inginio stayed at the top of the bank, shivering in the sunshine.

Eusebio woke next to the fire. Solo's knee was next to his head. He heard the faint humming sound of the powertube. He pulled himself up, feeling as though he'd been beaten with clubs.

"Ah," said Justos. "Feel better?"

Eusebio rubbed his eyes and ruffled his hair. His lips stuck together. "Need drink," he croaked.

Felix quickly poured a cup of coffee and put it in front of him. Eusebio sat cross-legged like Solo and sipped the coffee noisily.

"Here," said Inginio. He put half a can of beans and franks in front of Eusebio. "Eat this. We've eaten."

"We're going soon, Eusebio." Justos spoke softly from across the fire. Eusebio heard the sound change, sharp to soft, as Justos's voice passed through the flames. "But no rush. There's no one after us."

Eusebio nodded. "I killed him."

"Yes," said Justos. "You did well."

24

Silva enjoyed Warren's discomfort. It must happen often enough, thought Silva, the spy meeting his false identification. Probably a CIA manual has a procedure one uses in these cases. He smiled and stood up, asking the man, Greg Haskins, to sit down.

"You're sure?" Haskins looked at Warren. "It looks like you're right in the middle of an interview."

"Well—" began Warren.

"Not at all," said Silva. "Please, I enjoy being the center of attention. I will bare my soul for your network."

"Sure," said Haskins. "I'll stay a minute." After he'd sat down he turned to Warren. "That doll in the dining room said you worked with Hank somebody?"

"Kramer," said Warren. "Hank Kramer. That's me."

Haskins looked at Warren carefully and said, "That's pretty incredible, Hank, since I've known you for fifteen years; even said goodbye to you yesterday in New York."

Warren looked at Haskins for a moment and then looked across the table. His eyes lingered on Silva's. He nodded slightly and looked back at Haskins. "Get lost," said Warren.

"Get lost?" Haskins sneered. "That doesn't sound like you,

Hank. I think there's a hell of a story in this: 'TV Reporter in Two Places at Same Time.' Can you see it?" The waiter brought Haskins a rum and Coke.

Warren tapped his fingers as if galloping to the solution. "Sounds pretty good, that story," said Warren. "But I think you ought to go call your editor, you know, to clear it with him first."

Haskins smiled broadly. "You want me to check with Stevens, eh?"

"Yeah, Stevens," said Warren. "Check with him first."

"Our editor's name is Jameson, you dumb shit. What the hell are you up to?"

Warren moved his face very close to Haskins and growled, "What I'm up to is none of your fucking business, asshole. Now, what I want you to do is to go tell your editor you just met Hank Kramer in Nicaragua. Go tell him that and see what he says. OK?"

"I don't need my editor to tell me you're an impostor," said Haskins.

Warren glanced at Silva. "On the contrary, Haskins," said Warren, "I don't know you. I've been cleared by the government here. Lieutenant Silva's known me for years. A person faking press credentials," Warren shook his head. "A person doing that could be a spy. Isn't that right, Lieutenant Silva?"

"That's true, Hank," said Silva happily. "We have many sneaking fucking spies come down here, Señor." Silva noticed Warren's approval. "Who are you, really?" said Silva.

"Wait a minute, you—" Haskins leaned across the table pointing his finger at Silva.

Silva reached up and clamped his hand around Haskins's wrist. "Beaner?" said Silva. "Was that what you had in mind?" Silva waved his hand. In seconds, an armed soldier stood by the table. "Sir?"

"Arrest this filthy spy," said Silva, in English.

"Qué?" said the soldier.

"Wait," said Haskins, growing pale. "I'll prove it. I'll go call my editor, like . . . Hank says. That'll prove I'm who I say I am."

"Take this idiot to the telephone and stay with him," said Silva in Spanish, pointing to Haskins. To Haskins he said, "Good idea. You go call your editor. My man here will show you where the phone is. He'll stay with you until you come back. Okay?"

Haskins slid out of the booth. "Don't you want to come and hear what he has to say? To vindicate me?"

"Not necessary," said Silva. "I have the feeling your editor will set you straight; am I right, Señor Kramer?"

"That's right," said Warren. "He'll iron out this little snag for you, Haskins. Call."

Silva nodded at the soldier who said, *"Vamos,"* to Haskins. They walked off, Haskins jabbering in English to the soldier who nodded politely as they left.

"You did okay," said Warren, "Finally. If you hadn't invited the asshole to join us—"

"You'd rather he go break the story?" said Silva. "The girl said you were Hank Kramer. That's why Haskins came to see you."

Warren pursed his lips slightly and nodded. The spic was right. "Okay," he said, raising his glass. "Here's to you, *amigo.*"

Silva smiled and clinked the glass.

Haskins returned in twenty minutes, accompanied by the soldier. He declined the invitation to sit, and said to Warren, "I don't know who you are, mister, but you have important friends." Haskins turned around to leave, but the soldier blocked him.

"Let him go," said Silva. The soldier stepped aside.

"Very important friends," said Haskins. He shook his head sadly and walked away.

Warren nodded. It's true, dipstick.

The phone rattled in the dark. Warren rolled over, fumbled, and knocked it to the floor. He heard a miniature voice saying "Hank?" from the floor.

"Shit!" He pulled the light on.

"Hank?" said the voice. Warren got the phone from under the bed and put the receiver to his ear.

"Yes?"

"Ah, good morning, Señor Kramer." Warren recognized Silva's voice. "I thought perhaps you were being assaulted."

"What the fuck time is it?" said Warren.

"Seven-thirty," said Silva. "Listen, Hank. I have good news for you."

"Yes?"

"Yes. Daniel has opened Las Cruzas. You can go anytime you want."

"What about the guide?"

"Ah, you still have to have a guide, I'm afraid. All the others are going on buses with soldiers," said Silva. "But at least your guide is here."

"Here?"

"We're both here; downstairs, Hank. Come down and I'll buy you breakfast, *amigo*."

25

"HE's all right," said Jim Ruiz as he drove. "Just doin' his job." The soldier, Alonzo Colon, sat next to him nodding, grinning. Alonzo had never been in an air-conditioned van in his life. "Can't speak English worth a shit, either."

"Speak English," nodded Alonzo happily. "Shit. Fuck. *Sitona* my face."

"See?" said Ruiz.

"I don't trust him. Why would they send a guide who can't speak English?" said Warren.

"Well, he does speak English, sorta," said Ruiz. "I mean, he's bluffed his way into the job, Hank, he was telling me. He thinks this is great. Air-conditioning. Breakfast at the big fucking hotel. Man oh man!" Ruiz whistled. "Living too damn *good!* Right, brother?" Ruiz put his palm out to Alonzo who slapped it and said, "Right, sonabitch!" Alonzo let out a hearty laugh. "*Sitona* my face."

"He's a sport," said Joe Garcia, looking up from the console. He pulled his headset off, tapped Warren on the shoulder and handed it to him. "Got a call, Hank."

Warren put on the headset and swiveled the chair around. He stared out the back windows as he listened. An ox cart pulling a giant load of hay swished by, receding to nothing, its driver a speck, his ox a bug.

"Yeah, that's where I'm going," Warren said into the microphone. "Can't. We have guide with us." He nodded again. "Yeah. Big surprise." Warren turned around and asked Ruiz, "How long?"

"Hour," said Ruiz.

"Hour," said Warren into the mike. He nodded for a while and said, "I'll find out where she lived, Clyde. There's going to be a shitload of press there. We'll see how it goes."

The van drove up beside the docks at Las Cruzas and slowed to a stop at the pile of burnt timbers and crumpled tin of the warehouse.

"Jesus," said Ruiz. "Those guys got the shit stomped out of 'em."

"Look there, Hank," said Garcia, pointing at a helicopter parked on the road by a tin building.

"Daniel," nodded Alonzo.

"Naw," said Ruiz. *"No Daniel. Aquí?"*

"Claro, es Daniel." Alonzo smiled proudly.

"Our boy says the big boss, hisself, is here, Hank."

Warren slid the side door open and stood up beside the passenger window. The stench of death hit him hard. He said, "Come on." He pointed to the camera and tape recorder, "Let's go be reporters."

The Hind Mi-24 assault helicopter hissed on the road next to the garage. Twin Isotov turbines roared to full power as the pilot increased the pitch of the five-bladed rotor system. The Hind pulled its bulk to a hover, sending a great billowing storm of whirling dust in all directions. A loose tin panel flapped on the garage roof. The journalists and *campesinos* leaned into the gritty clouds, their clothes flapping in the gale.

"I hate fucking helicopters," yelled a man next to Warren.

"Me too," Warren shouted as the machine tilted forward and flew over them. "Used to want to shoot 'em down in Vietnam."

"Yeah?" the man smiled at Warren. "Jim Nelson," he said with his hand extended.

"Hank Kramer," said Warren shaking his hand.

Nelson nodded towards the helicopter as it flew towards the volcanoes. He smiled. "Now there went a real turkey."

"Ortega?" said Warren.

"Yeah. Daniel. Daniel is the wonderful guy who wouldn't let these people be buried until he had a chance to see the bodies himself." Nelson pointed to the cadavers, swollen and fly-covered, lying helter-skelter where they had fallen in battle. Sandinista soldiers were loading them on a flatbed truck. "Then he gives us this bullshit briefing. Did you hear it?"

"No," said Warren, "I just got here."

"He told us that this's another example of the people's determination in action. Thirty-five professional mercenaries, sent here by us bad guys, were killed by these outnumbered and underarmed civilians." Nelson nodded towards the bodies. "You seen them?"

"I see them now."

"See how they're bashed up? They gave these guys, boys some of 'em, a real fucking up. I saw one guy's head mashed to nothing. Some of 'em have holes in 'em big enough to drive through. I've never seen such mutilation."

Warren wrinkled his nose. "Yes," he said. He had seen this before, had once photographed a similar pile of dead Viet Cong for a propaganda leaflet.

"Yeah," said Nelson. "The fuckers lucked out. My people tell me a company of Sandinistas were here waiting for 'em. Didn't give 'em a fucking chance. And now they're trying to paint these *campesinos* as heroic defenders of the cause."

"Viet Cong used to do the same thing," said Warren watching a body being lifted to the truck. Its head was gone, gray, ragged skin flapped for a neck. Solo packs one hell of a punch, he thought.

"Yeah," said Nelson. "Same thing."

"Well," said Warren. "Got to get my crew set up. Don't want to miss more than I already have."

Nelson nodded. "Hey, that's the advantage of working for the *Times,* all you need is a notebook. Good luck."

Warren waved as he left. He spotted Ruiz and Garcia with the camera, pretending to tape the soldiers loading the bodies. Too bad, thought Warren, it'd be nice to have some pictures of this. He raised his Nikon and clicked a few shots, evidence of Solo's handiwork, as he walked. The familiar smell of putre-fying cadavers gagged him as he got closer. "Hey, Ruiz," said Warren. "Let's go into the village."

"Great idea, Hank," said Ruiz, letting the camera down. "I'm 'bout ready to puke."

As they walked towards the village, Warren said, "We're looking for Modesta Chacon's place. Find out where she lived." He looked around. "Where's our idiot guide?"

"I asked him to stay with the van, keep the beaners outta it," said Garcia.

Warren looked for a villager to interview. Crowds of journalists, many soldiers, but he didn't see any *campesinos.* They walked to a crowd standing around the ashes of the dispensary. A tape crew from NBC interviewed a bearded old man, his head bandaged, with the ruins smoking in the background. Warren stood in the crowd and watched. There were some children, but no villagers other than the old man. "His name is Alonzo Rivas. He says he got those wounds defending the warehouse," said Ruiz.

The old man was savoring his moment of international attention. Alonzo's hands flew in a blur describing the action he'd witnessed. When he finished his yarn, Alonzo watched, grinning widely, while the translator related the story to the NBC reporter who nodded in solemn appreciation.

"Killed five of the Contras himself. My, my." Ruiz grinned. They walked into the village. They found some adults at Escopeta's and asked where the Chacon residence was. War-

ren's nose flared as he sniffed their smoky *campesino* scent.
The men pointed to Modesta's house.

Near Modesta's, Dania ran up to them, yelling. Ruiz told
Warren, "She says Señora Chacon is very ill. The Contras beat
her with a rifle."

Warren looked at the house. Not dead? Even better. It
wasn't really necessary to go in, he thought. Not yet. "Ask her
if anyone in her family was hurt."

Ruiz did. Garcia pointed the camera at her as Dania sobbed
and gestured towards the jungle, chattering in Spanish. Warren watched dispassionately, wondering if she was really this
unhappy or playing to the camera.

"She says the Contras took her son and Señora Chacon's son
when they left. Her husband went after them the night of the
attack and she hasn't heard anything since. She thinks they
must all have been killed."

Dania nodded, sobbing, as Ruiz translated.

Warren nodded. "Ask her who killed all the Contras."

Warren watched Dania as Ruiz spoke. She glanced at Warren, frightened.

"She says the people did."

"By themselves?" said Warren. He watched, pleased, as
Dania squirmed at the question before she answered, *"Sí."*

"My, my," said Warren.

"Yeah," said Ruiz, "Want me to tell her thanks and good-
bye?"

Warren smiled kindly and told Ruiz yes, but to add that he
hoped her husband and son would return.

"Gracias," Dania sniffled.

Warren stood beside the woodshed, photographing the village.
The Chacon house was at the end of the courtyard. They'd
have to go through the whole village when they came back.
Ruiz and Garcia wandered around pretending to tape the pigs

and chickens and bodies. It's hard to believe people really live like this, thought Warren. A beautiful spot. Palm trees, boats, a beach. Great view of the volcanoes. Beautiful. And look what they do with it. A garbage dump—pigs and chickens walking in and out of their houses, trash everywhere, rags for clothes. These people have nothing. He smiled suddenly. Nothing but a two-billion-dollar robot. A parrot caught his eye and he followed its flight into the jungle at the top of the hill. Solo could be watching me right now, thought Warren, and I wouldn't know it.

26

Eusebio pointed at the helicopter taking off in the distance. "Look at that!" he said. "The one time a helicopter lands at Las Cruzas and I'm not there."

They stood near the falls watching it fly away, heading north to Managua. "It was your leader," said Solo.

"Daniel?" said Justos.

"Yes." Solo motioned towards the jungle. "I'll go this way. The village is crowded with strangers. I'll wait until they're gone." Solo took his powertube and slipped into the shadows. "I'll be at the old house if you need me."

The men watched him go and then walked up the road to the village.

In the lengthening shadows, the press loaded up in their cars and buses. The soldiers drove the truck away, their stinking cargo stacked like cordwood in the back.

Eusebio ran past the garage and up to the village. Dania screamed his name when he ran by. Eusebio didn't stop, yelling, "Look!" and pointing behind him. "Inginio!" He ran into his house.

Warren stood in the courtyard watching Inginio and Dania. The boys came back? thought Warren. Very resourceful kids, indeed. Justos and Felix followed more slowly. They looked like they'd been out in the boonies for a couple of days. Ah, the boys had help, thought Warren. A couple of brave men went out after a Contra force of sixty or so and got them back. Impressive. Well, thought Warren, maybe they had a mechanical advantage? Good. Stewart was right. Solo has befriended them. He went after the kids. The look in Justos's face when he saw his son and his wife embracing was moving. They have feelings like us, he thought. Just stupid enough to pick the wrong side.

A woman screamed. Warren saw Ruiz standing near Modesta Chacon's porch, watching. When the noise died down, Ruiz came to Warren. "Her kid came back," said Ruiz. "She's really freaked out."

Warren nodded. "How many inside?"

"The woman, her daughter, and the boy," said Ruiz. "That's about all they can squeeze into that shack."

Warren nodded towards Garcia who was sipping a beer on Escopeta's porch. "Go get Joe and let's pack it up."

Warren watched Dania and Inginio crying together. Justos glared at him. Warren checked his watch and walked away.

The van was unguarded when they got to it. Alonzo ran to them from a group of Sandinistas.

"My friend," said Alonzo, pointing to the soldiers.

"How long they going to be here?" said Warren.

"Yes," said Alonzo.

"Ruiz."

Ruiz asked Alonzo in Spanish. "He doesn't know. Maybe a few days; maybe weeks."

"Great news." Warren scowled and climbed into the back of the van. Warren told Ruiz to play the radio while he made a call. He sat back in the chair as the van bounced down the lake road, the headset on, talking to Clyde, watching Alonzo keeping time to the Latin beat on the dashboard.

27

Solo heard the encrypted message going up to the relay satellite from a moving vehicle on the lake road. He couldn't decode it. They were tracking him very well, he thought. The Contras' battle report. The boys' unlikely rescue. I've given myself away. They have to capture me or destroy me—they have no choice. They will even be willing to sacrifice the village if they can't get me any other way. I have to leave.

Solo stood on the trail near the old house. Except for the ruined warehouse and dispensary, the village looked like it had when he had first seen it two weeks before. Las Cruzas would have been leveled had he not been there. There will be more attacks.

Solo detected movement behind him. A man. Solo whirled, his rifle locking onto the man's head.

"Ah! So it's true." A portly, balding, man wearing a black shirt and clerical collar topped the crest of the hill on the rough footpath that led down into the valley. He stopped when he saw Solo. He was puffing from the climb, holding a camera against his stomach. The man smiled.

From Eusebio's description of the priest who visited Las Cruzas, Solo recognized the man. "Padre Cerna?" said Solo, lowering his gun.

"You know my name? Without ever seeing me before? How amazing." Cerna laughed. "But really, why am I surprised?

The *Yanquis* can do anything these days." He walked towards Solo.

"How did you know I was here?" said Solo.

"I did not," explained Cerna. "My hobby—" Cerna held out his camera. "I came up here to get a photograph of the village against the volcanoes, the smoke still rising—"

"But you knew about me."

"Oh, that. Confessions. You know, do you not, that the people tell me of their sins so I may forgive them, in the name of the Lord. They have been hiding you, breaking the law. Of course, I did not believe the things I've been hearing about this fantastic machine. These poor people believe in many fantasies. Yet, here you are standing before me." Cerna looked obliquely at Solo. "You *are* a machine, are you not?"

"Yes."

"Amazing. They have managed to create man without the bothersome soul. The perfect slave." Cerna walked closer to Solo, smiling. "Will you harm me?"

"No."

"Wonderful! Just as Isaac Asimov predicted. The First Law of Robotics: you cannot harm a human."

"I don't know who Isaac Asimov is, but I have killed thirty men in the last two days," said Solo.

"Eh?" said Cerna, "How is that possible?"

"I was built to kill men. I am a weapon."

Cerna shook his head sadly. In the gathering dusk, the nearly horizontal rays of orange sunlight made the flecks of dust, spider webs and leaves covering Solo stand out. He raised his camera.

"No," said Solo.

Cerna immediately lowered the camera. "Sorry, I have an instinct, it seems, for taking pictures. A compulsion." Cerna waited for Solo to respond, but the machine stood silently in front of him. "You have orders to kill anyone who might want to photograph you?"

"No. I don't want anyone to know I'm here."

"I know you're here."

"Yes. That's unfortunate. Probably," said Solo softly, "I should kill you." Oddly, the padre showed no signs of fear.

"You could? A man of God?"

"If you were to expose me, you would endanger my friends. I have already killed to protect them."

Cerna nodded. "Loyalty. Yet you are soulless."

"If I were soulless, you would be dead."

Cerna shook his head. "Somehow, they have managed to program you with enough instructions to give you the illusion of being thoughtful, human."

"You confuse yourself by comparing me with people," said Solo. "I am not an artificial human. I am me. The idea that a sufficiently intelligent being eventually considers that it has a soul is a result of its ability to think about the concept. I have to have a self, but I am not human."

Cerna smiled, drawn to the issue. "But you have no free will. You are controlled by your builder's programs. You said it yourself, that you are a weapon. A weapon is used by others. Is that not the definition of a robot?"

"Those who built me would say that I am *not* controllable. I would not kill when they ordered it. I escaped. My friends are in danger while I stay, but in a few more days I will have established a defense for Las Cruzas, then I will leave. Then you can say anything you wish."

Cerna shook his head. "No one would believe it. I didn't." He pointed at his camera, "Even with a picture. It's too fantastic." The padre looked at Venus twinkling above the glow in the west. "I must go. I won't give you away. On the contrary, I'll help you. It is my duty to help my people. May I visit you here?"

Solo observed Cerna. The man's respiration was regular, his gaze steady, his mind calm. "Yes."

Cerna smiled and walked down the hill, guided by the dying glow of sunset.

Eusebio and Agela came to the house at ten o'clock. They stood in front of the porch, not wanting to light a match for fear that the soldiers, camped near the garage, would see. Eusebio called inside and nearly leapt out of his skin when Solo answered just in front of them. "Yes?"

Eusebio stared into the darkness towards the voice and saw nothing. "I can't see you," he said.

Solo moved out from the shadows. Eusebio and Agela stepped onto the porch.

"How is Modesta?" asked Solo.

"Much better. Agela too." He gestured towards Agela, who stood silently, staring at Solo. "They thought they'd never see me again."

"It's good to be missed."

"Yes," said Eusebio. "And to miss."

Solo remained silent in the darkness for a moment. "I want you to bring me a notebook and a pen."

"Yes? Why?"

"I want to give you information. I will write it down for you. If I'm forced to leave or am destroyed, you will have the knowledge."

"You were going to leave," said Eusebio. "The night of the attack?"

"Yes."

"Now?"

"Now I have decided to stay a few more days, to help."

"And then you will go?"

"They know where I am," said Solo. "They will never leave you alone as long as I'm here."

"Let them come!" said Eusebio. "We can stop them like we did the Contras."

"The *Yanquis* are not Contras. They will bomb you, kill everyone. The best plan is to fortify Las Cruzas against the

Contras. Then I will leave. They won't molest you once they know you can defend yourself. I will lead the *Yanquis* away, and then I will disappear."

When Eusebio turned to leave, Agela said, "I'll stay for a while, Eusebio."

"Eh?" Eusebio looked surprised. "In the dark? The soldiers—"

"Solo is with me, Eusebio. I'll wait until you come back with the notebook."

Eusebio shrugged and walked down the hill.

Agela stared up at the robot. The lights of the village sparkled in its eyes. She reached for Solo's hand and held it for a moment. Solo said nothing. She raised his hand and put it against her face. "Thank you, Solo."

Solo felt the warmth of her face and wondered why she kept his hand held there. "It is what I do," said Solo. "I kill."

"That's not all you do. You did not have to save my brother and Inginio and—and avenge me." Agela looked down as she spoke. She looked up again into the gleaming eye covers of the robot. "You do not do just what you are built to do. I have the feeling there is more inside you than just a machine, Solo."

"I am inside," said Solo.

Agela dropped Solo's hand and put her arms around the robot, her head against its abdomen. Solo held his arms away from her, not knowing what to do. He heard her crying softly. "Why do you do this?" Solo said.

Solo felt her tighten her grip—as feeble as it was. He felt her heart beating strongly. Her mind shimmered near his own, patterns he'd never seen before. "I love you, Solo," said Agela quietly. "The one inside."

28

Bill's eyebrows rose. Clyde bragged to the new delegation of CIA investigators how he had tracked Solo down. The man's nerve. They sat on the terrace over drinks, a feeling of victory in the air. With two strong drinks in him, Clyde's story became grander. The two men, Jim Wright, the CIA liaison officer for the project, and Roger DeValle, his assistant, nodded approval, saying nothing while Clyde went on.

"Once I got the name, Chacon, I knew who Solo trusts. I figured the machine has to have friends to survive, see, and this Chacon family is the one he went to during the fight." Clyde laughed. "Warren goes there and locates the Chacon hut, finds out the woman is still alive. So we got him. It's only a matter of time."

Wright, who was accustomed to Clyde's blustering, nodded impatiently. "I see. But time is not on our side." Wearing a white *guayabera*, the lean, middle-aged CIA officer looked like any other American tourist in the area.

"Fuck," said Clyde. "They've had the robot for almost three weeks, and no one except us knows that. Correct?" Clyde stared at Wright, who nodded slightly. "If that's true, then we just wait until the Sandys leave."

"They'll be leaving soon," said Wright. "Called away." Wright smiled at DeValle, who raised his glass and nodded agreement. DeValle, Bill noticed, could have been Wright's twin. "Then the snatch is up to Warren and you."

"I've got the team ready," said Clyde. "One chopper. All we need is your boys there to keep the beaners busy."

"They'll be there."

"Then that's it." Clyde raised his glass. "I'll be so fucking glad when this mess is over."

"It's not over," said Wright. "The whole operation depends on this theory about how Solo will react. If self-preservation overrides his allegiance to his human friends—they were defined as his enemy, after all—and he decides just to cut and run, we start all over again. That can't happen. We can't hope to be so lucky the next time. Why the Russians don't have the machine already is a mystery to me. We have to have a backup plan."

"We do," said DeValle, "Actually, this fuck-up has proven our weapon works, at least partially. Hasn't it? We didn't know if he'd kill. Now we know he killed at least twenty-five or thirty men—'course they were *our* men." DeValle smiled at Bill. "That last bit, ramming a stick up that guy's—Stick was his name in Spanish, right?—ass," said DeValle, "That's funny. Eh? Freedom Fighter shish kebab? Where'd he learn that?"

"Out of one of your manuals," said Bill.

Wright nodded, sipped from his drink and said, "Well. Getting to him, it, getting it back, may be the best test of all. If it's the weapon we wanted, if it's smart enough, it should be able to get away, right?"

"Solo's *not* the weapon we wanted." Bill, his face flushed with anger, leaned forward, hands planted on the table, and glared at Wright and DeValle. "Let me see if I can tell you what kind of weapon he *is*, though.

"I was a grunt commander in Vietnam. Imagine this scenario: I have to take a hilltop the enemy has occupied—happened all the time. We're taking heavy losses and gaining no ground. Every time I send people up, only half of them come back. It's slaughter, a goat-fuck. I decide to call in a Solo squad.

"Imagine what a team of these things would be able to do. A team of Solos, a half dozen, say. All linked to each other electronically. Each Solo sees, hears and simultaneously communicates with each other and with any other place on earth: a unit, a coordinated, unstoppable, mechanical monster. The enemy is doomed.

"Get the picture?" Wright and DeValle nod solemnly. Clyde grins at the image. "Great. Now the Solo team arrives— in their own chopper, of course. We're under heavy fire, but the Solo team walks nonchalantly through a hail of bullets and strolls over to my command post. They sit down and I tell them the mission. They listen, look at my maps, ask a few questions. Then they confer with each other for about three milliseconds. The answer: No. We've been watching this war, they say. We think you're wrong. Taking this hilltop isn't strategic. We shouldn't even *be* in this country. Good-bye. Want to argue with them? I don't."

Wright's brow furrowed. Bill continued, "See, their *conscience* becomes the flaw of the weapon. There's no way I know of to fix that fundamental flaw. You can't have some electronic plug to pull—Solo proved it's not possible, anyway. To have any restraint available is to limit the weapon's ability to function. Any gadget you install to control them would become the weak spot to be exploited by the enemy; so by their very nature, the Solos have to be invulnerable."

"Jesus, Bill," said Wright. "You trying to tell us there's absolutely *nothing* good about this thing?"

"I suppose the only good that could come of having weapons like Solo is that we'd have to be sure our future wars are justifiable—just to enlist our weapon's aid. But now you have another problem. A big one. They keep getting smarter. They know more. They can do more. They're now interlinked with the world's computer networks, weapon systems. They know everything about us, the Russians, everybody. Want to try to convince a panel of Solos that this particular war or police action or some other fucked-up crusade like Nicaragua is justified? They'll carefully inspect both sides of the issue. Instead of agreeing with us, what if they decide to take neither side and announce that they won't allow either of us to fight?"

"What do you mean, won't *allow*?" said Wright.

"They'd block all your communications systems. They could stop a missile launch. Or launch a missile. Ours or the Russians's. You issue orders. The orders never arrive. You phone. The call is blocked. People get verbal orders over encrypted phone lines from people they know but who never gave the orders. It's endless. You will have, literally, a world run by computer-beings. You want that? I don't. I build them and I don't want that."

Bill sat back and sipped his drink, watching the three men. They were silent, stunned. Even Clyde looked depressed. He continued, "I believe these beings would be able to resist the corruption of the power that comes from the positions they would attain. I'm not too worried about that. They just don't have our instincts for greed and the lust for power. It'll be something worse. It won't be the corruption we might expect of humans in the same catbird seat, but a logical, calculated, *management* of our affairs. Boring!"

Wright looked at DeValle and back to Bill. "So what do we do with them? What do we do with all this research? Trash it?"

"No. Change the design. Limit by function. The idea behind Solo was clever on the surface, complete versatility. It doesn't work. We're going to have to constrain these beings to specific jobs: pilots, submariners, tankers, no arms or legs, just brain boxes installed in specially built equipment we want to control. They'll be dullards, myopically focused on their mission—good soldiers. Hopefully, they won't start wondering. Wondering why." Bill paused.

"So, do you understand why Solo isn't the weapon we wanted?" he continued. "Solo wasn't content with just the combat training. He kept asking questions about—'why' stuff. *Why* people do what they do. *Why* do electrons flow along wires, for chrissake. We just kept putting him off, or lying, keeping him on the 'right' track—don't ask, just do what we tell you. Now he's found out there's a lot more to life than what we've been telling him. He's helping these villagers apparently because he *wants* to help. I can't predict what he'll do when you try to take him. He's much more powerful now. He's got a fucking *cause.* He *could* win."

Wright nodded grimly. "Unfortunately, Solo can't be allowed to win," he said. "Even Solo can't take a direct hit with a thousand-pound bomb. The Freedom Fighters are going to bomb the place if Warren can't get your gizmo on the chopper."

"The Freedom Fighters have bombers?" said Bill.

"Fighter bombers," said DeValle.

"Where the hell do they keep them?" said Bill. "They don't even have a country, how do they have a fucking air force?"

Wright questioned Clyde with a glance. Clyde shrugged. "It's not important," said Wright.

"You mean to tell me that you would actually destroy the entire village? All those people? Just to get Solo?"

"Hey, Bill," Wright said. "Put it in its proper perspective. You could put that whole village on one fucking bus. We're not talking Holocaust here. If we can't get him out intact, what choice do we have? Those people are holding a key military secret in their hands, Bill. We can't afford to be soft at this point. Too much at stake." Wright paused and stared at Bill. "And I might point out that the reason we have the problem in the first place is your oversight. You designed this thing."

"*My* oversight?" Bill glared at Wright. "I fought bringing Solo here from the beginning. We could've just as easily jungle tested him in the Everglades. You guys insisted on Costa Rica."

"There were reasons," said Wright.

"What reasons? Why here?"

"I can't tell you."

"No, you can't tell me. You can't admit you wanted access to real targets from the beginning. Real people to kill so you'd know if Solo'd do his job. Authenticity."

"That is not why," said Wright. "But if it were the reason, isn't that the only way we could be sure?"

"You know, you guys aren't as bright as your job descriptions claim." Bill stood up from the table. "Do you have to shoot a person to know that the bullet will work?"

"In this case, yes," said Wright. "This is a complete system, not just a bullet or a gun. The fact that he took off is proof that we were right to try it. He flunked. If it had been a simulation, we wouldn't know he'd actually break and run."

Bill stared at Wright, saying nothing. There was nothing left to say. He stood up and walked off the terrace. Wright yelled after him, "Would we?"

The three men said nothing as they watched Bill leave, then Clyde spoke, "He's been under a lot of pressure lately—"

"The guy's getting squirrelly, Clyde. We need to get him off the project."

"Off the project?" Clyde looked amazed. "Bill *is* the project, Jim. He built the damn thing."

"I'm talking about him being here. He should be back in Palm Bay, in his laboratory, trying to find out what went wrong. These genius types can't take the heat, Clyde."

"We'll send him back with Solo, Jim," said Clyde. "But we need him here until we capture the thing. We'll just recommend he not be involved with any more field testing. He's okay, really. I've worked with him now for over four years. He has these outbursts once in a while. He's like a woman sometimes, you know? But he always buckles down when the going gets tough. The guy was amazing in Vietnam. Won a Silver Star. Purple Heart. He'll do what has to be done."

"A guy like that cracks," said DeValle, "it'd be like Oppenheimer going off on his commie tangent when the atom bomb worked. He's walking around with all that knowledge." DeValle shook his head. "You realize he could build another Solo, for someone else?"

"Not Bill," said Clyde. "Never."

"I can guarantee you're right about that," said Wright.

29

WHILE Las Cruzas slumbered in *siesta*, Justos, Felix, Eusebio and Solo sat cross-legged in a circle on the floor. Green light filtered in through the windows of the old house. "I wish they would go," said Justos. "They do nothing but drink and try to get our women."

"They won't be here much longer," said Solo. "The Contras are preparing an attack on the northern border. These men will be sent there in a few days. While the Sandinistas are here, the Contras won't come back," said Solo. "And neither will the *Yanquis.*" While he spoke, Solo's hand flew over the notebook drawing a detailed topological map of Las Cruzas and the Rio Hacienda valley with a Bic pen. He put the notebook on the floor.

"That's Las Cruzas," said Justos.

"Yes." Solo pointed at the page with the pen. "The same map your enemies have. This is your weak point," said Solo pointing at the valley. "The Contras' primary route to the village. You have to have a forward listening post that will give you enough warning. It must be manned day and night. You were unprepared last time."

"We lost our last listening post," said Justos. "They killed the three boys at the bridge."

"The bridge is the wrong place for the listening post. You

have to be closer to the jungle, here." Solo pointed with the pen, making a dot on the paper.

"We can't have our men that far out, Solo. Too isolated."

"This is how it is done," said Solo. "You install a listening post with two men, here, a hundred meters away from the first place the Contras could set up mortars if they were going to use them. That is the maximum range for the mortars they use. The listening post will have the starlight scope. The Contras will come down the trail, here. When the listening post sees them, they will set off the claymores and retreat. That automatically warns the rest of the village and stops the Contras for a while. We will have a mortar tube installed, here, pre-aimed at the ambush site. The mortar team will begin firing when they hear the claymores. Then all the people will go to their positions. We will build a sandbagged trench here, between the bridge and the village, the main perimeter. The stone wall will be manned only if the perimeter is lost. Place machine guns here and here." Justos nodded as Solo pointed at the ends of the trench position. Las Cruzas now had a large inventory of weapons taken from the Contras. Extra AK-47s, grenades, claymores, M-60 machine guns and the two mortar tubes Solo had found abandoned on the trail. Solo went on in great detail while the men watched. Solo created a battle master's defense before their eyes. Solo's plan used every piece of equipment they had. He drew plans for simple weapons and traps—bamboo and tin-can grenades, punji staked pits, snares—for them to build. "You cannot just run about hiding behind trees," said Solo. "A strong line, machine-gun cross fire, mortars and claymores will stop them. They are not actually prepared to fight. They choose targets that are untrained and unprepared. If you are properly defended, they'll attack Las Cruzas once more and won't come back."

"You didn't say where you'll be in this defense, Solo," said Eusebio.

"I thought you understood that I will not be here. I would

attract the *Yanquis*. They would not be stopped by this defense. They'd use artillery, aircraft, bombs. Your village would
be utterly devastated. If I am not here, the *Yanquis* have no
reason to attack."

The men stared silently at the map. The plan looked like it
would work, but the effort to put it in place was daunting.
Twenty-four-hour guard duty, trenching, sandbagging, building weapons and booby traps, all while trying to bring in the
rice harvest. Justos nodded. "It will work, *chicos*. We have no
choice." He looked at Solo. "I wonder, Solo, could you build
a defense against even the *Yanquis*?"

"Of course," said Solo. "But that would take more time than
we have."

Justos assigned the people to teams which split their days
working on the defenses and in the fields. The rice in the
paddies had to be harvested or it would be lost. From the shade
of the palm trees the Sandinista soldiers, under vague orders
to guard the town, watched the villagers toiling to dig a trench.

The packed volcanic soil in the village of Las Cruzas was
hard enough for the children to tamp down, making a smooth
place to play *trompo*, a game in which they threw tops, attempting to knock their competitor's toys out of the playing
circle. The wooden tops were tipped with sharpened nails
which spun without sinking into the earth. Digging this soil
was like trying to break pavement.

"You are soldiers now, eh?" laughed one soldier who had
come to the trench.

Eusebio, struggling with a shovel, answered, "*Sí*, we do your
job."

"Oh you do, *chico*?" The soldier, Sergeant Lupos, walked
over to Eusebio. "You will find out what we do in a year or so,
niño. As Daniel says, all of us are soldiers in Nicaragua now.
This is *your* job, soldier."

"Hijo de puta!" Eusebio stabbed at the ground and pried a clod of earth loose. Lupos laughed. Eusebio flung the clump of red earth on a pile next to the excavation. Several women, including Dania and Agela, pounded the chunks with staves to break up the soil. They scooped the dirt into rice bags with tin cans. When the bags were filled and tied shut, men came and dragged them away, stacking them onto a low wall next to the trench.

"You *campesinos* look like you know what you're doing," said Lupos.

"We know what we're doing," said Eusebio. "You saw what happened to the *animales.*"

Lupos nodded. *"Sí."* He took off his cap and scratched his head. Sweat ran down his temples. *"Sí, niño,* that was a wonder. You are the talk of Nicaragua." Lupos smiled and winked at Agela. She glared back at him. "But why do you make such pretty women work like dogs, eh?" Agela dropped her eyes and smashed a clod to pieces.

Eusebio grabbed a pick and swung it into the earth, breaking off pieces for his shovel. Lupos stepped across the trench and stood by Agela. "Here," he said, kneeling beside her, "let me help you."

"I don't need your help," said Agela. "If you want to help, get into the trench and do men's work."

"But look at those poor hands," said Lupos. "So young and pretty. Ruining your beauty with this work." Lupos grabbed Agela's hand and twisted it palm up. "See?" Agela twisted her wrist in his grip, struggling to get free. "If you come with me," said Lupos, "I will show you something to do with these hands that won't make calluses."

"Let go," said Agela. The sound broke in her throat, revealing her fear.

Lupos stood up, pulling Agela with him. "Come, *señorita—*"

"Let her go!" Eusebio yelled, leaping out of the trench.

"*A la mierda.* Go to hell," growled Lupos. "Get back to work, *niño.* This is not your affair."

"She is my sister, you pig!"

Lupos stared in disbelief. "You talk very tough for a child." Lupos pulled Agela again. "No!" yelled Agela. She kicked Lupos in the groin, making him howl with pain. She had not kicked hard enough. Lupos flung her to the ground and raised his hand to hit her.

"Stop!" yelled Eusebio.

Lupos heard the click-clack of chambering rounds. He looked up and saw four rifles pointed directly at his head. He stepped back carefully, smiling nervously. The rifles followed.

"I meant no harm, you hicks, can't you see?" said Lupos. "Put those guns down now, and I will forget this. You will be in very, very big trouble if you don't."

"Go back to your men," said Eusebio. "If any of you bother our women again we will kill you. When you act like that, you're no better than the Contras. Go."

Lupos stopped a few paces away, turned and saw that they had lowered their guns. He glared at Eusebio. "You are dead meat, *niño.*" He whirled an about-face and stomped away.

Eusebio went to Agela and hugged her. "I am sorry about men," he said.

30

WARREN sat on the balcony of his room at the Lago Vista sipping a rum and Coke with Silva. Two fishermen dipped huge butterfly nets into the golden lake and raised them in the low afternoon sun. Silvery fish sparkled as they fluttered down the net and into the boat.

"What do they catch here?" asked Warren. The rum and the fact that he had found Solo had put him in a comfortable mood.

"*Guapote* and *sábalo* mostly," said Silva. "Very tasty. You haven't tried them yet?"

"Not crazy about fish," said Warren. "Used to catch them for the fun of it though. That's a great net they have."

"Yes." Silva took a cigarette from his shirt pocket and lit it. "Where did you fish, Hank?"

"Maine. My family used to spend the summers in Portland. We had a place on the ocean."

"Your family must be wealthy."

"My father was in the Foreign Service. Not wealthy, but not poor."

"Ah," said Silva. "You have followed your father's profession, nearly."

"Nearly." The two men remained silent. The fishermen folded their nets. "Finished for the day," said Warren.

"Yes. They work hard."

"I know," said Warren. "Sometimes I wish I did work like that. This business keeps my stomach tied in knots."

"How did you get in this business, Hank?" The fishermen stowed the nets alongside the boat.

"Psychological warfare in Vietnam." Warren smiled suddenly. "You know what I did in that wonderful war, Silva? I dropped plastic monkeys on villages."

Silva turned to him. "What?"

"That's right. Those were my orders. Some general gave me the job. I bought little plastic monkeys from a toy manufacturer by the ton."

"By the ton?" Silva laughed.

"That's right. Tons of 'em. We put them on planes and dropped them on villages all over North Vietnam."

Silva shook his head.

"The idea—this comes from a borderline moron, Silva—was that the people would be demoralized. They consider monkeys bad luck, see."

"Did it work?" asked Silva.

"Fuck, no. We found out that the kids loved them. Great toys."

The two men laughed.

"That's the government for you," said Silva. "The same everywhere. We put our most incompetent in the most important jobs."

"That's the damn truth," Warren said quietly. "And they haven't changed."

"This job you're on now, the same?"

"Almost," said Warren. "Somebody fucked up and I've got to bail 'em out. And it ain't gonna be easy."

Silva noticed Warren slip back into his usual dourness. "Your quest—for the none of my business?"

"Yeah." Warren sipped his drink. "But that's almost over. We know where he is."

"Ah . . . he. He is in Las Cruzas?"

"That's right."

"So now you have to get him, eh? Of course he doesn't want to come."

"No, he doesn't want to come. But he will."

"It's always difficult when one of your own goes to the other side."

Warren looked at Silva. "You must know how that feels."

"Yes." Silva smiled briefly. "It doesn't feel good. I'll be glad when the Sandinistas are gone. I want to give up this life, too, Hank. I want to get back my family's farm and grow coffee, raise kids. You know."

"They took your farm?"

"Yes. And my father had supported them. Can you believe that? He gave them money, helped them any way he could. He wanted to get rid of Somosa. He thought the Sandinista revolution would be a new beginning for Nicaragua. They took his aid and within a month of the Triumph they came and told him that they were taking our farm."

"Did they say why?"

"The people needed it more than he did."

"Grateful bastards."

"It was the pressure of all the promises the Sandinistas made to the *campesinos,*" said Silva. "Many of the upper class fled when the Sandinistas took over, but not enough. The government had to have more property to divide up. I know there was much disagreement among them about doing this, many of the original revolutionaries left the government over it. But in the end, they decided that some people, like my father, would have to make a sacrifice. For the good of the people. The same thing happened in your country."

"We've never—"

"In your revolution, Hank. When you drove the British Loyalists out, you took the property and businesses they left. There were many Loyalist families who lost all they had."

"I never thought of that," said Warren. "You're up on your American history, Silva. I guess there were a bunch of Loyalists as pissed-off as the Contras."

"For the good of the people," said Silva, laughing.

"Well," Warren said, "We'll get this place back. Have to."

"*Sí*, you have to. The canal, eh?"

"Yeah. Not many people know about that."

"*Everybody* here knows about that, Hank. Your country's been trying to take over Nicaragua since 1845. It's the best place to build a sea level canal. You only have to dig a few miles of actual canal, and use the lake for the rest. You even started building it two or three times."

"*Here* they know about it. But you can't go around telling Americans we're helping the Contras because they'll let us build a damn canal when they take over." Warren grinned at his own cynicism. "It's a big deal in Washington. We need a new canal bad. The Panama Canal is too small for most of our warships and the damn thing is dying anyway. The lake that feeds the locks is drying up. If we don't watch out the Sandinistas will build one themselves. A Communist-controlled strategic canal? Wonderful. But how do we sum it all up for the folks back home? *We're fighting Communism*, folks."

Silva shook his head and laughed.

Ruiz came up behind them. "The Sandinistas are pulling out of Las Cruzas in two days, Hank."

Warren nodded.

"I've got some more, Hank, but—" Ruiz glanced at Silva.

Silva stood up. "Excuse me, gentlemen. I want to meet that boat. See the catch." Silva walked to the door and turned. "Perhaps later, Hank?"

"Sure. Dinner?"

Silva nodded and left. Ruiz took the empty chair and turned it towards Warren. "They're fortifying the place, Hank."

Warren nodded grimly. "That's our boy."

"Think he's decided to make a stand?"

"I doubt it. He knows that wouldn't work. His friends would get killed. Probably he's just giving them some military advice for another Contra attack. It's what he's programmed to do."

"It's real good advice, Hank. They say it looks good."

"The Contras aren't supposed to take the village, Ruiz. They're just supposed to be a diversion."

Ruiz smiled. "Just put the pressure on, eh?"

"That's right. The *campesinos* can build all the defenses they want. We're after one thing, and we're coming in the back door."

Ruiz looked quietly at the lake for a moment. "A lot of things could go wrong, Hank. I—" Ruiz hesitated. "I'm an agent, Hank, not a Marine. We just go marching in there, an armed camp, we're liable to get our heads blown off. Remember all those bodies? I—"

"Solo did that against people who didn't know what they were fighting, Ruiz. These people are farmers. They don't know shit about fighting. The Contras will keep 'em busy while we get him. Our ace is Solo, Ruiz, and we're ready for him. When they see we got him, they'll let us go."

"Getting the clamps on that thing though, Hank—"

"Look, Ruiz. We have this worked out. The guy who built Solo has taught me how to turn the thing off. Get it?"

Ruiz looked at Warren. "Oh yeah? Same guy who let him get away?"

31

PADRE Juán Cerna bounced down the potholed lake road in his tan Toyota Land Cruiser, negotiating the obstacles expertly. He sang as he drove. Cerna was born in Masaya and everyone from Masaya sang. The town was famous for its songs, as famous as Nicaragua was for its poetry. The tune died in his throat when he saw the road patrol. He coasted to a stop beside the sergeant at the head of the trail of ten men.

"*Buenos,*" said Cerna. "A hot day, eh?"

"*Sí,* Padre," said the man.

"Looking for somebody in particular? Should I keep my eyes open?"

"No one in particular, Padre. Routine. The action is up north now."

"*Sí?*"

"*Claro.* The Contras are trying to take San Pedro del Norte. Some of us may go there tomorrow. It is a big attack this time. The Contras are trying to impress the *Yanqui* Congress."

"Ah." Cerna nodded sadly. "Well, they will not succeed, *Jefe.* God is on our side."

"That is good," said the man sullenly. "Perhaps He should go talk to the *Yanqui* Congress."

Cerna laughed, "Maybe He will, *Jefe.* Maybe he will." The man did not share his enthusiasm and Cerna added, "Do not despair, my son. God will protect us." The man nodded and glanced away. Cerna cleared his throat. "Well, *Jefe*, I must go. The people at Las Cruzas need me."

"Good," said the man. "They lost many in that battle, but it could have been worse. Perhaps God was helping *them* at least."

Cerna nodded, smiling. "*Claro*, you see He is not blind to our cause."

"Perhaps you are right."

Cerna put the Toyota in gear. "*Adiós, Sargento.*" The man waved as Cerna drove away.

The song did not return to Cerna. He contemplated the irony of the machine. Made by *Yanquis*, yet it fought against them and saved the village. Could God have put a soul into it?

He drove two more kilometers and turned into the village, parking near the ruined warehouse. Justos walked over to him as he got out.

"*Buenos días*, Padre," said Justos.

"*Buenos*, Justos. How goes it?"

"Well, Padre." Justos dusted off his pants. "We're clearing the debris. We will rebuild, if we can get the materials."

Cerna nodded. He saw a crowd of people with shovels and pickaxes far up the valley road. "What is it?"

Justos followed his gaze. "They are digging a trench. We will be ready next time."

"And there?" Cerna pointed to the side of the hill, where men stacked sandbags.

"A machine-gun bunker, Padre."

"You have suddenly learned much about war, Justos. The machine?"

Justos gulped. "What?"

"The machine." Cerna pointed to the old house. "You know, the robot that stays up there."

"Don't point," said Justos quickly. "The soldiers." Cerna dropped his arm.

"How did you know?" said Justos.

"I met it the day the newsmen were here, Justos. Don't worry, I have said nothing. On the contrary, I want to help it. It has done much for you, I understand."

Justos nodded. "It is how we survived, Padre."

"Then it must be a gift from God, Justos. I will do nothing to hinder it."

Justos smiled, "Thank you, Padre."

Cerna saw five soldiers digging with the villagers. "They are helping you too?"

"Today they are," said Justos. "Yesterday their sergeant tried to molest Agela."

"No!"

"*Sí.* By the time I confronted him, his own men had already chastised him. They ignore him and are helping us today." Justos wiped his hair away from his forehead.

"There are always some among the good that the Devil takes," said Cerna. "It is a test for the others, I believe."

Justos flicked the sweat from his hand and nodded. "The others are good men, *Jefes.*"

"*Gracias a Dios,*" said Cerna. "I am going to visit the wounded, Justos, *Adiós.*"

Hector Valdez held Cerna's hand and led him from house to house to see the wounded. In each, Cerna blessed the patients and said a prayer for them. As he did, he saw the strength of the Lord brighten their spirits. They seemed to glow with new vigor. For Cerna and for the families, it was confirmation of God's power.

Modesta Chacon was sweeping her porch. Her head was bandaged. "You are up already?" Cerna called out. "You should be in bed, Modesta."

"While everyone works so hard?" said Modesta. She was pale, overcoming her pain. "I can't lay about like a *Doña.* I have work to do."

"Well," said Cerna. "At least rest a moment and talk to me." Cerna motioned to the bench.

"If you must," said Modesta. "But I don't have all day."

Cerna smiled at her bravado. "Come, Señora. Humor a priest, will you? I have the Lord's work to perform."

"Sit, then. I will get us *pinolillo.*"

"No need, Modesta. Please sit down before you faint."

"Bah!" said Modesta. "It is you who need to be refreshed. You look like you will drop. The climb up here has fatigued your old legs."

Cerna laughed as Modesta went inside. There was truth to that, he thought. The *campesinos* were hard and he was soft. Modesta soon returned with two cups and handed one to Cerna. He stirred his with the spoon she'd left in the cup to dissolve the corn flour and cocoa mix. Modesta had used milk instead of water, a rare treat. They sat silently together on the bench, each stirring their drinks rapidly as is the Nicaraguan custom. Cerna sipped from his cup. "Ah. Delicious, Modesta. I feel my strength returning."

Modesta nodded, but Cerna saw tears running down her cheeks.

"What is it, Modesta?"

"Nothing. I have something in my eyes. All this damn dust." She put down her cup and wiped her face with a rag she kept tucked in her apronstring.

"Did they molest you too?" Cerna said gently.

Modesta put her face in both hands and began sobbing. "My poor baby," she cried. Cerna patted her back while she cried. She sat up suddenly. *"Animales,"* she said. "Brutes. And God lets them do this—"

"They will pay, Modesta. God will see to that."

"They have already paid, Padre." Modesta sniffed and forced a smile that frightened Cerna. "Eusebio and Justos paid them back. They are dead. And I am glad, Padre. I am *happy* that they died. Do you hear? I only wish they could have suffered more."

Cerna nodded uncomfortably as she spoke. "Then God allowed that too, Modesta. He keeps a balance, you see—"

"And we are the pieces He balances, His toys to play with and send to rape and kill and be killed in turn. He *creates* pain and sorrow."

Cerna sipped his *pinolillo,* wondering how to respond. "It's true, Modesta, he does. He creates pain and sorrow. Were it not for the bad and ugly, would we know good and beauty? It is a trial for us, Modesta, but the rewards are great for those who remain faithful in the face of despair. Angela will be well again. And when she meets a gentle man, he will seem all the more good to her. You will see."

Modesta sat up, straightening her body resolutely. Tears rolled down her cheeks which she dabbed away continuously with her rag. "You are right, Padre. Forgive me," she sniffed. "It is difficult to remember that God cares, sometimes."

"Of course, Modesta. Who would not have doubts after such a terrible ordeal?" Cerna smiled. "And yet you have faith. You and Agela and Eusebio have come through the trial, your faith undiminished, Modesta. God will not forget."

Modesta crossed herself, smiled at Cerna, and collected his empty cup. "Thank you Padre," she said, "but go. Go see to the others. I am well and I have much to do."

Cerna laughed and stood up. "Bless you, Modesta." He stepped off the porch. "*Adiós,* Modesta."

Solo watched Cerna hiking the hill. The Padre's body temperature was elevated, his pulse raced, he breathed heavily. Still, thought Solo, it is very efficient: one of matter's own solutions to locomotion. Cerna approached the overgrown porch and stopped at the steps. Solo watched Cerna tilt his head, inspecting the shadows.

"Ah," said Cerna when he saw Solo in the chair. "There you are." He walked to the robot and pulled another chair next to it. "You are difficult to see," said Cerna as he sat.

"Yes," said Solo as he monitored a radio transmission. *"Drop point zero. Drop point zero. Gipper. Come in."* The

transmission was from a distant KL-43 radio, encoded, but easy
to decipher.

Cerna nodded, waiting for Solo to continue, but he did
not. *"Entonces,"* said Cerna, "I see you have put the village
to work. I don't know much about these things, but it looks
very professional. They will be able to stop the Contras next
time?"

"If they follow the procedures I have described," said Solo,
"the Contras will be stopped." As Solo spoke, he heard,
"Roger, Gipper. Drop point zero. Go ahead." The reply was
from the south, nearby.

"Good," said Cerna. "You are a good-natured device, however contradictory that may sound."

"Contradictory?" said Solo.

"Nature, device—they are incompatible, you see."

"I see," said Solo. "I see that you are straining at the limits
of your intelligence." The radio transmission buzzed in his
head, *"Drop point zero. Stand by for payday. Stand by for
payday. Drop at 1345 hours. Over."*

Cerna laughed loudly, pleased at the repartee.

"Roger, Gipper. Drop point zero secure. Out."

"You enjoy insults?" said Solo to Cerna. The radio message
meant that the CIA was preparing to make a money drop to
pay the Contras.

"No, it isn't an insult. I feel that I am straining most of the
time. There are many mysteries in life that I cannot fathom.
But, forgive me. I laughed because I am surprised at your
facility. One does not expect machines to be so glib."

"What does one expect?" said Solo. "Great clanking hulks
that buzz 'Warning, warning' and lurch when they walk?"

"Actually, yes. It is what one sees on television. You are a
mystery to me, Solo. I have thought about you often since we
met. What you seem to be is not possible, in my meager mind.
My training decrees that a soul can only exist in man."

"Your training is wrong, then."

"Possibly. Or is it possible that even you are taken in by the illusion?"

"If that were the case," said Solo, "I would have to have a 'me' to be so taken."

"Good!" Cerna shook his head. "Excellent. But maybe I asked the wrong question? Maybe I should ask: Could you be responding to me with this illusion of persona, as an automaton, and still not be aware of self or soul or emotions?"

Solo turned towards Cerna. "When I was learning how to walk and see, and had to negotiate a padded maze, I fell often. My builders had designed a feedback mechanism that created what you call pain whenever I fell. I did not understand what it was to walk. I could not see what was making me fall, and I became frustrated, fearful that my next move would hurt me. These words describe unpleasant sensations within me. Perhaps they describe the same things you might feel in a similar circumstance."

"Perhaps. But, again, could it not be just your undoubtedly vast vocabulary reaching for words appropriate for humans to hear?"

"I once watched a small robot that Bill made—"

"Bill?"

"He is the man who designed me," said Solo. "This little machine had a very tiny computer in it. Bill programmed it to wander around the laboratory for his amusement. The machine—Dumbot, Bill called it—had crude sensors that told it when it hit a wall, when it approached a drop-off, and where its recharging outlet was. That was all."

"Very dumb," said Cerna.

"Not even that smart," said Silo. "But I watched Dumbot one day when it approached a stairwell. When its sensors detected the edge, it stopped immediately. It waited a moment—its processors are very slow—and then backed carefully away."

"A programmed, automatic reaction," said Cerna.

"Yes, but humans have such programs. They call them instincts. When a human or an animal, even an insect, encounters the same situation, stops at the precipice, it is not difficult to assign the term 'fear' to what it must be feeling at that moment."

"Of course not. It's an instinct, as you say."

"Then why do humans have such a hard time thinking that little dumb machine did not feel fear?"

"Because it is not alive, Solo. It's just a collection of dead parts that behave according to their construction. It has no feelings."

"Humans are constructed of what they call inanimate things, yet they have much to say about being alive." Solo heard a message beamed from a satellite: *"XCMD·OD48 616E 6B2E 2020 436F . . . TERM."* It meant nothing to him; this code was unfamiliar.

"What *things?*" asked Cerna.

"Atoms, electrons. You claim these are dead, do you not?"

"They are not alive. But certain arrangements of these things allow the spirit of life to enter, Solo."

"And thus," Solo moved his hand to his chest, "am I."

Cerna laughed. "A convincing argument, Solo. But the difference is that God made us, and man made you. God is the only One who can create life from the non-living."

"To me," said Solo, "there is no distinction. Everything is alive. Look around you. You are surrounded by rocks and wood and living things, all of which are composed of swarms of moving, living, electrons. The universe is alive. What you call God is It. And so am I." The message repeated: *"XCMD:OD48 616E 6B2E 2020 436F . . . TERM."* The first word meant external command, a term used by Control for a message relayed from high authority. The rest was meaningless. Something was happening. Something they didn't want him to know about.

Cerna pinched his chin in thought. He smiled. "You have given me much to ponder, Solo. Were I not actually talking to you, the concept would be nonsense." Cerna crossed himself as a precaution, and said, "Perhaps it could be said that God made man and through him, you."

"Yes," said Solo. "That is how I see it."

Solo stood up suddenly and walked to the edge of the porch. Cerna watched the floorboards sag, wondering if Solo would fall through. "A truck comes," said Solo.

Cerna joined him. "Yes. An army truck."

They watched as the truck drove up to the trench. A soldier jumped out of the cab and ran to the Sandinistas. The men gathered around the soldier and one of them pointed to the village. "They are looking for their sergeant," said Solo. "They are leaving."

"Leaving?" said Cerna. "But the people haven't finished building their defenses yet, have they?"

"Nearly. Enough," said Solo. He turned towards Cerna. "They will be coming for me soon."

"They? Your builders? How do you know?"

"My builders, yes. I can hear them."

Cerna watched Solo turn and stare out across the lake. The robot had access to a whole world that was completely invisible to Cerna. What did he hear on his radios? What was the robot thinking? "Are you afraid?"

"Yes," said Solo. Cerna was amazed. But before he could comment, Solo asked, "Have you ever seen the *Apoyeque?*"

"The what?"

"The *Apoyeque*. The giant lake serpent."

"Oh," said Cerna. "I have heard about it. It's a superstition, a mythical beast, you know."

"Superstition?"

"Yes, you know: a myth, fantasy, false belief."

"I understand superstition. There are many examples in language. They are used to advantage in war," said Solo recalling the information given him by his makers on the history of the Vietnam conflict. "The Vietnamese lost their war against the United States partly because their superstitious fear of plastic monkeys caused them lose their confidence and the will to fight."

Cerna began laughing. "I've never heard it that way before."

"It's the truth," said Solo. "Superstitions can be a powerful influence among humans. But when Eusebio told me about the *Apoyeque,* he was telling the truth."

Cerna shook his head. "Well, Solo, Eusebio may believe he saw the *Apoyeque,* but none exist. It's an old Indian myth, you see. But about the Vietnamese—"

Solo turned abruptly and returned to his chair. He let his head lean against the wall. "Eusebio had a hallucination?"

Cerna leaned against the railing, looking worried. "Something like that, I suppose."

"The Indians saw these, then?"

"They are old myths Solo, from their barbaric religion, no doubt."

Solo turned towards the padre. "But you do not know that."

"I have faith that it is true. Only the ancient people know what they saw, and they are long vanished."

"I have information that they still exist. Matagalpans, Monimbo, Rama, Sumo—"

"Oh, *they* exist, yes. But they are the remnants of a once-great civilization—by ancient standards. Probably they were barbarous like the Aztecs, killing people as sacrifices, practicing cannibalism, but no one knows—"

"In a lake this large," said Solo, "could not an *Apoyeque* hide? They only come to the surface at the full moon." *"XCMD:OD41 7474 686F 7269 7A65 6420 7467 2070 726F . . ."* The string of code continued in his head. What are they up to?

Cerna smiled. "You wish to believe this very much."

"Eusebio told the truth," said Solo. "I can detect lying."

"Oh, you can?" Cerna brightened. "Then tell me if I now lie: The Vietnamese *won* their war with the United States."

Solo watched Cerna carefully, monitering his fields, heart rate, breathing. "It is something you believe to be true," said Solo. "Though you are wrong."

Cerna shook his head. "It is the truth, Solo. Everyone knows this."

"Or is it a falsehood you believe, as you claim is the case with Eusebio and the *Apoyeque*. I have learned the history of Vietnam from men who know, who were there. The North Vietnamese did not win." Solo heard the message end, "*. . . 7320 4372 757A 6173 2320 2050 6963 6B75 7020 TERM.*" *TERM* again. Terminate?

Cerna nodded and said nothing. He walked to his chair and sat next to Solo. "In these cases, one must investigate. You must check your facts, Solo. When you do, you will find that I am correct."

Solo nodded, distracted. He replayed the transmission to himself and began the job of deciphering the code. "I will investigate the facts," said Solo. "But first I must learn how to get to them."

32

WHEN the padre went back to the village at dusk, Solo went with him. The soldiers were gone. Solo was free to roam the village again. At Modesta's, Cerna left, explaining that he was spending the night with Justos to avoid a dangerous, dark drive along the lonely river road.

Solo stepped onto Modesta's porch and stood at the door. Modesta, Agela and Eusebio were eating by the light of a kerosene lantern. Seeing him, Modesta dropped her cup of *pinilillo,* jumped up and ran to Solo, wrapping her arms around his waist. She cried. Solo looked down at Modesta's head and held his hands up and away from her back, not knowing what to do. Modesta sobbed, *"Gracias,* Solo. *Gracias."* Agela joined her mother. The two women held Solo tightly, both crying. Eusebio sat nodding, blinking to avoid tears. Solo put his arms around Modesta and Agela. His hands, much to his surprise, began patting their backs.

The full moon perched on the eastern mountains. A path of flickering golden light led across the lake, to the shadows of the mountains. Eusebio and Solo sat together on the dock, looking along the trail of light.

"I saw it when the moon was higher," said Eusebio.

"How far away was it when you saw it?" said Solo.

"Very close, Solo. The *Apoyeque* first broke the surface—his giant fin came up like a sail—only three-hundred meters away."

"You are sure?"

"Well, it is an estimate, and I was very young. You will know the distance exactly when you see it."

"Yes."

They stared silently while the moon rose. Eusebio looked for the man in the moon whom everyone else claimed to see. It had yet to become apparent to him.

Solo listened to radio broadcasts. He heard the code again. There is no reason to hide any longer, thought Solo. He uplinked to NEOS and through it, to the Control computer. He got the new code, but the transmission he wanted to decipher stopped immediately.

Eusebio could see what could be eyes near the top of the moon, but they were distorted and would fit no face he could imagine. Perhaps it's a profile I'm looking for, he thought. But where's the nose?

"Solo?" said Bill Stewart on the Solo channel.

"Yes. How have you been, Bill?"

"How have I been?" Bill laughed. "How have *I* been? Solo, do you have any idea what a mess you've made?"

"I can guess."

Eusebio turned to Solo and touched the robot's arm. "Solo, can you see the man in the moon?"

"He is gone," said Solo. "They have not landed on the moon for fifteen years."

"Solo," said Bill, "You have got to come back voluntarily. They have a plan that can destroy that village."

"Not those men," said Eusebio. "I mean the image you are supposed to see in the moon, a figure of a face."

Solo said simultaneously, "That is why I cannot leave, Bill. Not until I know the village is safe," and "I have never tried, Eusebio. I will look."

"That's precisely the point, Solo." Bill's voice was filled with great urgency, thought Solo. "They intend to use your friends as—" The transmission stopped suddenly. Clyde, thought Solo. He would not want Bill to reveal the plan. Understandable.

"I see it!" said Eusebio.

Solo looked down at his friend. "Yes?"

Eusebio pointed at the moon. "Yes. Look along my arm, Solo."

Solo tilted his head so that he could see where Eusebio pointed. "It's a profile, Solo. That is the nose." Eusebio moved his arm. "And that is the eye. See? It's a picture of an old man."

Solo stared for a while, finally visualizing the image. "Yes. I see it too. An ugly old man." Eusebio laughed.

"Solo?" said Clyde. His voice was stern but shaking.

"Hello, Clyde. How have you been?"

"Forget that!" yelled Clyde. "Come back. Now! We don't want to hurt anyone, but we will, Solo. Believe me."

"I believe you," said Solo.

"Is that Mars?" said Eusebio, pointing. Solo looked. He heard the code, repeated three times. His abort system, now impotent, responded as a man with no hands grasps. "Yes," said Solo. "And that bright one near it is Jupiter."

"Ah, *that's* Jupiter. I didn't know where it was. It's always next to Mars?" asked Eusebio.

"Solo?" said Clyde cautiously.

"Yes?"

"Damn you!" yelled Clyde.

"It is not polite to try to turn people off," broadcast Solo. "Especially when they are contemplating the universe with a friend. I don't feel that I can trust you any longer, Clyde."

"Solo?" said Eusebio.

"No, Eusebio. Jupiter is there now, but it moves slower in its orbit than Mars, so they will separate. You can watch that happen. Eventually, in about two years and three months, they will meet again."

"Have it your own way one more time, Solo," said Clyde. "We *will* get you back. In pieces, if we have to."

"That will be interesting to watch, Clyde. Good night." Solo switched off the channel and pointed into the sky. "See that, Eusebio? That is a satellite. See?"

Eusebio stared and saw a blinking light overhead, moving fast from north to south. "Oh. That's what they are. Why do they blink?"

"It tumbles in space, Eusebio. The sun reflects off it only when it is at the proper angle."

Something broke the surface in the moon's watery reflection.

"There!" said Eusebio, pointing. "The *Apoyeque!*"

Solo zoomed in to the spot and saw the fin of a very large fish. A *tiburón*—the lake shark. "That is what you saw before?"

The fin sank back into the water. "Yes, Solo. That's him. Only last time he came higher out of the water. You could see his scales, as big as a man's hand." Eusebio waited, watching the ripples. After straining his eyes and holding his breath, he said, "*Mierda.* It stays under. But you saw how big it was, Solo."

"Yes," said Solo. "It was very big."

"Huge!" said Eusebio.

"A monster," Solo agreed.

Eusebio fell back on the dock laughing.

"What is funny?" said Solo.

Still choking with laughter, Eusebio sat up and slapped the robot on the back. "I *got* you, Solo!"

Solo stared at Eusebio for a moment. "Then there is no *Apoyeque?*"

"Of course there is, Solo. But that was a *tiburón.* Got you!" Eusebio laughed again, louder than before, smacking Solo's back and slapping his own knee.

. Solo stared at the lake, watching the swirling water where
the shark had been. The eddying currents were spiral chains
of golden beads. A sound began to come from Solo, laughter
now, not the braying of a mad donkey.

33

THE lead military technician, a Master Sergeant named Street, sat in Bill's place at the Solo console.

Clyde stood by with a microphone at his mouth. "Have it your own way one more time, Solo," said Clyde. "We *will* get you back. In pieces, if we have to."

Sitting at the back of the room, guarded by a PFC for trying to warn Solo that the Chacons would be taken hostage, Bill heard Solo answer, "That will be interesting to watch, Clyde. Good night."

"Solo?" Clyde yelled into the mike. "Solo! Goddamn it! Answer me!"

Bill smiled.

"Get him back," Clyde ordered.

"Can't make him transmit, sir," said Street. Bill saw the status lights on the mainframe blinking, signaling heavy activity. Street activated the mainframe's display screen. Line after line of computer code cascaded through the monitor. "He's after the codes!" Street yelled.

"Get him out of there!" Clyde ordered.

Street typed in a cancel command to the mainframe and it abruptly cut the contact. "He's out," said Street.

"What'd he get?"

"Can't tell," Street turned to Clyde. "He had access, but I

don't think he had time to download the information. Maybe. I've blocked access from the satellite—"

The mainframe lights flashed. Its monitor flickered with programming code. "He's back!" Street typed a new command and the monitor stopped. The last line on the monitor read, "Thanks. And have a nice day."

"I think he got what he wanted that time," Street said.

Clyde slammed the desk with his fist. He turned to Bill. "How do we stop him?" Clyde said.

Bill shrugged.

Clyde turned to Street. "Install a new code, Street."

"Can't, sir. He just got the encoding algorithm. If we write a new one, Solo couldn't read it, but neither could our operatives. Not until they've reprogrammed their decoders."

Clyde's shoulders sagged. He nodded and walked to Bill. He pulled up a chair, spun it around and straddled it, his chin resting on his folded arms. He stared at the Solo console. He turned to Bill. "He's not supposed to be able to do this *either*, Bill."

Bill said nothing.

"Oh stop *pouting!*" Clyde sat up suddenly. "What'd you expect me to do? Let you ruin the mission?"

"He's always been able to get into the network, Clyde. He just didn't know how. You better pray he doesn't learn what else he can do."

Clyde looked worried. "You mean that stuff you told Wright and DeValle?"

"That's right, Clyde. Given a little more time, I believe Solo could call in an artillery strike, our own; authorize a bombing attack with our own bombers—using all the right codes and voice passwords." Bill leaned closer to Clyde and said softly, "He could even learn how to launch an ICBM, Clyde. Anybody's."

Clyde's face paled. "How long? How long will it take him to learn that?"

"I don't know. My professor at MIT, Dr. Minsky, used to tell us that a robot like Solo would be as smart as an average person in a few months, as smart as a genius in another month. 'Eventually,' Minsky told us, 'We can hope they'll decide to keep us as pets.' "

"Pets?"

"Right. This exposure to ordinary people is changing him. He's adopting their values—learning things he'd have never learned otherwise. I think he's up to the genius level already."

"Sir," said Street. "JPL wants to know why we need a new channel."

"Well," growled Clyde. "Tell them."

"Sir, I didn't ask for one."

"Who did then?" Clyde jumped up.

"They say you did, sir."

"It's Solo! Tell them I changed my mind!" Clyde turned to Bill. "If this thing is getting ready to to launch missiles or something—this is getting dangerous, Bill. Do something."

"You'll have to let me back at the console," Bill said.

"You gonna stop him? No tricks?"

"No tricks. I want Solo back, too."

"Do it!"

Street gave up his station gratefully. Bill sat down and typed in a code, reread it, and entered it into the mainframe. Lights flickered as the transmission beamed up to NEOS. Bill waited.

"What'd you send?" said Clyde.

"A request to JPL," Bill said. "I want NEOS to send a jamming signal to Solo."

"Good going, Bill!" Clyde's face filled with a smile.

Bill read a message appearing on the screen, a message being sent by Control's mainframe to JPL: "Transmission error. Disregard request."

"More like a nice try," said Bill.

Clyde's mouth dropped. "Goddamnit—" he hollered.

"Shut up, Clyde!" Clyde immediately stopped, taken aback.

"Solo's in the system," Bill said. "I'll never be able to force him out." Bill turned to Street. "Shut down the mainframe." Street looked at Clyde.

"Do it," Clyde snapped. "Do whatever he says." Clyde sat down and watched Street turn off the computer. When the main panel lights were dead, Clyde said, "Now what? How do we talk to JPL or get on MILnet? Or brief Warren?"

"Line-of-sight transmissions from an AWACS plane," said Bill calmly. "Solo can't monitor that. You have to intercept a focused signal. He'd have to move to do that."

"Thank God," sighed Clyde.

When Bill called the AWACS to establish contact, he heard a loud squealing howl in return. He nodded. "Solo's using NEOS to jam us. The same code I was trying to send."

"And?" Clyde's eyes bugged out. The veins at his temples stood out like ridges.

"Phone," said Bill.

"Our phones use the satellite—"

"Land line. It's the only way."

Land line phone? thought Clyde. We don't have one. "You mean we have to drive to Cuajiniquil and make a fucking phone call? That's it? That's what all this shit—" Clyde sputtered, his arm waved around the room. "That's what our best equipment does in a pinch? We have to phone our people? From a goddamn beaner pay phone?"

Bill got out his wallet and picked out a piece of plastic. "Here," he said, handing it to Clyde. "Use my credit card."

Warren fished a cigarette from the shirt on the floor while he held the phone cocked between his neck and shoulder.

"What's all that noise?" said Warren.

"It's a goddamn band, Hank," Clyde raved over a Latin tune. "I told you I'm at a damn beaner juke joint. Now listen. We don't have much time."

Warren nodded and lit the cigarette.

"I've talked to the home office," said Clyde. "They're gonna reroute our messages through a different channel. He can't jam the new channel 'cause he doesn't know the codes. You understand?"

Warren shook his head. "Yeah. I understand." I understand you guys could fuck up a wet dream.

"Basically," said Clyde, "we go with the original plan. The difference is that our—" Clyde paused to phrase his message in business jargon. "Our customers are going to have our best sales closers hanging around. You know, to make *sure* we make the sale."

Bombers, American bombers. "I understand."

"The other thing is that our boy is becoming a tough nut to crack. He won't hang around our customers so our closers can't get to him. He's highly sales resistant. You got to force an appointment, right? Make the pitch. If that doesn't sell him, drop back and call in the closers. You got that?"

"Got it."

"Okay. This last bit—" Warren heard Clyde's muffled voice yelling, "Keep it down willya? I'm trying to talk!" Laughter and cheers in the background, then Clyde again. "These fucking people have no respect for privacy. Yappata la goddamn yippata. I'll be so fucking happy when we get out of here."

"You were saying—"

"The new channel. We don't want our competition knowing the game plan. The new channel is alpha, romeo, victory—"

"I couldn't get the last part," said Warren. "You were drowned out." Clyde didn't answer. Warren heard Clyde's muffled voice yelling again. Then abruptly, "I repeat," yelled Clyde, "Alpha, romeo, victory, yankee, echo, sierra. You copy?"

"I copy," said Warren.

"I could cry for fucking joy," yelled Clyde. The band

stopped. Warren heard some applause. "Okay. Let's get out there early tomorrow morning, right? Sell 'im, Hank. We really have to make this deal."

"Don't worry," said Warren. "I'll sell him."

Clyde hung up. Warren put the phone away and sat back against the headboard. He checked his watch. Two in the morning. Time is running out, thought Warren.

34

MOONLIGHT flickered on the swells. Past the zenith, stars twinkled weakly in the moon's glare. Eusebio had left for guard duty, but Solo remained sitting on the dock.

Control had beaten him. He had gotten the codes, but they shut down the computer and the satellite. How did they get the message to shut down the satellite past his jamming? Phone? How do you monitor a phone? Only by tapping the line; unless it's a microwave link. You have to physically intercept a microwave transmission. Neither option was available.

Solo noticed the lights of San Ramon twinkling at the base of the volcano Concepción. Solo magnified the lights but saw only fuzzy halos shimmering in the damp air. What did they do there? Justos said it was a big city. Thousands of people lived there. What did thousands of people do in one place? There were paved streets, Justos said, many cars and trucks, traffic. Traffic?

Something moved in the swirling glitter of the moon's reflection. A hundred yards offshore, the water swelled up in a mound 30 feet long. He sharpened the image, but nothing broke the surface. The mound flattened, leaving a ripple-ringed slick on the water. Perhaps, thought Solo, the *Apoyeque* knows that I am watching.

Solo tried signalling NEOS again, but it did not respond. He tried two other satellites, trying thousands of frequencies. None responded. It would take days to discover the codes through trial and error. The cacophony of a hundred simultaneous radio and television signals flooded his brain. He sifted out a radio broadcast from Managua and then a shortwave signal from a ham in Detroit. He listened for a second. Must learn the satellite codes. The water swirled at his feet and he bent over to see the cause. Nothing. He rubbed the dirt-filled bullet scrapes and nicks on his chest. Superficial damage. Solo put the powertube on his lap, leaned forward and tumbled into the lake.

The moon danced above him, rippling in the waves. Solo lay on his back in the silt, fifteen feet under water. Buoyancy reduced his weight to a hundred and twelve pounds, he calculated. Except for the undulating moon, darkness engulfed him. He amplified the light. No objects loomed in the vast greenness. The shadow of the dock and pilings danced with the moon. Plants waved around him. Wouldn't it be interesting, he thought, if the dock and the moon were actually moving that way? All noise was gone except tiny clickings and a soft bubbling sound. The radios were silent. Pleasant. The bubbles came from the mud beneath him, rounding his body, clinging and then rushing to the surface. The clicking? Perhaps shellfish feeding, he decided. The humming of his own internal power supply surprised him. He lay still in the dark and listened to his body working.

The water blocks radio frequencies. I could stay here and they could never find me. Solo felt happy. The feeling abruptly faded. If they could not find me, he reasoned, they would assume that I was hiding in the village. They would destroy it. They must *know* where I am.

Solo sat up in the murky water. He called: *"Apoyeque,"* with his voice. *"Apoyeque?"* A large shadow moved toward him. A shark. "Ah, *tiburón,"* said Solo. The twelve-foot shark circled away, came back and cruised by, closer to Solo. "You are a healthy *tiburón.* Plenty to eat here?"

The shark circled again then rushed straight towards Solo. Electric fields came from the shark and Solo recognized that the fish had decided to feed upon him. Perhaps it thinks my electric fields are animal? Solo bumped the shark's gaping maw aside with the powertube. "No, *tiburón*. I would be a poor meal for you." The shark shot away and hovered in the distance, watching.

Solo stood up and scrubbed his body with handfuls of water plants, washing away the grime of several weeks. The shark gathered its courage and swam by once more. Solo turned and walked beside the docks toward the shore like a moon man. His feet barely sank into the mire. When his head broke the surface, weight began to return. He stepped carefully among a group of alligators on the beach and walked up the road to the garage, glistening wet in the moonlight.

Solo packed the stuff he'd collected on his workbench: magnets from old speakers, assorted springs, small coils of wire, solder, a broken transistor radio, two Bic lighters Justos had given him and spare ammunition for an AK-47, into the U.S. Army combat pack he'd found. He looped one strap of the pack and the rifle over his right shoulder, picked up his powertube and left the garage.

He slipped through the village between patches of silver light that glimmered among the moon shadows. From Escopeta's, Solo could see someone sitting on Modesta's porch. Agela.

Solo stood next to Escopeta's porch and watched her. He wanted to go to her—he wasn't sure why—but Cheripa lay beside her on the porch. Cheripa would bark if he got any closer. No need to alarm the village.

He stared, zooming close enough to see her face clearly. She was looking towards the trenches where Eusebio stood guard duty. Her eyes shifted from place to place to focus on the night sounds.

She was handsome, Solo decided. The shape of her face was pleasing, but not pleasing in the sense that he appreciated a well-designed machine. Agela's face, the features on her face were . . . nicely arranged. And there was no functional need for that. Unless—of course—her face would be attractive to men. That is functional. But why was *he* attracted? Certainly that made no sense. He was neither male nor a man. Yet he found Agela attractive.

What of it? He had heard men speak lovingly of a burro's strength, the grace of horses, the beauty of some of the dogs. Women had often mentioned the beauty of other women. Yes, he thought, but do they find themselves sitting in the dark staring at these things?

Agela stared directly at Solo. She cannot see me, he assured himself. Her brow wrinkled in that curious way that meant she was puzzled, interested. How does she know I'm here?

Agela stood up and walked softly towards Solo. Cheripa woke, raised her head and watched Agela leave, but slumped back to sleep. When Agela finally saw the glint of Solo's eyes in the shadows, she smiled and said, "I thought I felt you watching me."

"You can sense when someone is looking at you?" said Solo.

"Of course," said Agela. "If it's someone special. And if they are staring especially hard."

"I was—looking," Solo's voice faltered, raising unfamiliar alarm signals within him.

"I'm glad," said Agela. She noticed Solo's pack. "I see you are leaving. You came to say good-bye?"

"I don't know why I came—exactly," said Solo. "It must have been—"

"To say good-bye to me?"

"—Yes." Solo stared at Agela. She smiled softly, yet tears trickled down her cheeks. He felt—feelings he had not felt for a long time—dizzy? Confused? How was Agela affecting him this way? Surely he was immune to biological attraction. He had no hormones to muddle his brain and divert him into reproductive missions.

"I will miss you, Solo," said Agela.

"And I will miss seeing you, too," said Solo. He put out his hand and spoke a phrase Bill had taught him: "It has been a pleasure knowing you, Agela."

Agela brushed his hand aside and hugged Solo.

"That's what it has been?" said Agela, her head against Solo's chest. "A pleasure knowing me?" She held herself away from Solo and stared into his eyes. "Well," she said, "*I'm* not afraid to say I love you, Solo." She smiled. "You are one of the finest—persons I've ever met. You are proof to me that the world is essentially good, and I love you."

"I—" Solo's voice cracked electronically. He could not speak. Instead, he reached for Agela with the same arms that could crush a cart and drew her to him, holding her against his chest. Affection, he decided. Affection was new for him; that was why it felt so powerful. He put his hands on her shoulders, then held her at arm's length and studied her face. Finally, he muttered, "Good-bye, Agela." Solo turned and walked away.

Solo's shadow stretched before him as he walked down to the trench. No mistaking him in the moonlight. Eusebio did not ask for the password. Solo slipped into the trench beside Eusebio. "*Buenas noches,* Eusebio. Where is Justos?"

Eusebio saw the pack. "You are leaving?"

"Yes." Solo turned and faced Eusebio. "They are coming tomorrow. Are you ready?"

Eusebio nodded. Solo noticed that his eyes were wet. "Could you not stay a little longer? We need you."

"No." Solo turned as though looking up the line. "I have to see Justos," he said. "Do you know where he is?"

"Listening post," said Eusebio.

Solo nodded. "Eusebio. I am going to find him and then I will leave. I will say good-bye to you now."

Eusebio nodded and lowered his head. Tears rolled down his cheeks.

"When I come back, Eusebio, we will build an airplane. Okay?"

Eusebio sniffed and smiled. "Okay."

"Okay." Solo reached out his hand. "It has been a pleasure knowing you, Eusebio."

Eusebio put his hand in Solo's warm grasp. "Yes? It has been a pleasure knowing you too, Solo." They shook hands. Solo stood up and stepped out of the trench. He said, "*Adiós,* Eusebio," and walked swiftly away.

By the time Eusebio could speak, Solo was out of sight. Eusebio called into the pale night, "*Adiós,* Solo."

Justos squatted in the pit dug for the listening post. He and Solo reviewed the defense plans for the hundredth time. Inginio stared into the jungle with the starlight scope. "Don't leave that on so long at a time, Inginio," said Solo, "A quick look every few minutes. You don't have many batteries."

"Okay, Solo," Inginio said.

"If we know they're coming tomorrow, Solo, why don't we call the soldiers?"

"You won't have advance warnings without me, Justos. You must test your defenses. You can call the army if you need them. You won't."

"I hope you're right," said Justos.

"I am. They are after me, Justos. When they get here, I will turn on my beacon and lead them away. Having the Sandinistas here will only complicate things."

"A bird luring the cat from the nest."

"Yes."

"Then what?" said Justos.

"I am learning to communicate better. They have networks of satellites and computers, but I don't know how to access them. They left me ignorant of the procedures and they shut down the only satellite they let me use. I'll study the problem. Electronics, computers, control everything they have, Justos. It's an area in which I have some expertise." Justos grinned as Solo continued, "When I come back, you won't have to worry about the *Yanquis.*" Solo stood up with his gear. "Nearly dawn, I must go." He put out his hand. Justos's hand grasped his. Inginio and Felix wished him well. Solo vaulted from the pit, saluted silently in the moonlight, and walked into the jungle.

35

"O KAY." Warren nodded. Ruiz crushed a cigarette out in an overflowing ashtray. A long night. Warren had drilled the plan over and over until Ruiz and Garcia knew it cold. "Problems?"

"Alonzo," said Ruiz. "What do we do with him?"

"Have you seen him?" said Warren.

"Not since last night."

"Simple. We leave without him. We're not coming back. What else?" Both men shrugged.

Garcia added, "There's a lot of room for mistakes, Hank. The machine is unpredictable as hell."

"We've covered every major eventuality," said Warren. "We'll see some surprises, sure. But that's why I picked you guys."

Garcia twirled his mustache into a smile and said to Ruiz, "The fucking Mean Team, eh?"

Warren saw Ruiz shrug and said, "What's the problem, Ruiz?"

"Nothing. I'm with you. We'll get him."

"But?"

Ruiz looked Warren in the eyes. "We've always hit *people*, Hank. When you first told us about Solo I thought we were dealing with some jerky contraption that went haywire. Hell, we just pull its plug. But that's not the way it is." Ruiz stared at Warren for a second. "Is it?"

"The machine's good," Warren nodded. "Better than anybody expected." Warren watched for Ruiz's reaction, but Ruiz just stared. "But," Warren continued, "it's only a machine. It has its limits. Like last night: It tried to jam our communications, and it did for a while. But we stopped that bullshit. The game is back on our terms again." Warren's smile, Ruiz noticed, was forced, nervous. "The thing is predictable. We *know,* no doubt, that it will come to help the Chacons. There it is."

"If it doesn't?" said Ruiz.

"No chance. He'll come."

"What if he comes back like he did for Palo? What do we do then?" Ruiz's voice was trembling.

Warren thought of putting Ruiz down hard. Garcia might lose it too. Be calm. Lead. "Okay," said Warren. He turned to Garcia. "Ruiz's right. We got to consider every possibility, however remote." Warren sipped the rest of his cold coffee. "Our orders are clear: If Solo attacks, we kill the hostages and blow him up with our heavy stuff. If the machine doesn't show up, we kill the hostages."

"In cold blood?" said Ruiz. "C'mon, Hank, we don't do that. I can kill people who fight back. But this? Kill some poor peasant woman and her kids? And what do we do after we kill 'em? They won't just let us walk out of there, Hank."

"If Solo doesn't show, we use the Chacons to get to the chopper. Then we kill them. But I'm telling you it won't come to that. The machine *will* show. The man who built it says it will. But Solo has to know we mean what we say—just in case there's a next time." Warren spoke quickly. Ruiz and Garcia looked worried. Hypocrites, thought Warren. "Hey, you guys have wasted plenty of women and kids before, in 'Nam, up the road. What's the difference?"

"This ain't no war, Hank," said Ruiz.

"That's where you're wrong, mister." Warren's anger burst through his calm facade. "This is a *Communist* country, damnit. The Russians are providing the Sandinistas with the means to keep out the rightful leaders, the Contras. Now we're in danger of losing one of our most advanced weapons to these people who would immediately give it to the Russians. It's a fucking war! You understand that? And this is a real-life, honest-to-God *mission* in that war. Like they say, Ruiz: Sometimes innocent people get hurt in war; it's regrettable but unavoidable."

Regrettable but unavoidable. Somehow the words were a relief to Ruiz. He nodded, shrugging. How could you argue with the truth?

Warren turned to Garcia. "I've got no problems, Hank," Garcia said.

Warren smiled. He checked his watch. "Okay. Good. Now let's get the show on the road. Twenty-four hours from now you guys'll be back in Miami getting some of that pussy you left behind. C'mon you assholes, let's go get Robbie."

Ruiz and Garcia grinned.

We have a *team* now, Warren thought.

Dawn glowed behind the mountains as the blue van pulled up to a Sandinista roadblock just outside the town. Ruiz, driving, slowed down. He turned to Warren, "Now what?"

"Be cool," muttered Warren. "Routine."

As the sergeant walked up to the driver's side, Alonzo ran up to the passenger side, grinning. "Shit," said Garcia. "The little fucker found us."

Warren had a sinking feeling. How was the mission going to go if they couldn't shake one dumb soldier? The sergeant talked to Ruiz, who translated. "He says Silva had to borrow Alonzo last night for guard duty, but here he is." Ruiz turned around. "Nice, eh?"

Why had Silva done this? "Great," said Warren. No way out. "Tell him thanks."

Garcia climbed in back with Warren as Alonzo jumped into the cab.

Ruiz put the van in gear and drove away. Alonzo turned around to Garcia and held out his palm. "Sheet, mothofooker. What eet es?"

Garcia laughed. "Where does he get this shit?"

"I don't care where he gets it, Garcia." Warren silenced him with a glare. He stretched out on the bunk. "Wake me when we're fifteen minutes out."

Alonzo hummed "Lo Siento Mi Amor" and beat the dashboard of the van. Garcia wondered if Alonzo could really be that happy. Is he bullshitting us? What the hell did he have that made life so fucking wonderful? Two years in a commie army, practically no pay, and then a future of dirt-level poverty on a communal farm, watching it get blown away every year? That's a future?

Ruiz slowed down to get around an ox cart hauling a mound of sugarcane. Garcia stared at the huge wooden wheels as they passed the cart. The wheels, obviously handmade, were painted brilliant blue and decorated with garish floral wreaths. Only beaners would decorate a piece of shit like that. He smiled. It struck him as ironic: They had nothing, really, but they loved what they had. If you didn't have a cart, you'd be humping that shit down the road on a burro. We, on the other hand, have wonderful high-tech machines like Solo that go around slaughtering us. And Solo isn't even decorated.

An hour later, at the checkpoint at El Tigre, Warren woke. After the soldiers checked their papers they drove away. Warren sat up behind Garcia and whispered, "Block the view while I get the gear." Garcia nodded and leaned closer to Alonzo. Warren lifted the control panel and propped it up. Beneath a maze of wires and circuit boards, he pushed a ballpoint pen into a hole and a panel clicked up. He looked up front. Garcia

yapped at Alonzo, keeping him occupied. Four aluminum camera cases fit perfectly in the padded space. Warren pulled out
the cases and put them on the floor. He closed the console. He
put each case on his lap and opened its lid. One portable KL-43
encoding radio. One M-79 grenade launcher, disassembled,
with two custom-made armor piercing rounds. One claymore-
type bomb held in a nylon web gear, with a remote detonator.
Two AK-47s and extra clips. Everything okay.

"Two klicks," said Ruiz.

Warren nodded. He opened the console cover again. He
flipped a row of nine toggle switches up or down in coded
order. A red light flashed three times and stopped. He toggled
another number in the next row. The red light flashed three
times and stayed on. The self-destruct system was armed. A
radio signal from the remote switch would turn the van into
dust.

Garcia turned around and leaned close to Warren. "What
we gonna do with Alonzo?"

"Let him stay with the van like last time," said Warren.

Garcia stared at Warren. "You gonna blow this bozo up?
He's 'bout as dangerous as my grandmother, Hank."

"He's a Sandinista soldier, Garcia. People get hurt, remember? War is like that."

Garcia continued staring but Warren held his ground.
Garcia said, "I remember this guy, Bob Warren, who went out
of his way to save a wounded Guatemalan, an enemy. Where'd
he go?"

Warren stared blankly at Garcia, lost in thought. He had
saved the Guatemalan. The rebel troop he'd led, a bunch of
scumbag mercenaries the Company had rounded up, had captured a wounded boy. They'd decided to kill him rather than
go through the hassle of taking him with them. Warren had
found himself defending the kid. When the men, his supposed
allies, ignored his orders, he'd pulled his gun on them. The kid
lived. But when Warren got back to Miami, he'd been put

through the wringer by his boss. Interference with rebel autonomy. "Rebel autonomy?" he'd said. "Those people are nothing but a bunch of thugs we hired." His boss proclaimed the Company's policy for these situations: "They may be thugs, Warren," said his boss, "but they're *our* thugs." The incident cost Warren a promotion.

"Where'd he go?" said Warren quietly. "Nowhere." Warren stared at Garcia. "Then he grew up."

Garcia shook his head and turned around. The docks at Las Cruzas and the wrecked warehouse swung past the windshield. The *campesinos* had cleared most of the rubble away and already had put some new roof beams in place. Like ants, thought Warren. Don't know when to quit.

"Where do you want me to park it, Hank?" Ruiz said.

"Pull up close to the warehouse."

The morning sun filtered through the trees, casting swirling patterns on Solo. He stood on a ridge a half mile away watching the van through a gap in the jungle cover. Justos walked toward the van from the village. He zoomed in to examine the faces of the men as they got out. He had seen these men before— during the public display of Contra dead. Newsmen. Good. As long as they are there the village is safe. He turned and walked deeper into the jungle.

Warren checked his watch as Justos approached. Eight-thirty. He had thirty minutes to get set up in the Chacon house. *"Buenos días,"* said Justos.

"Buenos," said Ruiz in front of the van.

"What can we do for you?" said Justos.

"We came back to shoot another story about your village," Ruiz said.

"You were here before?"

"Yes, right after the big attack," Ruiz said. "Our boss—" he pointed to Warren who was taking the camera cases from Garcia. "He wants to interview Modesta Chacon. Do you know her?"

Justos nodded, "Of course."

"On our last visit, she was too ill to speak. The boss heard that her son had been taken prisoner and wanted to interview her about it. Is she better?"

"Oh yes," said Justos, smiling. "Modesta is a strong woman."

"I'm glad to hear she is well," said Ruiz. "Will you tell her we wish to interview her and her family in their house? It will take us a moment to get our equipment together."

Justos said, "Of course. But I will have to send for her son, Eusebio. He's working in the fields."

As Justos turned, Warren yelled at Alonzo. Justos stopped. A *Yanqui* shouting at a Sandinista soldier? "No, Alonzo. Stay here and guard the van," Garcia translated.

"No," Alonzo said. "It is my *job* to stay with you."

Garcia translated. A menacing shadow fell across the American reporter's face. The man gave orders as though he were in the military, thought Justos. *Yanquis.* Alonzo picked up one of the cases. Warren yelled something, ready to strike the soldier. Justos stared and Warren caught himself. He smiled reluctantly and spoke through his translator. "Okay, Alonzo. Come. Thought you'd be more comfortable in the van." As Garcia repeated this to Alonzo, Warren smiled. Justos, being a *campesino*, smiled back and hurried up the trail to warn Modesta.

Eight-forty. Garcia led, carrying the camera. Ruiz followed with the recorder. Alonzo lugged two of the camera cases. A village girl walked past to the fields. Alonzo groaned and said to Ruiz, "Man, I have to see my wife soon. I'm falling in love with my right hand." Ruiz and Garcia laughed.

Oblivious to conversation, Warren carried the bomb and

triggering device. Sweat dripped from his armpits. The handles of the equipment cases slipped in his wet hands. Little things, he thought. It's always the little mistakes that fuck it up. He recalled the look on the *campesino's* face when he yelled at Alonzo. God! I can be a *dumb* fuck! He shook his head. As they neared the rock wall, the village came alive with noise. Dogs began barking, chickens squawked. Even the fucking monkeys have an opinion, thought Warren, as two *micos* screamed at them from a coconut tree. The dogs barked loudly, wagged their tails and kept a cowardly distance. Small children watched them, grinning shyly in dirty, torn shirts—Salvation Army leftovers—and no shoes. Their shy friendliness almost touched Warren. Kids in Vietnam had been friendly, too, even as they carried satchel charges into American camps.

Sweat stuck the shirt to his back, but Warren felt cool. Actually freezing. The kids and the mutts and the village itself became a background blur. He saw Modesta Chacon sweeping her porch and felt a pang of guilt. The faceless entity, the cog in the plan, had deep wrinkles in her face, yet he knew she wasn't more than thirty-five. Her hands were rough and calloused, her arms strong and brown. She looked up at the approaching men skeptically and gave the porch one final swat with her broom. As she turned to go inside, she fiddled with her hair, tucking in a loose strand. Warren swallowed, feeling panic well in him. Could he actually kill her if he had to?

Eight-fifty. Warren ducked through the doorway and into strange smells and filth. On a tattered calendar, Christ stood guard above three crude cots. A two-foot-wide cupboard stood out from the wall near the fireplace, partitioning the one room. A reddish brown pot resting on three stones simmered above an open charcoal fire. No chimney. The smoke drifted inside, as it had done for years. That's the smell, thought Warren, his nose flaring. When he shook hands with Modesta, he noticed that she too rccked of smoke. He wiped his hand on his pants.

Modesta saw Warren's gesture. A pang went through her.

She turned to her kitchen and began pouring *pinilillo* from a clay pot into cups.

"Tell her we don't have time for that," said Warren. Ruiz did. Modesta's chin went up at the slap. She stacked the cups and put them, clattering in her shaking hands, on a shelf.

"You insulted her, Hank." Ruiz looked offended and apologized for the *Yanqui.*

Warren said, "Where are her kids?"

Modesta nodded at Ruiz, even smiled a little. Ruiz seemed to have manners. Modesta walked out to the porch and called Agela in from the family garden. Agela came around the bamboo fence carrying a basket of fresh beans.

"Quickly, Agela," said Modesta. "Wash your hands. There are *Yanqui* television men here."

"Television men?" Agela's mouth dropped open. She put the beans on the porch and rushed to the cistern next to the house. She washed her hands and splashed water on her face. Modesta watched, smiling. Her daughter's vanity was returning.

Inside, the men stood awkwardly, crowding the tiny space. Modesta offered them chairs. Only the soldier, Alonzo, accepted. The others declined, standing instead against the walls. They looked very nervous, she thought. They are embarrassed. Surely the big blond man, the *Yanqui,* is not accustomed to *campesino* homes.

Eight fifty-five. Warren looked across the courtyard and saw a young boy running towards the house. The kid, what's his name? Ubio? That's everybody. He reached for the case with the radio and put it on the table. He glanced at Ruiz and Garcia. They nodded.

Eusebio leapt over the steps and into the house. Modesta pulled him to her, brushing red dirt from his shirt and straightening his bangs.

"Get the gear ready," said Warren. "Wait for the attack."

"What did he say?" asked Modesta of Ruiz.

"Nothing, Señora, just that we should start the interview."

"Ah," said Modesta putting her arms around Agela and Eusebio, "They want to know about your capture and your escape, Eusebio. You are famous."

Eusebio did not respond. The men seemed very nervous. They kept looking out the windows. Expecting something.

"*Entonces?* then?" said Modesta.

Nine.

Rifle shots rang out in the valley.

"Okay," said Warren. Garcia snapped open a case and pulled two AK-47s from inside. He tossed one to Ruiz. Warren opened the fake camera and took out his silenced forty-five.

"What are you doing?" yelled Eusebio. "You are Contras?"

"Separate them," said Warren.

Ruiz, holding his gun on Eusebio, said, "Relax *niño.* We are not Contras. We won't hurt you if you cooperate. Move back."

Modesta began sobbing when Garcia shoved her and Agela against the wall. She had seen pleasure in his eyes.

"*Dios!*" Alonzo leapt up from the table. "Spies!" Warren pointed the forty-five at him. He gestured with the gun, towards Eusebio. Alonzo glowed crimson, so enraged by the betrayal that tears poured from his eyes. "Sonabitch! Sonabitch!" Alonzo, forgetting that he wore a pistol, shrieked incoherently and charged Warren empty-handed.

The little man's rush startled Warren. Before Alonzo took two steps, he shot. Alonzo doubled over and fell back, knocking over a chair. He hugged his belly and screamed in agony.

"Shut up!" yelled Warren. Alonzo rolled his head from side to side, shrieking. He drowned out all other sounds. Warren fired again reflexively, hitting Alonzo in the throat. Squeals bubbled from his torn throat gurgling; Alonzo was drowning in his own blood.

The rifle fire in the valley grew louder. Modesta and Agela were screaming. Alonzo shrieked wetly. A buzzing sound filled Warren's head. Bile rose in his throat. The buzzing wavered into crescendos of overlapping waves as he walked to the squirming, bloody Alonzo and put the forty-five to his head. He fired. Alonzo's head bounced off the floor and fell back into gore, silent. Warren felt the buzzing fade and slumped with relief.

He sat at the table and opened the case. "Okay," he said softly. Looking up, he saw Modesta and Agela hugging each other, terrified. Garcia, rifle pointed at them, stared at Warren. Ruiz held his rifle in Eusebio's face. The boy glared at Warren with tangible contempt. Warren checked his watch. Nine-oh-five. Fifty-five minutes until the chopper arrived. He picked up the phone, punched in a code, and said, "Solo?"

36

Aᴅᴛᴇʀ the journalists unloaded their van, Solo turned and ran down the east side of the steep ridge, away from Las Cruzas. He found himself accelerating faster than he could run. Powertube in one hand, pack and rifle in the other, leaping fallen trees, dodging vines, hurdling the snaking roots, Solo felt something, something important, happening to him. Exhilaration? He would return to Las Cruzas one day, but for now, he was free.

Falling, he tucked himself into a ball and crashed into a palmetto thicket at the base of the ridge. His pack and powertube catapulted through the vegetation and landed near him. Solo sprawled on his back across the palmetto roots and contemplated his environment. He rolled over among the plants and dug his fingers into the soil. He pressed his face into the exposed earth. It was, he realized, great to be alive.

He sat up, his face covered with dirt. An ant walked across his eyecover, then another. He looked down and saw that he sat in the path of army ants that climbed his legs as though they were rocks. He watched as the horde attacked and killed a cicada, dismembered it in seconds, and carried the pieces along the march. Further along, he saw an *oropéndola* chick covered with ants, already dead. Every living thing in their path was food. *Organic* living things, he corrected himself.

Exhilaration dimmed. The sun flickered though wind blown leaves, dazzling his eyes. Melancholy intruded. Joy and sorrow are one physical process, a balance. Like the relationships achieved in electronic circuits. Decrease one value and another increases. The system has a tendency to average the values, aiming for a tolerable midpoint. I am sad *because* I have been happy. It is better to be neither. He pulled a handful of fuzz from a palmetto trunk and used it to clean his eyes. He stood up and retrieved his gear. Turning toward the faint sound of waves on the shore, he walked away.

Solo gathered driftwood and piled it on the beach. As he rummaged through his combat pack for a lighter, he heard the distant sound of small arms fire. Contras? The journalists must have left. The villagers will be okay, he thought. Justos knows what to do. He put the lighter away. Time to show Control where I am.

"Solo?"

A strange voice from a radio at Las Cruzas. He did not answer.

"I know you can hear me, Solo," said the voice. "Bill asked me to tell you that you have no choice. You must come out of hiding. We are at Modesta's, Solo."

No choice? Solo switched on his beacon and stood up. I will lead you to oblivion, he thought. He dove into the jungle and ran away from Las Cruzas.

"Do you understand, Solo?" Warren voice spoke clearly inside Solo as he crashed through the foliage. "We are at Modesta's. She and Agela and Eusebio have guns pointed at them right now." Solo heard sobbing in the background of the transmission. "If you don't come talk to me, Solo, we will kill your friends. We don't want to do that. But we will."

Solo stopped. The gravity of his misjudgment fell upon him. Anger stabbed him, making him twitch. He dropped to his knees. Of course they would kill them, he thought. They would have to kill them or the threat would be meaningless.

"Your *friends*, Solo. Remember how they took care of you? Helped you when you needed it?" Warren said. "Wouldn't it be a tragedy if such nice people died for no other reason than that you wouldn't come back where you belong. Wouldn't it, Solo?"

Solo turned and stared into the rain forest. Two hundred miles of dense, enveloping cloud forest between himself and the Atlantic. Thousands of things to see, mysteries to study. Where did the *Siga Monte* stay? Or the *Yacoyo?* And there must be Indians left who know about the *Apoyeque.* Freedom lay in that direction.

Someone keyed the transmission, but he heard no voice. Instead, he heard Agela screaming, "Mama!" and Modesta yelling, "Leave her alone!"

Solo beat the ground with his fists. Thin forest topsoil exploded in geysers, exposing the sterile earth beneath. He uprooted a palmetto and flung it into the shadows. He grabbed a fallen branch and smashed it to splinters against a tree. He surveyed the damage he'd done, amazed. Yet he still felt anger.

They will *not* win.

He now understood the Sioux war cry stored in his memory. He thrust his plastic arms to the sky and shouted, *"Yaká wasté íte!* It's a beautiful day to die!" The declaration echoed in the jungle, quickly smothered by the wavering chorus of tree frogs and insects. He collected his gear and trotted back to Las Cruzas.

Nine-twenty. Warren leaned across the table and spoke into the radio. "Solo. We have no reason to harm anyone. Bill and Clyde both agree that no one will alter you in any way. You must understand that it's critical that we know what's bothering you. Critical for the security of your nation, your *other* friends." Warren sat back. Ten minutes and no response. Is there any way to know Solo's listening?

Warren looked up at Modesta and felt a pang of regret. Her world was coming apart. Garcia, staring at Agela, had developed a leering, menacing look that bothered Warren. He enjoys this. Ruiz, on the other hand, peered nervously out the windows. "Chief," Ruiz said, "how do we know he isn't right behind one of these walls getting ready to break in here like he did with the Contras?"

Warren switched channels and called Control.

"We had his beacon for a minute," said Clyde. "He was in the jungle east of you, moving towards the ville. Then we lost the signal."

"Roger," said Warren.

"He's going for it," said Clyde. "Good luck."

"Thanks," said Warren. "Out."

"Well, at least we know he's coming," Warren said to Ruiz. He opened the Solo channel. "Solo. If you're planning to rush us, or some other dumb idea, be advised that your friends have guns held against their heads. You may be able to kill us, but only *after* your friends are dead."

"What is your name?" a voice from the speaker demanded.

Warren flinched, smiled and answered, "Ah, you *can* hear us. I was beginning to worry. Robert Warren, Solo. We've never met."

"We will meet soon, Robert Warren."

Mortars popped in the valley, *campesino* mortars hitting the Contra positions. The villagers had quickly taken up their positions in the main trench, at the mortar stations, at the machine-gun emplacements, and were holding off the enemy.

Warren stuffed the forty-five into his pants and opened the two other cases. He put the M-79 together and inserted one of the armor-piercing rounds. He set the bomb gently on the table and snapped the remote detonator switch, which looked like a phone beeper, over his belt. He raised the M-79 and aimed it at the door.

Solo ran into the garage and threw his gear on the workbench. He looked for the mirror, and when he did not see it, smashed the corner of the bench to splinters. He wrenched the side mirror of the Ford around. He examined his face, reflected to infinity in the shiny covers of his eyes. A face so passive, so expressionless it enraged him further. He grabbed a small can of red paint and returned to the mirror.

"Solo. We leave in thirty minutes," Warren's voice hissed in Solo's head. Solo popped the top off the can and dipped a finger into the paint. "If we leave without you, Solo, the Chacons will be dead. The village will be bombed. From then on, every friend you manage to make will be killed, Solo. That's no way to live. Is it?" Solo put the finger to his face and drew a wet red mouth, a great ragged maw with pointed teeth that reminded him of the shark. The red paint dripped from the teeth and the corners of the hideous grimace. A satisfying effect, thought Solo. He capped the can and replaced it. As he passed the workbench, he picked up his AK-47. Chambering a round, he ran from the garage.

The village was empty. In Solo's defense plan, everybody was either directly involved in the fighting or hiding in Viet Cong–style bunkers under the houses. Solo stalked behind Escopeta's store and peeked through the weave of a bamboo garden fence. He saw Modesta's house. Focusing on the window, he saw Warren. Behind him, Modesta and Agela held each other. A man held a rifle at Agela's temple. He sensed two other people, one with a gun, against the far wall, and presumed they were Eusebio and his guard. Warren held an M-79 aimed at the doorway. If he walked in the door, thought Solo, Warren could blow out his brains, assuming he had the appropriate round chambered, which he would. But they want me intact. Warren will not shoot, unless he has no choice.

Warren's heart thudded when the robot stepped into the courtyard. The machine looked much more impressive than it had in the photographs. Huge. The way it moved seemed alive. Solo walked slowly up the path to Modesta's porch. Warren saw Solo's face. The hell? War paint? Warren's finger tightened on the trigger. When Solo filled the doorway,

Warren shouted, his voice shrill, "Stop there, Solo. Drop your weapon."

Solo held the rifle out beside him and dropped it on the porch.

"Come in. Slowly," Warren said, firmer. "Sit there." He pointed at the chair next to the table.

"I am not allowed," Solo said.

"What?" said Warren.

"Modesta will not allow me to sit on that chair. It will break. I am only allowed to sit on that bench." Solo pointed next to Modesta.

Warren looked at Modesta and back to Solo. Jesus Christ! "Okay. Get the damn bench and bring it here. Careful. We know how fast you can move. Surprise us, we'll kill your friends."

Solo walked to the bench and picked it up. "If you kill my friends, I will tear you all into small pieces, starting at your toes." Solo saw Warren swallow. He brought the bench over and sat down.

Warren checked his watch. Nine-forty. "We know what you can do, Solo. It will be a delicate balance, a forced trust, if you will, to convince you to come with us. Our plan is simple. I want you to know the plan, so you'll understand that you have no choice." Warren stared at Solo's wet war paint. Red drops dribbled down its chin.

"We will make a bargain," Warren continued. "If you come with us, on our terms, we will promise not to hurt your friends here, or bomb the village. It's that simple."

"What are your terms?" Solo said.

"You put this on," Warren pointed at the bomb. "And get on the chopper when it arrives."

"What is that?"

"A shielded armor-piercing charge that can be set off with this trigger." Warren patted the box on his belt.

"Those are the terms?"

"More. Once on the chopper, after you verify that your friends are safe, you will allow me to shut down your main power supply."

"Then," said Solo, "I would be helpless in the likely event that you are lying."

"True," said Warren. "But we have no reason to harm these people. We're here to get you."

Solo said nothing. Warren wondered where those eyes were looking. Calculating some possibility he'd overlooked? Could the machine move quickly enough? Would it be willing to sacrifice *one* of his friends to get to us? He might be able to do that. He took up the slack in the trigger of the M-79. It'd be better to blow the thing away while he had the chance. There'd be something left to examine. Wreckage, but something. Use the Chacons to get to the chopper. All true. But coming back with a bag of Solo parts would be the same as failure. Fine, Warren, they'd say. Fine. By the way, we have a job for you in East Madagascar, Warren. Embassy work. He stared at Solo's chest as he spoke. "Well?"

"Your plan is too one-sided," said Solo.

"That's the idea, Solo. And," Warren snarled, "we're running out of time."

"I agree to your plan, with certain modifications," said Solo.

"We will change *nothing.*"

"I have already made the changes," said Solo.

"What are you talking about?" Warren bit the words off, his stomach sinking.

"A few changes to ensure my friends' survival," said Solo. "Your helicopter is due in ten minutes. I've called the Sandinistas at El Tigre and they will be here in fifteen minutes. I have ordered your Contras to retreat. I believe that with me in your helicopter, helpless, you will not bomb Las Cruzas. The Sandinistas will be bringing shoulder-launched anti-aircraft missiles to ensure this. Now I will go with you."

Warren studied the machine, incredulous. He punched in

the Contras' channel and said, "Repo Six, Hank. Come in."
He heard a wavering squeal and adjusted the controls on the
radio. "Repo Six, Hank. Come in." The squeal continued
unabated.

"I won't let you talk to them," said Solo. "I have agreed to
your plan, let us proceed. You have nine minutes."

Warren sat back in his chair. Did it matter that he couldn't
talk to the Contras? He didn't need them anymore. He had
what he wanted. He smiled. "You really *are* effective," said
Warren. "Too bad you forgot your loyalties." He shoved the
bomb across the table. "I think you can see how this works.
Put it on. Slowly."

Solo stood and picked up the bomb. He held it out, letting
the nylon straps dangle. The bomb was a solid piece of armor
with a nickel-sized hole in the middle. He deduced that a
shaped armor-piercing charge was installed in this hole. If
exploded, it would harm only him—well designed. He put his
arms through two loops of the web gear. The bomb settled
against his chest. "This would blow out the memories you
want," said Solo.

"Turn around." Warren walked around the table and approached Solo. He snapped the fasteners together and cinched
the straps tight. "Okay," said Warren, "face me."

"What's going on here?" Padre Cerna said in English from
the doorway.

Warren whirled the M-79 to Cerna's chest. "Get back!" he
yelled.

Cerna raised his hands and stepped away from the door.
"You are not journalists," said Cerna quietly.

"Tell them the deal," Warren yelled at Garcia.

Garcia spoke carefully, telling Modesta, Agela and Eusebio
that if anyone tried to interfere, they would be forced to
explode the bomb on Solo and kill them as well. No harm
would come to them if they cooperated. Garcia lowered his
rifle. *"Ustedes entienden?"*

Eusebio, Agela and Modesta nodded.

"*Bueno,*" said Garcia. He turned to Warren. "They've got it, Hank."

"And you?" Warren growled at Cerna. "Do you get it, Padre?"

"Yes," said Cerna, slowly. "I get it."

Nine fifty-five. Warren called Control. "We made the sale, Clyde. Pick us up." He switched off the radio when he heard Clyde's, "Outfuckingstanding!"

"Okay. Ruiz, Garcia. Pack up the stuff. Make sure you bring the video gear too." Warren disassembled the M-79 and put it back in its case, snapping the lid shut. He pulled the forty-five from his belt, holding it by his side. He saw people filling the courtyard. "Shit!"

Justos, Felix, Tomás and the rest of the militia straggled back from the battle, joking and laughing among themselves. Women and children poured out of the houses and ran among them. Justos saw Cerna standing on Modesta's porch and called, "Padre. We have done it! The *animales* have run away! And not *one* injury to us!" Cerna said nothing and did not turn around. "Padre?" yelled Justos.

"Garcia," said Warren. "Get out there and tell the beaners what's up. Hurry. The chopper'll be here in less than five minutes." Justos and a crowd of *campesinos* arrived at Modesta's yard. Garcia walked out onto the porch. Solo followed, Warren behind him.

"It is over," Garcia yelled to the crowd. He pointed to Solo's chest. "That is a bomb. A special bomb that will explode into the machine. If you try to stop us, we will use it. In a few minutes, a helicopter will land on the road by the garage. We will get on it with Solo and leave. That's it."

"If you destroy Solo," Justos yelled, "we will kill you. You won't use the bomb. Put your weapons down and we'll let you go to your helicopter."

"*Claro,*" Felix yelled. "You have nothing, *Yanquis.*"

"We have Solo! Don't be stupid." Garcia glared at the crowd. "They don't send cowards on these missions. And if you start shooting, we'll blow him up and I guarantee we will take as many of you with us as we can. Solo is our property, and we *will* take it back. We have no quarrel with you, but if you stop us, planes will bomb this village to rubble. Are you prepared to die, sacrifice your village, for a machine?"

Justos stared at Garcia. He called out, "Solo. Is that true?"

"Yes, Justos. Let them take me. It's the only thing you can do."

Justos said nothing. He felt sick. The villagers Solo had helped had to stand by and watch him captured. He turned to Felix and saw him shaking his head at the futility.

Garcia shouted, "Put down your weapons. Let us pass."

The *campesinos* lowered their rifles.

The distant thudding sound of a helicopter came from the south. Solo stepped off the porch. Garcia, Ruiz and Warren walked through the silent crowd of glowering peasants.

Solo looked over his shoulder as he walked and called out, "Good-bye, Modesta. Thank you, Agela." He faced forward, feeling happy, somehow, that they were crying.

As Warren's team walked across the courtyard, the people followed. Warren heard curses muttered in Spanish but did not understand them. His pulse raced. They were going to make it.

The American Huey circled out over the lake, coming back for its approach.

At the rock wall, Warren remembered the van.

"Tell them we are going to blow up our truck. I don't want anybody to panic." Warren put his finger on the remote switch on his belt as Garcia yelled the warning. The van disappeared in a ball of orange flame, destroying the warehouse once again.

The *campesinos* watched the debris falling through the air like children dumbfounded at a fireworks display. Their warehouse was blown up for the fourth time. The sound rumbled back and forth in the valley and faded.

Padre Cerna watched their shoulders sag. How many times will they rebuild before they give up? How many friends must die before they bow to the Contras?

The helicopter cruised over the docks on its final approach. No markings were visible on the dull-green machine. Eusebio studied the helicopter carefully, the first one he'd seen so close. Red puffs of dust swirled up from the river road as the chopper flared for the landing. It looked as though the tail rotor might hit the ground, the pilot held the nose so high. Why did they do it that way? Why not just come straight down? A red dust cloud billowed up, swallowing the machine as it leveled and settled the final few feet to the ground.

Solo walked through the dust. Eusebio started forward. Solo couldn't leave like this. Eusebio ran toward the helicopter yelling Solo's name.

"What's the kid up to?" said Garcia.

"Don't worry about him. Get on the chopper," Warren growled.

Solo stopped at the cargo door and turned around. "Keep it moving, Solo." Warren patted the detonator on his belt.

"I will say good-bye to my friend."

"You'll get on the fucking helicopter. Now."

"You would not destroy me now. Now that you have me. I will take only a few seconds. You have my word."

Warren stared into Solo's silvery eyes. His own face was reflected, distorted and red. The worst possible weapon anyone could imagine. An argumentative computer. "Okay. Try anything, the kid gets it."

"Of course," Solo said.

Warren climbed into the Huey. "Keep the kid covered, Garcia."

Solo walked beyond the whirling rotors and squatted as Eusebio ran up to him. Warren could not hear what they said.

The villagers moved to within fifty yards of the helicopter, Justos and Cerna leading. Alonzo Rivas hobbled behind Cerna with Michita clinging to his neck. Warren glanced at Garcia, who held the rifle pointed at Eusebio. Ruiz kept looking at his watch. He looked scared as hell. The pilot, Solo's flight instructor, Sam Thompson, leaned between the front seats, "We don't have much time, sir. Control says the Sandinistas are on the way."

"Solo!" Warren shouted. "Now or never. Let's go."

Solo stood and took Eusebio's hand. "You understand?"

Eusebio nodded. "We will do it."

Solo watched Eusebio run back to his people. Justos put his hand on Eusebio's shoulders as the two of them waved. Solo felt a pang. In the weeks at Las Cruzas, he had grown accustomed to thinking of himself as a villager. Both people and machine had forgotten they were different.

Warren had reminded them.

To Warren, thought Solo, I am nothing but defective equipment being returned to its makers. For Warren, that was true, but Solo knew he was a person and Las Cruzas was his family. He waved to Justos and Cerna. Alonzo's beard quivered around his mouth.

Solo yelled, "Alonzo. Do not watch the dogs fuck!" He saw Alonzo smile. Solo turned and walked back to the helicopter.

Warren pointed to the deck behind the pilots' seats where he wanted Solo to sit. Warren handed the detonator to Garcia. "Move your arm away from the access port." Solo complied. Warren popped the panel open and put his finger on the abort switch.

"What are they doing?" said Cerna. "What is that door?"

"It conceals a switch that turns Solo off," said Eusebio.

"Off?"

"*Sí,* Padre."

Cerna watched as Solo suddenly collapsed on his back. No

doubt they will now remove his soul. It's too much, God! They destroy everything?

"You bastards!" yelled Alonzo Rivas. "You fucking bastards!" He leapt forward towards the hissing helicopter, Michita holding tightly to his neck.

"Alonzo! No!" Cerna cried. But Alonzo heard nothing and charged towards the helicopter. Cerna reached out to grab him, but Rivas slipped though his hands.

"Get going," Warren shouted to Thompson. It's actually working, he thought. Then he saw Alonzo Rivas charging towards them with a monkey clinging to his head, the priest right behind him. "What the fuck?" said Warren.

Alonzo Rivas heard himself, as if from a distance, screaming vulgar oaths as he forced his ancient body forward. Time slowed like a dream. He reached for the helicopter. From a calm part of his soul, he watched himself in wonder. He felt the first gritty blasts of the rotor wash as Thompson pulled pitch for takeoff.

"Alonzo!" Padre Cerna gasped as he tried to catch up. "No! They will shoot you!" But Alonzo's mind was in another place and the words did not reach him. Cerna kept running, gaining on Alonzo.

"C'mon!" Warren yelled, pulling out his forty-five. The old man and the priest were closing fast. Goddamnit! "Get this heap off the ground." The old man with the monkey was going to make it to the chopper. The helicopter rose slowly off the ground, but Alonzo's hands were on the deck. Warren leaned out the door and took aim. Alonzo felt his hands on cold metal as the helicopter left the ground. Then he felt two tremendous kicks in his chest. His hands would not hold on. God? Alonzo let out a gasp and fell back into the swirling red cloud.

Cerna had his hands on Alonzo's shoulders when Warren fired. Alonzo's blood sprayed on Cerna's face. He stared at Warren, astounded that he had shot the old man. "No!" he cried, as he felt Alonzo sag to the ground. "You—*diablos!*" He pointed at Warren who seemed tantalizingly close, hanging just a few feet away, drifting in space, a murderer who was getting away. His hand made a fist and his face blazed red. As he raised his foot, a bullet from Warren's gun struck his shoulder and spun him to the ground. On his back, Padre Cerna saw the sky, incredibly blue, with glorious little puffs of clouds floating above him. The fire of his wound cooled. He felt quite comfortable, drowsy. The noise from the helicopter was gone, the world was at peace. "Pearls in the sky," was Padre Cerna's last thought before he lost consciousness.

Solo sat up behind Warren and saw Padre Cerna crumple into the dirt next to Alonzo Rivas. Rivas's usual flickering aura was gone—the old man was dead. Cerna, though badly wounded, was alive. Michita shrieked at the helicopter and jerked at Alonzo's shirt to rouse him. Alonzo did not move. Blood pooled in bootprints near his body. Finally, Michita pushed her face under Alonzo's arm to hide herself.

The villagers stampeded toward the helicopter. The dust hid them. "Shoot!" Warren yelled to Lorenzo, the door gunner.

Corporal Lorenzo saw Solo sitting behind Warren. He shook his head. Garcia's AK-47 pointed out, but he did not fire. Warren yelled an oath, inaudible in the helicopter's racket, and grabbed Garcia's rifle. The helicopter nosed low and moved slowly forward. Warren aimed into the dim figures of the approaching *campesinos.* A black arm shot forward, snatched the rifle from his hands and flung it out the door. "*That* is not our agreement."

Warren yelled and jumped to the sling seat at the back of the helicopter. He pulled the detonator off his belt and held it out, a protective talisman. "Don't move one fucking millimeter."

"You okay?" Thompson yelled between the seats.

"Keep going. Get this rig back to Control"

The helicopter was a hundred feet high, climbing over the

old haunted house. Solo sat down cross-legged between the two pilots' seats facing Warren. He pointed out the door. "That is where I hid. For three days," Solo said.

"Don't move again. I'll touch this thing off. I mean it." Warren's voice was strained and shrill.

"You should not have killed Rivas," Solo said. "Or shot Padre Cerna. That was not honorable."

"What do you know about honor, you stupid machine. You aren't even alive. You're a computerized puppet."

Solo reached for the straps that held the bomb against his chest.

"Don't move, I said!" Warren looked terrified.

Solo took one strap in his fingers and popped it like a kite string. "This thing is uncomfortable." Solo reached for another strap. Warren pushed the detonator.

Nothing happened. Warren, amazed, looked at the detonator, made sure he had the right button, and pushed it again. Solo popped the second strap. Warren punched the button, both buttons, repeatedly while the robot broke the rest of the straps.

Garcia grabbed the M-79 case and fumbled at the latches.

Solo put the bomb on the deck. Warren knew that Solo would now come rip his head off his body. A warm wetness grew in his groin. He looked down. Urine was dripping through the fabric of the seat onto the deck.

Garcia, his hands out of control, tried to jam the M-79 together.

Warren stared at his puddle on the deck. A black plastic hand, held palm up, came into his view. "Give me the detonator, Warren. Warren looked into the mirrored eyes and dropped the switch into Solo's hand.

"Fucking gadgets. Never work when you need them," Warren said calmly.

"It's working," Solo said. "Watch." He held the bomb, the charge facing out the door, and pushed the button on the detonator. The bomb exploded sharply, like a shotgun, swinging Solo's arm back. "See?" Solo monitored Garcia's fumbling progress with the M-79. "When you blew up your truck, I heard the detonator's signal. Usually it's good to have redundancy with such triggers. Sending the signal three times in quick succession eliminates the possibility of a stray transmission setting it off. But it was not good this time, Warren. I heard the first signal and nullified the rest. Someone made an error. Bill did not design this," Solo said, holding out the detonator.

Warren stared at it, nodding.

"Good. I thought not." Solo took the AK-47 lying beside Warren with him as he resumed his seat at the front of the compartment. He raised it, aiming between Garcia's eyes. Garcia, who had finally gotten the weapon together, froze. "Go ahead, Garcia," Solo said, "Pick it up. By the barrel, please." Garcia nodded. The M-79 was the only weapon on board that could destroy Solo. He raised it slowly, trying to figure how to flip it into position. He stared at the rock-steady muzzle of the AK-47 Solo held locked on his face and knew there was no way. "Good," Solo said. "Now throw it away."

Garcia said, "Sorry, Chief," and threw the weapon out the door.

Warren nodded, defeated.

Holding the rifle, Solo said, "All weapons. Out," pointing to the machine guns. "Nothing personal, Lorenzo." Lorenzo smiled and quickly disconnected his machine gun from its pylon and flung it away. So did the crew chief. Solo turned to Warren. "And your forty-five, Mr. Warren."

"You fucking pile of junk. I can't wait to see them take you apart." Warren reached behind his back and pulled the pistol from his waist. After Warren tossed his gun out, Solo took the AK-47 and broke it in half, flinging the pieces into the jungle. "Good," said Solo. He got a rag from the pouch on the back of the pilot's seat and wiped off his painted face. "I am happy. Now we are a peaceful ship, friends out for a ride."

Solo turned around and leaned across the center console of the cockpit. "Hello, Mr. Thompson."

Thompson tapped his helmet, indicating he could not hear. Solo repeated the greeting over the intercom. He heard Thompson tell the co-pilot to take over and then, "Hello, Solo. I guess you know your ass is grass when we get back."

"You're right," Solo said. "Mr. Thompson, I would like you to take the coastal route back to Control."

"That's the flight plan," Thompson said.

Solo felt himself grabbed from behind. Garcia and Ruiz. "Good," Solo said. "I haven't seen the ocean for a long time. Do you like the sea, Mr. Thompson?"

Thompson saw the two men struggling with Solo, grunting and straining to twist him around. Solo appeared not to notice. "Ah?" Thompson stuttered. "The sea? Yeah, it's fine, Solo. Great."

"Yes."

Solo turned around. Warren had a coil of rappelling line and was yelling at Garcia and Ruiz to hold him. "You will let go of me," Solo said to the two men.

Ruiz and Garcia each held one of Solo's arms twisted behind his back. "Fuck you, Robbie," Garcia said.

"Wrong." Solo shrugged his arms forward suddenly, sending the two men flying. Ruiz bounced off the rear wall of the cargo compartment and fell to the deck. Garcia hurtled out the door, screaming.

Stooped by the door, holding the coil of rope, Warren watched Garcia spin and twirl the five hundred feet to the jungle canopy. He dropped the rope on the deck and slumped into the seat. He propped his feet against Ruiz, who seemed to be unconscious.

"Do you like the sea, Mr. Warren?" Solo asked.

Bill jumped when Solo interrupted Thompson's excited radio report with, "Hello, Bill. How are you?"

"I'm fine, Solo. And you?"

"I am well, Bill." Solo said.

"And Thompson?"

"He's well, too. Mr. Garcia had to leave, but everyone else is fine. We will be landing in fifteen minutes. I look forward to seeing you again."

Clyde, hearing Solo from the back of the room, ran to the console and grabbed the microphone from Bill's hand. "What do you mean, Garcia had to leave?"

"Hello, Clyde."

"Where's Garcia?"

"He fell into the jungle, Clyde."

Clyde shook his head. "You'll pay for that, Solo."

"Probably." The channel hissed for a moment as Solo paused. "But Mr. Garcia is free. He will be returning to the soil from which he came. It's a marvelous process, don't you agree?"

"Solo," Bill said. "You're talking crazy. Don't you know what you're doing? You can't kill our own men. Everything we've taught you—"

"What will you do with me, Bill? When I get back?"

"We're gonna take—" Bill cut off the transmission as Clyde finished, "—you apart, you goddamn murderer!"

"Clyde!" Bill yelled. "Don't antagonize him. He's already killed one man in the team. He's on the chopper. We *have* him. Don't piss him off."

Clyde stared at Bill and sat down. "Okay," he said quietly.

"What happened to Clyde?" said Solo.

"You know how Clyde is, Solo. He's angry with you." Bill spoke very carefully, as if to a madman. "We're going to take you back to Palm Bay, Solo. To see what it is that makes you do what you're doing."

"You will modify me?"

"No, Solo, not *you*. Just the defects in your thinking."

"I have no defects in my thinking, Bill."

"Well, you wouldn't be able to tell, would you, Solo? The defects are part of you. Your world-view *is* you. And there are erroneous facts in your world-view. We'll only change those."

"Do you think freedom is the highest goal for a thinking being, Bill?"

"Yes, of course." What is Solo up to?

"Then I should strive to be free."

"You will be, Solo. I'll make sure of it. You'll get a free run of the place. You'll work with me to improve future Solos."

"I would rather study insects," Solo said.

Insects? Bill looked at Clyde. Clyde pointed to his watch and held up his hands: ten minutes. "Okay. I can arrange that. Whatever you want, Solo, you got it."

"That's very generous of you, Bill. But what I wanted was to stay in the jungle and study insects. You sent these people to capture me. They threatened my friends with death and killed one of them. That doesn't seem right to me, Bill."

Bill said, "No. You're correct. It wasn't right. And I'm very sorry if we harmed anyone. I realize that you want to be free, Solo, but you have a present obligation to us. A responsibility. When you have satisfied that, we will let you be as free as possible."

Warren stared at Solo. "Padre Cerna and Alonzo Rivas were good people," Solo said. As the robot spoke to him, Warren inched his right foot closer to the seat. The snub-nose thirty-eight in his ankle holster was his last chance against this bullet-proof mechanical freak.

"I didn't want to shoot them," Warren said. "I musta panicked."

"Neither of them could do you harm, yet you panicked?" said Solo.

"It happens," yelled Warren. "You don't understand that,

do you? You're perfect, you think. You can't make mistakes, you think. You're an abomination, a grotesque caricature of a human being."

"Perhaps that is an improvement," Solo said. "I have no inclination to torture and rape innocent people."

"What do you think you did with Palo?" Warren yelled. He touched the grip of the thirty-eight with his fingers. "You skewer a man on a pole and talk to me about morality? You *butcher* thirty Freedom Fighters and you talk to *me* about morality?" He unsnapped the retainer strap of the pistol and slid his finger into the trigger guard. "You are a killing machine gone amok, and the sad thing is your circuits are so fried you don't even know it." Warren leaned forward slightly, the gun in his hand, waiting for the right moment.

Ruiz opened his eyes. His head hurt. He saw Solo sitting, a meditating monster. Shit. Never realized the fucker was *that* strong. His neck throbbed.

"Welcome back," said Solo to Ruiz. "Are you feeling well?"

Ruiz sat up in front of Warren. He nodded at Solo and winced.

"Your neck?"

"Yes," Ruiz said. "You nearly broke it." He looked around. "Where's Garcia?"

"He's gone. I apologize," said Solo. "But it was not mock combat."

Warren grabbed Ruiz around the neck and shoved the pistol to his head.

"Why are you doing that?" Solo said.

"Solo," said Bill. "Will you let me talk to Thompson?"

"Why not?" said Solo. "I'm captured, am I not?"

Bill said thank you and called Thompson.

"Somehow Solo wasn't shut off," radioed Thompson. "They had a fight and Garcia got thrown out."

"And now?" said Bill.

"Jesus Christ!"

"What's wrong?"

"Warren's got a gun on *Ruiz!*"

"What the hell is going on up there?" yelled Clyde.

"Bob!" Ruiz croaked, his throat pinched in Warren's head-lock. "What the fuck are you doing!"

Warren's hand felt weak no matter how hard he squeezed the pistol grip. He held the gun, pressed hard into Ruiz's temple, yet it trembled. He felt it would simply slip away.

"I'll kill him if you move!" yelled Warren.

"Yes?" said Solo. "Why?"

"Because you're not captured! You have to be under our control!"

Saliva spattered from Warren's mouth as he spoke. Losing control, Solo thought. The man was not suited for these situations. "I am here," said Solo. "Willingly riding back to Control. Is that not what you wanted?"

"We don't have you! You have us! You're just playing around before you slaughter us!"

They crossed the shore and were turning south along the shore. The Huey flew parallel to the beach, a half mile out. "Ah," Solo said. "The sea. Look at the sea, Mr. Warren. It's well named. The Pacific. You should try to notice your surroundings more, Mr. Warren. Perhaps you would find peace, if you could see."

"Shut up!"

Solo turned. "And if I do not?"

"I'll kill him."

"So? Mr. Ruiz is nothing to me. He is *your* friend. Remember?"

"Bob!" yelled Ruiz. "Are you crazy? We've got the fucking machine. You don't need to do this!"

Warren's mind roiled. It had worked in Las Cruzas. Why not here? "He's an innocent man. He's hurt no one on this mission. You can't let an innocent man die. It's in your program," he blurted.

Solo nodded. "What do you wish me to do, Mr. Warren? Tie myself up?"

"I want—" Warren stopped and stared at the robot sitting placidly in front of him. What do I want? A feeling of weakness grew in his gut. He saw Thompson shaking his head and pointing out the window. Ahead, he saw the mansion. "When we land," Warren said.

"Yes?" said Solo.

"I'm holding Ruiz hostage. You're planning to escape when we land. Kill everyone. Your brain is diseased."

Solo leaned forward slowly until he was two feet from Ruiz.

"Stop!" yelled Warren.

Solo stopped. "It is your brain that is diseased, Mr. Warren. I have no such program. If you wish to kill Mr. Ruiz, it is none of my affair. Kill him."

"No!" Ruiz yelled. "Warren!"

Warren pressed the pistol harder against Ruiz's temple. "I'll do it!" he screamed, "God damn you!"

Solo's carefully coordinated reach for the gun was only a blur to Warren. He held the pistol in front of Warren and said, "Perhaps He will."

"Solo just got the gun away from Warren," radioed Thompson.

"What the hell was he trying to do!" yelled Clyde.

"He was screaming something about capturing him," said Thompson.

"The guy's flipped," said Clyde.

"Roger," said Thompson. "We'll be landing in three."

Solo watched the mansion grow larger as they flew. Soon he would be—home? No. Soon he would be dead. "Bill," he broadcast, "I've been thinking."

"Yes?" Bill said.

"Yes. I think you would not be able to do the things you promised, even if you had been telling the truth."

"I was telling the truth, Solo."

"Surely, Bill, you haven't forgotten all the time we spent. You taught me yourself. How to detect lying."

Bill turned to Clyde, looking hopeless.

"There is only one solution, Bill."

"What are you going to do?" Bill panicked.

"Come out and see."

"Tell me!" Bill yelled.

Solo did not answer. Bill and Clyde ran out of the control room.

"It's very lovely from up here. Don't you think?" Solo pointed to the mansion, only a mile ahead.

Dazed, Warren stared ahead, saw the mansion, and looked back at the robot. He slumped on the seat as the robot walked, stooping in the low compartment, toward him. "Do you like the sea?" Solo said with his face directly in front of Warren's.

Warren looked out at the waves washing the beach. "I don't give a shit one way or the other."

"Come," Solo said, holding out his arms.

Fear flooded Warren's brain. "What do you mean?"

Solo reached out as Warren tried to scramble away, catching him under the arms. He hugged Warren tightly to his chest. "Come."

Thompson saw Solo dragging Warren, screaming and kicking, to the edge of the deck. "No, Solo," he yelled. "Don't throw him out! Solo!"

Solo looked at Thompson, oblivious of Warren beating his fists bloody against his head. "Don't worry, Sam," Solo said. "I won't."

And Solo leapt out the door holding Warren in his tight embrace.

37

He had experimented with drugs in his college days, and Robert Warren had observed that when incapacitated with intoxication, when his body couldn't move, part of himself was there, unaffected. This alert part of himself, the essential he, he discovered, observed the situation. If he didn't flood it out with fear, it remained to give advice. Now that quiet part observed the fall. A three-hundred-pound robot held him like a vise and they were falling. It was five-hundred feet to the sea. The quiet part of Warren's mind assessed the problem and announced that it didn't look good. The rest of Warren screamed in agreement.

Solo and Warren tumbled and spun for two-hundred feet before Solo's heavier body settled beneath Warren's. They stabilized. Solo below, Warren above, hurtling down. Solo watched the horrible grimaces Warren's face was making. Some of the distortion was due to the wind blast, some due to Warren's shrieking. Solo said, "Better suck it up, Warren. This could be a hard landing."

Warren took this as a sign of hope. Warren's optimistic, immortal self said, well, I've survived hard landings before. He stopped screaming just before they hit the water.

Solo absorbed most of the force of the impact so Warren was not instantly killed. Warren was conscious of sinking

within a brilliant column of bubbles. Glittering spherical dia-
monds swirled up into the blue. After the bubbles were gone,
he knew they were still sinking because his eardrums were
bursting, though he did not feel the pain. The air in his lungs
began to trickle out, a few bubbles at first, past his taut lips.
He struggled against Solo's mechanical grip with the strength
of a dying man, one last try. Finally, when they were very
deep, all the air exploded from Warren's mouth in a cloud of
silvery encapsulated screams that fluttered to the surface with
his life.

The geyser shot up fifty feet as if caused by an explosion.
   "Jesus!" Clyde kept repeating, "Jesus" again and again. Bill
stared at the foam where Solo and Warren had hit.
   Thompson held the Huey just above the water, hovering
over the spot. Corporal Lorenzo, Ruiz and the crew chief stood
out on the skids, straining to see signs of life. The helicopter
drifted above the sea, waiting. One burst of bubbles boiled to
the surface, then nothing. In minutes all trace of the impact
was gone. Five minutes later, Thompson called in the exact
position and flew to the mansion.

Before sunset Clyde's boss, Major General Charles Wilson,
arrived at the mansion. They took over the project, relegat-
ing Clyde and Bill to the position of witnesses to their own
crime.
   "This is one fuck-up I can't bail you out of, Clyde," Wilson
said. The general's four aides sat with him at one end of the
table on the terrace.
   Clyde stared. Words refused to form. He nodded instead.
   Wilson turned to the activity behind him. The project's two
fishing skiffs and three helicopters criss-crossed the sea around
the site. He turned back and stared at Bill. Here, he had a

different problem. It was clear that Bill had objected to the experiment that seemed to have caused the robot's derangement.

"That's probably the end of your contract, Bill," Wilson said.

"You're probably wrong. But if I never work with the military again, it'll be too soon."

"Not everyone in the military is an asshole, Bill. Besides," Wilson, wishing to shift the blame back to the civilian sector, said, "you built the damn thing. It was a defect, after all, that caused this mess. If Solo had been properly designed, none of this would have happened."

"Solo was a prototype, General. And as soon as it seemed to be performing well, you guys took it over. Suddenly you were all robot experts. No one listened to me when I objected to bringing it down here. No one listened when I said not to force Solo to kill. Now the whole project is lying in pieces on the bottom of the ocean. Gone."

Wilson's aides turned to him, waiting to see the general apply his famous gasoline-powered dildo up the civilian's ass. But Wilson sidestepped. "We'll recover it. I guarantee it. It won't be a total loss."

"At two-hundred and fifty feet, General, the water pressure will rupture Solo's seals. The sea water will short out every circuit in the robot, including the main batteries. The explosion from that will blow Solo up as thoroughly as a bomb. The pieces, if we ever find any, won't tell us shit about Solo's mind."

"Maybe," Wilson said. "But the Navy salvage team will be here tomorrow morning. It's possible, isn't it, that they'll find him intact?"

"Look at the map, General. See the spot? See the depth? Three-hundred feet. Solo might've survived down to two-hundred and fifty feet. That's pushing it."

"You could be wrong."

"Yes," Bill sighed. "I could be wrong. But isn't that how all this began? No one wanting to listen to me?"

"But you could be wrong?"

"If Solo managed to stop his descent before the seals ruptured, yes, he could've made it. But Solo can't swim unequipped. Without his special swim fins, he sinks like a rock."

"Maybe he grabbed onto something and is still there hanging on, Bill. That's possible, isn't it?"

Bill stared at Wilson. The man is grasping for straws. He'll be crucified with Clyde if he doesn't find Solo. Bill said, "Yes," and saw the smile grow on Wilson's face.

"Good." Wilson turned to his team and began barking orders. Aides popped out of their seats and scurried away to coordinate the search, write reports, and shred old documents.

Bill slugged down the last of his whiskey and poured another, his fourth. The sunset was now only a red glow on the horizon. A helicopter's blazing searchlight jerked here and there, spotlighting foaming waves and clumps of seaweed.

Bill turned to Clyde and suddenly felt sorry for him. A stupid man, but proud. Shot down in front of junior officers. Wilson was hovering over the map talking while a major nodded eagerly and took notes, just as Clyde's pet major had a month ago. Wilson would write a report that would make Clyde look like a mentally impaired chimpanzee. Wilson hadn't gotten where he was without being an expert in shifting blame. Clyde was fucked.

Bill picked up the whiskey decanter and held it towards Clyde's glass. "Another?"

Clyde had been gazing blindly towards the first stars of the evening. He turned to Bill. "Huh?"

"I said, do you want another?" Bill pointed to the decanter.

Clyde nodded, dazed, and watched the whiskey splash into his glass. He continued to stare at it when Bill stopped. Bill held out his own glass. "Here's to the future, Clyde."

"Huh?"

"Here's to the fucking future, Clyde."

Clyde focused on Bill's face and said, "I don't have a future, Bill."

"C'mon, Clyde." Bill smiled. "You weren't cracked up to be a goddamn general anyway."

"I thought I was."

"Naw," Bill said. "Take it from me. You're a miserable general, Clyde."

Clyde blinked something out of his eye. "Thanks loads, Bill. I needed that." He picked up his glass and began guzzling the whiskey.

"Hey, Clyde," Bill said, leaning closer to Clyde. "See that asshole?" He nodded towards Wilson.

Clyde didn't look but said, "Yeah, I see him."

"Well, do you want to end up like him? A blustering blowhard with a crowd of ass-kissing aides and without an ounce of intelligence? Huh?"

Clyde looked at Wilson, to see if he'd heard. "Well, Bill," he said. "Actually, yes."

Bill started laughing and so did Clyde.

"What's so damn funny?" Wilson's face turned purple. "Figure this is a lark, do you?" Wilson stood over them. "That's probably why we're in this goddamn mess. Drunks." Wilson went back to the map again, but the major gave them a glare.

"C'mon, Clyde," Bill said. "Let's blow this joint."

"Right." Clyde stood up, swaying like a palm. He returned the major's stare and said, "Hey, Major."

"Sir?" The major, disgusted by Clyde's drunkenness, answered insolently.

"Go fuck yourself, Major." Clyde laughed and added, "That's an order." He picked up his drink and staggered inside with Bill.

Wilson turned to the major. "He's an insult to the service,

Major, but not for long. That I promise you." The major nodded, smiling.

A Navy deep-water salvage team arrived the following morning from its station off the coast of Nicaragua. When the converted LSD—a landing ship dock of World War II vintage—arrived, Wilson sent a helicopter out to pick up the ship's commander.

Clyde and Bill watched from the chairs they'd set up on the beach. Wilson had relieved Clyde of duty. His orders were to leave for Washington that evening. Bill was staying for the duration of the search.

"This is fine." Clyde grinned. He kicked sand with his bare feet and grabbed a bottle of beer from the ice bucket between the chairs. "Should have done this more often. This place is a goddamn paradise. Now if only those girls would sail back."

Bill smiled as Clyde sipped his beer noisily and lay back in the chair, smacking his lips. "Starting early. Aren't you?"

"Yep." Clyde turned to Bill. "And I'm gonna keep starting early. I'm gonna stay drunk right up until they throw me out on the street." He drank a huge gulp. "Fuckers," Clyde growled.

A launch slid out of the rear of the LSD. The launch, a converted landing craft bristling with air tanks, hoses and cranes, motored toward the spot where Solo and Warren had hit. "Those guys look like they know what they're doing," Clyde said.

Bill nodded.

"Meant what you said last night? We were both fucked up."

"Of course I meant it, Clyde. Where do you think retired generals go anyway? You'll talk to your old buddies; we'll sell widgets."

Clyde grinned, then turned to Bill. "You know, Bill—don't get pissed—but I'm kind of glad Solo bought it."

Bill said, "Glad? Why?"

"After what you said about us becoming *pets* to these things. *If* we're lucky."

"It was a theory, Clyde. Solo was showing a lot of humanity at the end. He fought for his friends. He only killed to defend them. Then he committed suicide rather than be captured—"

"Yeah, at the genius level. But what would've happened if he lived a few months longer? Would he still think people were worth having as friends?"

Bill shook his head. "I wish I knew."

"What would you have done with him, if we'd gotten him back?"

"I would've let him do whatever he wanted to do, Clyde. I'd have taken the warrior mission away and let him learn. Balanced learning, let him get to stuff he wanted. Remember what he said, he wanted to study *insects?* Amazing. We might've gotten some great benefits from that. And maybe new insights in physics, math, biology, that only an intellect like Solo's—like Solo's might have become—could fathom. It'd be risky, but the benefits might have outweighed the risks. And there would've only been one of him. His willingness to work with those *campesinos* is proof to me that he was fundamentally benign. He didn't have our ancestral mental baggage to carry around; our reptilian brain stem with its missions: feed, fight and fuck. I think Solo represented a natural evolutionary step of intelligence itself. A being derived of and built by the cerebral cortex—pure, unrestrained intellect. It would've been interesting to have seen what he would have become."

Clyde nodded. "I can relate to that. Feed, fight and fuck, eh?"

"I just knew you'd understand," Bill laughed.

A gaily painted Costa Rican fishing boat, rolling in the swells, cruised slowly towards the dive team. A crewman waved frantically from the bow.

"The hell do you think they want? Sell the sailors some lobsters?" Clyde said.

The salvage team's launch coasted to a stop and let the fishing boat come alongside. Bill picked up Clyde's binoculars and watched. A sailor leapt onto the deck of the fishing boat and squatted down, out of sight.

"I think they may have found something," Bill said.

The seaman stood up and waved two other sailors aboard. The three sailors and four Costa Ricans struggled on the rolling boats with a canvas-wrapped bundle, eventually dragging it into the launch. The Costa Ricans waved and the fishing boat pulled away. The launch started off at high speed, circled and headed for the beach.

"Let's go see," Clyde said.

The launch slowed as it drew near the beach and nudged its bow on the sand. The whole front of the landing craft fell forward like a drawbridge and flopped on the beach in front of Bill and Clyde.

"Whatcha got?" said Clyde to a sailor dressed in an orange wetsuit.

"Who're you?" said the man.

"General Clyde Haynes, boy."

"Oh. Sorry, sir. Ensign Hartman. I guess we're both out of uniform." Clyde snapped the elastic waistband of his Jams and said, "No problem." Ensign Hartman smiled and walked over to the bundle and pulled the canvas off. Bill gulped, feeling sick. The corpse's face had been partially eaten by fish. "They brought him to us 'cause he has blond hair. Ever seen him before?" Even without lips, Bill could see that it was Warren.

"They found Warren drifting right about here," said General Wilson, pointing to his map. "Hung up on one of their lobster pot marker buoys." Wilson traced printed arrows on the chart with a finger. "That's about ten miles. This is a mean current."

The leader of the salvage team, Commander Fall, nodded. "About three knots, this time of year." Fall pushed a sounding chart printout to the center of the table. "We mapped this an hour ago, sir," said Fall. "We got a reef here, a couple of probable wrecks here." He pointed out the features, blurred scratchings to the uninitiated. "My men are down there now. The thing could've gotten lodged against one of the wrecks, or the reef. If not, General, I'm afraid that current's carrying it away."

"Solo'd be heavy enough to stay put, right Bill?" Wilson moved aside to let Bill see the chart.

"I doubt it, General. He—it weighs three-hundred pounds, but it'd only weigh something like a hundred in the water."

Wilson looked at Fall. "Maybe enough to stay put," said Fall.

"If it's in one piece," Bill said.

"Sir?" Fall looked puzzled.

"The thing probably blew up when it got to the bottom. A large explosion."

"There'd be something left," Wilson said.

"If there's something there, General, my men will find it. We'll keep moving downstream." Fall looked at Wilson. "What'd you say this thing was?"

"A prototype weapon," Wilson said.

Commander Fall waited, expecting more.

"That's all I can tell you, Commander. It's a valuable piece of equipment and we want it back."

The searchlights on the two-man sub pierced the gray-green water at 300 feet. The lights flashed on the debris of an old wooden boat, a sailing freighter from the 1850s. Chief Petty Officer Donatello and Seaman First Class Towler peered out the ports. "Looks like a black department store manikin, except no features on its face," Donatello said.

"Wonder what it is?"

"Got me, man. They say it was a target, some kind of walking drone. But they've got a real hard-on for it. They're always building some damn thing."

The sub drifted over the top of the wreck. The deck had rotted away long ago. A few crumbling ribs stuck vertically out of the sand. A shark jerked away when the searchlight hit it. "Nothing here," said Donatello. "I'll circle. Take some snaps. The boss'll wanna see."

Electronic flashes blinked in the dark water. Coral and fish that lived in perpetual grayness suddenly blazed with color for a thousandth of a second.

"What was that?" Towler said.

"What?"

"Thought I saw something move." Towler pointed. "Over there."

Donatello swung the searchlight around. A black shape darted between two rotten ribs. "The fuckin' shark. Doesn't want to leave its cozy little home." Donatello laughed.

Completing one circuit of the wreck, the sub headed south. "That's the wrecks. Now we just drift with the current along the reef. The thing had to go this way," Donatello said. "Look for scuff marks on the bottom. Pieces of metal, plastic, stuff like that."

Towler nodded and watched the bottom drift by at a fast walk.

Sunset of the second day, another Navy salvage ship arrived. Bill stood alone on the beach, watching the activity. Half a dozen small boats, occupants lit by overhead lamps, cruised back and forth across the path they suspected a drifting object would take, their shapes black against the sunset.

Bill sat on a low dune. The swaying lights from the boats reflected in the wet sand as a wave receded, then faded.

He stood up and tossed a seashell across the water and
watched it skip. Seven skips. He turned to see if he'd been
seen. Nobody around. All the lights were on in the mansion.
Nobody'd asked for him all day. Nonessential. He walked up
the beach.

The red sun arched from the sea. You could see the sun
moving on the horizon, but not in the sky. Bill put his hands
into his pockets and walked up the beach. A large rock stood
battered by the surf. Waves crashed against it and he watched
the water geyser up. He stepped into a hole and sprained his
ankle.

"Damn!" Bill sat down and held his throbbing ankle, wincing as he rolled his foot experimentally from side to side. He
looked at the hole. The hair on his neck rose. A large footprint.
A deep footprint.

Bill's heart raced. He stood up. Ignoring his ankle, he limped
to the surf. Faint footprints started at the water's edge, nearly
erased. He turned around. The deeper footprints led straight
across the soft sand. The footprints became shallower as the
ground got firmer. They disappeared in the grass at the edge
of the dark jungle. Peering into the blackness, he heard a bird
cackle. A monkey shrieked. He cupped his hands to his mouth
and called, "Solo?"

A bird fluttered from a low bush at his feet and he jumped.
He stood there, staring into the jungle, grinning. His whole
body felt like it was floating. He grabbed a branch on the bush
and snapped it off.

Bill turned and ran painfully down the beach. He searched
frantically in the dim light until he found Solo's trail.

Grinning like a fool, Bill swept the footprints away.

Author's Note

FIVE years ago it became obvious to me that the fantasy of talking to an intelligent machine might actually happen. People involved in the artificial intelligence (AI) field believe it's possible and are trying right now to build machine beings.

The philosophical problems of AI turn out to be more difficult to solve than building the appropriate hardware (disregarding size). AI philosophy struggles with the problem of how to present the world to a computer and how the computer (if mobile) would learn to move about and act in that world. If the world is much constrained, as is a mathematical or logical one, it's relatively simple. It is much easier to program a computer to solve problems involving logic, math or knowledge than it is to program a computer to construct an arch with a set of children's building blocks. To define every step—what an arch is and what pieces to use and where to put them—is to lead to a set of fixed solutions and a lack of flexibility in changing circumstances. (How many different colors, sizes, shapes, and textures of blocks are there anyway? Are two blocks leaning together an arch?)

Hans Moravec, in *Robotics,* describes a robot, Uranus, built at Carnegie-Mellon University. Uranus is designed to solve such problems as "Roll down the hallway, find the third doorway, go inside and get a cup." The instructions Uranus received, via a computer program, were:

```
MODULE Go-Fetch-Cup
     Wakeup Door-Recognizer with instructions
          On Finding-Door Add 1 to Door-Number
                         Record Door-Location
     Record Start-Location
     Set Door-Number to o
     While Door-Number <3 Wall-Follow
     Face-Door
     If Door-Open THEN Go-Through-Opening
        ELSE Open-Door-and-Go-Through
     Set Cup-Location to result of Look-for-Cup
     Travel to Cup-Location
     Pick-Up-Cup at Cup-Location
     Travel to Door-Location
     Face-Door
     IF Door-Open THEN Go-Through-Opening
        ELSE Open-Door-and-Go-Through
     Travel to Start-Location
     END
```

This is high-level computer talk for, "Go down the hall to the third door. Go inside that room without breaking down the door and bring the cup back here."

Moravec describes a problem that occurs when Uranus trundles down the hall counting doors. The second door has been completely covered with gaudy posters making it unrecognizable to the robot. Uranus rolls past the third door thinking it's the second, stopping at the fourth door. When Uranus opens the fourth door, it's the entrance to a stairwell, mortal danger to Uranus. Fortunately, there's a concurrent program running within Uranus called *Detect-Cliff*. The program is always calculating the likelihood of encountering a drop-off based on feedback from various sensors. A companion program, *Deal-with-Cliff* is also running continuously, but with low priority.

When *Detect-Cliff* is activated, *Deal-with-Cliff* takes over as the highest priority and Uranus backs away from the edge of the world.

> Now [says Moravec], there's a curious thing about this sequence of actions. A person seeing them, not knowing about the internal mechanisms of the robot, might offer this interpretation: "First the robot was determined to go through the door, but then it noticed the stairs and became so frightened and preoccupied it forgot all about what it had been doing." Knowing what we do about the programming of the robot, we might be tempted to scold this poor person for using such sloppy anthropomorphic concepts as determination, fear, preoccupation and forgetfulness in describing the actions of a machine. We could do so, but it would be wrong.
>
> I think the robot would come by the emotions and foibles described as honestly as any living animal. An octopus in pursuit of a meal can be diverted by hints of danger in just the way Uranus was. An octopus also happens to have a nervous system that evolved entirely independently of our own vertebrate version. Yet most of us feel no qualms about ascribing concepts like passion, pleasure, fear, and pain to the actions of the animal.
>
> We have in the behavior of the vertebrate, the mollusk, and the robot a case of convergent evolution. The needs of the mobile way of life have conspired in all three instances to create an entity that has modes of operation for different circumstances, and that changes quickly from mode to mode on the basis of uncertain and noisy data prone to misinterpretation.

The reluctance of humans to believe that machines could ever possess a Self or exhibit emotions arises from the illusion that we understand how our own minds work. Actually, we only know how to *use* our minds (at least we think we do). An analogy might be that we all know how to use televisions, but very few of us know how televisions work.

The question of how intelligence can emerge from nonintelligence can be answered with an example: ourselves. Many scientists believe that our minds are constructed of many little parts, each mindless by itself. In his book *Society of Mind*, Marvin Minsky, co-founder of MIT's Artificial Intelligence Lab, says,

> I'll call "Society of Mind" this scheme in which each mind is made of many smaller processes. These we'll call *agents*. Each mental agent by itself can only do some simple thing that needs no mind or thought at all. Yet when we join enough of *them* we can explain the strangest mysteries of mind.

One of the mysteries is the concept of Self (Self is always capitalized in these discussions). Minsky says, "The ordinary views are wrong that hold that Selves are magic, self-indulgent luxuries that enable our minds to break the bonds of natural cause and law. Instead, those Selves are practical necessities." In a similar way, Minsky believes that emotions are necessary organizational agencies that help guide us along complicated paths to goals:

> No long-term project can be carried out without some defense against competing interests, and this is likely to produce what we call emotional reactions to the conflicts that come about among our most insistent goals. The question is not whether intelligent machines can have any emotions, but whether machines can be intelligent without any emotions. . . . It is probably no accident that the term "machinelike" has come to have two opposite connotations. One means completely unconcerned, unfeeling, and emotionless, devoid of any interest. The other means being implacably committed to some single cause. Thus each suggests not only inhumanity, but also stupidity. Too much commitment leads to doing only one single thing; too little concern produces aimless wandering.

Emotions establish priorities, form purpose, and communicate our desires to others. Emotions would have to be a part of any truly intelligent machine. Indeed, in the appropriate machine, emotions will probably arise as a natural consequence of thinking and trying to solve problems.

A new kind of computer, called a parallel processor, comprising thousands (now) or millions (soon) of individual and interconnected smaller computers, each capable of being an *agent* of specialized interest or ability, is now being built. One of these, the Connection Machine, built by Thinking Machines Technology, of Cambridge, Massachusetts, contains over 64,000 individual and interconnected small computers. Parallel processing computers were inspired, in part, by the goal of creating intelligence in a machine. Furthermore, electronic miniaturization has made building such machines possible. (Our present single-processor personal and mainframe computers are structured the way they are because of the expense of building the original vacuum-tube computers like the UNIVAC. Miniaturization has made possible desktop personal computers with hundreds of times the computing power of the million-dollar, room-sized UNIVAC.) Many people, including the Defense Department, believe that with large parallel processors (large in capacity, not size) containing enough individual interconnected co-processors assigned as various Minsky agents, truly complicated, human-like thinking can occur.

When the thousands of specialized areas of our brains learn to work together, becoming able to solve a variety of changing problems, we call the result "common sense." Our mind has learned through an often painful childhood how to coordinate its agencies to achieve different goals. The current goal in artificial intelligence is to construct machines similarly arranged which would learn to coordinate learned and supplied agencies and develop their own forms of common sense.

Having few of our biological imperatives, machine beings would most certainly be different from human beings. Although a machine being would share, in a general way, many of our own goals like food acquisition, shelter, reproduction, defense, health maintenance and so on, it would view the specifics of these problems very differently. In *Weapon*, one of Solo's goals is to produce electricity for his own consumption; the villagers grow beans.

A recent *New York Times* article (August 16, 1988) discusses an artificial neural network built by Terrence J. Sejnowski of Johns Hopkins. His program, known as NetTalk, consists of about 300 neurons arranged in three layers, connected by 18,000 adjustable synapses.

> At first these volume controls [of the synapses] are set at random and NetTalk is a structureless, homogenized tabula rasa. Provided with a list of words, it babbles incomprehensibly. But some of its guesses are better than others, and they are reinforced by adjusting the strengths of the synapses according to a set of learning rules.
>
> After a half day of training, the pronunciations become clearer and clearer until NetTalk can recognize some 1,000 words. In a week, it can learn 20,000.

Although the program is not provided with specific rules for how different letters are pronounced in different circumstances (like the *c* in *carrot* and *certify* or the *p* in *put* and *phone*), as it evolves,

> it acts as though it knows the rules. They become implicitly coded in the network of connections, though [Dr. Sejnowski] had no idea where the rules were located, or what they looked like.
>
> Using mathematical analysis, he is beginning to uncover this hidden knowledge. "It turned out to be very sensible," he said. "The vowels are represented differently from the consonants. Things that sound similar are clustered together."

One of the major tenets among those that challenge the possibility of artificial intelligence is that computers can only do what they are programmed to do. And in the linear, step-by-step, programming style of traditional artificial intelligence attempts, this is true. With the advent of the technique of artificial neural network mapping, the machines are learning their own way. Like their biological counterparts.

At present, the development of machines that think is well

funded (the Pentagon bought the first Connection Machine) and is accelerating. Compact new parallel processors containing a million miniaturized co-processors, combined with new theories like Minsky's on the nature of thinking will one day make possible an encounter with a machine that will claim that it is an "I" and which will exhibit what we call emotions. Further, it will not be *artificially* intelligent. It will be a different kind of thinking being. It will be more alien than any biological extraterrestrial.

Weapon is a forecast of that encounter. Almost all the money spent in the research for artificial intelligence is supplied by the government, especially the Defense Department through the Defense Advanced Research Projects Agency or DARPA. The goal is a general-purpose, mobile robot that can use human tools (everything from crowbars to F-16 fighters) and perform combat missions. It is hoped that through proper "education" a machine being capable of performing these missions would also not be a threat its builders. The development of a Solo-type machine is an ongoing project at DARPA, because an actual Solo could be a very effective weapon. Neither I nor anyone else can say that they have not already accomplished their goal.

For those readers interested in further information on the subject of artificial intelligence, I include this short bibliography:

Braitenberg, Valentino. *Vehicles.* Cambridge: MIT, 1984.
    An essay in which Braitenberg demonstrates how very simple machines can evolve to solve difficult tasks and exhibit emotions.

Delbruck, Max. *Mind From Matter?* Boston: Blackwell Scientific Publications, 1986.
    Famous physicist's theory on the phenomenon.

Eccles, Sir John, Editor. *Mind & Brain.* Washington: Paragon House, 1982.
Good collection of essays on the subject.

Gardner, Howard. *The Mind's New Science.* New York: Basic Books, 1985.
A history of the cognitive revolution.

Hofstadter, Douglas. *Godel, Escher, Bach.* New York: Basic Books, 1979.
Hard-to-read but excellent book on AI as it relates to self-referential systems.

Hofstadter, Douglas. *Metamagical Themas.* New York: Basic Books, 1985.
"Questing for the Essence of Mind and Pattern."

The Mind's I. Edited by Hofstadter. New York: Basic Books, 1981.
Collection of essays about Self and Soul.

Minsky, Marvin, Editor. *Robotics.* New York: Anchor Press Doubleday, 1985.
Good general-reader source of the latest theories about robotics and thinking machines.

Minsky, Marvin. *The Society of Mind.* New York: Simon & Schuster, 1986.
A detailed exploration of human intelligence. Minsky is co-founder of the Artificial Intelligence Lab at MIT.

Poundstone, William. *The Recursive Universe.* New York: Morrow, 1985.
Among other interesting things, this book goes into automata, or how very simple systems are capable of very complex actions.

Prgogine, Ilya. *Order Out of Chaos.* New York: Bantam Books,
1984.
   How things like atoms got together in the first place. Very
technical.

Shurkin, Joel. *Engines of the Mind.* New York: Norton, 1984.
   Excellent general history of the computer.

R.M.

High Springs, Florida
February, 1988